## Carl Hiaasen
### Bill Montalbano

# POWDER BURN

CARL HIAASEN is the author of seven novels, including the national bestsellers *Lucky You, Strip Tease,* and *Stormy Weather.* He also writes a twice-weekly metropolitan column for the *Miami Herald.*

BILL MONTALBANO is the author of *The Sinners of San Ramon* and the forthcoming *Basilica.* He was the *Los Angeles Times* bureau chief in San Salvador, Buenos Aires, Rome, and London, and a foreign correspondent for the *Miami Herald* covering China and Latin America. He was the recipient of more than a dozen awards for his journalism. He died in 1998.

D0063414

ALSO BY

## Carl Hiaasen and Bill Montalbano

*available from Vintage Books*

A Death in China

Trap Line

# POWDER BURN

## Carl Hiaasen

## Bill Montalbano

**Vintage Crime/Black Lizard**

VINTAGE BOOKS

A DIVISION OF RANDOM HOUSE, INC.

NEW YORK

First Vintage Crime/Black Lizard Edition, July 1998

ISBN    0-375-70068-4

www.randomhouse.com

Book design by Rebecca Aidlin & Cathryn S. Aison

Printed in the United States of America
10   9   8   7   6   5   4

*For Dart and Connie*

# POWDER BURN

THE FREIGHTER was registered in Panama, a formality. The name crudely painted across her square stern was *Night Owl.* Two months before it had been *Pacific Vixen;* before that, *Maria Q.*

She was 108 feet long and nearly rusted out. Once she had hauled coffee from Santos and fish meal from Callao; now she wallowed in senility, crabbing against the current, her diesels coughing. She showed no running lights.

The freighter changed crews as often as she changed names. That night it was nineteen young Colombians, adventurers from the tropical Caribbean coast where Drake once sailed. They lounged on the flaking deck, gambling idly for cigarettes, drinking beer. A scratchy loudspeaker played old Argentine tangos from Radio Rebelde in Havana.

The captain was older, a taciturn man who drank white rum from a bottle with no label and prized his M-1 rifle, Colombian army issue. He had many friends in Colombia, but none on his ship and none at sea that night.

The rifle hung across a yellowed undershirt. Its barrel brushed the wooden coping as he leaned through a portside window of the bridge and peered westward into the night.

On the horizon, the Miami skyline glowed under an amber halo from sodium vapor streetlights. The captain had heard much about the city; he wondered about it. Would it be big and noisy like Bogotá? Or small and lively, more like Cartagena? And the women? How were the *gringas*?

The captain rang the bridge telegraph to "Stop," and the freighter lost way. Instinctively her crew became silent. A few of them whispered, some of the new ones pointing toward the sleeping city.

The ship's radio crackled, faded and crackled again. On the tarnished bridge only the radio shone, a compact package of Japanese electronics, sophisticated, gleaming.

The captain gave his coordinates in Spanish, flicked the bow lights twice and darkened the ship again.

"*Ya vienen,*" one of the crewmen called.

Even against a stiff easterly breeze the captain heard the humming, like a distant swarm of bees deserting the mangrove coves in South Biscayne Bay. He counted three, no, four different engines, each with its own pitch, growing louder in the night.

Three crewman moved below quickly. A fourth stationed himself on the bow.

The radio spoke.

"Owl, what's your twenty? Come in, Owl, this is Pussycat. Could you give your twenty again?"

This time the captain spoke in labored English, repeating the coordinates. As he finished, a curt voice from another boat broke in.

"*¡Basta!*" it commanded. Then the radio was quiet.

"They are in a hurry," the captain told the guards on deck. "Be sure your guns are ready."

THE CRANDON MARINA docks were quiet; the sportsmen in their chalk white boat shoes and the playboys with their zinc-coated noses always left with the sun. The night belonged to the shrimpers, lobstermen and hand-liners, solitary men more at home with the lonely sea than with the painted city to the west.

A big Jeep International pulled into the lot and backed a sleek red speedboat down the ramp: a Donzi, twenty-six feet of screaming lightning. Three lithe young men in dark clothes hopped in. The roar of the big twin Mercruisers startled the drowsy resident pelicans and flushed two stringy cormorants from a buoy in the harbor.

The driver shoved the throttle forward. The bow of the boat stood up, then planed off under four hundred horses. The Donzi cleared the last harbor buoy and raced south, rooster-tailing a ten-foot spray. The Miami skyline glinted pink and ruby off the boat's mica hull.

"Lights!" yelled the smallest man.

"What?" The driver cupped a hand to his ear.

"Get your lights on. You want the Coast Guard tailing us all the way out?"

Balaos, needlefish and a big stingray skittered out of the Donzi's path. The third man sat in the jump seat, his back to the others, watching the spray fly from the huge inboard engines and trying painfully to set himself for the concussion of waves he could not see.

"How about a beer?" the driver yelled at him.

The third man shook his head. "No, thanks." His eyes fixed on the wake, a mile-long seam in the black water. The small man, a gun in the waistband of his jeans, leaned close to the driver.

"What's the matter with Ruis?"

"It's his first time," the driver said, grunting as the boat's tapered hull pounded off a swell. "He's just a little nervous."

"That's just great. Jesus! Why didn't you tell me?"

"Hey, it's no problem," the driver said, smiling. "This will be easy."

"Shit," said the small man. He heaved a beer can, half-full, into Biscayne Bay.

Twenty minutes later the Donzi anchored near Elliott Key, a boot-shaped island nine miles off the mainland. The driver flipped a CB radio to Channel 15, turned down the squelch control, and the boat filled with harsh static and Spanish gibberish from cars in the city.

"Idiots," he muttered.

The three men sat in silence for thirty minutes, the driver scanning the eastern horizon. The ungainly silhouette of a tanker moved south in the Gulf Stream. Occasionally the whine of a small boat broke the quiet.

Ruis, balancing like a rookie high-wire artist, stood to urinate off the side of the boat, and the driver and the small man coughed with laughter. "While you're up there, get the anchor," the driver said, then glanced at his wristwatch, a gold Rolex Oyster that had cost him twenty-three hundred dollars and one night's work. "It's time to move."

"See anything?"

"Not yet."

He aimed the Donzi out to sea and throttled up to thirty miles per hour. The hull pounded mercilessly in the offshore rollers, and all three men stood in the open cockpit to brace themselves. After fifteen minutes the driver cut back the engines and the bow dropped with a slap.

"Come in, Owl," a voice on the radio said. The reception was clear this time. The driver said nothing.

"Why don't they answer?" Ruis whined.

"Shut up," the small man said. "Just watch."

"Owl, come in," the voice repeated.

"There!" the driver exclaimed. He pointed northeast. Several miles away two lights flickered. One green. One white. On, off. On, off. Over the radio an answering voice recited numbers in Spanish. The driver of the Donzi didn't bother to write them down. He could make out the freighter's bulk even above the four-foot chop.

"Come in, Owl, this is Pussycat. Could you give your twenty again?"

"That guy's crazy," hissed the small man in the Donzi. "Tell him to shut the fuck up."

The driver snatched the microphone and spoke sharply in Spanish. "*¡Basta!*"

"OK," the small man said. "Let's do it."

Another boat beat them to the freighter. It was a Magnum, Gulf Stream blue and built to fly. Even in the dark the Donzi's driver could see the crew was American: tall, sandy-haired, tennis-shirted, two of them with pistols.

The *Night Owl's* Colombians, shirtless and sweating, passed the bales to the Magnum with the rhythm of a fire brigade. One of the Americans perched on the bow of his boat, relaying each burlap bundle to his partners. The bales, fifteen in all, disappeared into the fat hull.

"I wish they'd hurry," Ruis said nervously.

The small man said nothing but glanced angrily at the driver. This was the pussy's last trip, as far as he was concerned.

The Magnum roared away, the backwash rebounding in deep echo off the freighter's old steel hull.

The Donzi motored up to the *Night Owl,* and the small man tied on with a clove hitch. His hands clinging to the speedboat's plexiglass windshield, Ruis stared up at the freighter's bulging flanks. Framed above him against the night sky stood a lean Colombian with a rifle.

*"¿Cuantos?"* the crewman asked.

*"Veinte,"* the driver replied in Caribbean Spanish that had come with him from Cuba as a child. *"Y algo más."*

The Colombian nodded.

"You do the loading," the driver ordered Ruis. "I'm going aboard."

The Colombians began tossing the pungent bales to the small man, who relayed them to Ruis. Winded from the effort, Ruis awkwardly hauled each of the fifty-pound bundles below, cramming it as far up the Donzi's hull as it would go. After a few minutes the speedboat was nearly full.

"It won't hold any more," Ruis gasped. "There's not enough room up there."

*"¡Silencio!"* the small man commanded.

The driver stood on the deck of the freighter, talking quietly with the captain. To the south he could hear the sounds of more engines; more customers.

"Three kilos," he said to the captain. "We can pay cash now."

"Those are the rules. We aren't supposed to even carry this shit," the captain replied, handing a brown bag to the driver. "Grass is one thing. Cocaine is something else."

"But not too risky for you, eh? Or your brother?"

The captain's face darkened.

"Oh, I saw him in Miami the other day," the driver continued. "Big car, pretty *señorita.* Last time I saw him he was on this boat; now he's a big shot salesman."

"It's a big business, *compadre,*" the captain replied in a flat voice. "There's plenty of room for people who don't ask questions. Get the money."

Back on the Donzi, the driver extracted a small blue Pan Am

flight bag from a locked stowage shelf under the cockpit. The sides bulged.

"Hurry," the small man urged. "We're running out of room."

"Start the engines," the driver said. "Here goes."

Quickly he scrambled up the rope ladder to the freighter's deck. The small man turned the ignition key and idled the Donzi's engines back as far as they would go.

"Hey, where's he going?" Ruis demanded, wrestling with bale number thirteen. The small man moved against him and pressed a pistol into one of Ruis's hands.

"Let the other bales go. Turn your back on the ship, and put the gun in the front of your pants. Use it only if I tell you."

On deck, the Donzi's driver handed the flight bag to the Colombian captain.

"It's all there, Félix."

"*Bueno.* I will count it." The captain never took his eyes off the smuggler. One hand held the M-1, the other the Pan Am bag.

The driver monkey-climbed down the ladder, cast off the freighter's rope and went to the wheel of the Donzi. "Hang on," he yelled, slamming the throttle forward. The speedboat spun in an arc, hurling spray on the *Night Owl*'s deck.

The captain unzipped the flight bag.

"*Madre de Dios,*" he screamed. "*¡Come mierda sinvergüenza!*"

He dropped the satchel onto the wet deck and brought up his rifle.

"*¡Fuego!*" he cried. "*¡Fuego!*"

In the Donzi, the small man ducked when he saw flashes from the freighter and came up with his semiautomatic, firing. His hand shook.

Ruis never understood.

"Slow down! Christ! Slow down!" he yelled.

The speedboat accelerated like a rocket, throwing Ruis against the gunwale. The pistol dropped from his hand and clattered overboard. He clutched wildly for something to hang onto, but the Donzi plowed through a wave and bucked him up over the stern into the wake. From the freighter the splash sounded like a sack of cement.

"Jesus," the small man said.

Rigid at the wheel, the driver never looked back. His eyes teared from the sharp wind. The speedboat raced eastward, out of rifle range, toward the Cape Florida lighthouse and home.

"Shit," the small man exhaled. "Can Ruis swim?"

"I hope not—for his sake," the driver said, shaking his head. "*¡Mierda!* It was a mistake to bring him. . . ."

By now the small man had stopped trembling. "What was in the bag?" he asked.

"Tampons," the driver said.


ON THE FREIGHTER, the captain cursed and spit into the sea.

Ruis bobbed in the water while the Colombian crewmen watched silently. No one fired at him.

"*¡Socorro!*" Ruis cried. "Help!" His voice bounced off the hull like a dull chime.

"*¡Por favor! Tengo miedo!*" Ruis treaded water awkwardly. He was afraid to paddle toward the ladder, afraid to move a muscle in the sight of the rifles.

"Help!" he yelled plaintively. "*¡Tiburón!* Shark!"

One of the crewmen laughed harshly, but the captain silenced him with a grunted command: "Bring him aboard."

By daybreak the *Night Owl* was gone.

# Chapter 1

ALL OF HIS FRIENDS in Coconut Grove had gone to ten-speed bicycles, but Meadows thought that was absurd. He didn't race, and there wasn't a hill for three hundred miles. Three gears were enough. As a matter of fact, the sturdy brown Raleigh he was pedaling along Main Highway had only one gear; the other two had rusted to perdition long since.

It was summer, one of those afternoons when the clouds build over the Everglades and march with thunder and drenching rain out to sea.

The temperature stood at eighty-eight; the humidity, even higher. Sweat poured from him as he pedaled a narrow strip of asphalt alongside the road, protected from the traffic by majestic banyan trees, their thick branches casting a dappled shade over roadway and bike path. Lizards darted across the path. He heard the cry of a family of wild parrots that lived in an old royal palm near the bay.

The hotter the better, as far as Chris Meadows was concerned. It was the time of the year when all the tourists went home and left Florida to the Floridians. At least that was how it used to be. Now more and more people were moving in, calling themselves Floridians, and with each one of them there was that much less of Florida.

Meadows glanced over at the long line of traffic moving in the opposite direction past an ivy-covered church. Three cars in five had their windows closed, air conditioners growling. He felt sorry for the drivers. They missed the lizards, the parrots, the tantalizing breeze being sucked off the bay into the building clouds. In another hour they would miss the cloudburst that in a furious few moments would wash the streets, drop the temperature twenty degrees and reward all those wise enough to enjoy it with new sights, sounds, sensations.

Meadows was of two minds about the coming storm. On the one hand, he could pedal home before it and watch from his porch with a shot of Jack Daniel's as it beat on the bay, or he could take off his shirt and pedal home in the rain. Either would do.

Indeed, it would not have been hard to please T. Christopher Meadows that afternoon. The hospital in New Mexico had been a tremendous tonic. He had done it for the cab fare, liking the idea of science cloaked in white adobe on the sere shank of a mountain. The hospital was for children, and Meadows had suffered it: every block, every window, every angle. He had paced the hillsides around the growing structure, weighing, examining, analyzing. Then one day he had walked no more. The building belonged. Even the sallow consulting architects who made their living designing hospitals had found no flaws.

Usually Meadows made a point of being somewhere else when the time came to inaugurate buildings he had designed. It was curiosity that had led him to break his own rule in New Mexico two days before. He had left room in the vaulted hospital lobby for a cross on the wall facing the wood-framed doorway. Meadows understood that without the crucifix the hospital would never be complete in the eyes of the nuns for whom he had built it. To carve their cross, the nuns had improbably picked a wispy kid, self-taught, thin as a reed and spacy as hell. Meadows wouldn't have hired him to chop firewood.

Meadows had been wrong. He realized that the instant he had walked into the completed lobby. The boy had carved a breathtaking Christ, bony as himself, stretched in agony on the mahogany cross. The cross had seemed to envelop the lobby and everything in it; the anguished Christ had spoken more of forgiveness than of pain. Meadows had been astonished. And now, back home in Miami, the delight still warmed him.

THE BUSINESS DISTRICT OF Coconut Grove slept in the afternoon sun. Few people walked the streets. Meadows passed a darkened theater, an empty park, an earnestly fashionable line of boutiques of the sort that had made Coconut Grove so chic Meadows was thinking about moving out.

Meadows won an inviting smile from a jogger with whom he briefly shared the bike path: he, pedaling north, hair tousled, shirt open, feet bare, canvas shorts straining at the thighs; she, running south in a seventy-five-dollar outfit of satin and tie-dyed cotton, hair combed back and tied with a red ribbon. Pretty, Meadows thought, but a bit too obviously on the make. He had paced a few joggers in his day, one athletic activity prelude to another, but that was in the past now.

Meadows waved at a teller named Bert who stared morosely at the street from a drive-in window at the local bank. It reminded him that he had to pick up some money on his way home, even if it did mean passing the time of day with poor Bert. Bert had piles.

From what had once been a good neighborhood bar a blond youth appeared, wiping tears with a piece of blue silk. The silk matched his light T-shirt, which matched his pocketless jeans, which almost matched the tearful eyes. A circular gold pendant bounced uncertainly against the hollow, heaving chest.

Meadows let the bike coast. There had to be a second act. There was. The youth took a deep breath, marched back to the bar and pulled open the door.

"Bitch!" the young man screamed. "Cheating bitch. I hope he bites it off." There was a commotion inside the bar. The youth walked swiftly away, clutching the silk handkerchief to his face as though it were an ice pack. Ah, to be young and in love, Meadows thought.

Arthur stood at his usual corner, where the road turned east to dip toward the bay. Arthur was hard to miss. He was six-four in splay-toed feet that were indifferent to the burning concrete side-walk. He wore his hair in braids. A wrap of beige and white batik circled his waist and breached at his ebony calves.

"Hey, Chris," Arthur called.

"How you making it?" Meadows asked.

"Lean time, brother. The heat is after me every time I turn around. A man can't even stand on the street anymore without trouble."

To the very tense Miami police assigned to patrol the Grove, the theorem was simple: Anybody who stood on a street corner all day was peddling something—dex, ludes, weed, coke, even heroin. The cops rousted Arthur regularly, but they never busted him.

"What you need"—Meadows laughed from his bicycle—"is a defense fund."

"Shit."

"I'll get some T-shirts printed up. We'll stage a rally."

"Fuck off, whitey," Arthur said. "How about some chess later?"

"Not tonight. I'm working on a project."

"Make it pretty, Frank Lloyd."

Meadows encouraged the old Raleigh down the gentle slope toward the library. Arthur was a friend. Meadows had seen him first in a neighborhood greasy spoon, where the black man had been engrossed in a battered book of chess openings. Good chess companions do not come easy in Miami, but your average citizen does not casually approach strange ragged giants and ask them for a game. So Meadows had simply eaten and left.

A few days later, however, Meadows had been buying pencils and ink in an art supply shop when Arthur had approached him nonchalantly dragging a teenager in each ham-sized fist. It seems he had caught them popping the door locks on Meadows's aged Karmann Ghia. That night the two of them had played chess by the pool, and Meadows had learned to his dismay that he was overmatched.

"The man looks like a Rastafarian and plays chess like Morphy," Meadows said to his beleaguered king. "OK, I give up. Who the hell are you?"

"Just another refugee," Arthur answered. He was, in fact, a computer technician of some talent who had saved his money, let his hair grow and dropped out. At night he worked effectively as a bouncer in a small downtown jazz club. By day he manned his street corner in the Grove. Meadows had never asked what he did there. He wasn't sure he wanted to know.

"GOING TO PERU, Mr. Meadows? You seem to have just about cleaned us out of Incas," said the pleasant round-faced librarian.

"Ecuador. Northern branch of the same family, I'm told."

When the last Incas' sons had feuded, one had had his capital in Cuzco, the other in Quito. Would it have made any difference to the Incas, Meadows wondered, if they had known that under their empire lay reservoirs of oil that would centuries later become the lifeblood of civilization? Probably not—but tapping those reservoirs certainly had made a difference to the inheritors of the empire.

Out in the Amazon vastness, Ecuador had oil and, with it, sudden national wealth, instant inflation, unprecedented international status and membership in OPEC. Would Señor Meadows consider designing a building to house the oil ministry in Quito? A skyscraper, *por favor,* something majestic and symbolic of the new Ecuador. Meadows hadn't decided. He hadn't liked the pretentious, *nouveau riche* army officers who had approached him, but he was intrigued with the challenge: how to design a skyscraper consistent with the colonial heritage of mountain Quito and yet strong enough to resist the earthquakes there were nearly as common as revolutions in the Ecuadorean Andes? Before he made up his mind, he would do some homework. . . .

He had just decided the rain would catch him on the way home, and turned to ask the librarian for a bag to protect the books, when he was intercepted by one of the most beautiful creatures he had ever seen.

She stood squarely in his path, a half smile on her face, a twinkle in green eyes that seemed a mirror of Meadows's own. Her blond hair was cut to the shoulder. She wore a plaid pinafore, white socks and white patent leather shoes.

"Hello," she said.

"Hi."

"My name is Jessica Tilden and I am five years old."

"Oh. My name is Chris Meadows and I am thirty-six years old. How do you do?"

"Are you famous?"

"No, of course not. Who says I'm famous?"

"My mommy."

"Well, she probably means well, but she's mistaken."

Jessica Tilden thought that one over. Clearly she would have more to say. Meadows couldn't take his eyes off the little girl. There was something there in that pixyish, semimocking, I'm-not-through-with-you-yet expression. Something familiar.

"Don't you know it's not polite to lie to little girls?"

The voice came from over Meadows's shoulder. It sent a shiver down his spine, a pounding in his chest. He felt lightheaded, weak, vulnerable. Meadows turned.

"Hi, Sandy," he said softly.

"Hello, Chris."

Jessica was her mother's daughter, no mistake about it. Except that her mother's eyes were a bottomless blue and she wore a knee-length white cotton dress and sandals. The last time he had seen her she had worn a bikini and the blue eyes had sparkled with tears.

They shook hands, there in the library. The ultimate absurdity, to shake hands among strangers with someone you once loved. Meadows didn't know what else to do.

"Your palms are all wet, Chris."

"I'm sweating. I came on the bike."

"Yes, I saw it outside; that's why we came in."

"Gee, Sandy, it's been . . ."

"Almost six years."

"If she is Jessica Tilden, then you are . . ."

"Mrs. Harold Tilden of Syracuse, New York."

"Syracuse. Yes, well, I've been there. Nice town." It was not a nice town. It was an awful town; no architecture, no life, no sun, and he didn't give a damn about Syracuse anyway.

"How are things with you?" she asked with that gentle, private smile.

"I can't complain."

"The house?"

"Fine."

"The boat?"

"New engine, same boat."

"The coffee grinder?"

Oh, stay away from that, Sandy; that is too close to home. In the mornings, when the sun ricocheted off the bay into the bedroom, it had been his custom to get up and make coffee, beginning with shade-grown Costa Rican beans a friend shipped him from San

José. He was a fetishist, she teased. Anyone who abandoned her alone and languorous on a big bed in the morning sunshine to make coffee had to be. And a fool to boot, she liked to say.

"The grinder broke. I threw it away," Meadows lied.

"Oh? Somehow, Chris, I can't imagine you without your trusty grinder. Or is it that there is someone to make your coffee?"

"No," he said quickly. "I make it myself still."

Meadows struggled unsuccessfully to regain his poise.

"You . . . you haven't changed much, I mean not a bit at all. How have you been? All that time."

"It went so fast." She blurted it out, a set piece. "After we, uh, after I left Florida, I went up to New York and thought about finding a job. But I never got a chance. Almost as soon as I got there I met Harold and he . . . swept me off my feet." She smiled in apology for the phrase. "We were married in two weeks—can you believe it? Then, bang, along came Jessica right away, and well, Syracuse, when Harold's company transferred him there. Apart from that I haven't changed a bit. Big, old-fashioned country girl who likes the sun in her face and sand between her toes." The smile again.

Meadows had never understood why she had left him. He had finished his laps one day to find her hunched on the porch steps, head in her hands. He had had faint warnings that something was wrong, but never anything concrete. She had been distant, nervous, skittish, alternately voracious and chill in bed. He had put it down to women's problems and forgotten it; at the time he had been working hard on a town house for a millionaire in London.

She had refused to say anything sensible that day. She'd called him obdurate, imperceptive and self-centered, but that was not news to either of them. That afternoon she had left. He'd thought she would come back. She never had—until now.

"What brings you to Miami?" he asked finally.

"Fresh air and sunshine, like always. And I wanted Jessica to see the town where I grew up."

"Is"—Christ, he couldn't say Mr. Tilden. What in hell did she say his name was?—"is your husband with you?"

She spoke quietly. "Harold was killed last fall, a hunting accident. They were after deer. A silly accident."

"Oh. I'm sorry." Second lie in three minutes.

She was looking straight at him. The challenge was there, frank and direct. Before Meadows could accept it—did he want to accept it, almost six years later? And what about Terry?—the little girl came skittering around the corner, carrying a stack of books almost as tall as she was.

"Mommy, I want these books."

"Jessica, you are not a member of this library, and those books are for adults, not for children."

"I want them. You promised me ice cream. If I can't have ice cream, then I want these books."

"I'll buy you the ice cream, darling. The store is just at the corner."

Meadows had been thinking in high gear, only half hearing the mother-daughter exchange. He had to make a decision. Which? How? He needed some time to think.

"Look," he said, "maybe Jessica would like to go for a ride on the bay. I mean, if there's a nice day while you're here."

"I'm sure Jessica would love that," Sandy said. "We'll be at the Crestview until the end of the week. Give us a call—if there's a nice day."

Dammit, she had always been more put together than he. He couldn't shake her hand again, could he? Should he kiss her on the cheek?

She didn't wait for him to decide. Taking the girl by the hand, Sandy smiled, gave a half wave and left the library. Meadows walked slowly to his bike, unaware of much more than that his sweaty palms still clutched the plastic bag with his library books about the Incas.

The bank was two blocks from the library. It took Meadows three minutes and six years to get there. After Sandy there had been a cheerless procession of one-night stands for Meadows. Plastic women. Windup dolls. He couldn't even remember most of the names.

Until Terry. He had met her a year ago, a volcanic *Latina* with strength enough to turn the tides and beauty enough to make a poet weep. He smiled. It was no exaggeration, though. He had fallen hard for Terry.

And now here was Sandy, ripping open a scar thought to be

healed. Was it nostalgia that had brought Sandy back? Or was it Meadows? No, that wasn't what was important. There was something else. The equation didn't balance.

So Sandy had left him and gone to New York. That made sense. If you're looking for a change of life, it is harder to get farther from Miami than New York. But to meet some guy and marry him in two weeks? That was crazy, not like her at all. If anything, Sandy had been strait-laced, almost proper, the kind who would go to bed with you only if she thought she loved you. To meet a guy one minute, marry him the next and have a baby the morning after—what the hell kind of way was that to rebound from a love affair? Sandy was too smart for that.

Meadows parked his bicycle on the red-brick sidewalk outside the bank, then swallowed hard against a lump of lead that suddenly enveloped his gut. Could she have married quickly not as a means of burying an old affair, but as a way of legitimizing its result? Perhaps she had come, not to see Meadows herself, but to have the little girl meet him, so that one day the girl would understand. . . .

Meadows covered the few steps to the sidewalk teller in a mental fog. His head reeled, and Bert was no help.

Bert was a trial, a once-weekly test of endurance, a whining, shuffling, sweaty, living definition of dyspepsia. No doubt Bert's conception, too, had been a mistake, for thereafter everything else had gone wrong for him.

"If you have piles, you can't sit, right? So you have to stand all day. And what happens when you stand? Your arches fall, right?"

Meadows, Sandy-on-the-brain, had no compassion for Bert this afternoon. It seemed to take an eternity for the teller to open his drawer, count out four twenties and four fives. He put them in a neat stack, lined up the edges and counted them again. Meadows roiled with impatience. He shifted his weight from one foot to the other. The sidewalk reflected in Bert's picture window cage was burning hot. He should have worn shoes, Meadows thought. And where was the rain? He looked up and saw the first gray scout cloud nearly overhead. It wouldn't be more than a minute or two now. Somehow the thought of biking home alone in the rain didn't seem as attractive as it had a few minutes before.

"And the doctors? What do they know? They charge you a lot of money and never fix anything."

"There is no justice, Bert," Meadows muttered as he retrieved his money from the stainless steel drawer that at last shot forward.

"Now that's the truth. I was explaining to one of the vice-presidents here and he—look at that crazy bastard!"

Meadows had a disconcerting moment of dual imagery. He saw Bert's eyes pop open, his mouth constrict in a shocked O. At the same instant, through the glass of the teller's cage, Meadows saw a red blur whip past, a car, traveling at an impossible speed on a drowsy business street.

Meadows whirled to his right. He caught a rear-end view of the car, a Mustang, and what looked like two occupants. The car would never make the corner where the road turned toward the bay. It was going too fast.

The driver saw that, too. He swerved to the left, hunting for more room. He lost control. The car veered toward the opposite sidewalk.

Sandy Tilden stood there, hand in hand with Jessica. Jessica was eating an ice cream cone.

They had no chance. The Mustang hit them both simultaneously. But it was capricious. It tossed Jessica high into the air, a pathetic bundle of rags, the ice cream spinning away like a hailstone. The car dragged Sandy Tilden. She was under it when it glanced off a trash can. She was under it when it grazed the edge of a building. She was under it still when it came to rest against a light pole.

The bills, four twenties, four fives, dropped unnoticed from Meadows's nerveless fingers.

"God. Oh, God," he moaned. He did not move. He could not move. Nothing moved save a squat black sedan that slid quietly to a halt in the street opposite the Mustang, and then nothing more except the passenger in the sedan.

He walked with economy, deceptively, the way a good emergency room doctor will get where he is going quickly without wasting the resources he will need when he gets there. But the passenger from the black sedan was not a doctor. He carried a gun. To Meadows, forty yards away, it looked like an obscene black stick.

The passenger stopped about ten feet from the Mustang. He spread his legs, leveled the gun and fired a long, continuous volley into the Mustang. It was the only sound. Then the passenger turned and strode back toward his car in the same measured pace.

It was more than Meadows could comprehend. His mind, so intricate, so finely honed, could not function. He began running. He ran without thought, without purpose. He ran toward the Mustang and the black sedan.

He had covered perhaps half the distance to the carnage when the passenger noticed him.

A split-second subconscious image impressed itself, like a Polaroid, on Meadows as he ran. The passenger was tall and burly. He wore aviator's sunglasses. The face was oval and cruel, with pronounced ridges above the eye and prominent black brows.

The passenger raised his gun with a casual flick. He fired once.

Meadows hadn't the time to recognize the danger, nor did he recognize the searing, angry blow that snapped his right leg from under him and sent him, in an uncontrolled slow-motion pirouette, sprawling onto the hot asphalt.

He did not hear the screams when they came. He did not sense the fresh wind that announced the squall. And he did not feel the rain that consumed the orphaned ice cream and sent probing red rivulets coursing through the gutter.

# Chapter 2

"YOU ARE a lucky man." The voice came from the end of a long tunnel. Meadows, lying on white sheets in a white room, peered up through the voice at the swarthy man behind it.

"Why am I lucky?"

"The bullet just tore away some flesh. If it had hit the bone, you really would have been in deep shit. That was an Ingram he hit you with, a submachine, real nasty. You should have seen what it did to those two guys in the car."

"Who are you?"

"My name's Nelson."

"Doctor?"

"Cop."

With an effort, Meadows hiked himself higher on the pillows. The movement sent an arc of pain along his right side, but it also chased some of the cotton candy from his head.

Two men stood by the bed, one tall and blond and muscular, the other shorter, leaner and darker. "That's Pincus," the dark man said, pointing. "My partner." The blond man wore the first crew cut Meadows had seen in years.

"Good afternoon, Mr. Meadows. We would like a few minutes if you feel up to it, sir," said Pincus.

Meadows didn't feel like much of anything. He knew where he was. He knew his wound was more painful than serious. The big-busted nurse had told him that, had urged him to eat a lunch he didn't want and then had left him. He had lain there a long time, drowsing in the sunshine like an old man, seeking without much success to rearrange jumbled swatches of memory into a coherent beginning, middle and end. He had been shot, and now he was in

21

the hospital. That seemed plain enough. He did not ask about Sandy and little Jessica; he didn't have to. That much he remembered with a terrible clarity that would ache for the rest of his life.

The tall cop, Pincus, unexpectedly proffered a thin white envelope.

"This is your property. Would you sign the receipt, please?"

Startled, Meadows scrawled his name on a form the police officer supported on his notebook. He peeled open the envelope and inverted it. Four soiled twenty-dollar bills drifted onto his chest. Meadows stared at them dully.

"You had just withdrawn a hundred dollars from the bank when you were shot," Pincus said. "This is all we could find."

The dark cop laughed.

"You'll never see the other twenty. Somebody grabbed it off the street," he said. "And if it was me, I'd take about half of what's left and buy a bottle of whiskey for that big black dude."

"Arthur?" He knew someone had come running, had knelt over him, stayed with him, but through the haze of pain he had not been able to see who. So it had been Arthur.

"He had the bleeding pretty well controlled by the time the ambulance got there. If he hadn't been so quick, it could have been a lot worse," Nelson said.

Meadows winced.

"Do you want me to call the nurse?"

"No, I'm all right."

Smoke from the fat cigar wreathed the policeman's face. It nibbled at his mustache, poked at deep-set eyes and fingered his long black hair. He was a *Latino,* Meadows concluded, almost certainly Cuban. You had to tell by looking. His English was perfect.

"Sorry, not supposed to smoke in here," Nelson said with an airy wave of the cigar that was less apology than explanation, "but I figured you wouldn't mind—there's nothing wrong with your lungs."

"*Su casa,*" Meadows replied.

"*Coño, chico, hablas español. Qué bueno.*"

"*Sí, hablo,*" Meadows responded, and switched back to English. "Just now I'd rather not bother."

"No problem, *amigo,* I only want to ask one question. English is fine."

"Answer one first: Have you caught them?"

"No."

"Will you catch them?"

"We're trying," said Pincus, "trying hard."

"That means 'No, we won't,' doesn't it?"

"Probably," Nelson said with a shrug. "Maybe you can help. Can you describe the man who shot you?"

"Not very well. It's still a blur," Meadows said, looking away. "I remember he was a big guy, and he wore aviator glasses. And he had a very prominent brow . . . it was so fast. Mostly I was thinking about the girl and her mother."

"Rest on it then. If enough of it comes back that you want to try building a composite with a police artist, you call me."

"Probably Homicide will take care of that," Pincus remarked.

"I think he ought to call me," Nelson said curtly. "The first name is Octavio." He laid a business card on the table next to Meadows's bed.

Meadows glanced at it, then took a sip from a glass of water. "Do you understand what it's all about?" he asked.

"What's there to understand? Two assholes broke somebody's balls and they got killed. Bang-bang."

"Tell me about it. I'd like to know."

"Naw, you don't want to get involved. It's scum from top to bottom."

"But I already *am* involved."

"The hell you are. You're not even an 'innocent bystander'—like the two who were killed. You are just what the paper calls 'a slightly injured passer-by.' They didn't even use your name."

"The *innocent bystanders*"—Meadows controlled himself—"the woman and the girl, they were special people to me. Very close."

Nelson seemed to admire the smoke spilling from the red edge of the cigar.

"Shit, *amigo*, I'm sorry," he said softly. "I didn't know that."

Meadows knew anger then, ignited by loss and pain, exacerbated by the cavalier cop and his own feeling of helplessness on the hospital bed.

"The guy who shot me is also responsible for killing Sandy and Jessica. He ought to be in jail already, for Christ's sake. It was broad daylight!"

"It is easier to identify the plague, *amigo,* than to kill all the rats."

"What the fuck is that supposed to mean?" Meadows snarled.

Pincus, who had silently watched the byplay, stepped smoothly into the ripening tension.

"Mr. Meadows, there is a drug war going on in this city, and the incident in which you were involved is one aspect of it. Eventually we will dominate the violence, but our resources are limited, and we can't do it overnight. . . ."

It was a pat speech, Nelson thought. He had made it himself, less stilted, a dozen times. Now he listened in brooding silence. Dammit, he had walked into a minefield. He should have bothered to find out that there had been something between Meadows and the dead woman. No, Pincus should have found out. Pincus was the one who went by the book, wrote perfect reports and could conjure up a dozen conspiracies between home plate and first base.

Now, Nelson reflected, instead of a wounded victim who could possibly give him a glimpse of the killer, he had on his hands an outraged guy who looked mad enough to eat raw meat.

Meadows didn't seem the vigilante or the I-am-going-to-the-newspapers-and-the-mayor type, but it probably wouldn't hurt to cool him off just the same. Then maybe, once he had pulled his wits together, he would look through the mugs of dopers for the triggerman. If he was an architect, he should have a good eye. . . .

"Look, *amigo,* I don't know how much you know about the drug business—" Nelson began.

"I don't know *anything* about it. Why should I?"

"If you yell like that, you'll probably start bleeding again. But if you listen for a few minutes, we'll tell you enough about it so that you'll understand why a mother and her little girl got killed in the street and you got shot."

Meadows lapsed into glowering silence, but it was only later that he would begin to digest what they told him now. It was as if they were talking about some other universe. Meadows had no term of reference by which to judge what he heard. . . .

South Florida, as Nelson and Pincus described it, was the victim of its own geography. Its thousands of miles of beaches, hundreds of airstrips, the inviting emptiness of the Everglades—all beckoned the drug merchants.

"When it comes to law and order and justice and all those other beautiful things the Constitution promises, the United States of America ends just north of the Miami line. Miami is a free-fire zone, a no man's land—call it what you will," Nelson said.

"This is drug central, *amigo*. From spaced-out kids to pillars of the establishment—everybody's into it; everybody's getting rich, and some people are getting dead."

From the Caribbean came huge quantities of marijuana, particularly from Jamaica, where ganja was the biggest cash crop. From Colombia in South America came mountains more of marijuana and perhaps the most prized drug of all, cocaine, the rich man's high.

The Colombian smugglers had established networks to move small quantities of cocaine. It came in purses, in high heels, in bellies and rectums. Customs once found two kilos sewn into the corpse of a three-month-old baby. A young Colombian once fell over dead, getting off a flight from Bogotá. When the pathologists got to her, they discovered she had stuffed nearly a pound of pure cocaine into her vagina. The plastic bags had leaked.

"She never would have to work another day in her life. Instead, she went out on an eternal high." Pincus snickered.

However, as the market grew, Nelson related, the smugglers had grown bolder. Small quantities became tedious, more trouble than they were worth. The smugglers began sending freighter loads of grass and big bundles of coke through the Windward and Mona passages into the Florida Straits. Fast boats came from shore to offload. Airborne smugglers landed tons of grass on headlight-lit runways in the Everglades. One load was enough to pay for an aged DC-3 or a rusty tramp freighter a dozen times over.

In the past few years the drug trickle had become an avalanche of unprecedented proportions. It was enormous, unstoppable. If the risks were huge, so were the profits. Drugs made hundreds of blue-jean millionaires every year.

And new widows as well, for as the volume grew, so did the violence. For a long time the Colombians distilled the coke and ran it as far as Florida. There the Cubans took over.

Among the half million Cuban exiles in Miami there were some who remembered fondly the old Batista days when tough *hombres* ran the women and the slots and their own private armies. The Cuban multitude also held legions of lean young men who had learned to kill, to infiltrate, to run small boats at high speed on moonless nights. The CIA had taught them, in a secret, losing war against Fidel Castro. They had learned well—and they had taught their young, acquisitive, upwardly mobile American-bred cousins, nephews and children.

Drug money was easy money. But more and more it tended to be bloody money.

"Now the pros are in tight. They have no room for wise-ass amateurs. There are still some around, but soon the big boys will be calling all the shots."

The violence had begun in earnest when the offshore-onshore arrangement between the Colombians and the Cubans had begun breaking down. Cocaine greed had been the divisor.

The Colombians had decided to become farmer-to-market dopers, cutting out the Cuban middlemen. They had moved onshore, setting up their own networks in Miami to distribute Colombia's down-home produce. The Cubans had writhed at the intervention, defended their home turf with lead and moved offshore, buying wholesale in Colombia and transporting the coke northward themselves.

It would be messy, but simple, if the Colombians shot the Cubans and vice versa, but it was more confusing than that. Colombians also shot Colombians and Cubans shot Cubans, and if sometimes a beautiful woman and her little girl got caught in the middle, too bad.

"For every one we catch, another ten laugh all the way to the bank," Nelson concluded.

"And this time?" Meadows asked lightly. "Who was it this time?"

"It's hard to know," Nelson replied. "The two stiffs carried no identification, but from the looks of them I'd say they were Colombians. Judging from the gun that killed them, the hit man was probably Cuban. You can't be sure."

"It's completely mindless," Meadows protested.

"Sure. And senseless and lawless. And hopeless. And the next time your very proper host at a dinner party passes around the spoons you be sure and tell him that."

OCTAVIO NELSON'S HEAD ACHED, and his tongue protested the bitterness of too many cigars. He drove reflexively. The rush hour was peaking, but the traffic into the city wasn't bad. The sun, poised for flight over the Everglades, promised another couple of hours of daylight. Angela was working, so there was no hurry to get home. He would go back to the station and slog through some papers. It had not been a profitable afternoon, Nelson decided.

"Can anybody really be that naïve?" Pincus asked suddenly. He meant Meadows.

Nelson grunted. Meadows had been about as useful as another corpse. Something strange was going down among the dopers. Only that would account for the daylight chase through the Grove. Dopers liked to settle their differences alone, in the dark; it was more effective, and it kept the pressure down. Nelson needed to know what was happening. But he certainly would get no lead from the morose, angry young man they had just left.

"If he had been able to finger the guy who shot him, it would have helped," Nelson said. "And it would have been smoother, Wilbur, if we had known he was somehow connected to the woman and the little girl."

Pincus bridled at the rebuke. "Jesus, I checked him out six ways from Sunday. Our records, the feds' records, everywhere."

"Did you ask around the Grove about him?"

It was not hard to interpret the silence that followed. Nelson stifled a sigh of disgust. His partner was the complete twenty-first-century cop. If information were reduced to a form and filed in a computer, Wilbur Pincus would find it. If Meadows had ever married the girl, Pincus would have known it. If they ever had had drivers' licenses from the same address or applied together for credit, Pincus would have found out. But if they had been simply good friends, or neighbors, or lovers, Pincus was defenseless. Nobody had bothered—yet—to file that kind of information in a central archive.

"Forget it, Wilbur." It probably didn't make any difference anyway.

ROBERTO CALLED THAT NIGHT just as Nelson was getting ready to leave the station. There was no small talk; there hardly ever was anymore.

"I need a favor, *hermano*."

"What now?"

"My car. It's parked over on Brickell Avenue, near the toll gate. I need somebody to tow it in."

"Call a garage."

"It's not that easy. Nothing illegal or anything like that, I swear. I just can't go near it right now. I think the cops ought to do it."

"What are you up to now, *por Dios*?"

"I'll tell you about it later. It's just some silly misunderstanding, but you really ought to get the car off the streets. I can pick it up down at the pound in a couple of days."

"Is it your car?"

"Hell, yes, it's my car, a brand-new four-fifty SEL, Sahara beige; it's a beauty. Listen, the tag is PRW three-seventy-eight. OK? Thanks. I'll call you later."

Octavio Nelson cursed silently. He yanked open a bottom desk drawer, dragged out a fresh cigar, but off the tip and spit it out. Some men simply had brothers. Octavio Nelson instead endured an affliction named Roberto.

Some brothers drank together, remembered old times fondly, cosseted one another's kids, helped each other when help was needed. Roberto Nelson was not that kind of brother. He was the kind who helped only himself until things went wrong. Then he came sniveling.

Fat, cherubic, good-for-nothing Roberto, the eldest of them all, and the most spoiled; the one who most resembled that shambling, wispy figure of disarming smile and indolent air, his father. Dead how long? Twenty-five years as a storefront photographer in the sleazy streets behind the *Capitolio*. Twenty-five years of bad pictures; a sodden monologue on abandoned Ireland interspersed with Señora Sánchez-what-beautiful-children-you-have-surely-you'll-want-some-extra-eight-by-tens. Twenty-five years, and when the *mojitos* had finally drowned the brogue, it was Nelson who'd arranged for the funeral and Roberto who'd cried.

Nelson peered cynically at the steaming summer night. For a man who believed in justice he sure as hell hadn't seen much—in his family, his job or anywhere else for that matter. And it was not as though he hadn't looked. *Cristo,* how he had looked.

He thought he had found it before he was twenty; wet, shivering, hungry and supremely content in the Sierra Maestra. He'd carried a rifle, mined bridges and lived with men who'd spoken of freedom and a new order. *¡Muera Batista¡ ¡Viva Fidel!* Nelson spit at his wastebasket. Roberto had never come to fight.

"You go, *chico,* I'll take care of the family," he had said the night that a teenage revolutionary marched to adulthood with tears in his eyes. Take care of the family, *coño!* One more dance at the yacht club, one more weekend in the country, another quick roll in the hay. But, boy, had Roberto been there that January morning when the guerrillas marched into Havana. Nobody had had a nicer red and black flag, and nobody had clapped harder. That day it had been Roberto who had cried and the hardened young section leader who had watched in a mixture of affection, disgust and unspoken political disquiet.

Roberto had not been there either at a beach called Girón where Nelson, deceived by a revolution gone wrong and commanding exile troops this time, had begged from the shelter of a dead friend for air cover that never came.

But wild horses would not have kept Roberto from the Orange Bowl to cheer the young president who promised to return a bloody battle flag one day in a free Havana. Octavio Nelson had not stayed for the speeches.

At first Roberto had proclaimed himself a businessman in their adopted land. Now he announced to all who wished to listen and many who didn't that he was an executive. An executive of what? Will-o-the-wisp International, maybe. But something evidently. Roberto always had "a big deal cooking," as he liked to tell his brother in his flawless English. Roberto wouldn't even speak Spanish to his family. It didn't suit his image.

Good old Bobby Nelson. Big house on the bay, big boat, graphite tennis rackets, decorator wife, vacation cottage in North Carolina. Thank God he didn't have any kids; they would have sneaked into the Ivy League on minority programs and claimed to their class-mates to have been born on Beacon Hill.

His brother was a crook. Octavio Nelson knew that. Big crimes, little crimes, any kind of crimes at all that didn't require dirty hands. Roberto was always on hand with a charming smile, a brisk handshake and empty promises.

And now he was running dope. Leave it to Roberto, forever at the height of fashion—a dope runner like every two-bit blow-dried dilettante in Miami. Probably even had his-and-hers matching gold spoons.

How tricky for Roberto to have a cop brother who was always arresting dopers. Tricky but bearable. Octavio would always be a brother first and a cop second. Roberto knew that. He counted on it.

Octavio Nelson sat for a long time. Around him the business of the police ebbed and flowed. He sensed it, but he didn't see it, and he didn't hear it. Should he, this one more time, do his brother's bidding? If he did, it probably would be abetting a crime. If he didn't, somebody might get hurt, and it certainly wouldn't be cagey Roberto.

Finally, painfully, Nelson picked up the black phone on his desk. He called a friend in the police garage.

"Tommy, this is Nelson. Could you do me a favor? I need a car towed in tonight—a brown Mercedes on Brickell near the cause-way." He recited the license number. "I'll take care of the paper work on it tomorrow."

"Sure, we'll get to it; it's a quiet night."

"Thanks. And listen, Tommy, tell the boys to check under the hood before they move it. There might be a bomb."

# Chapter 3

ONCE, WHEN MEN were young and home was Cuba, the *lector* sat in a place of honor above the long rows of wooden benches. He did not look at the artisans or they, gracefully building rich men's toys with flashing fingers, pungent leaf and wicked blade, at him.

In the mornings the *lector* exhausted the newspapers. Slowly, clearly, loud enough for the most junior apprentice to hear him, the *lector* would read all the local newspapers: the news, the editorials, the sports, the comics. In four hours of spoken lullaby each *tabaquero* would make one hundred cigars.

The long hot afternoons were a more contemplative time. The *lector* read novels of history and romance in the afternoons. Another four hours, another one hundred cigars.

The *lectores* were gone now, obsolete as lamplighters, vanquished by radio. In Miami today the *tabaquero* radios play loudly: saucy Latin music, mournful laments for a lost homeland, blatant come-ons to a consumer society. In the afternoons, soap operas.

The hands that caress the velvet leaf are the same. They are still quick, still supple, as loving as ever. It is the ears of the *tabaqueros* that are not what they once were. They have survived the *lectores,* but they will not survive the century. And there are none to follow them, not in Miami. Young Cubans in Miami drive trucks, teach school, run banks, smuggle dope. They do not roll cigars.

It is the old men who come to work in Miami's storefront cigar factories, old men steeped in tradition, patience and pride. Three old men came to work most mornings at the Matanzas cigar factory in a quiet side street near the Orange Bowl. For a long time it had been four, until Pepín died. Now it was only three. Elberto could have come if he had wanted to, Elberto whose cunning hands had

31

made cigars for princes and presidents in Cuba. But Elberto was lazy. He had always been lazy. *Cabrón.* Now he played dominoes day and night, useless, like an old woman. Elberto liked to tease his friends who still went to work every morning.

"Fools," he would cry as he passed the bench where they waited for the bus. "You need not work. Let your Tío Sam pay for your *frijoles.* You have worked long enough. Don't you know where they pay Social Security? Come, I will show you."

Fools? It was Elberto who was the fool, thought Jesús. One day he would learn how important it was to make cigars at the Matanzas factory. One day he would watch with envy while all of Little Havana crowded around the Matanzas *tabaqueros* to shake their hands and slap their backs. Then Elberto would see who had been the fool.

It was Jesús who opened the rickety front door each morning, who made the *cafecitos* and laid out the savory tobacco leaves to be worked. The leaves came from the Dominican Republic now, and the wrapper from Cameroon, but the tobacco had been grown from seeds smuggled out of Cuba. It was better than ever, better even than the tobacco other Cuban exiles now grew in Honduras and the Canary Islands. Was it as good as Cuban tobacco? *Ni hablar.* Of course it was better. Jesús had never met a Communist who could grow tobacco, much less roll a good cigar.

It was Jesús who fed the chickens in the small plot of green behind the shop and who turned on the radio that was the pallid North American substitute for the *lector.* Pedro and Raúl teased Jesús that he must do all the housekeeping work because he was the baby of the shop. Jesús knew they expected him to do all the work because he was a natural leader, and he appreciated that. Jesús was seventy-four.

It was Jesús, too, who emptied the ashtray and dusted and switched on the air-conditioning in the small private office at the rear of the shop. The office was soundproofed, paneled richly in wood. It held a modern desk and a swivel chair and a telephone with many buttons. It looked a century newer than the rest of the shop, and it was the real reason the three old men came each morning to make cigars. The brave man who worked in that office would one day lead them all back to Cuba. And that was a secret that stupid Elberto and his almighty dominoes would never know. *Cabrón.*

The old men always listened to the same Cuban exile radio station, and it was the talk shows they liked best. They sat, like a family for dinner, around the scarred *tambol,* gleaming *chavetas* cutting and shaping the cigars, the gray heads nodding agreement with each new forecast of disaster for *el tirano.* Castro. *El verdugo.* Pig.

It was the old men's pride that they understood so much more than the exiles who needed the radio for their news. The man who worked in the back would always know first when there was news. A crop failure. A plane crash. Important sabotage. Defections. He always knew, and he would always tell the *tabaqueros* who screened for him and protected his lair.

Never any details, mind you. Details were secret. They could be dangerous. There were many spies in *el barrio.* A nod. A smile of victory. Thumbs up. A shrug. They were enough; the old men understood. It was a difficult struggle.

When the man came that morning, he was impassive. It was not hard to explain: The radio spoke of a new Cuban victory in Africa. How that must have hurt. He touched Jesús lightly on the shoulder, took a Churchill from Raúl's rack and disappeared without a word into the office. . . .

He made two phone calls that morning. The first was to an office in a skyscraper overlooking Biscayne Bay.

"Law office."

"Mr. Redbirt, please." The English was flawless.

"Who is calling, please?"

"My name is Jones, Morgan Jones."

"I'll connect you now."

"Good morning," he said, "I understand there are problems."

"Jesus Christ, it's about time you called. The whole goddamn thing is unraveling. I don't know what to do."

"Tell me."

"The shipments are all cockeyed. One week we can't find an ounce. The next week I'm up to my ass in the shit. There's cops and Colombians all over town. We can't tell who to buy from. We don't know what stuff is good. People are getting ripped off. Everybody's nervous, and the customers are getting restless."

"It is only a temporary problem. It will be resolved. You may reassure the customers from me that the problems will be resolved."

"Reassure them from you? I don't even know who the hell you are! How long do you expect me to run this kind of operation with a phone call every couple of months from somebody I don't know?"

"As long as I tell you to. That is how we have operated in the past. And that is how we will continue to operate."

"No way. Things are very complicated; people are getting killed. We have to meet."

"No, my friend, we will not meet. You will do as you are told."

"I can't. I—"

"Would you rather go back to chasing ambulances? Or perhaps you would like the police to learn about how you are a criminal lawyer in every sense of the word."

"Now look, I didn't mean . . ."

"Order will be restored."

"How long, for God's sake?"

"A month, perhaps a little longer. I count on you to keep peace until then. Supplies may be tight."

He hung up and painstakingly lit the fresh cigar. Then he made the second call. It was to Bogotá, Colombia. He dialed direct, station to station, and this time he spoke Spanish.

"Juan? This is Ignacio."

"How can I serve you?" There was sarcasm in the smooth, liquid Spanish that was the only thing about Colombia he admired.

"Let us not play games. These are serious times."

"Of course they are serious. Your animals shoot my people in the streets. They kill *gringos*. They rob my ships; they kidnap my mules. That is not just serious. That is madness."

"I know, I know. But you must understand that it is not my people who do these things. It is what the *gringos* call the freelancers. They are everywhere; children. Anyone who can drive a boat or fly a plane. They are like swarming ants. I cannot respond for them."

"Which is why I put my own people in Miami. I must know who I am dealing with. I will not treat with children."

"That is something we can work out. There is plenty of room for both of us—you there, me here."

"I am not sure that I need you at all, Ignacio. I have the goods here. We are the factory—without us you cannot live."

"And without the distributors you cannot live. Your people come here like farmers, with cowshit between their toes. They do not speak English. They do not understand *gringos*. They do not even know how to make elevators work. All they know how to do is to steal and shoot."

"In time they will learn."

"In time the police and the customs and the DEA will be on every street corner with big deals and bad money. It will be impossible to sell anything."

From Bogotá came only static.

"Look," he continued, "we can work together. If you need a few people here to make sure things go well, that some merchandise is shipped north, that is no problem. It is only Miami that I care about."

It was a major concession, and he heard the man in Bogotá expel a long sigh. Relief? He pressed.

"We need to dry up the freelancers and to arrange territories between us. It should not be hard if we are sensible."

"Very well. We can talk at least. Where shall we meet?"

"I prefer somewhere neutral. Panama. I know someone there you would like. She is very special, very young."

"You certainly know how to tempt an old man, don't you? Let me see . . ."

He could almost see the manicured fingers ruffling the pages of a parchment diary. The man would be in his study at the desk of eighteenth-century teak. Under the Goya a fire would be burning, for in Bogotá it is always damp and the man was old.

"Ignacio," the man in Bogotá said finally, "there is no way I can leave the country anytime soon. The Senate is in session; my coffee is almost ready for picking; there is a speech I must give; my favorite horse is running. One thing after another. You know how it is."

"Ignacio" relit the Churchill and pulled deeply, letting the smoke pour into his mouth and tickle his gums. He tried to blow a smoke ring. He never could make them round. But he was good at negotiation.

"Yes, of course, I know how it is. My new boat is nearly finished, and I cannot wait. I am like a little boy. You must see her: long and white and sleek and new—like my friend in Panama."

"Cartagena!" said the man in Bogotá. "In a couple of weeks I must go to Cartagena for a conference. We can meet there."

Cartagena. Ancient, ribald, lawless Cartagena, a city for adventure. A great Caribbean port where less than half of what left and less of what came in ever appeared on anybody's manifest. Every smuggler in the hemisphere loved Cartagena, and most of them had been swindled there. He could go to Cartagena inside a Patton tank and still be dead in six hours. The old man was teasing him.

"But of course, Cartagena is very hot at this time of the year, isn't it?" said the man in Bogotá. "I'll tell you what. Come here as my guest. My granddaughter is getting married. I'll send you an invitation."

"Well . . ." He let the word drag out until it was an acceptance and a refusal.

"Come here and come alone. I guarantee your safety," said the man in Bogotá.

"Done," he said.

"*Vaya con Dios,* Ignacio."

"*Igualmente,*"he said, and hung up.


IT WAS AN IMPORTANT DAY, a day of great events, Jesús could tell.

The man had gone into the office hunched and worried. When he emerged now, he seemed relaxed, almost expansive. He complimented Raúl on the Churchill and asked after Pedro's family. He told Jesús sales were good and urged him to find another *tabaquero* to fill Pepín's empty seat at the *tambol.*

The *tabaqueros* waited. Would he give them some news of the cause, something to warm their bony chests and scarred hearts? They needed to know that the cause was advancing, that little by little, the way a good cigar accumulates ash, the circle was tightening on the killer in Havana.

"*La lucha sigue,*"the man said at last, gently banging a fist against the old wooden table. The fight goes on.

The *tabaqueros* understood.

"*Hasta mañana,* Don José," the old men chorused. It was indeed an important day.

# Chapter 4

THE EARLY-MORNING light is Florida's freshest face, flawless as crystal, fleeting as tropical twilight. Chris Meadows savored the morning solitude. He made coffee and sat on the porch, half reading the paper but engaged more by the dancing shadows that announced dawn's eclipse by day.

Early rising was a legacy of the hospital, he supposed. He had been home a week now, and his leg had subsided into a manageable ache. He looked appraisingly through the line of royal palms at the pool. No swimming, the doctor had said, until the bandages were off.

Truth be told, Meadows didn't want to swim. He didn't feel like working either. It had been a lost week, a week of nothingness—two weeks if you counted the hospital time. Apathy was a stranger to Meadows, but he felt trapped in its cobwebs now and too mushy-headed to resist.

The day before, in a listless walk through the tropical acre that shielded his house from the road, Meadows had halfheartedly examined himself. Diagnosis: sorrow, anger and shock in about equal measure. So he was feeling sorry for himself. So what? He was entitled to it, wasn't he?

It was not as though anybody else gave a damn. Arthur had come by with a book of chess problems and a pocketful of wisecracks, a few neighbors had made sympathetic cluckings and he had had to proclaim himself fully recovered to forestall a visit from his mother. Beyond that, Meadows mourned alone in a cocoon of privacy. Terry would have helped—she would have helped a great deal—but when Terry lifted her bulky cargo plane off the runway at Miami International and pointed south, only God knew where she would turn up next.

Meadows overcame his ennui once each day to dial the number Nelson had given him, to ask if the killers had been caught.

"Nothing new," Pincus had said curtly the day before. Nothing new.

Awkwardly Meadows swung off the rattan sofa. Maybe if he went upstairs and sat at his worktable, he could summon up inspiration or at least some energy.

The house was wood, dark and weathered, with a fronting of native limestone. Meadows had bought it a few years before from a cracker family that had lived there in termited isolation for more than half a century. Meadows had dubbed the house his "cracker box" and set about rebuilding it in his own image.

The huge screened porch with its Sea Island hammocks faced the bay. Inside, Meadows had torn down the interior partitions, opening up the living area so it flowed into the porch, uniting the whole with polished oak floors and cypress ceiling beams. Doing most of the work himself, Meadows had built a second story, also of wood, also with its huge porch, and joined it to the first by a spiral staircase that seemed to float off the floor.

It was on the second floor that Meadows slept and gave birth to his architectural dreams. A skylight joined studio and bedroom, making the second story as light and airy as the first was dark and cool. A scarred drafting table dominated the studio. In walk-around mahogany display cases sat precise models of buildings Meadows had conceived—and some he wished he had.

Meadows was doodling listlessly that morning when Stella called. Stella was the dragon who guarded the small office Meadows kept in downtown Miami. He seldom went to the office, and she was the major reason.

Stella was an intense, aggressive female who should have been a politician: all style and no substance. She had the most commanding telephone presence Meadows had ever encountered—that was why he had hired her. What he had not discovered until after it was too late to fire her was that forceful Stella never got anything right.

At first Meadows had been dismayed. He had chided her, coaxed her, coached her until he was sure she understood. It was like translating from another language. If he asked her to book him on Western to San Francisco, she would say "Yes, sir, right away, Mr. Meadows," and call Eastern.

By now, however, Meadows had grown accustomed to Stella. In fact, Meadows's friends had his unlisted home number, everybody else called Stella. It worked fine. When Stella garbled a message, it usually turned out to be somebody he hadn't wanted to talk to anyway.

That day she reported that a client named Nelson Octavio had called. At least she got the phone number right. Meadows felt a pulse of excitement as he waited for Nelson to come to the phone.

"Nelson, it's Meadows. Have you arrested those guys yet?"

"No, *amigo,* we're still working on it. But we've got a lead, and I'd like you to give us a hand."

"Sure. What can I do?"

"They found a body last night in Coral Gables. It might be one of the guys you saw in the shootout. I'd appreciate it if you went down to the medical examiner's office and took a look. Won't take long."

"Where?"

"The county morgue. Downtown."

"Jesus. Can't I just look at a picture?" Meadows asked. "I don't want to go to the morgue."

"Sorry, but a picture is no good. All these scumbags look alike when they're dead," Nelson said. "The complexion, the hairline, the size of the face—none of that comes through in a mug shot. Really, it would be a big help. . . ."

All look alike when they're dead. Meadows saw Jessica's body again as it arched into the air, Sandy's as it dragged along the ground. "I'll be there," he said, and hung up.


THE MEDICAL EXAMINER'S office, Meadows discovered after a series of wrong turns, was a featureless two-story annex attached to Flagler Memorial Hospital. Buildings without architecture, Miami was full of them.

Meadows was intercepted by a laconic clerk who seemed as anonymous.

"I'm here to look at a body," he said.

"Are you next-of-kin?"

"Uh, no. Definitely not."

"Name?"

"Christopher Meadows."

The clerk leafed through a stack of pink carbons.

"We don't have a Chris Meadows. We have a Christine Reilly, but she's already been ID'd by her daughter."

"Meadows is *my* name. I was asked to come down here and look at a body that was found this morning."

"OK, whose body?" The clerk tapped a Bic pen on her desk. She had all day.

"I don't know. They didn't give me a name."

"Is this a joke?"

"No, Detective Nelson told me to come. He said he was going to meet me here."

The clerk mashed an intercom button. "Dr. Appel?"

"Yes, Lorie," a voice reverberated. It sounded as if the man were in Key West.

"There's a man named Meadows here wants to look at a body. Says Nelson sent him."

"Right. Send him back."

Meadows edged cautiously through one set of swinging doors, then another. He found himself standing in a vast room, walled in old tiles the color of lima beans. It took several moments before Meadows realized he was surrounded by human bodies.

They lay, one after another, on silver autopsy tables. Some were splayed open at the sternum, the skin stretched back and the chest cavity open like a Thanksgiving turkey. Meadows thought the corpses looked very small. The whole room smelled rotten and cold. He swallowed hard.

"Hello there."

Meadows spun around. Dr. Harry Appel stood behind him.

"Hello," Meadows replied shakily. "You scared me."

"Didn't mean to," Appel said. "Sit down."

Meadows sat. Appel, a tall man with tortoise-shell glasses, turned back to his work. In one hand he held a half-eaten ham-and-cheese sandwich. The other hand held a human heart, a small bloody violet balloon. Meadows thought he was going to be sick.

"I'd offer you a sandwich," Appel was saying, "but this is the last one in the house." The doctor noticed Meadows pale. "Oh, I'm sorry." He put the sandwich in a paper bag. "I normally don't eat on the job, but we've had a very busy morning. As you can see."

Meadows nodded weakly and looked at the floor.

Appel placed the heart on a scale and read the weight aloud into a Dictaphone. Then he took a plastic bag, the same kind sold as sandwich bags in any grocery store, and pinched an edge until it opened. He slid the heart in, twisted a metal tab to seal it and dropped the whole soggy package back into the chest cavity. Meadows watched, transfixed.

"I have to do this," Appel explained. "Used to be I could throw the organs away after I took lab samples. Lately, though, a lot of families insist that their loved ones be buried intact, with all the parts and pieces."

Meadows just nodded.

"So, you're here to see the Juan Doe?"

"Uh?"

Appel ran his hands under a faucet, rinsing blood off the diaphanous surgical gloves. He wiped them on his wrinkled green lab coat and motioned to Meadows. "I think your friend is over there."

He led Meadows to a table where a skinny corpse lay. The top of the skull had been cut away with a fine saw. It hung as if by a hinge, exposing the upper hemisphere of the brain. The skin was pulled down over the face into a wrinkled rubbery mask. The nose was in the wrong place. The mouth was a sneer.

Meadows stood six feet from the table, frozen.

"Oh, Christ," he wheezed.

"Don't worry," Appel said cheerfully. "I'll put this face back so you can see what he looks like." He replaced the cap of the skull on the brain, tugging the scalp into place. Then he pulled the skin up, tightening the facial features. Meadows now saw that the victim was a young man, probably a Latin. The face was narrow and bore a grubby trace of a mustache.

"I don't know him," Meadows said. "He wasn't one of the men I saw."

Appel shrugged. "I'm not surprised." He asked Meadows about the shootout in the Grove.

"I'd rather not," the architect replied. "Nelson can tell you what happened. Where is he anyway?"

"He called to say he couldn't make it," Appel said. "He mentioned that your girlfriend got killed."

"An old friend. Just the way it happened . . . I'm still upset about it. I still don't feel much like talking. The only reason I came down here was Nelson. He said this might be the guy who did all the shooting, but it isn't."

Appel peeled off his gloves. "I'm sorry about your friend. Nelson said you got shot up, too."

"In the leg. It's getting better."

"That's good," Appel said. "That's very good."

Appel was trying to be friendly. Meadows liked him. He wondered why anyone would become a coroner. He was intrigued by Appel's nonchalance.

"How did this one die?"

"Same old tricks," said Appel.

With a bare hand—that was the first thing Meadows noticed— Appel grabbed the corpse by the hair and lifted the head off the block of wood under the neck. He turned it on its side and pointed to a dime-sized hole, dead center in the back of the skull. "There. Bingo."

Meadows winced. "Why?"

"Take a wild guess." Appel sighed. "Shit, I get these guys in here every week. Latin male, late twenties, early thirties. Single bullet wound in the back of the head. No ID, no family, no friends. Takes us weeks to trace them. This one's a Colombian. A Juan Doe, and he'll probably be buried that way. He's an illegal. Do you know what they found on the body? Three thousand bucks."

"That's a lot of money to be carrying around."

"He also had a gram of coke and a Cartier watch. The guy had great taste in jewelry but bad taste in the company he kept."

Meadows took a breath and stepped closer. He studied the face again. "No, I really haven't seen him before."

"Were the men in the cars Cuban or Colombian?"

"I don't know. They were Latin . . . well, dark-skinned. I just don't know. They were yelling at each other in Spanish, but there was so much happening." Meadows flashed on the scene again, just as in his dreams: the noise, the smoke, the screams, then dizziness. The cops had said ten or eleven seconds were all it took.

"You want to look at a Cuban?" Appel asked.

"Another drug murder?"

"Yep. Came in this morning." Appel went to another table. The corpse was in a heavy black body bag. The words *Metro Fire Rescue* were stenciled in red near the feet.

"A stinker," Appel warned as he unzipped the bag. "Better hold your nose on this one."

Meadows fumbled for a handkerchief and mashed it over his mouth. The corpse was ghastly: bloated, greenish, fetid. The clothes were torn, and the flesh of the abdomen was shredded and white.

"Sharks," Appel explained. "They found this one off Cape Florida. Three clowns from New Jersey were out dolphin fishing on a charter boat. They trolled right over the body and snagged it. Pulled an outrigger down, and they fought it for fifteen minutes before they realized it wasn't fighting back."

"God, I couldn't possibly tell you if I knew that guy or not," Meadows said, fighting waves of nausea.

"He's been out there three weeks," Appel said. "He died the same way as the Colombian: thirty-two semiautomatic in the back of the head." The medical examiner zipped the bag up. "You know what's interesting, though, is that this one got beat up first."

"Was it a robbery?"

"Don't think so. Beat up, as in tortured. Broken ribs, some kidney damage. They really did a job on him."

"I'm sorry, but I can't tell what he used to look like," Meadows said.

"Oh, we got an ID on this one." Appel handed the architect a clipboard. The police report was on top. Meadows read it all, fascinated, but feeling like a voyeur.

The dead man's name was Ruis Juan González. Age: twenty-six. Single. Address: 1721 Brickell Avenue. Meadows knew the building, an ugly condominium two blocks off Biscayne Bay.

Appel pointed to a line in the police report. "This is the best part," he said.

In the space marked Occupation the cops had written: "Import-export business."

"That's from his sister," Appel explained. "She said her brother was very big into coffee tables from Colombia. Sold them in a shop down on Flagler Street."

"But he really was a smuggler."

Appel laughed. "Yeah. He really was a smuggler." He watched Meadows closely. The architect was examining the homicide report as if it were one of the Dead Sea Scrolls.

Appel sat down at his desk. Meadows noted, with astonishment, that the doctor's coffee cup was fashioned from what seemed to be a human skull. Appel noticed Meadows's discomfort and chuckled. "Want some Sanka?"

Meadows shook his head.

"Do you know much about the dope business?" Appel asked.

"Just what's in the papers," Meadows said. "I talked to Nelson after the shooting. After the murders. He said it was probably just a rip-off, that was all, and everyone started shooting."

Appel fingered his sideburns, flecked with gray. A bit premature, Meadows thought. The doctor couldn't be more than thirty-five, thirty-six.

"There's a small war going on," Appel said evenly. "They're killing each other left and right. We get at least one a week in here, just like I showed you. Colombians, Cubans, a few stupid Anglos. It started about a year ago, and at the time it was all very neat because it was fratricide. Dopers killing dopers. Nobody seemed to care. Then some innocent people started getting in the way."

"Like . . ."

"Like your friend and her little girl." Appel lit his pipe and didn't say anything for a while. Meadows looked at the room full of bodies. He counted nine.

"Oh, most of these are naturals," Appel said, waving at the tables. "Routine stuff. Some old lady on the beach is insisting I do a post on her husband. He was seventy-four. Now I know he died of congestive heart failure; I *know* it. But she's convinced he got poisoned by the boysenberry pancakes at this cafeteria downtown. She's already hired a lawyer, for Chrissakes! Pancakes."

Appel and Meadows laughed together.

"I could never do this sort of work," the architect muttered.

"No, probably not," Appel said, not unkindly. He thought of Sandra Fay Tilden. He didn't tell Chris Meadows that he himself had done the autopsy.

"I've been down here five years, and I've never seen it so bad," Appel said. "They brought in one of these jokers the other day and I counted eleven machine-gun holes. Machine guns . . . think about that."

"Why a war?"

"Greed," Appel said. "The money is beyond imagination, probably even more than doctors and architects make." The coroner grinned. "Coke," he said.

"Cocaine?"

"That's it. That's why these assholes get killed. That's why your friend got killed. She got between the salesman and the merchandise and never knew it."

Meadows stood up to leave. "I'm sorry that I couldn't find one of the killers here today."

"Don't get your hopes up," Appel said sardonically. "Most of these murders are never solved. No one talks." He pointed at the dead Colombian. "That's the price you pay if you do."

"Did Nelson say if they had any more leads?"

"Didn't say." Appel shook Meadows's hand. "It was nice meeting you. Hope I didn't spoil your appetite for the day."

"I'll be OK."

Meadows stepped into the parking lot, and the harsh afternoon sun blinded him. He breathed deeply. Full of rain and summer heat, the air felt marvelous in his lungs after an hour in the stale autopsy room.

# Chapter 5

THE PHONE was ringing when Meadows returned from the morgue.

"Chris, thank God. It you don't come here instantly and rescue me from these miserable curs, I shall never speak to you again."

"Terry!"

*"Perro de mierda. ¡Cállate, carajo!"*

"Terry, where are you?" From the receiver came snarls, barks, a howl.

"I have just brought two dozen mangy dogs from Panama to a place called the Miami Shores Kennel Club. I should have dumped them out over the Caribbean instead. Filthy brutes."

"I'll be right there. Wait in the lobby."

"I will not wait in the lobby. I will wait in the bar, and if you are not here in twenty minutes, I shall run off with the first man there who tells me he hates greyhounds."

"Twenty minutes."

Meadows hustled back to his Karman Ghia and pointed for the expressway north. The steering wheel was nearly too hot to grasp. Meadows hardly noticed. Terry was back.

Terry the wildcat. Meadows had never known a woman like her. She was to Sandy as a hurricane was to spring rain.

They had met at a party in New York the year before, one of those East Eighties parties so full of earnestly meaningful phonies that Meadows had taken one look and nearly headed for the door. Instead, he had sought out a quiet corner, and there she'd been. . . .

"MY NAME IS María Cristina Betancourt Issuralde," she said after a moment, apparently deciding he wasn't one of the bores. "People call me Terry."

"Chris Meadows." He offered his hand awkwardly. "How do you get Terry from María and all the rest?"

"It's a nickname—short for *Terremoto.*"

"I am moved."

Terry rewarded him with a grin, then, after a few minutes, said suddenly, "Will you please take me away from this horrible party? Take me to eat. I'm starved."

"Sure," said Meadows, delighted and somewhat nonplussed. "Chinese food?"

"Anything."

Over dinner they talked, or rather mostly she talked and Meadows listened. She had been born rich, Terry confided between mouthfuls of Peking duck, and she bored easily. She was the eldest child of a South American land baron who owned huge tracts, and passports to match, in Argentina, Paraguay and Brazil. Terry had skied at Portillo and swum at Monaco. She spoke English, Portuguese, Spanish and French interchangeably. She had been to boarding schools in England and a university in France. She had been wooed by playboys and tycoons. And she had rebelled.

"There I was one day, twenty-two years old. I had known about men since I was sixteen. I had known about the world since I was born. So I asked myself: 'María Cristina, what are you going to do with your life?' It was nasty question.

"'Marry a millionaire and screw the gardener while he counts his money? Run off with a sports car driver until one day he makes goulash of himself against a concrete wall?' No, *señor,* that was not for me."

"I'm surprised you didn't find a good revolution," Meadows ventured.

"I thought about that, it is true—and believe me, I look terrific in khaki fatigues and a beret. But I will tell you something about my part of the world. The revolutions all promise freedom and justice. South America is a continent of great promises. But what they deliver is nothing. And I will tell you something else. Take away the rifles from those tough *hombres* and they are nothing. A woman might as well go to bed with her teddy bear for all the good they will do her."

"I didn't know," Meadows replied weakly.

"Revolutionaries destroy. I am a builder. So I looked around for something I could build, something romantic and challenging. I thought about it for a long time, and then I decided. I went to my parents, and I told them. My mother called for her confessor. My father yelled and threatened to whip me, but deep down I think he was very pleased, for we both knew I was more like him than his sons, my brothers.

"I went to school and studied to be a pilot. Never has anyone studied so hard. And then I borrowed the money for a plane—an old Convair. I found a copilot, and I flew that plane anywhere there was cargo.

"Río Gallegos. Puerto Montt. Cuiabá in the Mato Grosso. Potosí, in Bolivia, where the mountains are cruel and the runway is short. My company is called Cargas Aereas Nacionales, CAN. I fly where I say I will fly, and I charge what I say I will charge. CAN do! Now I have four planes, and the money I spend is my own. My father is proud of me; my mother dares not criticize. Tonight I flew race horses to New York from Venezuela. Before that it was Brazilian tractor tires to Tegucigalpa. In a few days, who knows?"

SHE'D TRANSFIXED HIM. Beside her Meadows felt earthbound, pedestrian.

"I don't know why you hang around with me," Meadows teased one day after a joy ride across the state in a rented single-engine plane had left him green.

Terry had laughed deeply and bitten his ear.

"*Pobrecito*. I should have told you it would be bumpy. I'm sorry. That was a terrible thing to do to my protector."

"My protector." It was a private joke, a shard of that first night in New York. They'd left the restaurant three hours later and wandered aimlessly through the streets of Chinatown, talking.

The mugger had found them near the river. Meadows gave him what money he had, almost with a shrug, as though it were a form of taxation people who walk at night must be prepared to pay. But the mugger had wanted more than money.

"You go for a walk, big boy. The girl stays."

That had been too much. When the man advanced, waving a chain, Meadows charged blindly and seized him in a bear hug. For endless minutes the two men grunted in a clumsy wrestling match until their momentum carried them crashing into a steel trash bin, and it was the mugger's skull that caught the corner. The chain clattered to the pavement.

Terry had tugged at Meadows's elbow, but still enraged, he'd stooped down and methodically stripped the man of his clothes, mugging the mugger, leaving him in underwear and socks and moaning half-consciously. He'd thrown the clothes into a sewer, then bought himself two Irish coffees to stop the trembling. That night he and Terry had made love for the first time.

MEADOWS'S REVERIE CARRIED him onto I-95, through the long elevated curve that skirted downtown Miami, past the blackened sentinels of despair that the riots of 1980 had posted in the Liberty City ghetto. The dog track was only two blocks off the 125th Street exit, and the matinee was in high gear by the time Meadows arrived. The clubhouse seemed to rattle like an airplane hangar as the crowd cheered another skinny hound to the finish. Meadows rehearsed what he would tell Terry about the shooting.

She was hard to miss in the tawdry bar, tall and bronzed, hair like pitch and eyes to match. To Meadows's surprise, Terry seemed to be studying a race program. As he moved toward her, though, first his gaze, then his path were blocked. Was the couple in front of him dancing? No, they were wrestling.

"Gimme the ten!" snarled a tall black man in a Panama hat. "You tol' me to bet that dog. It's your fault I lost."

He clutched a belligerent woman by the elbows. In one hand she deftly balanced a plastic cup full of beer; in the other she kept a death grip on a crumpled ten-dollar bill.

"Get your fuckin' hands off me!" she shouted. "You touch me and I'll run to your goddamn wife."

They twirled in a woozy minuet until a fat security guard waddled up and collared them both. Meadows slid onto the barstool next to Terry's and sneaked an arm around her waist.

"Nice place you have here," he whispered, "but welcome home anyway."

"*¡Por fin!*" The embrace took Meadows's breath away.

"Let's get out of here," Meadows said into the great black mane. "I have lots to tell you."

Terry surveyed him hungrily. "Ten minutes, one race. I have made a bet."

"I thought you hated dogs."

"I do when they shit all over my airplane. But not this one. Look." She gestured to the program. "Here, number three, Fly Baby. It must be good luck for me."

They found a seat twenty rows up, far from the race track. Meadows noticed glumly that they were surrounded by garrulous retirees from a nearby condominium. Having spent their youth, but not their savings, in Queens and Charlestown, they fled to Florida, first for the winters and then forever. Great climate, but not a damn thing to do but to await death over the bingo table or to sign up for the bus trips to the dog track. Meadows tuned out their chatter.

Two minutes before race time the grooms emerged from the kennel area. At the end of each leash was a lean greyhound capped tightly with a muzzle. The dogs were impossibly mean, he knew, sometimes even stopping in the middle of a race to fight each other. The inbreeding that had made them fast as a freight train had also made them monumentally stupid. Each dog in front of him now wore a cloth number and walked in a desultory gait two or three paces behind the groom.

"You picked a name. How does everybody else know which dog to bet on?" Meadows asked.

"That's how," said Terry, pointing. The number seven greyhound was hunched unabashedly in a squat, fertilizing an orchid bed near the home stretch. A cluster of drunks down on the rail gave a hearty ovation.

"Jesus!" Meadows laughed. "Great sport."

"*Ay Dios,* everyone will bet that dog now." Terry sighed. And sure enough, by post time the odds on the seven greyhound had dropped to five to three.

The dogs bolted from the gate in hot pursuit of a bogus rabbit nailed to a moving boom. Meadows tracked Fly Baby as it grabbed an early lead, faltered, move up once more before getting bumped to the outside and finished fourth, out of the money. The whole thing took forty-nine seconds.

*"Mierda,"* muttered Terry. The number seven dog won by three lengths. "Let me go to the bathroom, and then we will leave. I'll meet you at the finish line."

Alone, Meadows scanned the payday crowd. Below, six rows down, was a pretty young woman. From the back she resembled Sandy Tilden. Meadows found himself straining to see if a small child sat at her side. Of course, there was none. When the woman turned sideways, she did not look like Sandy at all, and Christopher Meadows looked away.

He limped down to the rail for a better glimpse of the greyhounds. From the grandstands they all looked alike; up close he noticed marked differences in size, musculature and gait. The grooms looked bored stiff. So did the dogs.

"Stop it now. I was here before you."

Meadows turned to his left in time to see a pudgy snowhaired old man move nose to nose against a tall young Latin. "Now this was my spot, son. Move down a little bit, please."

His adversary was built like a refrigerator.

"Who the fuck do you think you are?" the young man demanded. He had the face of a ferret. Another husky Latin stood behind him, laughing. A third had his back to the fracas. He was studying the greyhounds. Meadows noticed he wore a cream-colored suit.

"Now I don't want to fight . . ." the older man was saying.

Meadows searched the crowd for a sign of Terry. When he looked back, the old man was out of breath and off the ground; the punk had hoisted him by the shoulders.

Meadows did not move. His heart rattled against his ribs, and his legs felt like sand. He saw it quite clearly, tucked into the young man's belt . . . the bluish butt of a pistol. Then the third man turned around. The face of the man took Meadows's breath away.

There it was. Oval and brooding. Those fierce, deep eyes, coals and ice.

It was him.

The eyes flicked past Meadows as the man in the cream-colored suit said something harsh to the other two and gestured sharply. The young *Latino* sullenly put the old man down and walked toward the ticket lobby with his two companions. The old man slapped wanly at his rumpled clothes, speaking to no one in particular. "Stupid goddamn hoods. Think they own this country . . ."

Meadows could only stand transfixed.

Terry appeared then. "Chris! You're pale! Is something wrong?"

Meadows grabbed her arm.

"Let's go. Let's go," he muttered. "I'll tell you later."

Meadows and Terry moved upstream against the crowd, which was pouring back to the grandstand from the ticket windows. His eyes searched the seats as he shuffled impatiently toward the exit.

There.

In the last row up, they sat together. Meadows counted four now. The three biggest ones were laughing together. The fourth, the dapper one in the suit, held a pair of small binoculars to his eyes.

He had been scanning the park, but now he stopped. He wasn't looking at the greyhounds. He was looking directly at Christopher Meadows.

"What is it?" Terry asked. "Chris, you're pushing me."

"Hurry. Please."

That night, when he tried to draw that face from memory, the shape came easily in smooth, circular strokes. The sharp eyebrows and heavy Neanderthal ridge of the forehead were not exact, but acceptable.

What Meadows could not seem to replicate were the eyes. He fiddled with them for what must have been a half hour, faltering and starting again, before he was satisfied.

When he was finished, Meadows knew what the eyes reminded him of, so dark and dispassionate and deadly. They were not the eyes of a man at all. They were the eyes of a shark.

# Chapter 6

THE LINCOLN sat in front of El Hogar, a cramped storefront restaurant on Southwest Eighth Street in Little Havana. A Sorry We're Closed sign hung in the door window, but small candles still burned in the red table lanterns inside. There were but four customers.

Outside, in a dingy blue Dodge less than a block away, Detective Octavio Nelson closed his eyes. They had been sitting on the Lincoln for an hour with no sign of the owner. Nelson was sure the man was inside El Hogar, but he wasn't sure it was worth the wait. Another headache was coming on like a noisy bus.

"I heard Shafer got off today," Wilbur Pincus said.

Nelson nodded and sucked on a cigar.

"I told you it was a bad search," Pincus said.

Nelson glared at his partner. "I knew he had at least a kilo in the trunk. I took the chance."

"How'd you tell it in court?"

"Routine traffic stop."

Pincus shook his head. "I bet they took you apart on probable cause, right?"

They sure had, Nelson thought to himself. He hated to lose a shithead like Shafer. Shafer could have been flipped. He was an Anglo. He'd been scared out of his mind. Nelson had known it the minute he'd put the handcuffs on. But the judge had said it was a bad search. "Totally illegal" were the words he'd used. So Shafer walked.

"At least I cost him a kilo of coke," Nelson muttered.

Pincus snorted. "We took a whole course in probable cause up at

Tallahassee. Lasted two weeks. Maybe you ought to sign up next time."

"Right," Nelson said. "You bet."

The car was like a sauna. He flipped on the radio and tuned in a Miami *salsa* station.

"Don't you think you ought to leave the squawk box on?" Pincus asked. "In case they try to reach us."

"Naw. We're on surveillance."

The front door of El Hogar opened. Nelson sat up. Just one of the waitresses on her way home. The lights in the restaurant remained on.

"What did you find in that car?" Pincus asked suddenly.

"What car?"

"The Mercedes you hauled in a couple weeks ago."

Nelson tightened. "How'd you know about that?"

"I saw the tow sheet on your desk."

Fucking Mathers in the garage. He should have known better. "Nothing," Nelson said. "The car was clean."

"Who'd it come back to?"

"I don't even remember. Some doctor, I think. He got bombed one night and forgot where he parked. It was nothing."

Pincus seemed to buy it.

The car had *not* been clean.

Roberto Nelson's Mercedes-Benz sedan had contained 5.7 grams of cocaine hidden in a metallic key box beneath the steering column. Octavio Nelson had found it after a ten-minute search, weighed it and field-tested it himself on a lab kit he had bought one day at a Coconut Grove head shop. Then he flushed the powder down the john.

He'd never made a report on the coke or even on the tow job, an oversight the boys in the police garage were not likely to forgive soon. He'd given Mathers the same bullshit story about the doctor.

Then Roberto, idiot Roberto, had waltzed into police headquarters and copped the keys off Octavio's desk on the fourth floor and driven his goddamn Mercedes off without a word. They would see about that later, he and Roberto.

In the meantime, there was Wilbur Pincus, Iowa-born-and-bred, a babe in Miami. Pincus was a book man. He dressed by the book, talked by the book, made out all of his A forms by the book. The first time Nelson had caught Pincus shining his shoes, he'd immediately put in for a new partner. His complaints were ignored. Pincus, unfortunately, was a pretty good cop.

Nelson had tried another approach. He'd worked on Pincus until he planted the idea that the young cop should go to work for the federal Drug Enforcement Administration. Nelson had even gone so far as to provide three glowing letters of commendation, two of them signed by police captains who had been dead for years.

The DEA had been interested. Pincus had come out of his first interview with flying colors. Two days later, however, a DEA agent working in Hialeah had been shot down by one of his own men during a busted Quaalude deal. That afternoon Pincus had withdrawn his application. He'd told the feds he'd rather work with Octavio Nelson.

After all, all the other captains got fat behind desks, chewed out the sergeants, fucked the secretaries and worked up office pools on the Dolphin games. Not Nelson. Here was a big shot cop who really loved street work. Pincus had been impressed. Nelson was sloppy, to be sure, and a bit crude, but he was a cop Pincus could learn from.

Pincus truly felt that way until he'd discovered Nelson had been trying to dump him. The humiliation had been devastating. For two days he'd trod from floor to floor in search of Captains Donnelly and Lopez, to thank them for their letters. A rookie motorman had finally told him they were dead. That Nelson would actually counterfeit recommendations and mail them to the *DEA*— Pincus had been thunderstruck. He'd said nothing to Nelson, but the partnership had become a study in simmering friction. The other narcotics detectives watched closely to see which of them would surrender to the other's style. The heavy money was on Pincus.

Then came the Aristidio Cruz beating, and the whole bureau waited for the lid to blow. But Nelson and Pincus both acted as though it never happened. For Nelson, it was forgettable. For Pincus, it was a trauma, never far from his troubled thoughts. . . .

"What if these goons go out the back door?" he asked now, motioning toward the restaurant.

"They won't," said Nelson, turning up the car radio again.

At a corner table inside El Hogar, Domingo Sosa, the man known as Mono, seemed lost in himself while his three companions joked.

"How much did you lose today?"

"Four hundred," said one.

"Three eighty," said another.

"*Perros de mierda.* I tell you, the whole thing is fixed. They put drugs in the Gainesburgers. Some of them could barely walk around the track, much less run."

"We go to jai alai next time."

"Ha, that's worse. I had a friend who was a jai alai player. He said he never won if he made love to a woman the night before. For three weeks he went to bed alone. He won almost every night. Everybody in the fronton started betting on him. He was a big star. He said he was serving so hard the other players never saw the *pelota* until it was past them."

"Did you go and bet on him?"

"No, *chico.* I never trust a man who can't get laid for three weeks."

"What happened to your friend?"

"He damn near went crazy. Now he screws every night before the match. He's a shitty jai alai player, but I bet on him every time I go."

Ignoring the laughter, Mono motioned to the waitress. "Another pitcher, *señorita.*" He looked sternly at the other men. "No more of this. We must get back to business."

"The *gringo* at the dog track?"

"Yes."

"You are sure it is the same man?"

Mono nodded. "Did you see the way he stared?"

"So what?" One of his men, who looked like a peasant, shrugged. "Many people were staring."

"I recognized him," Mono said flatly. "He was the man down in the Grove that day when the woman was hit by the car."

"But you shot him."

Mono glared. "In the leg."

"Are you sure?"

"Absolutely."

He had learned his ballistics from the best of the CIA. He had trained on a beach in the Florida Keys—a mock invasion during a stinging rainstorm; nighttime target practice with the tracer rifles; blasting coconuts out of the palm trees with a .45 pistol at lunchtime. Six months' worth of training.

Mono had made many friends among his fellow soldiers-in-training. Two of them had died at the Bay of Pigs. Another, who had gone to jail for seventeen years on the Isle of Pines, had wished he had. He'd been freed, blind and half-crippled, and Mono had been at the airport when the chartered Eastern jetliner had brought him into Miami from Havana. The two men had wept together like children. Mono's henchmen had never seen him cry, but they understood.

Over the years Mono forgot nothing of what the CIA had taught him, least of all how to shoot. Now he was cursing himself: You should have killed that *gringo* when you had the chance. You should have aimed for the chest and squeezed the trigger. Instead you aimed low, not out of compassion but out of common sense— the important difference between aggravated assault and first-degree murder.

Mono had never dreamed he would see the *gringo* again or that the *gringo* would see him.

"Suppose you are right," said the peasant. "So what? Do you think he even saw your face? And if he did, do you suppose he would come looking for you?" The man chuckled and lifted his beer.

"I think you're full of shit," said one of the other men, whose ear was deformed, a grotesque knob. "I saw no one staring at you. Forget about it."

"No," Mono said. "Find out who the man is. Ramón, you have a girlfriend who works in the admissions office at Flagler Memorial. Call her. Tell her to check all the gunshot wounds that came in that day. Tell her you are looking for an Anglo in his thirties, thin, brown hair. He was hit in the knee or thigh." Mono patted his calf.

"I will get the name," Ramón answered.

"Get everything you can," Mono said.

"Then what?" the peasant asked.

Mono went on, "This is a private matter. You will do this as a favor to me."

One of the others snorted a laugh. He was drunk. Mono's face darkened, and the muscles in his neck tightened like a rope. Under any other circumstances he would have smashed the foolish punk with his fists, leaving him bloody but wiser. But now he needed him, and he said nothing.

"*El Jefe* said no more shootings," Ramón reminded. "He was furious about what happened in the Grove."

"He will not know about this," Mono replied sternly. "Find out what you can."

"Then what?" asked the man with the cauliflowered ear.

"Nothing," Mono said softly. "Then *nada*. I just want information."

He opened a thumb-sized plastic vial and tapped a small pile of white powder onto the flat side of his American Express card. He used a table knife to cut the powder into four perfect lines. The others watched silently as Mono rolled a crisp new hundred-dollar bill into a makeshift straw. He sniffed three of the lines in quick succession, then offered the fourth to Ramón.

On his way out of the restaurant Mono stopped to hug Oscar, the owner. "Thank you for your hospitality. You are a good friend."

"You are welcome, Señor Sosa. Anytime."

Of course, it was always *Señor* Sosa. Oscar wouldn't dare address him by Mono, a street name. The monkey.

Señor Sosa had once done him a great favor. Just a small debt, but how foolish. A drunken night when Oscar had agreed to join some friends for the cockfights in Key Largo. Money had flown like the rooster feathers, and when it was over, the restaurant owner had been dismayed to find himself three thousand dollars down. Of course, he could not pay.

Señor Sosa could, on the spot, from a roll of bills so large it filled his hand like an egg. He'd never mentioned the money again. All he'd ever asked of Oscar was to keep El Hogar open late whenever Señor Sosa and his friends wished to talk business. He was asking more and more these days.

"Oscar, you are having no more gambling problems, I hope?"

"Oh, no. I have given up. I don't even play *la bolita* anymore. Not even for one peso."

"That is good," Mono said avuncularly. "If only you could talk some sense to these baboons. They dropped a fortune at the dog track today."

Southwest Eighth Street, Calle Ocho, glowed a hazy orange beneath the sodium crime lights. The streets were deserted, save for an occasional speeding taxi on its way back to the boulevard. Mono stood for a moment outside El Hogar. His heart raced slightly. He did not feel like driving home; he felt wide awake.

His three companions slid into the gold Continental. Domingo Sosa did not follow. Instead, he walked briskly across Eighth Street and climbed into a gun-blue BMW parked in a space marked Handicapped Only.

"*Adios*, Mono," shouted one of the men in the Lincoln as it raced away. Drunken idiots, fumed Sosa, mashing the accelerator three times to warm the engine. Then he slipped the BMW into first and drove off in the opposite direction.

Octavio Nelson and Wilbur Pincus scrunched low in the front seat of the old blue Dodge. They stayed that way until the Continental passed them. Cramped together almost flush under the dashboard, Nelson could smell some kind of mint on his partner's breath.

"Let's go," Pincus whispered eagerly.

"Be still."

Nelson waited until the Lincoln's engine was but a hum in the distance. When he sat up, he noticed bleakly that the BMW had vanished, too.

"Shit," said Nelson, gunning the engine. The Dodge protested with a stall. "Oh, shit." He turned the key again and drove off as fast as he dared, hoping to catch a glimpse of Mono's taillights and afraid to look over at his partner.

THEY MIGHT have gone to Rio. Meadows later wished with all his heart that they had. It would have changed almost everything.

From the dog track, Meadows and Terry had driven to a small condominium Terry owned on Key Biscayne, an island twenty minutes south of the city. Along the way Meadows had recounted, as rationally as he could, what had happened in Coconut Grove and what he had seen at the track.

"I should have called the cops right then. They'd have caught the killer."

"Probably not, *querido*," soothed Terry. "If he recognized you, then he and his friends probably left as quickly as we did. Besides, it is better not to take chances with people like that."

"I suppose so," said Meadows, unconvinced.

"*Dios,* how I wish I had been here. You have been through hell, *mi amor.* Look, suppose we go away someplace for a couple of weeks? I will make your wounded leg better and your middle leg sore. I promise."

"Can CAN do without you, *Capitán?*"

"It will struggle along. I have hired a new pilot, and Pancho can break him in as well as I."

"Sold," said Meadows. "How about Brazil? I've always wanted to go to Bahia."

"*Vamos.* I know it well, and I promise not to introduce you to any of my boyfriends there. . . ."

They had gone no farther, though, than Key Biscayne, for the next night Terry had been summoned. One of CAN's Convairs had broken down in Costa Rica with no hydraulic system and no way to move its cargo. Terry would have to go herself, with another plane:

60

condoms to Peru, lumber to El Salvador and color televisions for traders in São Paulo.

"I will be back in ten days," she promised Meadows on the way to the airport.

"Oh? How do you plan to do that? Rent a Concorde maybe?"

Terry leaned across the front seat and gave him a kiss. "We need more time together," she said. "No more long trips for a while, I promise."

His idea had been to go back home and amuse himself with the Ecuadorian project, but he found he'd lost his appetite for it. His house would be empty; there was too much cluttering his mind. No sense wasting drafting paper on thin ideas.

He was distracted, first by Terry and now by the sketch of the killer, which felt like cold lead in his pocket. When Meadows left the airport, he guided the Karmann Ghia onto the expressway and headed east, toward the meager downtown skyline of Miami. It took only ten minutes to find the city police department.

Meadows stood in the parking lot. Out of habit, he gave the new building a once-over. The earth tones made it warmer, all right, but the windows were so small, like Leavenworth. Maybe the architect was trying to shield the office workers from the merciless afternoon sun. It was still too institutional, Meadows decided. The police probably felt right at home.

Inside, Meadows paced the slippery lobby floor, rehearsing what he would tell Octavio Nelson when he gave him the sketch. Would the detective laugh? Would he tell Meadows that he was hallucinating, that the Coconut Grove killers were long gone from this country?

Meadows sat down and stole another look at his drawing.

Two uniformed cops shoved a drunk through the lobby. "Lemme alone," the man whined. "Lemme go home." Meadows could see where the handcuffs had chafed the man's wrists. He wondered if anything more would happen when the cops had the drunk all to themselves.

IN THE FOURTH-FLOOR offices of the Vice and Narcotics Unit, Detective Wilbur Pincus hunched over his tiny desk and wrote in a small brown notebook. Carefully obscured under his right arm on the desk was a miserably faint photostat marked Vehicle Incident Report–Nonaccident.

Pincus had gotten the report from a friend in the police garage. There was no supervisor's signature on the last line, so the report would never be filed. There was, however, a significant bit of information about the Mercedes 450 SEL sedan.

In his notebook Pincus printed in short, precise strokes: "PRW 378 fl." He folded the photostat and ripped it into strips, tossing them into a waste can.

Pincus picked up the phone.

"Communications."

"Is Dennis on duty this afternoon?"

"Who's this?"

"Pincus in Narcotics."

A few minutes later, a new voice came on the line. "Hey, Detective, what can I do for you?"

"Can you run a tag for me, Dennis?"

"No problem. Fire away."

Pincus read the Mercedes's tag numbers to the dispatcher.

"Call you back in five minutes," Dennis said.

As Pincus hung up, he felt a hand on his shoulder. His mouth went dry, and he turned in his chair.

"Excuse me . . . I didn't mean to startle you. . . ."

"It's OK," Pincus said.

"I'm looking for Octavio Nelson," the man said. He was tall and sandy-haired, familiar. Although he had a good physique, Pincus marked him instantly as an academic, Ivy League.

"Nelson isn't here right now."

"I'm Chris Meadows. I think we met once before."

"Sure," Pincus fumbled. "In the hospital, right?"

"Yeah."

"You're feeling better, obviously. I didn't recognize you."

Meadows smiled wanly. "It was probably all the tubes running out of my face."

"Can I do something for you?"

"When is Nelson coming back?"

Pincus leaned back to look across the office at a wall clock. "Probably not at all this afternoon, Mr. Meadows. He's working a homicide way down in Homestead, so he'll probably go straight home afterward."

"How about tomorrow?"

"Bright and early," Pincus said. "I'll tell him you're coming by. Are you sure I can't help you with something?"

"Uh, no, no, that's OK," Meadows said. "I'll talk to Nelson tomorrow."

Funny guy, the detective thought as he watched Meadows leaving. Wonder if he remembered something about the shooting? Happens often enough after the trauma wears off. Probably should have pressed him some more . . .

The phone made him jump.

"Got your ten-thirty-nine," said Dennis in Communications. "The name is Nelson, Roberto Justo. You want the DOB and all?"

"Everything," Wilbur Pincus said, forgetting Meadows. "Everything you got there."

THE TRIP BACK to his house from downtown Miami was only ten minutes, but Meadows drove slowly, distractedly, and nearly missed his turn off Main Highway.

He wondered if he should have given the sketch to Pincus. The guy looked every bit as sharp as Nelson, more professional in fact. The square, smooth face, neat, if not too short, hair, blue suit—everybody's favorite FBI agent right off the television.

But Nelson was Cuban. Like the killers. It was precisely for that reason that he wanted him—and only him—to study the sketch. A man like Nelson was sure to know his way around the hot streets of ' Little Havana, whereas Pincus . . . well, that didn't look to be his specialty. Tomorrow was time enough.

He parked under the canopy of lush trees in front of his house. An outdoor spotlight, automatically timed to flash on at dusk, illuminated the walkway to the front door in a tunnel of white light. The moths and mosquitoes fluttered excitedly in and out from the shadows, and Meadows hurried into the house.

On the drive home, suddenly, fixed clearly in his mind, had come an image of the Ecuadorian oil ministry, what it should and *would* look like. It gave Meadows a rush just to think about starting the drafting. He had not felt so much enthusiasm since the shooting.

Meadows flipped a switch on the wall, and overhead fans began to purr. "To work," Meadows said to himself, "but first, a swim."

He peeled off his shirt, kicked off his trousers and ambled to the porch. The wind had died, and the bay was smooth indigo glass in the night.

Meadows noticed that the light in the swimming pool was on. He did not remember leaving it that way, but then again he had been forgetful these past weeks. Could it have been the pool service? What day do they come? Meadows wondered. It must have been them.

The pool was clean and clear. The underwater spotlights threw an iridescent aqua glow on the dense foliage in Meadows's backyard. The architect slipped out of his undershorts, savoring the privacy. Just me and the sleeping sparrows.

Meadows walked to the deep end, squatting twice to check the right leg. No pain. He stood erect on the diving board, letting his eyes measure the four quick steps.

A small branch, dropped from one of the old oaks, lay at the end of the diving board. Meadows retrieved it, his steps springing on the fiberglass platform. He tossed the branch into a hedge, and it landed with a rustle. The racket flushed a small chameleon, brown and mottled. Terrified, it ran full bore, its tail straight in the air, on a beeline for the swimming pool.

"Watch out, little fella." Meadows laughed.

The tiny reptile skittered into the pool, and suddenly the lights flashed. In that fraction of a second, Meadows heard a sound like the ripping of a stiff piece of linen. Then a wave of heat rose off the pool, and it was pitch-black.

Meadows inched back off the diving board, trembling, naked and unarmed. He waited fearfully for a noise, for footsteps hurrying through the yard, for a cold voice.

But the night was silent.

Slowly, in small steps, he moved toward the house until he was seized by his own fear and adrenaline. He broke into a run, but not before the architect saw it floating in the clear hot water: the twisted, blackened corpse of the chameleon, as crisp as a dead leaf on a quiet lake.

# Chapter 8

OCTAVIO NELSON surveyed the pool, then peered out at the bay, where a rusty shrimper labored south, nets streeling. He drank deeply of the still night air, hot, humid, salty.

"Beautiful place," Nelson said. "Setup like this must have cost you a bundle." He bent down to the spot where the electric cable snaked through the areca bushes into the shallow end of the pool.

"Clever," he muttered, as though to himself. "Those guys are usually not that clever. One little foot in the water and *ciao*."

Nelson decided not to call the boys from the lab. They would find no fingerprints, no discarded tools, no trace of whoever had so carefully and skillfully rigged a swimming pool for death. Nelson walked back to the wooden porch steps, where Chris Meadows sat with his elbows on his knees, knuckles white around a glass of amber liquid. On the phone Meadows had been tightly in control, but just barely. Little wonder. This was a no-nonsense hit, and by rights he should be dead.

"Once again you're a lucky man, *amigo*," Nelson said softly.

Meadows swirled the ice in his glass. The Jack Daniel's was his third. He did not speak for a long moment, as though not trusting himself to speak. His face was the color of the limestone that ringed the pool. His button-down white shirt was wringing wet.

"Not an accident? No chance it was an accident?" Meadows asked finally.

"No accident. A professional job. Somebody wants you dead."

Meadows stood quickly, violently, whiskey and a lone ice cube sloshing from the glass. His words came with a rush.

"And so I'm lucky. That's what you call it when somebody is

nearly murdered for the second time in a few weeks by a killer he doesn't know and doesn't want to know. That's lucky."

Nelson walked into the house and poured himself four ounces of Mount Gay rum. He had been right to send Pincus home, to have come alone. Drinking on the job! Imagine! Wilbur would go right to the chief with that. Nelson lit a cigar and leaned against the redwood beam supporting the porch roof.

"I'm afraid you're a loose end. Those scumbags don't like loose ends."

"But, Jesus Christ," Meadows said, "I haven't done anything to them."

"That's not required. You must know something you shouldn't. You are an impediment." He drew the word out slowly, a syllable at a time. "A loose end. Simple as that. What is it you know?"

Meadows shook his head, as though to clear it from a blow. The nonchalance of it all was appalling. Somebody had tried to kill him, and here on the porch was some Don Juan Caballero cop drinking his rum and matter-of-factly ascribing rational behavior to irrational action.

"Look, who are these people?" Meadows demanded. "You must have some idea. And if you do, why don't you go out and arrest them, for Christ's sakes! How many chances do they get? All that stands between me and a pine box is one small lizard who was not, to use your term, lucky."

The outburst, curiously, made Meadows feel better. When he continued, his voice was more normal.

"How did they find out who I am and where I live?"

"I have been wondering about that myself," Nelson said. "Your name wasn't in the papers after the shooting. But it was on the police report, and it was certainly in the hospital records. I'd say the police report; anybody can look at them. Tell me again what happened last night. Slowly. You weren't making much sense on the phone."

Haltingly, with false starts, pauses and an almost lack of inflection, Meadows recounted the incident at the dog track. But Meadows thought as he spoke, and by the time he finished the obvious was there before him.

"So I recognized him, but he also recognized me. Right?"

"That's how it went down," Nelson agreed. "And then they went and found out who you were."

Meadows was incredulous.

"Recognizing the killer de facto made me such a threat to him that he decides he has to drop by and electrocute me in my swimming pool."

"De fucking facto."

"How could he know it would be me who went into the water? Sometimes friends swim here. Sometimes neighborhood kids come by after school. He couldn't have been sure it would be me."

"That's right, he couldn't. It was a gamble, but a safe one. He'd be far away by the time it happened. Like I said, you were lucky."

"But there was a girl here with me only last night. I mean, it could have been her." Meadows was agitated now. Delayed reaction.

Nelson shrugged.

"*Amigo,* I don't make the rules. I'm just telling you how the game is played."

Meadows turned suddenly and hurled his glass into the woods behind the house. It slammed against a tree trunk and shattered. Meadows turned on Nelson.

"Listen, this kind of shit does not happen in a society of law. We are civilized. This is not a jungle."

Nelson moaned inwardly. He should have sent Pincus after all. Pincus had illusions, too. Pincus and Meadows, a lovely couple. He could see them now, standing at attention to salute the flag; swapping patches around the campfire at a Scout jamboree, pledging truth, loyalty, obedience, promising never to jerk off or drive drunk or run dope on a hot summer's night. Spare them, Lord, for they are innocent. Octavio Nelson downed his rum with a single swallow and turned to look for more.

"Let me make you another drink," Nelson said. "It will soothe the nerves. You've been through a terrible thing."

Nelson dawdled over the rum bottle, back turned to Meadows. He made a great production of adding ice cubes to his glass, one at a time, slowly, allowing Meadows to collect himself.

"Who is he?" Meadows asked. The voice was cold and ugly now. Nelson did not turn around.

"I don't know."

"I'll show you who he is." Meadows seemed full of nervous energy. He bounded up the porch steps and rushed to a table near the bar. Nelson heard a drawer protest as Meadows yanked it open. Then Meadows was beside him waving a single sheet of paper.

"This is him—the man responsible for Sandy and the girl, the one who shot me. I drew it last night. Now you can arrest him, can't you?"

Nelson laid down his rum and took the paper carefully, holding it at the edges. From the corner of his eye he watched Meadows pour a stiff shot of bourbon.

"God, that is well drawn," Nelson said. "You do have talent, don't you?"

"Do you know him?"

"Too well. Everybody calls him Mono. The nickname suits both his intelligence and temperament. He's a torpedo, an enforcer."

"In other words, your friend the monkey is a killer."

Nelson nodded.

"Why isn't he in jail?"

"He has been, and maybe will be again someday."

"Why not now?"

"We have lots of suspicions, but until this instant we have had nothing solid. Mono usually works on contract—so much a hit when it looks as though things are getting out of hand. Mono *es muy macho.* He killed his first man as a teenager in Havana. Everybody in the *barrio* is afraid of Mono. It's impossible to get a Latin to testify against him."

"But that's wrong," Meadows insisted.

Nelson exploded. "Wrong? Of course it's wrong. But you know something? It is also right. The people in the *barrio,* most of them don't have fancy educations like you have. But they are smart people, just the same. And they know the two laws of the dope business as well as they know the Ave Maria. They don't teach that kind of thing at college, do they?"

Nelson drained his glass and filled it again. The once-robust Mount Gay bottle was dying. He must have drunk eight ounces already.

"Two simple rules, *amigo,* the new commandments. Rule number one: Always get even. Rule number two: Never talk to the cops. People like Mono are better at enforcing those rules than most judges are at enforcing the law. What do you think about that?"

Nelson drank again, more slowly, wincing as the sharp, bittersweet rum ignited in his gullet.

"Do you have any cigars?"

Meadows motioned toward a humidor.

"H. Upmann! Well, I'll be damned. Are you sure you're not a doper, *amigo?* I thought only dopers had enough money to smoke Upmanns."

Intuition told Meadows it was not the time to say he bought the cigars on a trip to Cuba. In Miami it never paid to say that one had visited Cuba. A lot of people thought that was treason. No, he could not tell a Cuban exile cop that he had gone to Fidel Castro's Havana to lecture on architecture, not when the cop was getting progressively drunker in his living room. Not when he himself was wobbly and disoriented by a second encounter with a barbaric subculture he'd never known existed. It would not do at all to argue that architecture, like art, was universal and ought to be unfettered by ideology. That was a topic to explore subtly around a fire, with friends who had been trained to think and to debate. And what would such friends say of the new commandments? Always Get Even. "Really, Chris, how atavistic." Meadows could almost hear Geoffrey Brown's professorial voice. "A ridiculous throwback to Old Testament morality: an eye for an eye." And Scott Hansen, the painter whose bright canvases masked a morbid conservatism. Did he know that the second commandment was Never Talk to the Cops? "One more evidence of the decline of the society, the unraveling of the social fabric. A straw in the hurricane of dissolution. Military rule will come to this country. Wait and see." That is what Scott Hansen would say.

Meadows himself said nothing as the lean and angry policeman lit the Cuban cigar. He listened in silence as Nelson, like a frenzied teacher who has been cursed to be heard but not heeded, delivered a chilling, staccato homily on the cocaine commandments. What he heard through a bouillabaisse of Jack Daniel's-Mount Gay-H. Upmann dismayed Meadows. And sickened him.

Luis Garces, said Nelson, ah, yes, now there was an instructive example of getting even. Tough, cunning Luis. Poor Luis. He was an unlettered boy from the Colombian countryside with quick wits and quick hands. He came up to cocaine from picking pockets. Some of the best pickpockets in the world came from Colombia. There has been a university for pickpockets in Bogotá for more than three hundred years. Meadows didn't know that, did he? And Luis, good pickpocket though he was, was smart enough to realize that there were more pesos in one kilo of coke than there were in a thousand pockets. He stole enough to buy some travel documents and made his way to Miami. Could have retired to a condominium on Miami Beach and lifted an occasional bangled pocketbook from blue-haired ladies. But not Luis. He was young, and he was ambitious. Not long after reaching Miami he found himself a partner. Luis and his partner went shopping for coke, and one day they found it. Luis got all dressed up and passed himself off as a buyer from New York. Came the night to make the buy, and they didn't buy the stuff; they stole it. A sweet little sleight of hand, Luis being so good with his hands. They got away with the coke, OK, *amigo,* about a pound, but they made a big mistake: They didn't kill the guys they stole it from. Luis and his friend, playing in the big league with little-league pickpocket rules. If you're going to steal coke, Meadows, you have to make sure nobody chases you afterward. Because they will chase you. They chased Luis and what's-his-name. Caught them one night on the street downtown, near one of those banks that's always changing their name. Luis and his friend, they never even got a chance to pull their guns. Bam. Down they go. Hurt bad. But not dead, not by a long shot. So we bundle them off to Flagler Memorial, where it would cost you and me a couple of hundred bucks a day but dopers get fixed free. Luis and the other guy, they don't know nothin'. Was I shot, Officer? Are you sure I didn't walk in front of a truck? After a few days it looks like they're both going to be OK. Anyway, one day Luis and this other scumbag are resting up in their nice soft taxpayer beds when what happens? The guys who shot them come back to finish the job. How about that, huh? Persistence. These scumbags burst in with automatic weapons and blaze away. Luis gets hit a couple of times. His partner gets made into Swiss cheese. There are doctors fainting and nurses screaming and patients having heart attacks and every cop in the city running around the hospital with enough firepower to retake Havana. One of the shitheads gets away; we never could figure out where he went. The other one gets as far as the roof. There is a big fight up there with SWAT and helicopters and the whole goddamn cavalry. Well, the guy gets blown away finally, but a cop gets hit, and so his buddies rush him back downstairs. If you got to get shot, a hospital is not a bad place to have it happen, right? Wrong. They get back down with the cop, and there's nobody to take care of him. You know why? They are all working over pickpocket Luis. Hurt so bad he was. Poor Luis. Well, the lieutenant of the cop that's shot goes bananas. He jams his pistol down the throat of the head doctor and says, "You treat my cop first, motherfucker, because if you don't, I'm going to shoot you first and then the scumbag Colombian lying there on the table." Boy, was there hell to pay after that. But in the end the cop survived, and even Luis survived, and all that happened was that the lieutenant was transferred some-place where he didn't command troops anymore. The brass have shat on him ever since, but there's not a cop in the county who wouldn't lay himself down for that guy. Everybody's dead, everybody's even.

But that's not the end of the story. It's only the beginning because you know where poor twice-shot-but-not-dead Luis the pickpocket is right now, *amigo*? He's on death row up at the state prison in Raiford. One day they are going to fry Luis, and do you know why? He got out of the hospital, went back to Colombia cour-tesy of his sucker Uncle Sam, and then he turned right around and came back to Miami. And one night Luis walked into the living room of the asshole that shot him and blasted him to kingdom come. Murder One, and Fingers Luis is down the tube. But you got to admire the little sucker. He got even.

And *that*, everybody understands, is really the most important thing of all. Oh, of course they are all in it for the money. But you can make lots of money pimping, too. The *machismo* is even more important. The dumb Anglos hanging around the fringes don't understand that, and sometimes that's what gets them killed. If you want to run dope, you got to be *macho*. That's the long and the short of it. Fancy clothes, big cars, foxy *chicas*—that's all window dressing. If you are not a tough *hombre*, none of the rest of it counts. If your *compadre* gets shot by some other assholes, you go out and shoot them. If you don't, you might as well go back to picking pockets. Nobody will deal with you. Ever wonder why little girls and their mothers get killed in the Grove and ritzy suburban dames get cut down in shopping centers by animals with bad teeth and no English? *Machismo,* that's why. Why think when you can shoot?

"What? No more rum!" Nelson was standing with his back to the empty fireplace. His cigar had gone out again, and he relit it tenderly.

"There's another bottle. And I could use another one, too," Meadows replied quietly. He felt like a little boy who has heard his first ghost story. Clammy and prickly. He did not want Nelson to leave. He did not want to be alone.

Then Nelson told him about people who talk to the cops. Angel Arellano.

He was a Cuban, a nice guy, really; we went to the same high school in Havana. Angel was a hanger-on. No big deals, probably because he had no balls. But he was always around, always ready to drive a truck or run a boat. Just enough to be useful, enough so they'd throw him a bone. Angel made a nice living out of it, too. He had a sexy little wife and a daughter who was as cute as could be. They bought a house out in the suburbs. Man, he was proud of that house. It had natural ceiling beams, you know, like the house of some big shot architect. Angel, he loved those beams. He sanded them and varnished them and did whatever else you do to beams if you are a rich architect or a Cuban hustler on the make. Everything was swell for Angel until we caught him one night with a kilo of uncut coke—eighty-seven point nine percent—the genuine article. There was no chance in the world it belonged to Angelito. He was just baby-sitting it for somebody else, and we knew that, but we sure as hell never let on to Angel. By the time we got finished with Angel he believed he would never see his wife, his daughter or his precious beams again. So we turned him, made him into a snitch. We let the first batch go through smooth as silk, as though nothing had happened. Nobody ever knew we nabbed Angel cold and had let him go. But he belonged to us.

If you pick up a doper, *amigo,* and then let him go without any charges, that's the kiss of death. Everybody knows he has turned.

His own mother wouldn't write insurance on him then. But we were real careful with Angel, reeled him in a little bit at a time. We made some pretty good busts out of it and always in such a way that there was never any connection with Angel. Then it went sour. Hell, who knows how or why things like that go sour? But it went real bad. Angel went home one night, and there were his wife and his daughter, hanging from those ceiling beams he loved so much. Poor bastard.

Meadows was shell-shocked. "Are you powerless to control these people?"

"You are looking at the first line of defense, *amigo*," Nelson replied with a short laugh at what was not meant to be funny. "Powerless, no. Hamstrung, yes. Frustrated, totally. It's too big, too hard, too complicated. What seems so important for you—what *is* a matter of life and death for you—is really only a sidelight to the big show." Nelson gestured toward the oak and mahogany chess set. "You are being pursued by a knight. And you are barely a pawn. I'm after the king, and I would give my soul to get him."

Nelson's teeth gleamed wolfishly. He was feeling the rum.

"You see, *amigo*, I am a pioneer of a new branch of police science. Not homicide, not narcotics, but narcocide. Maybe pioneer is wrong. More a gypsy. I pitch my tent at one drug murder after another. Sooner or later one of them will lead me to the king."

"Who is he?" Meadows ventured.

"A Latin, certainly, probably a Cuban. He works out of Miami, and I think he is in trouble. I think the king and his Cubans had the local distribution and transshipment of coke locked up until a few months ago. About seventy percent of the shit that leaves Colombia comes through here, right? Well, from what we hear, a couple of months ago the king began to lose control. The Cubans got hit from two sides: too many Anglo amateurs pissing in the pond, running around like little kids in a schoolyard; too many Colombians getting off the boat to deal in Miami. Right now things are so confused out there you wouldn't know what you were buying if it was your brother who was selling it.

"So the king is wounded, and that's when I want to hit him. On the street they call him *el Jefe*, and every snitch in town knows that I want him, that I'll deal with the devil to get him. It looks like *el Jefe* is trying to clean up his act, and I think maybe Mono is his cleanup hitter. So I stay close to Mono. Sooner or later he'll take me to *el Jefe*."

Nelson dragged on Meadows's cigar.

"When I find out who he is, I will track him, and when I find him, I will shoot him." It was a promise.

"You mean, arrest him," Meadows corrected.

"Shoot him, I said."

"You can't do that. You're a cop."

Nelson's voice dropped to a feral whisper. "The law and justice are not synonymous, *amigo*. Not in this country, not in my country, not in any country. Never have been. Never will be."

"That is absurd," Meadows replied. "You can't have one without the other."

They argued for a time, a *pas de deux* in which naïveté and cynicism danced without embracing. Intellectually it was a draw. As a matter of reality it was Nelson who won.

"Will you testify against him, *amigo?*" Nelson asked suddenly. Meadows never saw the bait or the cruel hook it obscured.

"Against who?"

"Mono. He shot you and then tried to kill you here again tonight, although we'll never prove that one. But he shot you, and you can identify him. That's a crime, and justice demands he go to jail. But you'll have to testify. Without that, no conviction, no jail, no justice."

"Of course I will testify," Meadows responded.

"*Bueno*. Then I'll arrest him. And I'll get you all the police protection you want."

Meadows nodded, and Nelson set the hook.

"And I'll bet you anything that inside of six months you are as dead as that lizard out there. That is not conjecture."

Meadows felt sick. He could taste the whiskey rising in his throat. He had trouble catching his breath. Sweat sprouted on his throat. His mind tried to reason, but what it saw was the tiny lizard, gaily jumping: jumping to eternity. It suddenly occurred to Meadows that Nelson's horror stories had been more than boozy hyperbole. They carried a message to Meadows that he had not understood. With chilling clarity, Meadows saw that Nelson did not want to arrest Mono. And he accepted as conviction that to seek justice against Mono in a courtroom would be to sign his own death warrant. When Meadows spoke, it was a croak.

"Look, maybe . . . is there some other way? I mean . . ."

Octavio Nelson peered at T. Christopher Meadows with the same kind of detached superiority he had shown the lizard. Then Nelson smiled wickedly, his eyes masked by the fire-red *O* of the cigar.

"Good thinking, *amigo*. Testifying is a good way to commit suicide."

Meadows felt as though he had been reprieved: a coward allowed to leave the battlefront.

"What do I do?" he asked weakly. He sounded pathetic, even to himself.

"Leave. Get out of town. *Vete*."

"Just cut and run?"

"There is no other good choice. If you stay, you are a sitting duck. If you leave, time is on your side. You are not a major character in this show, and that puts time on your side. Sooner or later they'll forget about you. Another loose end is bound to take your place. Big things are happening, and you won't be worth killing long."

It would be wrong to run. Meadows knew that. But every fiber screamed at him to go. Sandy and Jessica were dead, and nothing would bring them back. He himself had already suffered enough. It would be running away from a fight, true, so what? Fighting was senseless, and he hated it, avoided it except when there was no alternative—like that night in New York with the mugger. Here there was a clear choice. He could accomplish nothing by staying. And probably save his life by leaving.

"How long would I have to stay away?"

"A couple of weeks. It's hard to say. Keep in touch." Nelson ground his cigar into an ashtray and headed for the door.

Meadows felt awful.

"I still think I'm right. If you decide to arrest him, I'll come back," he ventured.

Nelson waved his hand airily.

"Don't worry about it. Mono is one of those guys who ends up floating in the bay. He'll never get his in a courtroom."

A silence grew, became awkward.

"Do you want a ride to the airport?" Nelson asked.

"No, thanks. I'll make a few calls to friends in New York, and I have the house to close up first. I'll make the last flight."

"Why don't you go fishing? I love fishing," Nelson said. He stared at the sleeping bay with black eyes that were a universe away. "We used to fish a lot in Cuba when I was a boy, me, my father and my brother. I'll never forget the day my brother caught a big shark and was so scared he wouldn't even cut the line. Just stood there, frozen, with the rod in his hand and the shark rapping the side of the boat.

"I never go fishing anymore; there's never time. Now to get away, I dream instead. You know what I dream, *amigo*? I dream that one day I'm going to round up all the cocaine cowboys in this town and I'm going to take them to the Orange Bowl. It would be quite a crowd. Then I'd line them up, and I'd walk down the line like a platoon sergeant. To the guy at the front of the line I'd say, '*Oye, José,* do you remember how your *compadre* Luis got shot so many times they couldn't count the holes? Well, this *hijo de puta* who did that is named Carlos, and he's here in this line with a big grin on his face.'

"Then I'd walk down along the line to Carlos, and I'd say, '*Hermano,* I never could understand why they made your buddy Paco suffer so bad. If they had to kill him, that's one thing; we all understand that. But could you ever figure out why they cut him and made him scream toward the end? Did they have to jam the coke up his ass, and why did they laugh when he started to scream? It was terrible, let me tell you. And did you know that the *cabrón* José who did that to your friend is right here, right now?'

"I'd make six or seven stops like that, walking down the line.

"Then, *amigo,* I would toss a couple of loaded submachine guns out there on the fifty-yard line in the Orange Bowl, and I would walk out and lock all the gates.

"And an hour later I would go back inside and finish off the wounded. Then I would go fishing.

"You like fishing, Meadows? Do me a favor. Go fishing."

# Chapter 9

ONCE MIAMI INTERNATIONAL Airport dwelt in lonely splendor in the moist flatlands between the city and the Everglades. Now it is surrounded entirely by the tropical metropolis it serves, one of the busiest terminals in the world, a north-south funnel where every minute is rush hour. Flights to Santiago and flights to Seattle. Refrigerators for Grand Bahama and millionaires for Aspen. Christopher Meadows had never known the airport in its youth, in the days before cheap air conditioning made Miami a magnet for northerners who learned that final escape from bitter winter was worth the long summers.

It amused him, nevertheless, to know that Miami International remained an official refuge for the burrowing owl and that rabbits, raccoons, squirrels and tropical birds of a hundred varieties lived in the grassy fringes alongside the giant runways. Meadows prized the airport. It was fifteen minutes from everywhere; eleven minutes by back road, to be exact, from his Coconut Grove haven.

He drove slowly that night, deep in thought. He had plenty of time for the last New York flight, and for once there had been room. He was tired, washed-out. Too much too quick, and too much Jack Daniel's to boot. It would take a good night's sleep and a long walk in the morning to restore mental order from the jumble of fear, curiosity and Tennessee whiskey.

Afraid? Jesus! There by the pool, with the lizard, he had come within an ace of wetting his pants. Meadows had never known fear like that. In the street, with Jessica and Sandy, there had been no time for it. Was Meadows a freak, to have lived nearly four decades without ever knowing that sudden bowel-wrenching emotion? Or was he simply the product of a society so well ordered that fear had become as anachronistic as smallpox?

That was it, of course. And that was the argument he should have used on the cop. Without law, without justice, no man is safe from fear, and fear has no place among civilized men. Put that in your smelly cigar and smoke it, *amigo* Nelson.

Meadows's world held no one like Nelson. Tough, cynical, ruthless and probably very effective. Meadows pitied the criminal flotsam that fell into Nelson's hands. Like going to bed with a bobcat. A psychiatrist would have a field day with Nelson, would peel him layer by solid layer, like an artichoke. And in the process would no doubt destroy him as a good cop. To allow people like me to live without fear, Meadows concluded, society produces people like Nelson. . . .

But Meadows had coped, hadn't he? He hadn't wet his pants. He hadn't fainted or run in circles. He had called for help, and he had dealt rationally with the strange man who had come to help him. With Nelson's macabre prodding he had taken the only logical decision open to him. It was not a hero's decision, but it was a sensible one, an architect's decision made after measured analysis of form and stress. Meadows was running away, and he could live with his flight.

Terry was something else again. Could he live with Terry? Was that what she wanted? She had left a lot unsaid at the airport, and that in itself was saying a lot. Meadows savored Terry as a rarity among women: She never engaged the tongue without first putting the mind in gear. So he was meant to think about Chris & Terry, twin hearts on a tree. Well, he would think about it. And while he thought, he would go see Dana. He already felt terrible about that. Damn Terry. Like Nelson, she, too, had set him up.

Dana had offered to meet him at La Guardia, but he had refused. Airports made him nervous. All he ever wanted from them was to be allowed to get in and out as quickly and painlessly as possible. He hated airport greetings only slightly less than he hated airport farewells. He would take a cab to Dana's brownstone in Brooklyn Heights.

Calling Dana had been almost a reflex action for Meadows. New York without long-legged Dana was like New York without Chinatown. Once he and Terry had gone to New York for a weekend, and Meadows had worried absurdly the whole time that they would bump into her. She would not have fared well. Terry was a fighter.

Meadows drove up Twenty-seventh Avenue, his attention only partly on what he was doing. Paint stores, drugstores, a muffler shop flashed by in the night, all shrouded and locked tight. The only life in the streets came, as it always did, in the *barrio*. Traffic picked up there, and many cars brandished red, white and blue Cuban flag decals on a bumper or back window. Swarthy men in guayabera shirts clustered in gesticulating knots before shops that dispensed cigars, *cafecitos* and memories. A black and gold Trans Am cut Meadows off near the Flagler Street intersection. He took no affront. *El barrio* had its own unwritten traffic rules, and no prudent man drove there without anticipating some spontaneous display of *brio*. A red light that stopped traffic dead in staid Coral Gables was only a *gringo* challenge to *machismo* here. Meadows shifted down mechanically and swung around the Trans Am. The Ghia coughed in protest. The car was twelve years old, and it had been a long time since all four cylinders had fired properly.

Meadows disliked automobiles. They were dangerous, expensive and unreliable, and he drove one only because there was no alternative in a city where public transportation was as lackluster as its architecture. Besides, for table-flat Miami four cylinders was too much power. On the other hand, the damned thing would probably stop running altogether before long. As he approached the airport, Meadows made a mental appointment to have the car fixed. It was a promise he made religiously about once a month.

Growth had driven the airport to reckless extremes. Once a spacious ground-level parking lot had beckoned before the terminal building. Now there were five monster garages that were an affront to architecture: windowless, soulless, concrete mazes the only virtue of which was efficiency. Meadows hated them, but he had mastered them.

That had come after the time he had returned from a two-hour flight from Washington only to spend ninety-three minutes by his watch searching for the wretched car. Never again, he had vowed, and concocted a formula for parking survival that he shared with no one. It was simple: He always left his car in the last slot on the top level of the garage closest to the airline on which he was leaving. Sometimes, if he came back on a different carrier, it meant an extra walk—but at least he always knew where the car was without having to think about it. Like the owls and the rabbits, Meadows had learned to adjust to changing times.

The flight to New York was on Eastern. That meant parking garage number three, a hard left as soon as the Ghia conquered the ramp to concourse level. Traffic was light that night, even inside the airport. The Ghia followed a Dade County policeman on a Cushman three-wheeler up the approach ramp. The cop went straight. Meadows turned left into the garage and began the laborious climb to the top. He never saw the sleek Trans Am that slid in behind him.

The top level was empty, a few cars parked in gap-toothed clusters, but not a sign of life. Meadows had his choice of parking spaces. He left the Ghia against the far wall, pulled an overnight bag from the back seat, decided against locking the car and began walking toward the elevator.

He was thinking of Terry and Dana when the Trans Am crested the ramp to the top level. The daydreaming almost cost him his life.

It came hurtling at him like a torpedo, a rushing, roaring black hulk. What saved Meadows was the squeal of its radials as the big engine accelerated.

He had one flashing glimpse of the machine rushing toward him. Instinctively he hurled himself aside. His leather bag landed under the rear end of a dusty Chevrolet. Meadows landed with his nose to the retaining wall, his chest in a slick of oil. His wounded leg screamed in agony. He saw stars.

It was over in a second. With protesting brakes, the Trans Am howled to a stop a few spaces away from Meadows's Ghia.

Meadows pulled himself painfully to his feet from the hot concrete floor. He felt like an old man. Nothing seemed broken, but his leg hurt like hell, and there was a six-inch scrape on his left arm. The oil had ruined his shirt. His pants were ripped. His head ached. Most of all, he was angry.

"Dumb son of a bitch!" he yelled. This was the last straw. He had been shot. He had nearly been electrocuted. He was being run out of town, and now some stupid bastard had nearly run him over. Limping, Meadows stormed toward the Trans Am. One punch, he thought, and then throw the car keys off the roof. If anybody deserved it, it was this schmuck.

The driver's door of the Trans Am opened slowly as Meadows approached. Domingo Sosa, the man called Mono, got out.

Casually, with studied indifference, with the movements of a man who has all the time in the world, Mono stretched. He worked his shoulders. And then he turned to face Meadows.

*"Buenas noches, caballero,"* Mono said.

Mono wore white shoes, white pants and a white belt. He wore a white silk shirt open nearly to the waist. From his neck hung a thick golden chain. His bushy black mustache was artfully trimmed. His shiny black hair was combed straight back. On his left wrist he wore a large gold watch. In his right hand he held a long knife. The knife shone dully in the fluorescent lights.

Meadows saw all this without seeing. Never had he experienced such twin currents of anger and shock. His knees trembled. His right eyelid began to tic. He almost vomited. Yet he was so angry he almost threw himself at Mono. He might have—but he didn't. Christopher Meadows whirled and ran.

His leg ached from the first step, a searing, tearing pain that embodied his fear. He must stop. No, he must run. It was more of a limp than a run as Meadows approached the garage elevator. He could not stop. To stop was to die.

Gasping, Meadows reached the elevator. His hand clawed along the pastel wall for the down button. It lit at a touch. The indicator light atop the door showed the elevator on level three. Meadows could hear it begin to move. He looked back. Mono was about thirty yards away, running softly with effortless strides.

Meadows forced his hands against the elevator doors, as though to pry them open. Then he heard the elevator stop. The indicator read four.

Meadows shivered. His whole body felt chill, as chill as a corpse in the morgue. His breath came in great sobs as he pushed himself away from the betraying elevator and staggered toward a gray metal door marked Stairs.

The door was stiff. It would not move. Meadows pushed with all his strength. Finally it gave, opening into a barely lit, cavernous concrete stairwell that smelled of damp and urine.

Mono reached the door a moment later, before it could close. As Meadows started down the stairs, his leg felt as though it were on fire. Every step grated in the fillings of his teeth.

The garage stairs zigzagged down to the concourse level; two landings per level. Each set of stairs had ten steps. Meadows clutched the dirty handrail to help himself down the stairs. After six steps Mono was only a few inches out of range.

On the eighth step Meadows tripped. His weak leg collapsed, and he fell onto the landing. Rolling once, he crashed with his back against the unfinished cinder-block wall. He lay there, gasping like a landed fish, defenseless.

Mono was in no hurry. He looked down at his victim like some Aztec priest measuring his next sacrifice, gauging where to thrust the killer knife. Mono seemed to be enjoying himself. He had killed in more public places. In this little-used stairwell no one would even hear the screams. Supremely confident, he took a white linen handkerchief from his pocket, wiped his brow and then carefully laid the handkerchief on the third step as a buffer for his immaculate white pants. Mono sat down.

"*Ahora te cago, gringo,*" he whispered. "You are feenesh."

Meadows, as still and as tense as a trapped animal, shouted at him, "You can't do this to me! What have I done?"

"For me you are unlucky. That is enough. Will you die like a man or crying like a woman?"

Mono tossed aside the cigarette and sprang lightly to his feet. He even remembered to pick up his handkerchief. Perhaps that is what triggered Meadows, the ultimate indignity of watching his executioner carefully replace his handkerchief in white pants.

Meadows didn't move quickly, but in his arrogance Mono anticipated no movement at all. Meadows levered himself up along the wall until he was in a half crouch. When Mono came at him with the blade, Meadows did not rise but pushed off against the wall with strength he never knew he possessed.

Meadows aimed his right shoulder at Mono's groin. He felt the knife rip his shirt as the shoulder went home. As Meadows drove forward, Mono jackknifed above him. They slammed against the concrete steps, Meadows on top. He heard Mono grunt as his spine absorbed the jolt. He heard the clatter of the knife as it fell.

The impact nearly knocked Meadows out. It stunned Mono. Meadows lay for a moment atop the killer in an obscene embrace. Then he rolled away, and something pricked his good leg. Meadows reached down and picked up the knife.

Mono lay unmoving. Meadows's only thought was to escape.

He could not go up the stairs—Mono blocked the way—so he started down at a shambling pace, leg flaming, arm bleeding, head aching. His right hand grasped the banister; his left held the knife.

Meadows had nearly reached the third level when Mono was on him.

Savagely the killer tore at Meadows's neck. Meadows turned, elbows bent, and Mono's momentum carried him into the knife. Meadows felt the knife slash through something soft. Mono lurched back, away from the pain that suddenly enveloped him.

The knife came free, still in Meadows's nerveless hand. A gush of warm blood sprouted from Mono's chest and drenched his white silk shirt.

Meadows ran again. He jerked open the stairway door and burst into the garage. It was deserted, a graveyard of cars. Still clutching the knife, Meadows started down the ramp. He was drained, exhausted. He felt unclean, and he needed help.

He had gone only a few paces when a wave of nausea engulfed him. Meadows tottered between two parked cars and fell to the pavement.

It seemed as though he lay there for a long time. Finally he pulled himself to a sitting position, leaned against the ramp wall and breathed deeply. He tried to cry for help. All that emerged was a hoarse croak.

Gradually Meadows's brain began functioning again. Mono was badly hurt or dead. There was no longer any urgency. He could pull himself together and seek help at his leisure. The nightmare was over. All he needed was to find a policeman and explain his story. Mono would haunt him no more. If he was not dead, he would go to jail.

Meadows had only to sit somewhere visible and to wait until a motorist or the cop on the Cushman drove past. It was over. Mead-

ows laughed a bit hysterically at the prospect and prized himself
forward to sprawl against the back of a car.

Five minutes passed. Another five. Then Meadows heard the
sweet sound of the sewing machine engine that could only mean
the cop who patrolled the garages. The machine was just entering
the garage. It would come up slowly, a level at a time. Meadows
willed the cop to hurry.

He would have to call Dana to say he wasn't coming. Too bad,
but it wouldn't hurt her to sleep alone for once. There was no reason he couldn't go right home to the Grove. A hot shower, a couple
of drinks, and in the morning he would decide whether to see a
doctor. He was hurt, but he was functional.

And that—by Jesus—was more than anybody could say for that
motherfucker Cuban in the stairwell. The cocaine mob would have
to find another killer.

Meadows heard the Cushman clearly now. It was on the second
level and climbing. The cop made Meadows think of Nelson.
Wouldn't Nelson be pleased to know that Mono had gone out in
the same violence by which he had lived. One less scumbag for the
Orange Bowl, eh, *amigo?* Meadows felt lightheaded.

But there was something. Nelson . . . Meadows shook his head to
clear it. Mental alarms sounded. A thought formed, dissolved,
formed again. Pickpocket Luis . . . enough firepower to retake
Havana . . . hanging beams . . .

Then Meadows had it, and he groaned aloud with despair.

Nothing had changed.

Meadows, wide-eyed, naïve, an innocent bystander, had come to
the airport because he was literally running for his life. And now he
had even more reason to run. He had killed the killer. In the
cocaine jungle Nelson had sketched so powerfully there could be
no greater insult, no greater crime, no more surpassing summons
to vengeance.

If Meadows reported the body in the stairwell to the police, there
was no way on earth he could avoid being publicly identified as the
killer of Mono. That would be his death warrant. Always Get Even.
Never Talk to the Cops.

He would have to remain silent. He would have to disappear.
Then no one would ever know it was the shy architect who had, in

terror, dispatched the fearful Mono. Only he would have that satis-faction.

As the police three-wheeler neared, he sank behind the car that had supported him, crouching in the shadow of its hood. The Cushman passed him going up. A couple of minutes later it whirled back down. The policeman driving it had seen nothing, suspected nothing. Who would check out a deserted stairway at this hour on a quiet night?

Meadows felt a great weight lift from his chest. Now he was truly free. So there was justice after all. *Adios,* Señor Mono. May your death have come hard. May the shades of hell rejoice in your com-pany. There is nothing to link me to you.

There was the knife, of course, but that was easy, wasn't it? There had to be a dozen places in the garage where he could safely dis-card the knife. No one would look for it very hard. Where could he hide it? Not under a car; cars move away. Not in the stairwell. He could throw it out the side, but it might fall somewhere easy to see. It might even hit somebody. He could hide it in the ashtray by the elevator, but even if it fitted, ashtrays must be cleaned occasionally.

Damn, but the garage was an austere, functional place. Meadows wondered fleetingly who had designed it. If he ever—God for-bid!—had to design a garage, he would see to it there were places where a law-abiding man could hide a knife.

Meadows thought of crawling under a car and jamming the knife into the muffler or between the springs. But he had been on the ground too much that night already. Besides, the knife would prob-ably fall out just when the car stopped at the booth to pay the park-ing fee.

In the end Meadows decided to lose the knife in a flowerpot by the elevator that held a scraggly ponytail palm. Once he had to hide from a passing car, but he made a good job of it. He dug a deep hole at the back of the pot with the point of the knife and stuck it in the earth, handle down. Carefully he packed dirt over the tip and arranged the palm fronds so that they obscured the burial ground.

It was a long way up the ramp to the top level, and every step pounded. But there was a spring in Meadows's limp. He would look back on the nightmare as a maturing aberration. He would be better for it. He would never speak of how the terror had ended with the ripping of cloth, the awful sensation of the knife going home. In time, perhaps, he would even convince himself he had thrust with the knife, rather than witlessly, accidentally, allowing the killer to impale himself. Or perhaps he would one day feel remorse at having taken a human life, at having allowed his intellect to fail him.

Meadows felt no remorse as he passed the stairway door at level five. The door was closed. Meadows stopped to retrieve his overnight bag from where he had flung it.

Now, once he moved the car, there would be nothing whatsoever to link him to the garage or the grisly corpse in the stairwell. Meadows headed for the Ghia. Then he froze in his tracks.

Mono's big black and gold Trans Am was gone.

# Chapter 10

THE OLD MAN from Bogotá walked among his flowers. They were beautiful, and he was proud. In the high Andean valley the flowers stretched for nearly half a mile in all directions. Mostly they were carnations, red, pink, white. There were also mums, daisies, pompons and delicate roses of many hues. They grew in string-encircled beds under a giant polyethylene roof to protect them from rain and hail. Dusky, flat-faced girls in blue smocks tended the beds, tended the flowers, one at a time, trimming unwanted growth, catching the delicate buds with rubber bands to keep them from opening too fully too soon.

"The altitude, climate, temperature, sunlight—everything here is ideal for raising flowers," the old man boasted. "What you see are more than six million flowers. When they are ready, they will be cut and flown overnight to the United States. It is a big business. Each girl is assigned a specific bed to work. When her flowers are of the highest quality, she is rewarded."

"The flowers are very beautiful," the old man's visitor said.

They had driven out to the flower farm, an hour from Bogotá, on the morning after. It had been a sumptuous wedding, elegant, tasteful. The poise and charm of the old man's granddaughter had more than compensated for the awkward groom. A lucky man, said the guests. She is not the most beautiful woman in Bogotá, but of course, money has a beauty of its own. The bride's brother, the one with the haunting black eyes, had performed the ceremony from the main altar of the cathedral. He had even trimmed his beard; wasn't that the least he could have done with the metropolitan bishop there on the altar with him? Three hundred waiters in white coats had dispensed a hundred cases of French champagne, fifty pounds of Iranian caviar and five hundred pounds of Caribbean lobsters to 1,200 guests guarded by 300 policemen, 423 private bodyguards and a company of infantry commanded by one of the guests but deployed out of sight of the colonial *finca* Bolivar once owned. A catty social page reporter from *The New York Times* had assembled the box score. Bogotá's *El Tiempo* called it "the wedding of the century" but left out the part about the policemen, the bodyguards and the soldiers. The bride's mother wore a beige Givenchy of Chinese silk. The bride's father wore a Savile Row morning suit with a perfect white carnation at his lapel. Everyone deferred to the old man from Bogotá. He was the patriarch, and it was his money that had paid for the champagne, the caviar, the soldiers and the bishop.

"Seventy percent of my employees are single women under twenty-five," the old man said. "Without the flowers many of them would be whores or maids. When they come here, they have no skills. They know nothing."

The old man and his visitor stopped to admire a bed of red carnations that blazed with color and bristled with health. The girl who tended them had small bones, high breasts and a voluptuous mouth. A red and white plastic name tag on her smock proclaimed her to be Dorita. The two men watched in pleasure as the girl bent, her back to them, to trim a plant.

"They are not paid much by American standards, but it is more than they could make anywhere else. It gives them pride. It keeps them out of the city; it keeps them young and tender," the old man confided.

*"Venga,"* he summoned the girl.

Turning to his visitor as the girl made her way through the rows of flowers, the old man gestured at the flowers and at a flat green pasture beyond them.

"Do you see the difference? Here on a few hectares I give work to nearly a thousand people. I make money, and so do they. Over there twice as much land goes unexploited. My neighbor keeps a small herd of cows and gives work to a half dozen cowboys. That is the tragedy of Latin America, my friend."

The old man's visitor said something appropriate.

"How old are you, Dorita?" the old man asked the girl in Spanish.

"Sixteen, *patrón*," the girl replied. Up close she was quite beautiful.

"Are you happy here?"

"*Sí patrón.*"

"Your flowers are lovely. You are doing a good job."

"*Gracias, patrón.*"

The two men walked out of the carnation shed into the morning sunlight. The old man took his visitor's arm.

"It is time to talk business, Ignacio." He could feel the younger man stiffen.

"In Miami or in Bogotá, in a tuxedo at a wedding, you are who you are. When we talk business, you are Ignacio, are you not?"

The man from Miami had to bite his tongue not to say "*Sí, patrón.*" The old fool. He said nothing.

"I am listening," the old man said.

"There are two problems. We must redefine the distribution, and we must better control the supply."

"Why is that my problem?"

"Because all the merchandise in the world is worthless if the market is not well served. The system now is as backward and as inefficient as your neighbor's farm. You know that as well as I do."

"And yet, Ignacio, my neighbor's family has run that farm in the same fashion for nearly four hundred years."

"That is no answer. There is too much violence, too much confusion. The police are everywhere—we cannot buy them all. We could lose everything."

"*You* could lose everything," the old man countered quickly.

"If I lose, you lose, don't you see? You cannot distribute effectively in the United States from two thousand miles away. And the people you send to try, they are as ignorant as your flower girls."

"Perhaps," the old man said. "Of course, Ignacio, what you conveniently do not mention is that the profits in the United States are much greater than the profits for us here in Colombia. We send high-quality merchandise, and then it is diluted and diluted some more. Each time it is diluted the price doubles. We cannot dilute here for obvious reasons—the merchandise becomes bulkier and much harder to transport. But we are not stupid. We can dilute cocaine with sugar in Miami as well as you can. It is really the same old story—Latin America has always been cheated by the United States, hasn't it? We sell our raw materials for a pittance and the *gringos* finish them and make all the money. That is why we are poor and they are rich."

"OPEC dealt effectively with the *gringos,* did it not?"

"Is that what you have come to suggest, Ignacio? A cocaine cartel?" The old man laughed, and bits of saliva flecked his white mustache.

"Not a cartel but a partnership between producer and distributor. There is profit enough for all. *Los yanquis* will pay anything for their precious white powder."

The visitor from Miami warmed to his task.

"Look, you control about seventy percent of all the merchandise that leaves Colombia, do you not?"

The old man said nothing. It was a shrewd guess.

"And the other big shippers are all friends of yours who will listen if you tell them there is a better way to do business—more profit and less risk. Is that not true as well?"

The old man remained silent.

"What I propose is a partnership in which we share profits and assure greater profits through two simple strategies. First, we organize the distribution efficiently so that everyone has an agreed territory and there is a standard of quality and a standard price."

"And second?" the old man asked.

"We limit the supply until it is just below the demand."

"Interesting."

"And there is a third point as well."

"Which is?"

"While we work out the agreements, we shut down the supply altogether for a month or so. That will panic the freelancers and force them to the surface."

"What will that accomplish?"

"While they are milling about in confusion, we will make an example of one or two for all the rest to see. They will not trouble us further."

"That might work," the old man conceded.

"It will work," his visitor insisted. "As evidence of my good faith I have taken the liberty of setting an initial example already."

The old man looked at him quizzically.

"Do you remember the three *hijos de puta* who tricked your freighter captain one night a little while back? You caught one. We took the other two."

"Ah, yes. Capitán Veredo. He had served me for a long time. It was a pity. He will rest easier if they are dead, too."

The old man and his visitor talked for a long time that morning in a restored farmhouse with a commanding view of the flowers. Girls in household livery of white blouses and plaid skirts brought venison, truffles and exquisite Chilean Riesling so dry it puckered the mouth.

It gradually became apparent, as the old man understood the beauty of the alliance, that he would agree to meld two organizations, competitors until now, into one powerful unit. That would make the two men dominant and impregnable. The visitor could hardly contain himself. He would take back with him to Miami that afternoon an agreement that would in time make him rich beyond his wildest dreams. The violence and disorder that had plagued and weakened him would vanish forever. It was the most exciting day of his life. It was the stuff of history.

"*Bueno,* Ignacio, I believe your plan will work. I will curtail the supply and give you some weeks to implement your part of the bargain," the old man said.

"I think we should meet once more to make sure all the details are understood," his visitor said quickly.

"Yes, I was going to suggest that. When you are ready, let me know and I will come to Miami—my wife gets shopping fever every few months. She will be pleased if I accompany her once." The old man permitted himself a thin smile. "You have a good brain, Ignacio. In a way I am sorry that all of my daughters married long ago."

"I am honored," the visitor said.

"Before you go, permit me a gesture of good will."

The old man clapped his hands, and the flower girl named Dorita appeared. She had changed her blue smock, and now she wore the same plaid skirt and white blouse as the serving girls. It was a difference of degree. The blouse was sheer, rouged nipples straining against the soft fabric. The skirt was slit high up the naked brown thigh.

"Go with my friend, Dorita," the old man from Bogotá called softly. "I am tired today, and it is he who will reward you for your beautiful flowers."

"*Sí, patrón,*" the girl said.

# Chapter 11

"BORSCHT. Hot borscht in the summer, cold borscht in the winter—with plenty of sour cream. The best thing when you are feeling low." She said it with an assertive shake of her blue-rinsed head. There could be no doubting.

"Chicken soup?" she sneered. "Chicken soup is overrated."

"Thanks," said Christopher Meadows. "I love borscht."

Her name was Sadie. She was the queen of the Buckingham, and she had arrived with morning.

"Mr. Meadows, Mr. Meadows, wake up! It's your neighbor, Sadie. Time for breakfast."

He had bolted upright like a startled deer. For a few seconds he hadn't been able to remember where he was, or why. Then the memory had come flooding back.

THE TRANS AM WAS GONE.

For a second time Meadows dropped his overnight bag in a heartbeat of dismay. It was impossible. Mono had come alone, and now Mono lay in a pool of blood in the stairwell. The car had to be there, next to Meadows's own Ghia. But it was not.

Then Meadows saw the trail of blood. He traced it from the stairway door, drop by blackening drop, to where Mono's car had stood. There drops had formed a small puddle.

Mono was alive!

Meadows whirled in fright, prepared to see again the Trans Am bearing down on him. The emptiness of the top level mocked his panic. Nothing moved. The garage was deathly still.

All of Meadows's cunning evaporated. Logic deserted him. He

ran as fast as his wounded leg would carry him to the Karmann Ghia. The keys! Which pocket? Shit! Here! Which key? Here! Thank God, the same key for the door and the ignition.

Meadows threw himself into the seat and jammed the key into the switch. The car lunged forward and died. He had forgotten to depress the clutch. With his right foot he pumped madly at the gas and tried again. The car would not start. Finally the engine caught, and he jammed the transmission into reverse to back away from the wall. He guided it backward in a wide arc, eyes fixed on the rear-view mirror, awaiting retribution. The garage seemed endless, an eternal tunnel, twisting in a dark blind maze as Meadows descended to the exit.

When he finally got there, Meadows had to brake sharply to avoid rear-ending a fat black Cadillac stopped to pay the toll. He looked desperately for a way around the car. There was none.

Only one toll lane open, the others all sealed with black and yellow wooden barriers. Could he crash one? He could try. He slipped the Ghia in reverse. Then the Cadillac moved.

Meadows lurched up to the toll booth. Where was the fucking parking ticket? There, between the bucket seats, where he had left it an eternity ago. He thrust the ticket through the window.

A sign lit up: $1.00.

"One dollar," recited the attendant. She was as fat as the Cadillac.

Meadows fumbled for the money. He always carried his bills in a side pocket. He had nothing smaller than a twenty.

"Keep the change," he ordered, and drove off into the night.


WITH THE MEMORY came the pain. His leg hurt like hell. The drying scrape on his arm had stuck to the long-sleeved shirt he had put on in the car. Meadows regarded himself with distaste. He lay disheveled, ragged and fully dressed atop the bedspread of an ancient mattress that sighed for mercy.

"Mr. Meadows. Mr. Meadows! Your tea is getting cold!"

Who was this harridan? Against his better judgment, Meadows limped to the door. There stood a vision in frizzy curls and pancake makeup. A garish ring of red circled her mouth. One painted eyebrow danced higher than the other. She was barely five feet tall, and nearly as wide. A housecoat of many colors struggled to contain her. Meadows's head began aching immediately, and Sadie watched him curiously.

"It's nearly nine o'clock, Mr. Meadows. We breakfast early here at the Buckingham." She carried a metal tray with steaming tea in a chipped mug, two gnarled pieces of toast and a jelly glass holding an amber fluid that fizzed. He later discovered it was celery soda. Sadie firmly believed there was nothing celery soda and borscht would not cure.

"How did you know my name?" he stammered.

"Izzy, the desk clerk, told me. Everybody knows. It's not often we get late-night guests at the Buckingham. He says you came in looking as if you had been run over. Poor man. Of course, you can't believe everything Izzy says. You know how he lies. He claims he was in the ghetto in Warsaw. Ghetto, schmetto. Izzy comes from Newark. So why lie already?"

She winked conspiratorially. With an elephantine pirouette she deposited the tray on the wooden hulk that passed for a dresser.

"You've got to watch that Izzy," said Meadows dryly. His improbable morning caller was like the sight of land to a drowning sailor.

In the night he had stumbled upon the Buckingham, unseeing, uncaring. Pausing only to change his bloody shirt, Meadows had driven as far as the nearest expressway would take him from the airport. He had found himself in the shabby south section of Miami Beach, a refuge for people who were too poor to live on the tawdry strip farther north, and too old to enjoy it.

In the darkness the motel had looked like all the others. The bald and scrawny desk clerk who had awakened to his call—it must have been Izzy—had registered Meadows without comment.

Sunshine revealed the Buckingham to be a paint-peeling monstrosity, an elderly survivor of the Art Deco age. Once it had been white. Now it was flamingo pink, trimmed in turquoise. It was two stories high, built around an internal courtyard. Atop the second story stood a dome of chipped concrete. Sadie confessed that it was the observatory, unused these last fifty years because there was no telescope. When it had been built, the Buckingham had had a sea view. Now, like the telescope and the youth of its denizens, the beach was gone.

Sadie and her friends lived off memories and illegal hot plates that regularly blew the fuses. They dwelt amid a jungle in the courtyard and a parody of art in the hallways. Every few feet there was a niche, and in every niche the crumbling bust of some personage who had obviously been important to the horror's early owners: Lindbergh, Beethoven, Schiller, FDR, Eisenhower, Groucho Marx(!), Lincoln, Rickenbacker, Babe Ruth, Mae West.

For a day, Meadows did nothing but sleep, eat and wallow in a four-legged porcelain tub. He quickly discovered that the maternal care and breakfast were inventions of Sadie's. "The management is not responsible for the contents," Izzy proclaimed. Sadie chirped incessantly; Meadows endured it as a welcome shred of homeliness in universe-turned-alien.

It was too easy, eyes closed, seeking sleep on impertinent springs, to slip back into the nightmare: to confront questions again for which there were no answers.

Was Mono alive? He had to be. If he had moved his car, Mono could not be dead.

And if he was alive, the word must now be out among his friends that it was the *gringo* patsy who had stabbed him.

Or would Mono be too *macho* to confess to that? Maybe he could not bear the shame of it. Perhaps he would prefer to recover and to bide his time; to return himself one day to finish a job he had thrice botched.

Maybe Mono's thirst for revenge would dominate. Meadows could see Mono lying bandaged in some dark *barrio* apartment, a fellow shark bending close to hear his words. "It was the *gringo*. Get him for me, *chico*. Get him!"

If Mono was alive, Chris Meadows was either a dead man or a fugitive. There were no other possibilities.

Why hadn't he died? Meadows tossed on the lumpy mattress.

If nothing else, he was safe at the Buckingham. That afternoon, trailing a two-wheel shopping cart and lascivious winks from Izzy, Sadie had brought him food after a pilgrimage to the kosher supermarket.

On the second morning she brought him a copy of the *Miami Journal*. When Meadows could find no mention of a stabbed body at the airport, he threw down the paper in disgust. Then he called Nelson and lied to him.

"Do you think if I had gone to college, I too could be a globe-trotting architect?" Nelson teased when Meadows said he was in New York and had been to see a play the night before.

"I am here by necessity, not design," Meadows replied testily. "What do you hear about *el mono?*"

"Nothing. How about you?"

Meadows was instantly defensive. "Why should I hear anything?"

"Oh, I dunno. I thought maybe you bumped into him again. Maybe he went to haunt you along the Great White Way."

A weak joke, but too close to home for Meadows. "Listen," he said sharply, "when you left my house the other night, I went right to the airport and got on a plane and came up here—just like you said I should. You find that murdering bastard and throw him in jail—don't hassle me."

"No offense, *amigo,*" said Nelson. "Just hang on for a little while and things will blow over."

Fool, thought Meadows. Blow over! There was no way anything would blow over. Not while Mono lived. Meadows came close to blurting out the truth. He needed help. The Cuban cop was a slender reed, perhaps, but who else was there?

"Listen, Nelson, there's something . . ."

"Just sit tight. Give me your number there, and I'll call you if anything good happens."

"No," Meadows said quickly, "I'm going out into the country with a friend. I'll call you tomorrow."

"*Bueno,* save the taxpayers money if that's what you want. I'll be around."

Meadows had never felt so lonely. He was restless. Did he dare go for a walk? No, it was better to hide in the ruins at the Buckingham.

Meadows called Stella, who cooed and cawed and read him about twenty messages. Eight of them were from Dana, each angrier than the last.

"I'll take care of these, Stella. If anybody else calls, tell them I've gone out of town for a few days."

"Very well, sir. But you really ought to call the ministers from Salvador, Mr. Meadows. They are very anxious to hear about their oil building."

"Ecuador, Stella. The building is for Ecuador."

"Why would they tell me Salvador?" she asked petulantly.

Stella, Meadows reflected, was the only constant in his jumbled universe. He called his mother in Massachusetts and told her he was going to the Caribbean. He called a colleague in California who wanted help with a new government complex and put him off. Then he spent two hours trying to get through to CAN's one-room headquarters in Asunción.

"*La Comandante no está*. She flying," a secretary told him.

It was the same story with Arthur. No, Arthur was gone for a few days, a groggy voice explained when he called the jazz club downtown. Down to Jamaica. Wanna leave a message? Meadows hung up.

He ventured into the overgrown garden to sit for a while in the sun. He was promptly ambushed by Sadie and two crone-friends. They chattered around him, and he nodded every now and then, like a bored husband who simultaneously reads the paper and talks with his wife.

ON THE AFTERNOON of Meadows's third day at the Buckingham, Sadie appeared with a request. He was glad of the interruption. For the first time in his life he had succumbed in ennui to television soap operas.

"Mr. Meadows, it would be so nice if you could join us tonight for dinner. Once a week, you know, we sit down together and share what we have. Kind of potluck."

Meadows was touched.

"Of course, I'd be glad to come. But I have nothing to bring."

"For that you shouldn't worry. I bought some bologna for you."

Late in the afternoon Meadows called Nelson again. There was a long wait before he came to the phone.

"Good news, *amigo*. Mono is dead."

"What!"

"It happened a couple days ago, but nobody found him until early this morning. He was alone in his car in a vacant lot. Stabbed once, apparently, and bled to death."

"God!"

Meadows felt the world turn, a queasy mix of despair and glee. He pressed Nelson for details. From what he knew and what he heard, Meadows was able to piece together Mono's last agony.

Somehow Domingo Sosa had managed to drive away from the airport. He'd made it only two miles, not far enough—obviously— to find help, but fortunately far enough to get into the city, away from the crime scene.

Nelson admitted that the police had no leads to the killer. "It looks to me, *amigo*," he said, "like it's safe enough for you to come home."

"I can't believe it," Meadows said. "Now that the pressure is off, I may stay up here a few more days and really enjoy myself."

"Is she pretty?"

"Out of this world," Meadows said with forced enthusiasm. "When I come back, I'll tell you all about it—and bring you a box of cigars."

"*Adios,*" Nelson said, chuckling. "*Buena suerte.*"

Meadows set the phone down gingerly. Part of him wanted to weep, and part of him wanted to dance, bum leg and all. He had *killed* a man. It was no nightmare.

The architect studied his hands. He could almost feel it, the knife, in a damp palm. The noise came back, too, the muffled *shtup* of the blade splitting fabric and then flesh. Then Sosa's belly blooming red.

Meadows had *killed* a man.

And now he was safe.

Where should he go? Anywhere. Anywhere at all.

If Terry was flying, there was no prayer of finding her. New York? Why the hell not? He picked up the phone.

"I shouldn't even be talking to you," Dana scolded.

"Don't get snooty. I am coming tonight, by midnight. I expect you to be there."

"At the airport?"

"In bed. Leave the door unlocked."

"Have you been drinking, Chris?"

"Not yet."

Meadows sang in the shower. He scrubbed his nails. He washed his hair. He shaved to within an inch of his life. He allowed himself the luxury of deciding what to wear.

He wouldn't even call for a reservation. He would just go to the airport—Fort Lauderdale. No way anybody would get him back to Miami International anytime soon.

He emerged from the bathroom dripping wet, a skimpy white towel around his waist. He had decided to go classically: a fine white shirt, striped tie, light blue blazer, camel slacks and black loafers. Could he buy flowers at La Guardia?

There was a knock on the door.

"You can come in, Sadie, if you want to, but only at your own risk. I'm nearly naked," Meadows sang out.

The door opened quickly, and Octavio Nelson stepped through it.

"You are under arrest, *amigo*," Nelson said softly. Meadows caught a quick glimpse of Sadie in the passageway, an arthritic hand clutching a bony breast.

"What?" Meadows croaked.

"For the murder of Domingo Sosa."

# Chapter 12

MEADOWS FELT the room spin. Dots danced in front of his eyes. He tried to speak; could not. He clung grimly to the towel. It was all the defense he had. He felt naked, betrayed. His brain scratched for a fulcrum. It found none.

"I don't know what you're talking about," he managed finally. It was the hoarse whisper of an old man.

"Do me a favor, *amigo*. Put some clothes on, and try not to sound stupid, OK?"

Meadows grabbed his trousers and shirt off the bed and stumbled into the gloomy bathroom. He dressed mindlessly, slowly, willing away the implacable presence in the bedroom and the cheap cigars that had come with it.

Fear and anger, the emotions that seemed to have dogged him like malaria since that afternoon in the Grove, played hot and cold along his spine. He was a fool. He was helpless. He was trapped. And he had to get away.

The bathroom window. If he knocked out the cheap screen, he could squeeze through. Terry . . . Bahia . . . oh, God. Run.

The bathroom door. Lock the door. Knock out the screen. Go through the window.

Meadows's hands reached for the open door.

"If it's the window you're thinking about, *amigo*, I already checked," came the mocking voice. "There's only one way you can run in the alley outside. I'll be waiting."

Meadows's outstretched hand wilted lifelessly to his side. He leaned back against the cool tile wall. He could not run. He could not even fight. Senseless, so senseless.

Nelson sarcastically recorded Meadows's return. "Well, there he is, dressed to kill."

Meadows glowered silently.

"You sure surprised me, *amigo.* I figured you were mad enough to kill Mono, but I never dreamed you could do it. Killed by some architect who doesn't know coke from sugar. Jesus, that's a laugh. Wait'll his friends find out."

Meadows began to speak, to protest.

"No, don't say anything. You'd only make it worse. I'm supposed to tell you that you shouldn't say anything without a lawyer. Get a good lawyer."

Nelson toyed with his cigar, rolling it in his fingers, watching the thick smoke dart in and out of the circle of light from a floor lamp. The silence grew. Finally Nelson sighed.

"Shit, *amigo,* don't think I like doing this. I know you got caught up in something you never wanted and don't even understand. But facts are facts, *carajo.* Mono's dead, you killed him and you left a trail so easy to follow that Pincus will probably write his dissertation about it."

Meadows silently gauged the distance to the door. He couldn't make it in a straight shot, not with Nelson half in his path. Could he take Nelson? Probably, but it would have to be fast. But Nelson was a cop, and therefore, he had a gun. If Meadows sprang, would he have time to get it? Probably. Would he shoot? Yes, he would shoot. No way out.

When Nelson spoke again, it was in a low monotone, as though he were reading from a telephone book or reciting from a macabre rosary.

"You made a lot of mistakes. Mono would have done it better if he had killed you. Mono at least was a pro."

Meadows listened, disbelieving. He stared at a spot in the Buckingham ceiling where water had cracked and discolored the plaster. He said nothing, fascinated in spite of himself by Nelson's recital.

"A milkman found Mono in the car over by LeJeune. A milkman! I didn't even know there were any milkmen left. Anyway, you remember those nice white seats in the Trans Am? Mono had a thing about white, I guess. The seats looked like they had been dipped in red paint. The cops who found him said they had never seen so much blood. Of course, it was dried. It looked like some-body spilled a can of red talcum powder, they said. Jesus, they'll never get those seats clean.

"Anyway, it's pretty clear to us right off the bat that Mono wasn't killed in the car: no sign of a struggle, and nobody could have stabbed Mono like that without a fight. The ME says he'd been dead about two days.

"So he was stabbed someplace else and drove to where he died. About three blocks away there's a Cuban clinic that never asks questions, so we know where Mono was going.

"But where did he get stuck? That's the first question, *amigo,* and it's not hard to figure out. See, Mono's a pro, and when he left that parking lot at the airport, he didn't race away from the toll. He paid what he owed, and he took a little paper receipt that says, 'Thank you. Have a nice day.'

"Once we find that little piece of paper we call the airport cops, and they say, 'Funny you should call because something strange must have happened in the parking garage the other night. We found a puddle of blood in a parking space, and we followed the trail into a stairwell, and lo and behold, there's a whole lake of blood on the landing.'

"We know Mono got it at the airport, so the next question is: Who else was at the airport that night? About a million people, that's who.

"But it's not really as hard as that because I turn Pincus loose, and he's a tiger on things like that.

"Only one of the million people at the airport that night pays twenty bucks for a dollar's worth of parking and leaves without his change, Pincus discovers. That toll collector lady is no dummy. When somebody with shaking hands passes her a twenty and doesn't wait for change, she writes down his license plate number on the bill.

"That's really all Pincus needs, *amigo.* He cranks up the comput-ers, and in about fifteen minutes he knows that the car belongs to one Meadows, Thaddeus Christopher. No wonder you call yourself Chris.

"But where is Thaddeus Christopher Meadows? Well, that's easy, too. He's in New York. He must be in New York. He calls me up and says he's in New York, doesn't he?"

"That might fool me, *amigo,* but it doesn't fool Pincus. He calls up Eastern Airlines and talks to its computers. They say a Mr. Meadows, initial C, was a no-show on the last flight to New York the night Mono got killed."

Meadows knew what came next: the phone call.

"We do a routine trace," Nelson says. "Shocking! Meadows, initial C, is not calling from Manhattan. He's calling from some fleabag hotel on Miami Beach."

"It wasn't like that," Meadows cried, tossing his head back and forth the way a quadriplegic might try to dislodge a leech.

Nelson sucked on the dead cigar. "You're not a totally stupid man," he said after a moment. "I won't tell you we've got a first-degree murder case against you, because we don't."

"Why the hell would I buy an airline ticket if I was trying to set the guy up?" Meadows protested. "Why would I hand that lady a twenty? And why would I come here, for Chrissakes?"

Nelson nodded. "Good points. Self-defense is what I suppose your big shot mouthpiece is going to argue. Then the prosecutor will ask: Why didn't he call the cops? Why did he hide the knife? Why did he pretend he was in New York?" Nelson shrugged amiably. "We don't have a first-degree murder case, *amigo,* but we do have a case."

Meadows stifled a moan.

"Suppose we go for second-degree or, assuming we get a pussy prosecutor, manslaughter. What does a trial like that do for an architect's career? Real lousy publicity, no? You might spend the rest of your life dreaming up pretty gymnasiums or bait-and-tackle shops."

Meadows closed his eyes and swallowed hard. Nelson spoke slowly, hammering every word.

"That's not the worst of it, my friend. The best lawyer in Miami can snow a jury, but he will never convince Mono's friends that you were merely an innocent victim. Or that their brave *compadre* deserved such a death. So it boils down to this: Guilty, you go to jail, a very nasty place. Innocent, and you're dead two days after you're back on the streets."

Meadows was beyond shock. Heads you win, tails I lose. He wished his mother had taught him better how to pray.

"As far as I'm concerned, the worst thing," said Nelson, "is not that Mono is dead—who cares about that dirtbag?—but that you made him die at precisely the wrong time. I tried to tell you at your place the other night: Mono was never important as Mono. He was a fucking drone, Meadows. He interested me only because he worked directly for *el Jefe*, the ringmaster of the whole fucking cocaine circus."

"And that's your prize? Your big promotion?" Meadows sneered.

"I want him badly. Domingo Sosa would have led me to him eventually. It had to happen."

"Who *was* Sosa?"

"A killer," Nelson replied. "He moved down from Union City. He had steady work. You were just a little overtime. It must have been quite a fight."

Nelson watched Meadows's eyes for an admission. The architect stared back, saying nothing. Nelson could see the fear. Intuition alerted him to the fury that underlay it.

"Mono brought some helpers," the detective said. "Charming fellows; like lobotomized linebackers. I almost eyeballed them myself a couple nights ago on a surveillance in Little Havana. I'd love to know who they are because I'll bet they're about to become *el Jefe*'s new enforcers now that Mono is dead."

"Newly promoted killers."

"Sure." Nelson tapped ashes onto the threadbare carpet. "They stick together. In their line of work it's not easy finding people you can trust. They are here, that much I know." He began to stand up. "Well, my friend, time to go."

"I know who they are," Meadows said dully.

"What!" Nelson sat down again quickly.

"They were at the dog track with Mono. It was pretty obvious who was boss."

"Do you know their names?"

"No."

"Could you describe them?"

"Yes."

Nelson was excited now. "*Madre de Dios,* tell me what they look like!"

"Why should I?"

Nelson slapped his thigh in exasperation. He leaned back in the chair and made a ceremony of relighting his cigar.

"I don't blame you, I guess. Use what you know when you need it most. Maybe you can talk to the state's attorney."

Nelson puffed the cigar. Meadows coughed. Neither spoke.

Meadows abandoned the idea of flight: too risky. There had to be some other way, some way out. He thought frantically.

Nelson, too, was thinking: To arrest Meadows would please only Pincus and the police department gnomes who assembled crime statistics. *Pobre cabrón.* The gnomes should give medals to citizens who kill killers. . . . He came to a decision. Screw Pincus and the gnomes. Meadows could recognize Mono's companions. That mattered most.

"You know, *amigo,* you ruined a three-month investigation by killing that scumbag. If you could help me get things back on the track, maybe we could strike a deal."

"I'm not interested," Meadows said quickly, but Nelson saw the flash in the architect's eye.

"Even if we could agree that Mono's death goes into the books as one more unsolved drug murder?" Nelson said.

"I didn't murder anybody," Meadows replied stubbornly.

"Let's say I believe you. And then let's say as a token of good will you do me a favor."

Nelson had Meadows's attention now. He could almost see the gray cells churning back from the brink of despair.

"Then?"

"Then you go your way and I go mine. Mono's dead. Nobody knows who did it. Too bad. *Que descanse en paz.*"

"Just like that," Meadows said.

"Well, a few people in the department would have to know that while one of my sources was working for me, he happened to kill *el Mono*—and I'd have to sit on Pincus. But that's all. Nobody in the department will weep for him."

"Yeah, sure. And whose word would I have for all that?"

"Mine."

*"Yours!"*

Nelson fought against the color that rose to his cheeks. He was close now. Patience.

"Maybe it's not much." Nelson contrived a shallow smile. "But then"—hard now, to the gut—"have you got anything better, *amigo*?"

Meadows stared at the yellowed ceiling. He could see himself in handcuffs and, later, as the star attraction in some pompous court-room. He could see himself stuffed with cocaine and swinging from a varnished wooden beam. No, he had nothing better than the cocky Cuban cop, even if that meant he had nothing. Meadows was tired of being punched. Given a little rope, he might find a way to punch back.

"What do you want?"

"Tell me about those men you saw with Mono. Could you sketch them, like you did Mono?"

"No. It was Mono who interested me."

"Would they recognize you?"

Meadows mentally reran the scene at the dog track. The lighting had not been good. There had been a crowd. The thugs were not likely to have picked him out. He meant nothing to them.

"They might, but I doubt it."

Nelson sprang quickly from the chair.

"OK, you've got a deal. Get up. You've got a tie, haven't you? Take a shower first; you stink of sweat."

Cold water helped Meadows restore his equilibrium. Nelson wanted him to do something that was reckless. Surely he would not be content with a description of the junior killers or even a sketch. Nelson would want more, much more.

The architect in Meadows pleaded for caution. It was stupid to deal with the devil, even if he was not lying. Take your chances on the courts. It *was* self-defense.

And fatal not to deal with him, said the bruised and terrified man that was also Meadows. What difference can it make? A drown-ing man doesn't care how deep the water is.

When Meadows emerged from the shower, there were no prelim-inaries.

"The deal is this. I will deposit you, tonight, in a public place where Mono's friends will be among several hundred people. You will identify them. You will get to know them so well that your sketches of them would make their mothers swoon with delight. If possible, you will learn their names; your Spanish is good enough for that, right?"

Meadows snorted. "A couple of sketches."

"There's more," Nelson said quickly. "I think the man I call *el Jefe* will also be there, somewhere in the crowd. He will surely make contact with Mono's associates. He needs them now, badly. Watch and listen very closely. Get him for me, Meadows. Bring me a sketch of *el Jefe*, and Mono is forgotten. My word of honor."

"How can you be sure he will be there?"

"I know my people."

"Then why don't you put one of your bushy-tailed narcs in there with a camera? Pincus would blend in about as smoothly as I would."

Nelson raised a hand. "Let's just say this is my investigation, OK? Where I am sending you tonight, I could never go myself. Why? Because I've probably arrested relatives of half the people there and shared dinner with the rest. Now I'm getting tired of this conversation. Let's go."

A hundred questions sprang into Meadows's mind. What setting, how many people, what kind of light, how much freedom of movement—the kinds of questions an architect might ask a client before he sat down to draw.

"What kind of place is this?" Meadows said.

"You'll see."

Two other questions, both vital.

One was whether Nelson would keep his word. There was no sense asking that, so Meadows asked the other.

"Suppose I'm wrong? Suppose Mono's goons *do* recognize me. What then?"

Nelson shrugged.

*"Que sera, sera,"* he said.

# Chapter 13

WILBUR PINCUS did not show up at the Dade Community College for Police Management 202. Instead, he left his two-bedroom apartment about nine and drove his well-polished 1977 Mustang coupe toward Miami Beach. With Nelson out picking up the architect, there was something Pincus had to do.

As he crossed the MacArthur Causeway heading west, the young detective surveyed Biscayne Bay, glass calm under a brilliant summer night's sky. The sight left him breathless; he wanted to stop just to watch the ivory white yachts rumble south in the Intracoastal.

A group of fishermen clustered on one of the bridges. As Pincus drove past, he noticed one of the rods bent double under the silver muscle of a terrific game fish. He fought the urge to pull over and enjoy the battle.

Pincus came to the turnoff for Hibiscus Island, an exclusive dollop of real estate halfway between the Miami mainland and the beach. A heavy-lidded security guard scuttled from a wooden gatehouse and waved him down.

"I'm going to see Mr. Nelson," Pincus said.

The guard peered into the car and nodded. "Need your name," he said, lifting a clipboard.

"Wilson. Gregory Wilson."

The gate opened, and the Mustang cruised through.

Pincus already knew the address by heart. It was an easy one: 77 North Hibiscus. A quick call to a friendly clerk at the tax appraiser's office had bought him more: five bedrooms, four and a half baths, a swimming pool on two acres, waterfront, of course. Purchased eighteen months ago for $195,500.

Pincus found it all very interesting, but nothing so much as the curious fact that Roberto Nelson was able to put down $100,000 on the house. Octavio Nelson never talked about his brother, and Wilbur Pincus was beginning to understand why.

The house at 77 North Hibiscus was ringed with an eight-foot sandstone wall. A red phone hung by the wrought-iron gate— nothing out of the ordinary for the sort of people who lived on these islands, but damn unusual, Pincus ruminated, for a cop's brother.

Pincus eased off the accelerator as he passed the gate. A pair of headlights emerging from Nelson's driveway caught him squarely in the eyes. Pincus sped off.

In the rear view he saw a car pull out. It was not a beige Mercedes, but a small sports car. Pincus pulled into another driveway and turned around. By the time he reached the gatehouse the other car was halfway across the bridge, heading for MacArthur. Pincus broke a few traffic laws catching up. He fumbled in the glove compartment for some eyeglasses. The car, in front of him now by only six lengths, was an orange Alfa Romeo. The tag was also orange, a dirty orange. Either New York or Pennsylvania: GDU 439.

The driver was a man. Pincus noticed the cut of the hair, the size of the head, the way the fingers drummed on the dash; the guy was playing his stereo. He wasn't paying attention. The driver ran a red light at Bayshore Drive, and a Metro bus driver flicked him the finger.

Pincus got stuck behind the bus and lost the Alfa Romeo. At Biscayne Boulevard the young detective made a right turn and started hunting.


ROBERTO NELSON had been sitting at the bar of the Royal Palm Club for twenty minutes when the stranger came in. He was tall and muscular, and his radically short blond hair was damp with sweat. He wore small round glasses with tortoise-shell frames and he sat alone at the end of the bar farthest from the band.

"New talent, Joanie," one of the barmaids said to her partner. "I'll see what he wants to drink."

Roberto Nelson paid no attention. He drummed on the bar,

glancing occasionally at the pudgy lead singer with the gelatin breasts.

Soon a thin dark man sat next to him. Roberto grinned and leaned over to whisper. The two men rose together and threaded through the tables toward the rest room. When they came out, a full five minutes later, they were met by the stranger with blond hair.

"'Scuse me," Wilbur Pincus said shyly, stepping aside to let the men by.

"It's OK, bubba." Roberto Nelson smiled.

Inside the rest room, Pincus entered the toilet stall and locked it behind him. He waited for half a minute, but no one else came. Then he crouched on one knee to examine the tile floor. Flecks of dried urine near the toilet bowl. Some hairs. Scuff marks. And there . . .

Pincus pressed the palm of his right hand to the tile. It came up spangled with tiny ivory crystals.

THE BATTERED DODGE swept across the MacArthur Causeway and threaded Douglas Road toward Little Havana. Meadows and Nelson rode in heavy silence. To Meadows, there seemed nothing to say. Nelson seemed preoccupied. Once the police radio squawked, and Nelson spoke briefly.

"Five-six-one-five," summoned a metal voice.

"Five-six-one-five."

"There's suddenly a lot of movement on that Morningside surveillance. Can you come?"

"Negative. Can't you handle it?"

"Yeah, I think so, except that I can't seem to raise one-one-seven-eight."

"Stern and García," Nelson muttered to himself. "That's not like them." He addressed the microphone again.

Meadows listened with half an ear, his head filled more with roller coaster reflection than radio traffic.

Nelson wheeled into a cluttered parking lot underneath a flickering red neon sign that said Guayabera Grocery. From the parking-lot side of what looked to Meadows like a cluttered general store, an off-balance, belt-high counter yawned drunkenly. A waitress with bottled red hair swayed in the window to the sounds of the born-in-Miami beat called *salsa.*

*"Dos cafecitos, querida,"* Nelson ordered. *"Y bájame el radio. Tengo que usar el teléfono."*

The music shrank inside its green plastic box as Nelson went to the phone, and Meadows licked tentatively at the scalding brew. He felt resigned, as though all emotion had been purged from him. Nelson would not tell him where they were going; all he would say was that it was a public place that would allow Meadows to wander freely and inconspicuously and to leave quickly if necessary.

"How can you be sure all of them will be there?" Meadows had repeated.

"Because I am Cuban and they are Cuban. That's how I know," Nelson had replied enigmatically. "Relax. No one has ever had a softer chance to walk away from a murder charge."

Nelson's face was drawn when he returned to the counter, his lips a thin, tight line. He swallowed the coffee with a gulp and headed for the car behind a taut *"¡Vamos!"*

They drove deep into *el Barrio,* past a noisy bar that promised *Chicas Topless;* past a municipal ball field where wiry kids with olive skin backed up paunchy father-shortstops; past a vest-pocket park where keyed-up old men slapped dominoes on the smooth tops of square white tables. An old-fashioned butcher shop flashed by; a factory for hand-rolled cigars and a *botánica,* whose spotless display window offered prayerful saints and wizened cock claws, both guaranteed to ward off evil.

They stopped, finally, on the darkened apron of a gas station that obviously had been abandoned for a long time. Regular 52.9, said the twisted sign atop a rusting pump.

"This is the place," said Nelson, gesturing to a well-lit one-story brick building across the street.

Meadows squinted to make out the lettering on the discreet black and white sign: Hidalgo & Sons.

"Jesus Christ!" Meadows said. "It's a funeral parlor!"

"That's right. Open all night. Best sandwiches in Little Havana."

"I'm not walking into any damned funeral parlor."

Nelson's fist tapped impatiently on the steering wheel.

"We already played that scene, *amigo.* Either you walk into that place and do a little favor for me or somebody carries you into a place just like that much sooner than you would like. Think it through."

Meadows did not have to ask whose corpse the Hidalgos were cosseting that night. He knew. He knew, too, that Nelson had maneuvered him with exquisite planning and logic.

"We gave back the body this afternoon. They'll bury him tomorrow. Tonight is the *velorio.* The family will stay all night—it's an old Cuban custom. Everybody who knew him will be here between now and about eleven o'clock. It would be an unforgivable insult not to come. Honor is foremost with these people. Remember that."

"And will they be grieving and asking for the forgiveness of sins?" Meadows snapped.

"The grief will be genuine," Nelson said. "Among both men and women. Latin men are not afraid to cry."

"Then I'll stand out like a sore thumb among all those sniffling *machos,* won't I?"

"I worried about that, but it will not be too bad. That's a big place. There are four bodies in there tonight. Four *velorios.* One of them is for an old Anglo-Cuban. Some of the mourners will look more *gringo* than Cuban. No one will pay any attention to you."

"Christ!" said Meadows.

"I have two people inside; that's standard procedure for scumbag *velorios.* They're looking for the same thing you are, but they're looking blind. That phone call I made was to tell them to keep an eye on you. Don't try to find them. Don't be obvious. Look around thoroughly, and get out. I'll be waiting. I won't move. *Buena suerte.*"

"Thanks a lot," Meadows said. He wiped his hands on the soft fabric of his pants and walked around the car.

"*Oye, amigo,*" Nelson called. "If I knew who they were, I wouldn't need you. And if I didn't need you, you'd be in jail."

Meadows's first impression was that he had stumbled into the intermission of an off-Broadway play. A gust of chill air greeted him behind two gold metal doors that sighed open as he approached. In a hallway about thirty feet long and fifteen wide stood about a hundred well-dressed people. They all seemed to be speaking at once, and there was no mistaking them for Americans. They spoke with their eyes, their hands, their whole bodies. Mourners' knots formed and dissolved in an almost stylized pattern of *abrazo, besito* and gossip.

If there was reverence, it certainly was not hushed. In one corner, next to a gold papier-mâché fountain in the shape of a leaping dolphin, a woman of extraordinary beauty held court. Five, six, seven dark-suited young men swirled around her, knights beseeching favor. She was charming, imperious, untouchable.

From a doorway with marbled Formica lintels a dowager mourner emerged like a battleship under steam: broad of beam, black-clothed, white-haired, makeup streaked with tears, chattering nieces and nephews her darting escorts.

A child of about six, pigtails restrained by pink ribbons, wandered anxiously underfoot. *"Mami, Mami!"* she wailed. Two middle-aged men stood spread-legged, cigar to cigar, arguing loudly. Politics, Meadows's rusty Spanish told him. The men's wives turned away, as though on cue, to amuse one another with midwives' tales they had recounted a thousand times.

A strikingly handsome man, elegant in a three-piece black suit, yellow rose at his lapel, an establishment mustache curried till it squealed, preened in *macho* counterpart to the beautiful dolphin girl. He bussed four cheeks, shared six *abrazos* and shook three hands with stiff formality in the minute Meadows spared him.

The smell of death assailed Meadows. Calla lilies, gladiolas, carnations, chrysanthemums peeked from the four rooms that opened off the hallway. Their aromas mingled with the scents of perfume, sweat, cigars and formaldehyde.

Meadows felt light-headed. Before him, through the haze, the smell and the noise, lay the centerpiece of the room: a white-robed plaster Virgin Mary with two lambs at her feet, praying above an electric candle. Two flags, one Cuban, one American, flanked the Virgin in drooping salute.

Meadows stood irresolute. Where to go? How to begin? He had to go in, but every fiber screamed at him to get out. Finally he turned left and headed for the first of the four body rooms.

It was a mistake. About twenty people sat in metal folding chairs with red plastic seats facing the coffin in a niche at the far wall. The mourners sat in quiet dignity, silent reproof to the cocktail chatter that followed Meadows through the door. No head turned when he entered. The flower stench was overwhelming.

Meadows took four paces into the room and stopped. Wrong one, dammit. The coffin sat in lonely eminence, two spotlights illuminating its closed lid. It was tiny, toylike. It could have belonged only to a child. Meadows fled.

Heart pounding, head resting lightly against the thin white plasterboard wall, Meadows weighed his next move. He studied the people entering and leaving the other three rooms, his vision constantly intercepted by the swirling mob of mourners in the hall. He had to hurry; Nelson would be worried. He must have been here nearly twenty minutes already. He looked at his black-faced Rolex—a perfect mourner's watch. Four minutes had passed.

"You don't look Cuban," she said.

Meadows turned quickly, startled by the intrusion. "I'm not," he blurted.

"I know. I can always tell; something about the eyes and the set of the head."

Frank black eyes stared appraisingly at Meadows. She was even more beautiful than the dolphin lady. She wore a dark blue suit of superb cut and a white silk shirt, knotted in a loose bow at the neck. Her taste identified her to Meadows as an outcast.

"Pretty awful, isn't it." It was not a question.

"Yes," said Meadows. "Oh, yes."

"They're 'doing' my aunt's friend in there." The shiny black hair tossed at the room Meadows had assigned number four.

"A rosary. I couldn't stand it—the hypocrisy. My aunt hadn't spoken to the woman in ten years, except to say nasty things. Now she's in there weeping over her Ave Marias."

Meadows nodded. The child in number one, the aunt's friend in number four. Two down, two to go.

"My name is Sofia," the girl said.

Meadows mumbled something sibilant.

"Steven?" the girl asked.

"No, no," Meadows said quickly, casting frantically for a name. "Sean," he said in desperation.

"Where do you come from?"

Oh, Christ.

"Akron," said Meadows. "Akron, Ohio, heart of the Midwest." Why doesn't she go away and leave me alone? he thought.

"That's nice," the girl said uncertainly.

Meadows could see she didn't think it was nice at all. He was delighted—he had never been to Akron.

"What do you do for a living, Sean?"

Why doesn't she let up? Another time, another place, *señorita.*

"I'm in floor covering."

"Is that interesting?"

"Oh, yes," Meadows said in desperation. "Fascinating. People don't realize just how important the choice of a floor covering can be. Color, texture, resiliency. Things like that make the environment and can influence one's view of oneself and society."

It was a speech he had heard once from a gay decorator, but it worked. Meadows had her now. He watched the smile fade, the eyes glaze.

"Yes, well, I have to go," she said. *"Hasta luego."* And she was lost in the crowd, fleeing not only the rosary now but also asbestos tile and wall-to-wall carpeting.

Meadows pushed off the wall and headed for room number two. He didn't have to go in, and he cursed his stupidity. A black-bordered plastic wallboard, the kind in which skinny white letters were inserted one at a time, bore the name Don Richard Lorenzo Edwards de Gutierrez. This had to be the Anglo-Cuban Nelson had told him about. A nameplate would be outside all the rooms; he should have looked.

Meadows took a deep breath and pushed open the door to room number three. Mono's room.

Mono lay in a rich brown casket draped with a banner that said *Brigada 2506,* a tribute from the Cuban exile brigade whose invasion had failed at the Bay of Pigs.

The casket was open. Mono wore a white suit. His eyes were closed; his mouth was composed, his hair, neatly combed and lacquered in place. To Chris Meadows, Mono looked cruel even in death.

There were fewer people in this room, perhaps a dozen in all.

Meadows wondered which two worked for Octavio Nelson. There was no sign of the thugs Meadows sought.

He should have left then. But as his eyes cast about the room they fastened suddenly on three young boys, the eldest about ten, who fidgeted on hard-backed chairs in the row closest the coffin.

Three children. Sweet Jesus! Why did Mono have to have three children? Meadows grabbed at the moan, but some of it escaped into the quiet room. It might have been a sigh, a cough, a clearing of the throat, a calculated permission-to-enter? I-have-come-to-mourn-him-too.

Heads turned. Meadows felt himself go pale. Mono's widow—who else could it be?—rose stiffly from her chair and turned to face Meadows. Ten years ago she might have been pretty. Traces of insouciance lingered in a face traced now by tears. She had grown dumpy, afflicted by the sagging breasts and rice-and-beans ass that are trademarks of Cuban women over thirty.

"Ay, ay, ay," the widow keened as she approached Meadows.

"No, no," Meadows gasped.

It must have sounded to the widow like a murmur of sympathy. She embraced Meadows, crushing him tightly against her. Meadows could hear the dress fabric groan as she smothered him. He could feel her girdle and her thick thighs. He could taste her tears. It was like being hugged by a bear. Meadows dared not tear himself away. He stood perfectly still, unwitting and unwilling comfort to the new widow.

Over her shoulder the sewn-shut eyes of the dead killer vowed retribution.

Later Meadows would never be able to recall how he had extracted himself from the widow's cloying embrace. His last memory as he rushed from the body room was the image of the three young boys, staring wordlessly at him.

Meadows bolted into a neutral passageway to collect himself. He heard the sounds of plates, the whoosh of an espresso machine. Nelson's words returned to him: ". . . best sandwiches in Little Havana." Why not, if people mourned all night? Why not food in a funeral parlor?

The lounge was bright and airy: a half dozen wood veneer tables, a display case with cold drinks, a coffee machine and a cash register, its ring discreetly muffled. One Cuban waiter in a tuxedo stood behind a counter, gracefully carving a thick leg of pork. At the espresso machine a second waiter argued with a mourner.

"*¿Cómo que no hay cerveza?*" the mourner demanded.

"*Lo siento, señor, pero no tenemos aquí.*"

Beer. The thought of a sparkling cold glass of beer tugged at Meadows's throat. How nice it would be. He shared the mourner's disappointment. If there were sandwiches, there also ought to be beer.

Then Meadows's thirst vanished, and his heat leaped into his parched throat at a vision from the dog track.

The mourner was one of Mono's thugs.

Meadows looked hard: ferret's eyes, small, bulbous nose, ginger mustache, sharply etched cheeks meeting at a small mouth with big lips. Stocky build, about twenty-five, dark complexion. As the killer turned from the waiter, Meadows's portrait was complete. The man's left ear was deformed: a cauliflower ear. Meadows pictured the man in boxing trunks, a welterweight.

Meadows signaled the sandwich maker. "*Cafecito por favor, y agua,*" he said slowly in *gringo* Spanish.

The killer walked slowly toward Meadows's table. Meadows watched anxiously through fingers of a hand thrust quickly to his forehead, as though to massage it. Cauliflower Ear passed without a glance and went to sit at the table nearest the door. Meadows was committed now; there was no other way out.

When the waiter brought the coffee, Meadows swiveled slightly for a better view and was rewarded. Mono's second assistant was sliding into the spindly chair across from Cauliflower Ear.

"*El viene,*" the second man said.

A thrill ran through Meadows. "*El viene.*" He is coming. Who is coming? Who would drink coffee with two killers at a funeral parlor on this particular night? *El Jefe.* Nelson had been right.

Swiftly Meadows registered the second killer. By the time the man had lit a filtered cigarette with a gold Dunhill, Meadows could have drawn him in his sleep: older than the other one, about thirty-five, and bigger. Massive shoulders, about twenty pounds overweight, black hair thinning, round cheeks, pronounced brows, bad teeth, sallow complexion, peasant's hands, obsidian eyes that showed little intelligence. His nose had been broken and badly set. Funny, Meadows thought, the boxer's nose is not broken, but the peasant's is.

A dapper, well-dressed man of about fifty entered the lounge. His gaze swept over Cauliflower Ear and the Peasant. Meadows tensed. This was it. Here was *el Jefe*. He began filing the man's features away in his memory. Then the dapper man moved on without speaking and ordered a sandwich. Not him after all.

A woman entered; then another man. Neither paid the slightest attention to the two killers at their table near the door.

Meadows felt himself becoming angry. Come on, come on, dammit. I want out of here. How long can I nurse a two-ounce cup of coffee? To relieve his tension, Meadows rose from the table and took a soft drink from the glass-front display case.

When he turned to walk back to his chair, *el Jefe* had arrived. Could it be? Meadows sat down, stunned. The man standing over the table, lecturing the killers in soft, rapid-fire Spanish, was the matinee idol with the rose in his lapel that Meadows had seen in the hall.

Fragments of the monologue drifted to Meadows's table. His disused Spanish strained to translate. He hunched forward, trying to hear. He caught a word here, a phrase there. But there was no mistaking the tone. *El Jefe*'s anger was written on the Peasant's furrowed brow and in the right foot that Cauliflower Ear tapped nervously on the linoleum. Neither uttered a word.

It happened very fast. To a casual observer, the three men might have been exchanging the time of day. Without knowing what to listen for, a passer-by would have understood nothing. There was no greeting. Meadows didn't get it all, but he heard enough. There could be no mistake.

"Mono was a fool . . . Not the Colombians, I promise you . . . The Colombians will soon work with us . . ."

After what could have been no more than ten or fifteen seconds, a rising commotion drowned the diatribe. Everyone in the lounge heard a thud from the hallway. A woman screamed. Men's voices rose in alarm and confusion. Then came the staccato tat-tat-tat of a woman running on high heels. Meadows overheard only one more chilling phrase: "That business down in the Grove was stupid."

In that instant a well-dressed woman burst into the cafeteria, cast frantically about with wide eyes, caught sight of *el Jefe*'s back and screamed, "*¡Venga! Rápido. Es Doña Ines.*"

In those terse moments with the thugs the man with the rose had seemed wild, atavistic. Then, as Meadows watched in amazement, his features rearranged suddenly into a mask of suave concern. It was an extraordinary performance. That face in place, *el Jefe* turned to meet the distraught woman and quickly left the room.

At their table, the Peasant ground his cigarette into the floor and stood up sharply.

*"Fue el gringo. Vamos a visitarlo."*

As the killers left without paying, Meadows felt the aluminum of the soft-drink can begin to yield under the pressure of his grip. It wasn't hard to figure out which *gringo* they were going to visit.

Still, it was not so bad, Meadows reasoned. An hour or two at the drawing board, and all three men would come to life. With the sketches Nelson would have all he needed. The killers would be in his pocket then, and *el Jefe* would follow.

The crowd in the central hallway had resolved itself into a babbling knot around what Meadows presumed was an old woman who had collapsed. He slipped through the door without trouble, curiously elated and pleased with himself. Caught in a terror not of his own making, a pawn—to use Nelson's term—Meadows had acquitted himself well. He had what Nelson wanted; in fact, in one macabre interlude he had achieved more than Nelson and all his professional pawns.

He had found *el Jefe*. There could be no thought of any criminal charges against Meadows now. He had done his job. The rest was up to Nelson. Meadows would go away for a few days, and when he came back, it would be all over. He searched the street in both directions—above all, he didn't want to bump into the killers now—and walked across the intersection to the darkened gas station where Nelson was waiting.

But Nelson did not wait there. There were only the broken

pumps, a pregnant gray grimalkin and the smell of decay. In agitation Meadows walked to the corner. He found only a faceless line of traffic.

A squall sprang out of the night sky, and Meadows huddled in the doorway of a bakery. He waited there for what seemed a long time, but Nelson never came.

# Chapter 14

T. CHRISTOPHER MEADOWS lay in a coffin of burnished wood. His flesh was as white as talcum, as rigid as steel. The mourners came in solemn procession. "So young, so sad, so tragic," they said, and each laid an empty cup of Cuban coffee on the coffin lid. The lawman came late. A tarnished star glinted from his forehead. He leaned close, and when he thought no one was looking, he ground his cigar into the corpse's folded hands, just to be sure.

T. Christopher Meadows could feel the pain, just as he could smell the yellow roses and hear the empty lamenting and see through lids sewn closed by a mortician's apprentice. But he could not move. He could not even cry. The lawman watched expressionlessly as the cigar burned the white flesh with the smell of embalming fluid. He shrugged. *"Adios, amigo,"* he said, and tossed his cigar on the teetering mountain of empty cups.

The widow wept. She wore a black bikini and the white peaked cap of a pilot. "Ay, ay, ay," she wept, and embraced the mourners in turn, tight, grinding embraces that climaxed when the widow directed each mourner's hand to her firm cocaine breasts.

The man with the shark eyes came from the espresso machine to say the rosary. *"Gringo, gringo, gringo, gringo,* feenesh, unlucky *gringo,* feenesh." Blood spewed from his coffee cup and gave birth to a whirlpool on the corpse's chest.

The mourners never understood that the shark-eyed rosary man was the killer and the corpse his victim. They watched without comprehension while a gust of indifference toppled the mountain of coffee cups and they fell, one by one, into the whirlpool. Taxi! cried the corpse. I must get away. Why are there no taxis in this fucking city? Taxi! Taxi for a *gringo.* Please.

Meadows awoke with an erection, every pore open. The pale blue sheets clung to his body. His mouth felt like steel wool. Flares of pain chided his intemperance with every blink. A breeze had sprung up off the sea, rattling the venetian blinds. That was what had awakened him. Rattling blinds, toppling coffee cups. Meadows shivered.

Meadows rolled out of Terry's bed, heading for the shower. *El Jefe,* the Peasant and Cauliflower Ear hated him from the wall opposite the bed where he had pinioned them with thumbtacks. Again, Meadows shivered. No more pisco, he promised himself.

The empty bottle of the deceptively clear, seductively smooth Andean *aguardiente* lay at the foot of the kitchenette table where Meadows had worked through the night. He had drawn to remember, and he had drunk to forget. As he'd done so, a part of Meadows's brain had analyzed the Gothic night with the myopia of a jeweler assaying a gem. Every analysis had floundered on the same unanswerable question: Why had Nelson left him?

Meadows's new-found assurance had dissolved in those first few minutes outside the funeral home. He was alone. What should he do? Was he still a fugitive from a murder charge? Where should he go? Not to the Buckingham, surely. He couldn't go home. The Peasant and Cauliflower Ear had gone home. Should he try to leave Miami? He could, but if he was a fugitive, the police would be watching. That left Terry's apartment on Key Biscayne. It was the only refuge he had.

In a city notorious for its poor public transportation, Meadows had walked the rain-fresh streets for twenty minutes in search of a cab. Taxis do not cruise in Miami. They lie in wait. Meadows had found one, finally, in front of a hospital. He pounded on the window to awaken the driver, who, faithful to the tradition of all Miami cabdrivers, switched on the meter before unlocking the door to let him in.

Why, Nelson, why? He had asked himself that a hundred times that long night. He found no answer now in the finely chiseled features of *el Jefe* on the paper before him or the finely numbing lash of the pisco in his gut.

After he had showered and jolted his quarreling nerves with black coffee, Meadows examined the three sketches again with a critic's eye. He was pleased to see that neither confusion nor alcohol had cheated his skill. The broad-faced ferret looked exactly as Meadows had seen him: huge, stolid and dumb. The dominant pug characteristic had come through nicely in the second sketch, the head half turned to show the cauliflower ear.

The drawing of *el Jefe* was the best of the three, Meadows decided. Breeding, distinction, magnetism were all there. The deep-set eyes promised depth and intelligence. The mouth was a trifle too small, though, and not sensual enough. Meadows fixed it.

Then he tried to call Terry to say he was using her apartment. She lent it out sometimes, and the last thing Meadows needed right now was a gaggle of South Americans on their annual pilgrimage to the great PX in the north.

Predictably Terry was nowhere to be found, and the secretary at CAN's main office in Asunción, Paraguay, seemed even thicker than usual.

"When will she be back?"

"Long time no back."

"Tell her to call Chris at her house."

"What her house?"

*"Su casa está quemada,"* said Meadows, summoning his best Spanish and hanging up in disgust.

Meadows washed the dishes, made the bed, threw out the dead bottle of pisco, found Terry's keys and coaxed life from the old clunker Ford she kept in the building garage—just in case. Then he went back upstairs, drank a glass of ice water and realized suddenly he had nothing to do. He tinkered with the sketches. He turned on the television and turned it off again quickly. He tried to read. Terry had a good collection of Latin American literature, and Meadows picked up an English translation of García Márquez's short stories. The Colombian wizard's sense of timelessness suited Meadows's mood perfectly, but he tossed the book aside after a few minutes. He had enough mythical reality of his own to cope with just then.

Meadows kept coming back to Nelson. His disappearance was perplexing, outrageous. Several times he had picked up Terry's beige bedside phone to dial police headquarters, only to stop himself.

Nelson had set a mouse loose in a nest of snakes and then had abandoned him. Why? Something was wrong. No matter how Meadows juggled the pieces they would not fit.

Nelson should have waited. If the sketches were so precious to the case, nothing would have driven him away.

The logic eluded Meadows. Was Nelson trying to set him up? Suppose Nelson were allied with the dopers. Suppose the whole mission at the funeral parlor had been a charade, Nelson's way of feeding the killers their victim. . . .

Meadows recoiled at the thought. It was a possibility, but it did not square with his intuitions about the cynical, intense Cuban.

There was one other explanation: Nelson had used him for bait. Knowing Meadows would be recognized by the killers, Nelson had waited outside the funeral home for the architect to be dragged out, like a gaffed fish. And when Meadows had emerged alone, Nelson had simply waited some more, keeping his distance to see if the minnow really would get away. It was plausible. More than that, it was probable.

Meadows could not swallow the rage. Nelson, who had railed so bitterly about the impotence of the law, had found a cruel but clever way of subverting it. Give the *loco* dopers a target, someone scared and naïve enough to wear a bull's-eye on his own chest. Then step in and pick up the pieces. If one of those pieces happened to be broken . . . *que sera, sera.*

Meadows walked out to the balcony and surveyed the ocean's horizon, purple under distant clouds. Nelson's scheme had failed; the detective would get no more chances. Next time, Meadows thought, the plan will be mine.

OCTAVIO NELSON was not in a good mood.

"How's García?" Pincus asked.

"He's OK."

"Where'd he get hit?"

"Left shoulder, left knee."

"I heard it was the chest," Pincus said.

"You heard wrong."

"I heard it was his own gun."

Nelson lifted a mug of steaming coffee to his lips. "Yeah. That's right," he muttered sourly.

What a fucking nightmare, Nelson thought. When the dispatcher at Central broadcasts an "officer down" call, you simply do not stop to ask questions like: Did your hotshot cop shoot himself? Was he playing quick-draw? Did he fuck up? You don't ask; you move because the next time it could be your ass out there full of bullets.

But the call had come—one of his *own* men—so Nelson had muscled the old Dodge clunker into its very best bat-out-of-hell routine and torn away from that funeral parlor so fast . . .

And, inside, a terrified architect had been trying to do him a dangerous favor. *Damn.*

Christopher Meadows had been gone, of course, by the time Nelson had returned. The detective had driven the streets for nearly an hour, peering at figures slouched in doorways, aiming his Q-beam spotlight into the cat-ridden alleys of Little Havana. Still, no Meadows.

The incident had been catastrophic enough, but now here was Pincus, typing up his accursed eight-by-ten index cards and asking questions about Meadows.

"I don't understand," Pincus said.

Nelson turned his back to rummage through a drawer. "You seen my cigars?"

"What happened at the hotel?" Pincus pressed.

"He was gone," Nelson said curtly. "He took off."

"But what about the trace?"

"Ah!" Nelson beamed, holding up a fresh H. Upmann, courtesy of the Christopher Meadows collection. He gnawed off the tip and ceremoniously began firing up the cigar. Pincus said nothing; he knew he would have to wait for his answer.

Soon Nelson was enshrouded in smoke. The words came this time with contented patience. "Wilbur, the trace was fine. The address was good. All your information was good. It was nobody's fault. Meadows must have got spooked and ran, that's all."

"But how?"

Nelson shrugged. "Whatcha typing?"

Pincus ignored him. "Did he leave anything?"

"Two shirts, a new toothbrush—you know, the kind with the angled bristles—a can of Right Guard. Fascinating stuff really. It's all in a bag in my locker, if you're interested."

Pincus smiled officiously and shook his head. "I wonder how he knew you were coming."

"He had just killed a man and nearly got himself killed for the third time inside of a month. That would put my nerves on edge, too." Nelson's voice was taut; his story seemed frayed.

"Were the people at the hotel any help?"

"Oh, yes. Spent an hour telling me what a polite, wonderful fellow our architect friend is. They had no idea a crime was involved, and I didn't tell them. They wouldn't have believed it."

Pincus went back to his index cards, glancing up from the typewriter now and then to venture an idle question. Nelson tired of the game very quickly.

"Don't ask me if I checked his house. He's not there, and he's not stupid enough to go there. Look, Wilbur, the guy is very bright, and he's got lots of money. He could be anywhere right now, from Key West to Paris. He's scared out of his Ivy League brainpan, and I don't blame him."

Pincus shrugged. "I bet he's still in town."

Nelson groaned and shook his head.

"He won't go near that airport again," Pincus asserted.

"Good point," Nelson said sarcastically. "What are you telling me, that the guy can't drive fifteen miles up to Lauderdale, or charter a Beechcraft out of North Perry, or lease a fucking Bertram and cruise to Bimini? Wilbur, this guy is not stupid. He's scared, that's all. I think he'll call again. Soon."

Actually Nelson wasn't sure at all, but he glared at Pincus when he said it. Damn this kid. He won't let up.

"Are you just going to wait for him?"

"Christ! Wilbur, what in the fuck do you want me to do?" Nelson erupted. "At best this is a lousy manslaughter case, and at worst it's self-defense and we're not even going to get an indictment out of the state attorney. You want me to run up a few hundred miles tracking down some panicky little architect with wet pants, and in the meantime I'm looking at six open homicides, not the least of which is some hotshot English professor who comes in today with seven holes. From a machine gun, no less. Now *that*, Wilbur, turns my crank." Nelson pointed his chin at the ceiling and let loose a vaporized geyser of acrid tobacco smoke.

The two men sat across from each other with the postures of weary boxers, tired but ready for the next left hook. Pincus was enormously glad when Nelson's phone rang. It gave him a chance to extract a creased spiral notebook from his coat jacket. He flipped the pages until he found what he was looking for. His writing was precise, a virtue among cops. The notation said: "Buckingham Hotel. M.B. 555-3200."

As soon as Nelson lumbered off to the john, Pincus made his phone call. The desk clerk sounded like Myron Cohen.

"Is Mr. Meadows a guest there?" Pincus asked.

"Oh, no, not anymore. Are you related?"

"I'm a business associate. Do you know where he went? It's most important."

"No, no . . . hang on. Sadie! Sadie!" The clerk's voice faded away into a distant quarrel. An old woman came on the line.

"Yes? Can I help you?" she asked.

"I'm looking for Christopher Meadows. My name is John Lake. I'm a business associate," Pincus said.

"Yes, yes, Izzy told me, Mr. Lake. I'm sorry, but Mr. Meadows is not here. Now God forbid I should say something out of line, but I think you must know that Mr. Meadows is in some kind of trouble."

"Oh, no," Pincus said with expert sympathy. "What makes you think so? Did Chris leave in a big hurry?"

"Yes, young man, you might say that. He left with the police. It was unbelievable, such a nice young fellow."

"The police? I don't understand. Did you get the officer's name?"

"Let me ask Izzy. He's the one who let him up the stairs. Hold on, please." Sadie left the phone for a full minute; Pincus strained to hear her harping at hapless Izzy.

"He forgot. I'm so sorry, Mr. Lake. Izzy's memory is very poor. Very poor."

"That's all right," Wilbur Pincus said, "but Chris *did* leave with a policeman?"

"Yes, yes, I saw them go out the door myself. He was a big man,

Mr. Lake, a detective. Izzy saw the badge himself, but as I said, he can't think of the name. I'd know him again myself, though."

"Do you recall what he looked like?" Pincus asked tentatively.

"Yes, Mr. Lake, but I can only remember the mustache and the cigar. He was Cuban. I'm sure he took Mr. Meadows to jail. It was very upsetting."

"I'm sure it was," Pincus said thoughtfully. "Thanks for everything, Sadie."

MEADOWS COVERED HALF A MILE of tepid green ocean in a powerful, churning crawl. What he lacked in grace and efficiency as a swimmer, he made up in effectiveness. Swimming was his most treasured vice. The heat that enabled him to swim nearly every day of the year had been decisive in his decision to establish himself in Miami.

Far off the sandy beach Meadows rolled over on his back and thought about the man he knew to be *el Jefe*. A consummate actor. A man of charisma, of substance. And no doubt, in the face he showed to the outside world, a man of charm. Who was he?

Meadows decided to find out. It was the only way to begin to find a way out of the narrow and obscene canyon in which he languished: Nelson baying from one rim and the cocaine killers from the other. With *el Jefe's* identity, at least Meadows would have something to bargain with. But how to find out?

By the time he returned to Terry's apartment Meadows had it: Clara Jackson.

Clara Jackson was a police reporter with a national reputation at the *Miami Journal*. She thrived on violence and on implacable contempt for the editors she worked for. Meadows had met her when she'd dated a contractor friend, and he had found her remarkable. Clara had led a grand tour of the *Journal's* department-store news room with running commentary. Later, over dinner, all of them— the contractor, Meadows and Sandy—had listened with a mixture of revulsion and awe while Clara Jackson had talked about her job. The topic then, as now, was murder.

"Clara, hi. This is Chris Meadows. We met many years ago when—"

"Sure, I remember. The architect," Clara cut in. "That was back when I was seeing . . ."

"Jack—"

"Renner, right. We all had dinner. I remember what you said about the *Journal* building. You called it the world's largest Sunoco station."

Meadows laughed. "Just a joke," he said.

"The truth," Clara said. "How have you been?"

"Not good." Briefly Meadows told her about Sandy's death and how he had witnessed it—but said nothing of his own continuing terror.

"God, I'm so sorry. I wrote that story about the girl and her mother, and I didn't even realize who it was."

"Her last name was different when you met her."

"I'm so sorry," Clara said again. "Goddamn cokeheads. They're maniacs, Chris, every one."

"I need a favor," Meadows said. "I drew a sketch of a man—"

"The killer?"

"No. But one of them who is . . . involved."

"Did you give it to the cops?"

"I intend to, Clara, but I want you to see it, too. I'd like to send you a copy."

There was a pause. Meadows could hear a half dozen electric typewriters clacking smoothly in the background.

"I'll look at it, Chris, but . . . well, I have to be honest. Most sketches are useless. Even police artists make everybody look like Mr. Potato Head."

"Just take a look. Please," Meadows implored. "I'll send it over in a cab this morning."

"OK. Listen, Chris, I really got to run. I'm having a war with one of the junior editors here over a story that's supposed to be on the front page tomorrow."

"More drug killings?"

"Oh, no. Just some crazy husband who shot his wife with a spear gun and pinned her to the refrigerator. Asshole editor thinks it's too gory and wants to bury the story on the inside, so I gotta go."

Meadows placed the sketch of the suave man at the funeral parlor in a brown office envelope and sealed both ends with wide strips of duct tape. He printed Clara Jackson's name in capital letters on the front but did not write his own.

He gave the Yellow Cab driver twenty bucks and prayed that the man was honest. Once the package was on its way, he felt washed with relief.

The next day Meadows swam and walked the beach. He could feel his strength returning and with it his sense of mental balance.

He was a fugitive, but it was not the police who pursued him, he was sure. Just one lone-wolf cop. And two gunmen who killed for a chimera with a rose in his lapel.

Meadows feared them, but his panic was gone. He would let time be his ally. He was safe where he was. He had plenty of money, and he had no hurry.

He would wait until Nelson and the dopers found new distractions, like hounds bored by a stale scent. Let them gnaw one another in their own private frenzy. Meadows would be gone.

If Clara Jackson came up with a name for the doper king, Meadows might even be able to take some sweet revenge long distance. He'd send copies of the sketches and an appropriate anonymous note to the FBI and the DEA. To everyone but Octavio Nelson. Let him find out from the feds who his precious *Jefe* was. That would sting, wouldn't it? And then maybe Nelson wouldn't be so cavalier with the next bumbling civilian who crossed his path.

Meadows was learning something about himself. He had known abject terror for the first time in his life. He had been bounced from pillar to post at the whim of a demonic puppetmaster. And by Jesus, he had survived. In spite of himself, perhaps, but he had survived.

Late that afternoon he called Clara Jackson to see how the opening salvo in his campaign of character assassination was being received.

"Did you see what they did with my story?"

"No. Which one?" Meadows answered, rattled.

"Speargun Spat Ends in Tragedy."

"Oh."

"Page Three C. I really lost that battle," Clara said.

"Did you get my sketch?" Meadows asked anxiously.

"Yeah, I got it. What kind of a joke is it supposed to be?"

"I don't understand."

"You sent me a drawing of José Bermúdez."

"You know him?" Meadows's pulse raced. Bingo.

"Everybody knows him, Chris. He's one of the most dynamic, prominent, up-and-coming, et cetera, young Cubans this town has ever seen. In another couple years he'll probably be the goddamn mayor."

"Clara, are you certain?"

"Chris, Bermúdez's picture is in the paper every other day. The editors of our Spanish editions have just about canonized him. Bermúdez has tons of money, and he's a sucker for every charity around. He cuts more ribbons than the vice president."

"That doesn't mean he's not mixed up with the dopers, does it?" Meadows said, reeling inside. "Maybe that's where all his money came from."

"I tried that idea on two sources, Chris, one local and one federal. They practically laughed in my face. Bermúdez is the original straight arrow. No files anywhere."

Meadows was crestfallen. "Maybe it's not the same guy."

"Maybe not," Clara said. "Your sketch was sure as hell on the money, though."

"Could you send me his photograph, Clara? Just to be sure. I'd be happy to pay for it."

"I'll just swipe one from the files. We've got a hundred of them back there," she said. "I'll get some clips together and put the whole thing in the mail this evening. I think when you read this stuff, you'll see what I mean."

Meadows gave her his Coconut Grove address, then blurted: "Do you know anything about a Detective Nelson?"

"There's a couple of them."

"This one is with the city of Miami. Narcotics," Meadows said. "Stocky, tough, a bit rumpled."

"Octavio."

"Right!" Meadows exclaimed.

"You hit the daily double today, Chris. Nelson is squeaky clean, from what I know. He's made some huge cocaine busts in the last two years."

"That doesn't mean he turns it all in," Meadows cracked. He could hear Clara typing in the background.

"Octavio Nelson is a fanatic," she went on. "A couple years ago he got shot during a bust and nearly died, but not before he put two dopers away for good. Two Colombian pros."

"So you never heard anything bad about him?"

"A few little things," Clara said. "Last year there were two brutality complaints that probably had some basis in fact. Nelson roughed up a couple of nickel-and-dimers in his car. He used that big flashlight they're all issued. Nothing came of it. They jumped bond anyway." Her tone of voice told Meadows that the incidents were of minor journalistic significance. He thanked her for the information, hung up and submerged into his swirling thoughts.

He was certain of his information, sure of what he had lived and seen. Clara Jackson, who could find out more with a dozen profane phone calls than he could in a year, was certain that Meadows's drug kingpin was a pillar of the community.

The thought of being wrong didn't gall Meadows. He knew he was not wrong. Meadows thought fleetingly of taking his story to someone who might care. The state attorney? Federal officials? Wouldn't they see justice done? Clara Jackson didn't think they would even listen to him. And even if they did, could they possibly protect his anonymity?

Besides, in the cold light of day, what facts did Meadows have that would persuade anyone? That Bermúdez had talked in a funeral parlor with two men Meadows knew to be killers? There was nobody in that grisly purgatory that night that the unctuous man with the rose had *not* talked to.

Meadows did not even know the killers' names. And before he talked about them, assuming anyone would even listen, he would have to explain what had happened in the parking garage at Miami International. And that would leave T. Christopher Meadows, AIA, up shit creek.

MEADOWS NEARLY DID NOT GO to Coconut Grove the next day to retrieve the picture Clara Jackson had sent him. Being on Key Biscayne was tolerable, but getting on and off was torture. On this day Meadows needed to get to the mainland, and if luck was not with him, he knew, he could spend the better part of the morning on the journey.

There was only one way in and one way out of the key, which meant that the causeway became the island's lifeblood and the frequent scene of the worst vehicular madness Meadows had witnessed north of São Paulo.

The bridge nearest the mainland was a drawbridge. It rose at the imperious behest of any plutocrat with a mast tall enough. Thousands could swelter for an eternity in the afternoon sun while some uptown slob in white shoes steered his ketch through the bridge, a doff of his gleaming white cap to the cracker who tended the infernal machine from a hutch atop the center span.

"How's the traffic?" had become to the insular Republicans of Key Biscayne a salutation more common than "How's the family?" by the time Meadows first knew the island.

But Meadows was not intercepted by the bridge that summer afternoon. Traffic was light. He slid across to the mainland as smoothly as if he had sailed across the bay. The damn thing is probably broken, he thought, as he crossed the grated center span of the drawbridge.

Even the traffic in Coconut Grove was tolerable, but as Meadows neared his house, he grew cautious. He drove twice around the block, slowly, looking at the parked cars. Nothing. He could not see the house from the street because of the foliage, but there was no one watching from the street. Of that he was sure.

Meadows parked Terry's Ford a block away, scaled the four-foot limestone wall and approached the front of the house through the trees, shrubbery and undergrowth that were the silent sentinels of his privacy. He stopped at the mailbox, extracted a buff *Miami Journal* envelope and a Mailgram from the assorted trivia of bills and leaflets, and stuck them in his back pocket.

Even before Meadows reached the house itself, he knew something was wrong. He crouched for a long time behind a cabbage palm, but he heard nothing. So he went in. And immediately wished he hadn't.

They had destroyed the house and everything in it. Systematically, viciously, calculatingly. Vandals run amok.

They had begun with his books, it seemed. Books of art and literature. Architectural reference works and leftover college textbooks. Dictionaries and paperbacks. Some lay shredded on the floor. The rest lay on the bottom of the pool.

The glass cases that housed his architectural models—what Meadows called his ego gallery—had been shattered. The models themselves had obviously puzzled the intruders. They had destroyed them capriciously. One had been burned; the top of another, a multitiered housing development, had been ripped from its base. A third had been stepped on.

Meadows's Haitian paintings had been slashed with a knife, except one, coated now by what looked like dried ketchup. The entrails of Meadows's leather living room furniture littered the floor. The blades of his ceiling fans had been snapped, one by one.

The kitchen was a lake where cheese rind floated next to soggy bologna. The tap was still on, and Meadows let it run. Water from the bathroom cascaded by the staircase and seeped along the oak floor, out the door and into the pool.

Over by what had been his stereo system the oak was scarred where filter-tip cigarette butts had been ground into the wood. Cauliflower Ear and the Peasant had obviously waited a long, impatient time for the *gringo* to come.

Meadows touched nothing. He stood silently in the living room, cataloguing in his mind a barbarism that his eyes sought to censor. A terrible rage consumed him.

In the debris he spied the cut-glass figure of a troubadour he had bought in Venice many years before. It was miraculously unbroken. He picked up the delicate statuette and fondled it. Tenderly he set it back in its place on the mantel over the fireplace, where someone had smeared human feces and food and mustard.

The phone rang. Meadows stared at it for a long moment. Then he spun on his heel and strode out the door without looking back.

# Chapter 15

MEADOWS WAS out of breath by the time he reached the top of the stairs, clutching the key to Terry's condominium. He surged through the door, slammed it behind him and double-locked it with finality. His shirt was soaked. He hunted for the thermostat and twisted the dial to sixty-five degrees. He turned on a small table lamp but purposely avoided disturbing the drapes covering the wide picture window that presented such a grandiose view of the Atlantic. Below were a pool and a small park, Meadows recalled. And people.

No, the apartment should remain dark, closed up.

The package from Clara Jackson was still under one arm as Meadows went to the refrigerator and foraged for a beer. He found a can of Bavaria, a tart Colombian brew, and in it a reason for small rejoicing. It was ice-cold, but even better, it was strong.

Meadows collapsed on a fat throw pillow, decorated with a radically vivid Panama mola, then gulped half the can before surrendering to curiosity and ripping open the brown envelope from the *Miami Journal*. During the breakneck ride from his desecrated home in the Grove to Terry's place on Key Biscayne, Meadows had kept the envelope on his lap, fingering it nervously. He could feel the stiff photographic paper inside. Clara Jackson had come through, somehow raiding the *Journal's* sacrosanct photo morgue for a picture.

Now Meadows looked at it and could hardly be silent. His sketch had been accurate indeed. The man in the photograph, beaming so self-consciously at a chamber of commerce spaghetti luncheon, was the silky man at Mono's wake. The man with the yellow rose.

José Bermúdez.

Meadows felt vindicated. The conversation at the funeral home could not have been misinterpreted. Sandy had died because of this man. Mono had merely been the bullet; Bermúdez had been the trigger.

A sheaf of Xerox-copied newspaper clippings accompanied the photograph. Meadows could hear Clara Jackson's chirpy voice as she stood over the machine, watching it spit out copies: Surely this will convince the paranoid architect that he's wrong.

Meadows finished off his Bavaria and cracked open another can, the last one. Then he sat down at the kitchen table to read about the extraordinary, esteemed Señor Bermúdez. . . .

"Banker José Luis Bermúdez was honored Friday by the Greater Miami Chamber of Commerce when it presented the exile leader with its annual Statesman's Award for his service on behalf of South Florida's Latin business community. . . ."

Clip date: December 17, 1979. The article ran beneath the photograph now on Terry's kitchen table. The biographical material was impressive, and the weight of it afflicted Meadows with new doubt.

Bermúdez was forty-four years old, born in the Matanzas Province east of Havana. He was the son of a wealthy landowner who had turned acres of free-growing royal palms into acres of rich and highly prized Cuban coffee; who had given the best of everything to his three sons, his wife, his friends; who had panicked like a race horse in a burning barn after young Señor Castro had come down from the Sierra Maestra to take Havana. Bermúdez, his wife and two of the boys had made it to Miami with more of the family money than was thought possible in those frantic days of flight. The third son, Luis, had died in the revolution.

A feature article, written for the *Journal*'s Spanish editions and translated rather clumsily for Anglos, told more of the banker's history. How José's father grew dim and withdrawn now in Miami's Little Havana, spending his days at the hysterical funerals of old Cuban patriots and his nights dizzy with rum. Puerto Rican rum, at that. How the old man's friendships had brought José, then only twenty-five, a minor officer's job at a new Cuban-owned bank on Coral Way. The law degree that José had brought from Havana had been shelved forever; banking fortunes had exploded as hundreds of thousands of his countrymen had poured into Florida to build new lives. All of them had needed money, and exile banks had opened their arms. José Luis Bermúdez Modero had become a wealthy, important man.

Meadows riffled through the clippings. On Cuban holidays—and who could keep track of them all?—Bermúdez seemed to be everywhere: the street dances in Little Havana; the domino park on Eighth Street; the Torch of Freedom on the boulevard, listening fervently to heated speeches.

It simply made no sense. Bermúdez was a man who did not need the drug business. He had a six-bedroom house in Coral Gables (featured once in the *Journal's* fawning home style section), three clonelike children and a stunning wife. His name did not appear in Miami newspapers without the prefix "prominent Cuban businessman" or "noted Miami banker" or "exile leader."

Meadows paced. No wonder Clara Jackson did not believe him. José Bermúdez was dead wrong for the part.

And he was perfect.

Could there be a better camouflage? Meadows mused. He envisioned a cop, say Wilbur Pincus, plodding about Little Havana, asking rude questions about Señor Bermúdez. The reply would be scalding stares, curses at such umbrageous suggestions. "Do you have nothing better to do, bastard, then harass honorable men? Get out! You are insane to bother Señor Bermúdez."

The thought of such futility made Chris Meadows very tired. On Eighth Street they would laugh at his theory of José Bermúdez, cocaine broker. They would laugh, too, in the offices of Octavio Nelson.

Meadows stripped off his clothes and rummaged through Terry's closet for a pair of old cutoffs he had left there. He permitted himself a peek through the curtains. The pool was churning with children and teenagers; sunning mothers sprawled nearby on canary patio furniture. Beyond was the Atlantic, indigo in the distant Gulf Stream and a radiant aquamarine where it lapped against the key.

Meadows struggled against desperation. "A prisoner in paradise," he said with a sour laugh to no one. He could never go home. Home? They'd damn near fried him in his own swimming pool, then savaged his house. He grew sick, thinking of the wreckage and the filth. The message of their actions was horrifying.

What would Terry counsel? Call the police, Chris. The police who'd abandoned him at the funeral parlor, tossed him fat and high like a frigging clay pigeon. The police, Octavio Nelson and friends, were as much the enemy as the dopers. And perhaps more deadly.

Meadows was resolved to get out of Terry's condominium as soon as possible, for her safety as much as his own. If Meadows was being watched, he could lead the killers far away from her at least. If they had not yet found his hideaway, he might still be able to disappear. That was a possibility, Meadows thought coldly. It would take them time, the killers, to track them down. Probably a full day of sifting through whatever they'd stolen from the house. There were many names, many phone numbers.

Meadows thought of Terry, of Arthur, of all his friends, and shivered.

And he thought of Octavio Nelson. When the rogue detective set his mind to the task, it would not take long—maybe twelve hours?—to find the frightened architect at an exotic girlfriend's apartment. Meadows glanced at the door, half expecting to hear a cop's perfunctory knock.

He gathered the material about José Bermúdez and stuffed it back in the envelope. Hastily Meadows leafed through the other mail, showing no interest until he came upon a Mailgram from Quito, Ecuador. He used a kitchen knife to slit the envelope:

SEÑOR T. CHRISTOPHER MEADOWS: BY THE TERMS OF YOUR CONTRACT, YOU WERE TO PRESENT TO THE ECUADOREAN OIL MINISTRY A PREDESIGN PROPOSAL ONE WEEK AGO. SO FAR WE HAVE RECEIVED NO PROPOSAL AND NO EXPLANATION OF ANY KIND FROM YOUR MIAMI OFFICE. OUR GOVERNMENT IS VERY EAGER TO COMPLETE THIS PROJECT ACCORDING TO THE TIMETABLE WE DISCUSSED LAST SPRING. ANY FURTHER DELAYS WILL FORCE US TO CANCEL OUR CONTRACT AND SEEK THE SERVICES OF ANOTHER ARCHITECT.

The notice was signed by a deputy minister of development. Meadows paid no attention to the name. He crumpled the Mailgram and threw it in the general direction of a wastebasket.

To hell with them. His studio was a shambles. He was afraid to show his face at the downtown office; Nelson certainly had the place staked out by now. No, the project was impossible. It hit Meadows like a foul wind: He might never work as an architect again. He grieved for his career, for his own spirit.

His universe, Meadows recognized with despair, had dwindled to two stark choices: to run or to retaliate. Running made more sense. Meadows could disappear anywhere: Chicago, New York or—more ambitiously—Europe. He had a few good friends in Brussels. Good friends would ask few questions and smooth the way. But then what? Tend bar, drive a taxi, sell encyclopedias for the rest of his life? Say it was only a few years until Mono was forgotten, until Nelson was gone, or dead, or in jail himself. Returning to Miami would be difficult. Getting back into architecture would be impossible. A career loses momentum and fades. Meadows had seen it happen to friends. Five years out of the mainstream, and they ended up designing elementary schools and post offices.

To run was sensible, but it was not appealing.

Meadows stood before a wall mirror in Terry's bedroom. His sandy hair was ragged around the ears. His eyes were like radishes. The facial lines, incipient and vaguely distinguished in the best of circumstances, seemed now like sharp cracks in cement. He looked like hell.

The telephone rang. Meadows eyed it nervously. It seemed to quiver on the nightstand. He grabbed the receiver on the fifth ring.

"If you are sleeping in my bed, it had better be alone, *querido*."

"Terry!" Meadows fought back tears. He wanted to tell her everything, beg her to fly home so he could curl up in her arms and sleep for a month until the nightmare ended.

"I miss you," he whispered.

"Good," she said, "but speak louder—this is a terrible connection."

"Where are you, and when are you coming back?"

"I am in Honduras, in San Pedro Sula. And I have bad news. The mechanics have made a stew of the Convair. There is cargo stranded everywhere. I am afraid it will be at least two weeks before I can get back."

"Oh." Some of the disappointment was counterfeit. He needed time to get away, and he wanted her safely out of the line of fire.

"Please hurry," he said softly.

"I will," she said. A burst of static came over the line. "Listen, I must go. Take care of yourself. I'll call again if I can. OK?"

"OK."

"Bye."

God, he missed her, Meadows thought, prowling the empty apartment.

He settled down to reread the Bermúdez clippings. Meadows's life was in shreds and this man, one greedy son of a bitch, was to blame. A slick politician with a politician's perfect smile. The chamber of commerce, sweet Jesus, the Statesman's Award.

He *was* the one.

Meadows replayed the scene in the funeral home.

The Peasant, Cauliflower Ear. And him. What had he said? "That business down in the Grove was stupid."

Stupid.

Christopher Meadows decided he would end it himself. How, he didn't know. It would be done in his own way and, God willing, in his own time. It would not make things right again, he knew, but it would make things just.

He moved swiftly through Terry's apartment, searching, making a special effort at stealth as if someone could ever have heard his spongy footsteps on the carpet. He checked the double mattress, the cluttered and sweet-smelling drawers of her mahogany bedroom chest, even the glass bookcase. Finally he opened the nightstand and there it was, right next to her goddamned birth control pills: the gun.

Meadows lifted it as if it were nitroglycerine. The blue steel of the barrel was cold to his touch; the grip was coarse, almost corrugated. Meadows noted the name etched above the cylinder. Smith & Wesson. At least he'd heard of it, but whether it was a .38 or a .45 or a .357 he had no idea.

It was a gun, and it worked. At least that's what Terry said. Meadows was sure she knew how to use it. She carried a sidearm on most of her flights to Latin America, an extra shotgun when she flew into Bogotá.

But Terry wasn't here to make the introduction.

Meadows fumbled with a small lever until the cylinder flopped open and six bullets spilled onto the pink satin bedsheets. He gathered them in one hand and dropped them back in the drawer. Only because he remembered it from a television cop show, Meadows held the gun up to the light from the bedroom window and checked the chambers. All empty. He snapped the cylinder and walked to the living room.

The pistol was oily. Meadows set it on a table and wiped his hands on his cutoffs. He turned on the television set and flipped through the stations, settling on one of those raucous afternoon game shows. He turned up the volume, gauging how much would shut out noise without annoying the neighbors.

Then Meadows sat himself down in front of the television and fondled the gun until his hands knew every curve, every notch, every shaft, every possible angle. For two hours he practiced raising his right arm stiff and straight, bracing his left hand under the right and pulling the stubborn trigger. Ssssnap. Ssssnap. Ssssnap. The hammer moved more slowly than Meadows imagined it would. Would it be the same when the gun was full of bullets?

"Can I have a minute of your time?" asked an unctuous face on the tube.

Christopher Meadows raised the pistol until the announcer's nostrils were fixed squarely under the sight. Ssssnap. Ssssnap. Ssssnap.

# Chapter 16

THE TWENTY-STORY OFFICE BUILDING near the Miami River was like all its big brothers around the country. Promptly at 5:00 each afternoon it emptied as though someone had pulled a plug. The drones rushed from the air-conditioned lobby, braved brief assault by the sweltering afternoon sun and plunged into the air-conditioned boxes that would take them home. Machines reinforced the routine. At exactly 5:15 computers shut down the escalators and turned off the air-conditioning.

Lane Redbirt prided himself on his appearance. As he rode down on the elevator, he caught a refreshing glimpse of himself in the mirror. His light double knit was well cut, with flared pants and a tight, *de rigueur* vest. His blond hair was carefully sprayed; his blue eyes were alert. Redbirt knew he was the perfect image of a young lawyer on the make. He enjoyed that.

When the elevator stopped on the fifteenth floor to load more passengers, the girl edged closer to the young lawyer.

"I'll bet it's a scorcher out there, Mr. Redbirt," she said.

"Near ninety, I think, Virginia," he replied. She was his secretary, and she typed well enough.

On the ground floor the modish crowd from Redbirt's office clustered for a moment to exchange Friday afternoon banalities.

"Have a nice weekend."

"See you Monday, if I make it."

"Bring me some fish."

"I'll have the Mitchell brief ready first thing Monday morning, Virginia."

"Fine, Mr. Redbirt, I'll be waiting for it. Have a nice weekend."

"You, too."

The secretaries and the paralegals scattered for the parking lot, and the law partners strolled with more measured pace to their own cars, which waited in covered executive parking.

Lane Redbirt lingered behind the rest. He stopped at the lobby newsstand to buy cigarettes and breath freshener. By the time he reached his Porsche it was 5:09 and the parking lot was nearly deserted.

The brown Toyota pulled up sharply alongside him. "Hurry, Lane, I'm so horny I can't wait," she called from the driver's window.

"Ginny. I . . ."

"Do you know what I'd like to do tonight for a change?" She told him what.

Redbirt's groin tingled. "Give me one hour. I have to make a stop."

"An hour is too long, the way I feel right now."

"Fifty minutes," he lied.

"I'll start without you," she challenged.

"Wait for me. I'll be there as soon as I can."

Redbirt went back into the lobby, easily evading the gaze of the wizened security guard. He summoned the elevator and pushed 18. Virginia was as unimportant to him now as his wife.

"Morgan Jones" had called just after lunch. And as usual, he had caught Redbirt off guard.

"I have thought about what you said the last time," said the voice named Jones, "and you are right. There is too much disorder."

"It's not disorder; it's madness now," Redbirt wailed. "Nobody understands what's happening anymore; the whole thing's crazy. You said it would get better. It's worse. Deal me out. Whoever you are, deal me out."

"Just now? When your patience is about to be rewarded?"

"What do you mean?"

"I will explain that when we meet."

"When we meet?"

"Yes, my friend, I have concluded you were right about that, too. We will meet this afternoon."

"Where?"

"In your office, after everyone has left. I will come precisely at five-forty, and I will leave at three minutes to six. Wait in your office, and leave the front door unlocked. Is that clear?"

"Yes."

Lane Redbirt was impatient. He swiveled in his black leather chair to stare at the wall clock. It was 5:20. So he was being granted a seventeen-minute audience with the disembodied voice whose sporadic calls over the past two years had changed his whole life. Morgan Jones coming to announce peace in our time, was he? Well, Lane Redbirt would be ready for him. No more messenger boy–distributor. No more dealing by dead of night with spics who smelled of garlic. No more pussying around. No, sir, Your Honor. Whether Morgan Jones realized it or not, he was about to surrender his trump card: his identity. If he wanted Lane Redbirt selling his shit, from now on it would be on Redbirt's terms.

At 5:22 Redbirt could contain himself no longer. He had popped an upper about three o'clock. It was wearing off. From the bowels of a filing cabinet he withdrew a small plastic bag. One line, Redbirt thought. Just one line now to fire all the cylinders for the good Mr. Jones. Later, with hungry Virginia, he would really quench the thirst.

"Anybody home? Hello. Anybody home?"

The voice came from the reception area, shattering Redbirt's musings. He looked again at the clock: 5:23. It could not be Jones. If a man announces he is coming for seventeen minutes, he comes on time. Redbirt hurried from his office.

"Thank God somebody's here. I've been wandering all over the building, looking for a lawyer who doesn't run home at five o'clock."

The man wore an impeccable seersucker suit and carried a smart attaché case of brown leather. Redbirt knew him instantly.

"Oh, Mr. Bermúdez. Hello, I'm Lane Redbirt."

"I'm delighted to meet you, Mr. Redbirt, and I apologize for bursting in on you, but I need a legal opinion, and I need it urgently."

"I was just leaving, Mr. Bermúdez, I'm sorry. If it can't wait until Monday . . ."

"No, it can't wait. That's the point. I have people coming to my office upstairs in a few minutes to sign a contract, and there is one phrase I cannot understand. Our attorney has taken it into his head to go golfing. It is a game he will remember for a long time, I promise you."

"I'm sorry, I have to—"

"Please, it will only take a minute. Look, three hundred dollars for three minutes' work. I'll pay cash."

Redbirt looked at his watch. It was 5:24.

"It will have to be literally three minutes, I'm afraid. Come in, please." It was a gamble, but a good gamble, Redbirt decided. The executive offices of José Bermúdez's banking empire occupied the whole twentieth floor. Some people thought the man would be Miami's next mayor. Lane Redbirt suddenly decided that he himself would make a fine city attorney.

Bermúdez sat in the chair before Redbirt's desk and laid the attaché case on his lap.

"I can't tell you how I appreciate this, Mr. Redbirt," said Bermúdez, extracting a sheaf of papers. "Do you do much corporate work?"

"A fair amount," Redbirt lied.

"Then this should be child's play for you. Here, Clause Thirty-three. Does it mean we are protected in *all* cases?"

The clock said 5:26.

Plenty of time. Redbirt focused on the fine print of what seemed to be a fairly standard loan agreement. Bermúdez sat expectantly before him, hands crossed demurely athwart the attaché case.

"Mr. Bermúdez," Redbirt said, "this couldn't be simpler. Your protection is as ironclad as the law can make it."

"I know."

"If you know, then what is the question?"

"I have no question."

"I'm sorry, I don't understand."

"I said I would come at five-forty. I came early."

*"You?"*

José Bermúdez smiled. "It is quite simple, really. I see a bright young lawyer in the elevator every now and then. I make some discreet inquiries, and I discover that he is an ambitious man who is already strapped for cash. So 'Morgan Jones' calls and offers a private little cocaine deal that is too good to refuse. That is the beginning. Simple. I could have worked it with any one of a hundred young and ambitious professionals in this city."

Redbirt's astonishment gave way to admiration. Bermúdez, of all people. What a scream! This would be easier than he thought.

"You're the last person I would have guessed . . ."

"That is how I want it," the banker said, nodding in satisfaction. "Now listen. I have solved all the problems. In another few weeks the merchandise will begin flowing at a standard quality and a fixed price. Only those who are authorized will deal."

"Jesus, you've cornered the market!"

"Enough of it to make life comfortable."

"My God, how?" The stakes would be tremendous. Lane Redbirt struggled to find a diplomatic way of asking how much was in it for him. No, he thought, I won't ask. I'll demand. He wondered in silent congratulation whether Bermúdez understood how fatally he had exposed himself now. He was at Redbirt's mercy.

"I like your style, Lane," Bermúdez said unexpectedly. "I want you as a full partner."

Redbirt was speechless.

"The market will be orderly, and we will not be greedy. I believe it should be worth about three million a year. Each."

Redbirt could only nod.

"From now on we work together. Let me see what records you have kept, and I will assimilate them into the overall plan. We will study it together."

"They are hidden."

"Of course, they are hidden. Get them."

Numbly Redbirt stumbled to a filing cabinet and extracted a file marked *DeFalco* v. *DeFalco*.

"There's nothing deader than an old divorce case," Redbirt joked weakly. "Everything's in there under 'List of Witnesses.' Names, dates, amounts, the whole thing."

Redbirt slumped back into his chair as Bermúdez rifled the file. God, he needed another snort.

"Excellent. I am glad to see my instincts about you were well founded. I will study these over the weekend. Let us meet again Monday. Would the same time be convenient for you?"

"Uh, sure, Mr. Bermúdez."

"José."

Bermúdez slipped the DeFalco file and the loan agreement into his briefcase. "Now I must go. There's only one more thing: Now that you know who I am, you must never, under any circumstances, contact me directly. Just wait for 'Morgan Jones' to call. Is that clear?"

"Perfectly. I will never call you, Mr. Bermu—José."

"I know you won't, Lane."

It was over in a second. Bermúdez slipped a silenced Beretta from the attaché case and fired once. The bullet took Redbirt between the eyes.

Bermúdez replaced the gun, brushed an imaginary speck of dust from his lapel and rose to leave. He was halfway to the door before he realized his mistake.

Wiping his hand in a clean white handkerchief, he rummaged swiftly through Redbirt's desk. The tape recorder was still spinning. Bermúdez flushed. He took both spools and glowered with scorn at Redbirt. Then he shot the corpse twice more, once for each ball.

"*Gringo de mierda,*" said José Bermúdez, mayor-to-be.

The wall clock said 5:40.


LATER THAT NIGHT Bermúdez let himself into the darkened cigar factory in *el barrio*. Once more he had two calls to make.

The man Chris Meadows knew as the Peasant answered on the first ring.

"We are ready now. You may begin," said Bermúdez.

"*Muy bien.*"

"I will be sending you some more names."

"It is no problem."

"You have two weeks. Work quickly and well, *hermano.*"

"In Mono's memory," promised the Peasant.

The old man in Bogotá was slower to the phone, but no less obliging.

"Things are moving nicely here," said Bermúdez.

"I am very pleased, Ignacio. Here as well."

"Will you be coming for dinner?"

"Whenever you say."

"Two weeks from tonight."

"It will be my pleasure. But not spicy food, please. My stomach rebels."

# Chapter 17

WHEN HARRY APPEL called Monday morning to say he had an interesting new homicide victim, Captain Octavio Nelson wanted to retch. It was no way to start a week.

"This one's special, for a drug murder. White, young, affluent," Appel reported. "Shot late Friday, by the looks of it. You'd better come see for yourself."

"Shit." Nelson sighed. The architect, had to be. And it was Nelson's fault, deserting the poor bastard like that. What seat-of-the-pants insanity, sending him into Hidalgo's to eyeball those pukes! Jesus, what if Pincus ever found out about that little brainstorm?

Nelson was morose by the time he got to the medical examiner's office. Appel led him directly to the morgue, where a bare pale corpse gleamed on an autopsy table.

"I'll be damned," Nelson said.

"You were expecting somebody else?" Appel said.

"Yeah. Who is this asshole?"

Appel lifted a clipboard and read aloud: "Dale Lane Redbirt, attorney at law. Age: thirty-four. He lives at—"

Nelson waved an arm. "Who? Who? I said."

Appel shrugged. "You're the detective."

"Harry! Tell me what you know."

"It's a small firm, even smaller now, Smith, Turner, Redbirt and Feldman. They do mostly criminal defense work. Redbirt here specialized in hookers and two-bit possession cases. In either event he often accepted fees in services rendered, if you know what I mean. His law partners say he was doing OK, no F. Lee Bailey, but pulling in maybe thirty thou a year. Has a wife, two kids and a secretary who screws anything that walks, him mostly."

149

"Sounds like the all-American dream."

"Right," Appel said. "Except for the new Porsche and a refinished thirty-eight-foot Bertram. And how about a condo in Vail? And, oh, yeah, there's this." Carefully Appel opened a small brown envelope and turned it upside down in his hand. A heavy gold bracelet slid into his palm like a small glittering viper.

"Solid gold, of course. Cost about five grand," Nelson mused. "You think he was freelancing, right?"

"Nelson, that is only an opinion." Appel grinned. "I'm just a coroner."

Nelson studied the body. He counted three wounds, one in the face, two in the scrotum.

"Not nice," Nelson said. "No more screwing around for you."

"He got shot in his office over near the river. The weapon was a Beretta, not the usual Cuban doper's choice. A Colombian preference."

Nelson asked, "And his wife?"

"Truly bereaved."

"His partners?"

"In shock."

"His friends?"

"Catatonic. Total disbelief."

"Any drugs in the blood?"

"Some coke, a touch of speed," Appel said. "Nothing lethal."

Nelson and Appel walked out of the dank morgue. "Can I have some coffee?" the detective asked. "It's been a lousy morning."

"Captain?" It was a thin red-haired secretary in one of the office cubicles. "You partner phoned. He wants you to call him . . . some report you forgot to sign."

Nelson groaned. "See what I mean?"

He and Appel drank in silence for several minutes. Appel scribbled some notes on an autopsy report, stopping only to hit the intercom button and fire directions to scattered employees.

"It was not robbery," he said finally.

"The gold chain?"

Appel nodded. "They would have snatched the bracelet."

"Anything else?"

"They didn't touch the office, and they didn't take the cash."

"How much cash?"

"Two grand, and change."

"Dopers for sure," Nelson concluded.

"Yup," said Harry Appel.


TWO HOURS LATER Nelson slouched in a phone booth in Coral Gables, sweating like a pig. He was almost out of quarters.

"*¿Oye, gusano, qúe tu sabes?*"

"Hey, *Capitán, cómo estás, chico?*"

The punk's Spanish was atrocious. Nelson switched to English. "Know a lawyer named Redbirt?"

"Used to. I heard he bought it over the weekend."

"Word gets around, don't it? *¿Qué pasa?*"

"I'm broke, Captain, that's what's happening. Help me, and maybe I can help you."

"Fifty is all I got," Nelson said.

"*Tu madre!*" the worm sneered.

"A hundred. *No tengo más.*"

"*Bueno.*" The worm blew his nose. Nelson held the receiver away from his ear. He flicked the soggy stump of his cigar into the traffic of LeJeune Road.

"Your lawyer friend is the first of many," said the *gusano*. "The snow is going to melt for a while."

"Says who?"

"*Los Cubanos.*"

"Oh yeah? And our friends from Bogotá and Cartagena? They all retired all of a sudden?"

"Believe it or not, it's all been settled. No more fighting in the family. *Hay paz.*"

"I don't believe it," Nelson grunted.

"It's what I hear, is all," the worm whined. "Things are going to be very tight for a while, is what I hear. Where do I get my money?"

"What about Redbirt?"

"He had good connections, dealt a lot of coke. He was working his way up. A lot of the downtown crowd bought from him because he was, you know . . ."

"*Gringo.*"

"*Sí, gringo.*"

"Your money will be in the usual place," Nelson said coldly.

"*¿Cuando?*"

"Tonight; six o'clock. You got anything else for me?"

"*Nada.*"

"Still pulling those b-and-e's around the river?"

"Not me, *chico.*"

Nelson hung up and fished in his pockets for more change. All he came up with was three pennies; Wilbur Pincus would damn well have to wait.

WILBUR PINCUS thought about what he had: He had caught his partner in two lies.

Captain Nelson had lied about the Mercedes-Benz to cover up for his brother, a brother who obviously was into cocaine. At precisely what level of enterprise, Pincus was not sure, but it was lucrative, if judged by the price of Bobby Nelson's house.

Pincus was deeply troubled. Octavio Nelson surely knew about his brother. But how much? For how long?

The second lie was equally disturbing, maybe more so because it could never be explained away as family loyalty.

The missing architect was nobody's wayward brother.

Pincus knew Meadows had been hiding out in the Buckingham Hotel when Nelson arrived. Witnesses had seen both men leave together, yet Nelson had told him that the architect had spooked off before he got there.

It was a total lie, and it angered the young detective.

Now Meadows was missing, and Pincus couldn't shake the gut feeling that he was gone for good, that hunks and snippets of his lean flesh would be feeding the pinfish in Biscayne Bay for a long time.

These thoughts clogged his mind as he sat in his Mustang, parked in the grass under the mossy arms of a ficus tree. Pincus squinted toward a bench on the other side of a city park. Every few minutes he would lift a small pair of Nikon binoculars to see better the face of Roberto Nelson as he tossed popcorn to a flock of brazen pigeons. This was the sort of idle nonsense at which men like

Bobby Nelson would not be caught dead unless an important moment was at hand.

Pincus was distracted by a muffled voice behind him. Instinctively his eyes went to the rear-view mirror and his right hand crawled down his leg to an ankle holster that cuddled a small pistol. He saw two men on the ground behind his car.

"Come on, Johnny, let's go into the toilet," one said in a shy, low voice.

"Just do it here and get it over with," said the other.

Pincus straightened up in the driver's seat. He fiddled with the mirror until both men were in clear view, embracing clumsily under the shade tree.

"Fuck," Pincus said. From where they reclined the men obviously could not see him in the car. Pincus was surprised they had not tried to break in and use the back seat. His first impulse was to storm out of the car and bust both of them for lewd-and-lascivious, but of course they would scream and fuss, and Roberto Nelson would get very curious about the racket across the park. Likewise if Pincus were to honk or start his engine. He decided he couldn't afford to burn the surveillance, so he would be silent. He tried to tune out the sloppy moans and lifted his Nikon again.

He noticed that Roberto Nelson now had company on the bench. Pincus braced his elbows on the steering wheel to steady the binoculars. The other man was a skinny Latin with long, wavy hair and sunglasses; he waved his arms wildly at Roberto Nelson, as if agitated. Nelson appeared to respond coolly, touching his friend gently on the arm as if to calm him.

The two men rose and walked toward a parking lot where Pincus earlier had watched Nelson park the beige Mercedes-Benz. Halfway there, Skinny Friend stopped walking while Nelson continued to the car.

"Not too rough, Johnny. Easy! I'm getting blisters on these fuckin' roots."

Pincus winced at the noise behind him as Johnny's friend started grunting. He could no longer see the two writhing lovers in the mirror and supposed their passion had carried them under his wheels.

Roberto Nelson and his friend were walking together again. Pincus saw that Skinny was carrying a denim beach bag now and that Roberto was toting a thin brown briefcase. They stopped in front of the bench, where Roberto grinned, slapped his customer amiably on the shoulder and walked way. Pincus lowered the binoculars. He had seen all he needed.

As soon as both men were gone, Pincus shoved the key into the ignition and stomped on the gas pedal. The Mustang growled and belched a faceful of blue fumes from the exhaust.

"Hey! Christ, watch out! Don't back up, man," the man named Johnny yelled from the ground.

Pincus slipped the transmission into reverse and eased off the clutch.

"I said no, fuckhead!"

Suddenly Johnny was on his feet, glaring through Seconal eyes into Pincus's face. His friend, leaf-covered and sheepishly disheveled, scrambled behind the trunk of the big tree to zip up.

"What the fuck is the matter with you?" Johnny screamed. "You coulda killed us."

Pincus put the car in neutral and took his foot off the accelerator. He reached up to the sun visor and pulled out a laminated police identification card. Johnny leaned forward tentatively to read the name.

"You boys shouldn't fuck in the park," Wilber Pincus said.

"Officer, we didn't know there was anybody here, I swear."

"What if this was a car full of Girl Scouts?" Pincus asked sternly. "What if I was your mother? Come to the park to feed the pigeons only to find my son boffing a wino under the ficus tree."

"Jesus," Johnny muttered.

Pincus replaced his ID in the visor. "Do you know what it sounds like? All the moaning and groaning and howling, I mean, how the hell am I supposed to enjoy my lunch with that kind of shit going on? I don't ever want to see you here again."

"Right," Johnny said, backing away. "Yes, Officer. I've got to go now."

"Good idea," Pincus said sharply. "And find another place to fall in love. I'll be back here tomorrow, me and the Girl Scouts."

"Yes, sir."

MONEY WAS a big problem.

Christopher Meadows reasoned that Octavio Nelson or the Cuban goons were watching the bank and monitoring his checking account. He took no chances. On the day he decided to go underground Meadows visited four small shopping centers and, using his plastic bank card, collected a hundred dollars from each of the mindless automatic banking machines in the parking lot. It would take Nelson weeks to trace the withdrawals, and success would bring him no closer than a mall that was fifteen miles from Terry's apartment. Meadows never visited the same machine twice.

He estimated his resources at approximately nineteen thousand dollars in two savings accounts and the checking account; he believed he could make all of it last a year if he had to, but that was only if he didn't spend anything on cocaine. And Meadows was determined to pay whatever was necessary for as much as he could lay his hands on.

In Fort Lauderdale, Meadows opened a new checking account under the name Christopher Warren Carson and began depositing funds. For identification he obtained a Florida driver's license under the same name; it took him only five minutes and a discreet twenty dollars to convince a sallow clerk at the Department of Motor Vehicles that he had lost the original on a snorkeling trip.

Meadows moved out of Terry's apartment into a motel room about five blocks from the Fort Lauderdale beach. The distance insulated him—physically and psychologically—from Nelson and the dope lunatics in Miami. In Lauderdale Meadows felt he would also be less likely to encounter old friends—and freer to do the necessary socializing.

The first night out nearly ended in disaster.

He had chosen Tony's, an after-midnight disco with a five-dollar cover and a snowy reputation. Meadows sat alone at the bar, spellbound by the young crowd but repelled by the jackhammer music. After an hour of gawking Meadows realized he was blending in about as smoothly as an anthropologist in the Amazon.

He tried to loosen up, finally striking up a flimsy conversation with a man named Guy, who had come to the disco with two women. After a few strong drinks Meadows found them both quite breathtaking, even the one who made popping sounds with gum in her mouth. Soon the architect began telling amusing stories; Guy and the girls were in hysterics. One of the women, a model for a men's magazine, had stories, too.

"One time they were doing a photo layout on circuses, and they asked me to pose naked with these midgets. All of them were made up just like clowns, and we were standing in the big top with about ten thousand people screaming in the bleachers. And I was supposed to ride through the middle of them on a unicycle, with no clothes, remember. Now I don't mind taking my clothes off, not for that kind of money, but I can't ride a bicycle worth a damn. You can imagine what happened when I got on the unicycle."

Meadows nodded sincerely.

"They are *very* hard to ride, especially naked. And the midgets were no help," she related.

Meadows was afraid Guy was going to come in his pants.

"That's nothing. Cindy, tell Christopher about the time in Las Vegas with the man from the United Nations," Guy spluttered. "Honest to God, it was the ambassador to someplace, right, Cindy?"

Meadows was numb. After a few minutes Guy turned to him and asked, "You wanna do a couple lines?"

"You bet." Meadows was drunk, and Guy's words pinballed around his head. He followed him from the bar to the rest room, where Guy entered one of the stalls. Meadows stood in front of a urinal, leaning his forehead against the grimy tile to prop himself up.

"Hey, hurry up," Guy was saying. "Come here."

Meadows splashed some water in his face. Guy pulled him into the stall and locked the door. "Sit, sit," he whispered excitedly. Meadows slumped on the toilet seat and watched Guy take something out of a pocket and hold it up for self-approval. "Good stuff, buddy."

Guy unraveled a packet no larger than a postage stamp. Meadows noticed it was a one-dollar bill, folded into a neat square carton. In the middle was a tiny mound of chalky powder. Guy tapped the crystals onto a small rectangular mirror. Then he reached under his shirt and came out with a gold razor blade on the end of a necklace. He used it to cut the cocaine into inch-long lines.

"Is that real gold?" Meadows asked.

"Twenty-four carat," Guy replied. "Hold this." He handed Meadows the mirror. "You got a C-note?"

Meadows shook his head. Guy fished in his pocket until he came out with a twenty-dollar bill, which he deftly rolled into a stiff green straw. "It's all yours," he announced.

"No, you go first," Meadows said nervously.

Guy was hungry for the stuff. He touched the straw to the mirror, leaned over, placed one end up his right nostril and inhaled evenly, sliding the twenty-dollar bill down the mirror until one line of the powder vanished. Then he pressed a finger against the side of his nose, tossed his head back and sucked in deeply. Afterward he bent down and snorted another line the same way.

"Your turn," he said to Meadows.

Meadows was burning up, and his shirt stuck like tape to his chest. Wordlessly he took the mirror and tried to imitate Guy. On his first snort Meadows faltered and sniffed only half the line up his nose. "Man! Don't waste this shit," Guy muttered. Meadows nodded and finished up the line. He offered the last one to his new friend, but Guy shook his head. Someone walked into the rest room, and Guy put his fingers to his lips. Meadows trembled; he pictured some vice cop peering under the stalls, spying two pairs of feet and kicking the door down with a fury.

Meadows heard the sound of a man urinating and relaxed. Quickly he lifted the mirror to his nose, lined up the straw and inhaled again. The performance was still something less than convincing. Guy snatched the mirror and sucked down a few errant crystals until the surface was clean. They waited until the other man left, and then Guy said: "Let's go. I've got to give some of this to the girls or they're going to be pissed. How do you feel?"

Meadows felt nothing. "Terrific," he said anyway. They went back to the bar.

"It's about time," Cindy said with mock impatience. Guy handed her the cocaine in its snug currency purse. "Thank you," she sang, swirling off to the ladies' room with her friend.

Meadows ordered another whiskey. He noticed something sweet dripping from his sinuses into the back of his throat. Guy sat silently next to him, smiling and swaying slightly to the music. When the girls returned, they started chattering at once. Meadows didn't think it was funny, but he found himself laughing at everything. He felt good. Very good. Cindy's eyes glowed. She asked Meadows to tell another story.

He recounted the plight of a Colombian pickpocket, an unfortunate soul who had chosen as his victim one morning a very important *gringo,* the son of the United States ambassador. No sooner was the wallet out of the young man's designer jeans than the bodyguards, his own countrymen, had seized the thief and by way of punishment amputated one of his hands for all to see on the streets of Bogotá. . . .

Cindy moved closer. "That . . . is amazing," she said heavily. "When were you in South America?"

"Last year," Meadows replied. "On a job."

"You sell real estate in Colombia?"

"No, it was an architectural project."

"But you said you were in real estate."

Meadows was lost in her; he couldn't stop himself now. "That was a lie. I'm an architect."

Cindy laughed guardedly and tugged on Meadows's sleeve. "Come on. Why would you lie about that?"

"Because people are trying to kill me."

"Right."

Guy and the other girl were off on the dance floor somewhere. Meadows put his arm around Cindy and pulled her close. "Where do you live?"

"I'm staying at the Deauville," she said.

"Let's go."

"I can't. What about Guy?"

"He's too short for me," Meadows said, kissing Cindy on the

cheek. Her perfume was wonderful; he could not remember ever wanting to screw somebody so much. "Let's go back to your place and make love," he said. "I've got some better stories. You won't believe what's happened to me."

"That's very sweet," Cindy said, patting Meadows's hand like an aunt, "but I can't, really."

Suddenly Guy and the other girl were back at the bar.

"Big day tomorrow, girls. Time to hit the road," he announced. "Christopher, it was a pleasure." Guy stuck out his hand. "We've got an early flight back to Washington tomorrow, so I've got to get these dolls home."

Then Meadows was alone, left with a powerful hunger and puzzlement. It had to be the dope. He drove back to the motel and spent the next two hours pacing and sketching. Finally he fell into a solid, dreamless sleep. He spent the next day fighting off depression and trying to sort out what had happened. He was worried about his reaction to the drug; for a few moments in that loud dark lounge, his emotions laced with high-grade coke, Meadows actually had been in love with that crazy model. Fascinating stuff, he told himself later. Dangerous stuff.

It did not take him long to realize that, without an introduction, all he was ever going to get for his efforts were a runny nose and, occasionally, a willing woman. He needed more, and he needed it fast. It was difficult making the phone call, but Meadows was washed with relief that night when he saw the big man amble into the lounge. Arthur Prim broke into a grin when he spotted his friend at the bar; his huge hands seized Meadows warmly by the shoulders.

"Where've you been, man?" Meadows asked. "Hey, miss, this gentleman would like a Tanqueray. Right?"

Arthur nodded. "It's a long drive up here, Chris. Whatsamatter, you gettin' bored with the scene in Miami?" Arthur wore jeans, sandals and a tight yellow T-shirt that cried for relief across his huge chest.

"You're getting a little shaggy," Arthur said.

Meadows shrugged. They had talked at length over the phone. Arthur knew the situation, and he had agreed to help.

"You still up for it?"

"It's the only way I can see," Meadows said. "I know it's risky."

"Hey, man, don't forget, you're talkin' strategy to a man who regularly whupped your ass in chess."

"I'm never going to live that down," Meadows said, laughing.

Arthur's smile dissolved, and he took a long, thoughtful sip of gin. "There are," he said softly, "other ways."

"Sure, like what? The cops?"

"Sheeeeit, no." Arthur winced as the sax player in the band assaulted a high note. "Chris, I got some friends . . ."

"That's what I'm counting on, buddy."

Arthur shook his braided head. "I'm not talking friendly friends. What I'm telling you," he went on, lowering his voice, "is that if you tell me who did all this shit to you and the lady, I'll put the word in the right ears. You dig?"

"I couldn't live with that," Meadows said.

"Oh, so it's *living* you're interested in?" Arthur chuckled darkly. "You white boys sure got a crazy way of doin' it."

"Arthur, come on."

"This music sucks," he said, gulping down the last of the Tanqueray. "There's a blonde at the end of the bar. She came in with a tough little Cuban guy, but she's probably looking at us right now. Her name is Patti. Buy her a drink. If she wants you to meet the Cuban, you will."

Arthur stood up and fished in his jeans.

"No, it's on me. I'll let you buy me one when this is all over," Meadows said. "One more favor: Could you hire a couple kids to clean up my house? It's a mess."

They shook, Arthur's slab of a hand enveloping Meadows's. The big man did not let go for several seconds.

"I want you to call me and let me know," he said, moving toward the exit. "I don't want to read about it in the fuckin' papers."

After he was gone, Meadows glanced down at the bar at Arthur's couple. The man was darkly handsome and built like a fireplug. The woman was tall with a fickle weekend tan and dark blond hair to the shoulders. Meadows smiled in appreciation and was dazzled when the woman smiled back. He turned to his drink, wondering what to do now.

"Need a refill?" the barmaid asked. Her name was Barb; a name tag said so.

"Yes," Meadows said, "and I'd like to buy a drink for the lady down there." He watched Barb walk down and talk to the blonde, who shook her head. Meadows held his breath. Barb turned and shrugged at him. Feeling like a foolish teenager, he swung around on the barstool and pretended to watch the band. The blond woman came and sat next to him.

"It wasn't meant as an insult," she said. "I'm just not thirsty right now."

"It's OK," Meadows said. He guessed her age at thirty-four or thirty-five. Her hair was silky; her eyes were a stormy green, approaching blue.

"My name is Patti."

"Mine's Christopher." Meadows found himself looking back over her shoulder. "Where's your boyfriend?"

Patti laughed. "No boyfriend. That's Manny. My girlfriend's husband. He's dancing with somebody. Would you like to dance with me?"

"I'm afraid I'd just embarrass you. Are you sure I can't buy you a drink?"

"Perrier is fine," Patti said. "Where you from?"

Meadows gave her the real estate story and said he was from Atlanta. She told him she was from Pompano Beach and asked if he was married. Meadows said no, definitely not.

"I'm separated," Patti volunteered. "My husband is a lawyer. He's in jail right now, but that's not why we're separated. What I mean is that even if Larry didn't get caught, I would have left him. We weren't getting along."

"I'm sorry."

"Aren't you even going to ask what he got busted for?"

"OK. What?"

"Dope," Patti said.

"Grass?"

"Mostly, but he was getting into coke and ludes, too. We lived the grand life, all right. Big home on the Intracoastal, matching Corvettes . . . too bad he was such a greedy shithead."

Meadows got the feeling Patti wasn't losing much sleep over poor Larry.

"Know what he did? He and three buddies went out one night on a big Bertram sportfisher docked up at Hillsborough. The *Margie Doll* or *Maggie Doll*, something like that. The guy at the fuel dock asks where they're going, and Larry, the dumb shit, says they're going out all night swordfishing. This dockmaster is no idiot, so he mentions to this friend of his in the Marine Patrol that a bunch of young hotshots are taking out a big Bertram for a night of long-lining. And the Marine Patrol officer thinks this is hysterical because there isn't a fisherman in his right mind who goes sword-fishing in January off Hillsborough. It isn't even swordfish *season*. So the Marine Patrol mentions this to a buddy of his in Customs, and to make a long story short, when the *Maggie Doll* comes back into the inlet at four A.M., eight jillion drug agents are waiting for her. And there's my Larry, bless his dumb heart, snoring away on top of five thousand pounds of Colombian weed. He's up at Lowell now, doing two years. He's very mad at me because I won't visit him, but I made up my mind. I'm through with him. There's a good chance he'll be disbarred because of this."

"Sounds likely," Meadows said.

Patti lit a cigarette and looked around. "I wonder where Manny ran off to." Meadows spotted the stocky dark man at a table with two women. Patti saw him at the same instant.

Meadows steered the conversation back to drugs. "You didn't mind that your husband was smuggling dope?"

Patti looked up from her soda water. "Jesus, it wasn't heroin or anything. He was selling to doctors, accountants, lawyers like himself. The year before he got popped, his income from the law practice was only twenty-three thousand dollars. He made another hundred and thirty-five thousand selling grass. I went from a shitty two-bedroom apartment in Pompano to a seven-bedroom house on the Intracoastal. Did I mind? No. Don't tell me you don't toot a little yourself."

"When I can afford it," Meadows said.

Patti smiled. "What about if it's free?"

"Absolutely." My mother would despair, Meadows thought bleakly, and Terry would bust a gut.

"Well, I've got a little coke at my place if you want to share it," Patti said expectantly.

"What about Manny?"

"Manny's busy with his new friends," she said sardonically. "Come on, it'll be fun."

Meadows paid the tab. They rode to Patti's place in her car, a black Firebird that had seen better days. The sand-colored house was handsome in floodlights, and Meadows quickly assessed the design: a one-story Mediterranean layout with heavy emphasis on dark tropical woods. He guessed the price at $200,000.

"It's beautiful," he told Patti as she walked him through the front door.

"You'll get a tour later," she said huskily, leading him into a bathroom of alabaster tile and deep wine-colored shag. The powder was stashed in the hollow plastic handle of a man's razor. Patti handed him a pinch that topped off a small gold spoon. This time Meadows did not resist, and it had nothing to do with being drunk. The coke kicked in instantly.

Patti took Meadows to her bedroom and opened the curtains on a spectacular view of the Intracoastal Waterway, slick under a clear tropical sky. A channel marker winked a dim red eye from a distant bend in the dark waterway.

Meadows stood for several moments at the window, wide awake and excited. His heart hammered in his ears. He willed himself the concentration of a diamond cutter; tonight there could be no confessions.

"That's very good dope," he said awkwardly. He thought it seemed the gracious thing to do.

"The best," Patti answered as she sat on the bed. "It's getting late, Chris. Take off your clothes."

# Chapter 19

SHE WAS awake early. Meadows held his eyes closed, concentrating on the morning sounds. He listened to her footsteps from the bathroom to the kitchen. Soon he smelled coffee. His stomach stirred irritably, but he didn't move from the bed.

Meadows permitted himself his old identity for a few moments. He longed for Terry's comfort, seethed over losing the Ecuadorean oil ministry project, prayed that his parents and his friends were not calling out the National Guard to hunt for his body. He had left word at the office and with his service, inventing an architects' convention and other obligations that would officially keep him out of town for weeks. He had also cabled friends of his parents in New York, asking them to assure his relatives that he was alive and well.

Meadows rubbed his sore eyes and stared up at the bedroom ceiling and wondered if he was out of his goddamn skull. This is Disneyland, he told himself. It will never work. If he could corner José Bermúdez today, tonight, this minute, and do what he planned—who would believe his story later? Or understand?

"Hi there," Patti said.

"Morning," Meadows said, propping himself on his elbows. "You been up long?"

"Just a little while. I thought I'd give you a nudge before the races start."

Meadows fell back on the pillow. "What races?"

"The speedboats. Every kid in Fort Lauderdale gets a boat for his birthday, and I think they all take turns racing behind my house. The racket is awful." Patti sat down on the bed and put her hands on his chest. "Did you have fun last night?"

"It was wonderful," Meadows said. For the first time in weeks he was telling the truth.

"That's good stuff, huh?"

"Yeah," he said, burrowing back into the sheets. "Where'd you get it?"

"From Manny," Patti said. "Come on, let's eat some breakfast."

They had omelets on a small shaded patio. A breeze stirred off the Intracoastal. Two magnificent Hatteras fishing boats thundered past the house and sent deep curling wakes against the concrete sea wall. Copper-skinned young men with sun-bleached hair could be seen in the cockpits, working at the fishing rods, rigging baits for dolphin and sailfish. With the offshore winds, Meadows imagined the Gulf Stream was probably as calm as a lake.

"This is a wonderful house," he said to Patti.

"Larry said it was practical. Seven bedrooms for two people! Practical." Patti took a sip of hot Jamaican tea. "I do like the place though. See that?" She pointed to a dock that ran parallel to the sea wall. "You can put a thirty-four-footer there and still have room for the Donzis. We needed a pier like that."

"You had boats?"

"Different ones. The walkway that comes up from the dock leads right into the garage. This house has a three-car garage, but we never once put our cars inside. You understand?"

Meadows nodded. "The pot."

"You can't very well stash five tons in a glove compartment." Patti stretched one of her legs across Meadows's lap. It was smooth and tan. She wore a man's long-sleeved shirt and a pair of silk panties. Whenever she turned her head to the water, her blond hair caught the sun.

"So while Larry's gone, you've got the whole place to yourself?"

"For a while," Patti said. "Until the IRS finds a way to get it. They're very curious about how an attorney making the kind of money Larry did could afford a setup like this. They make me go downtown every other week to answer questions."

"What do you tell them?"

"I play dumb wifey. Larry never told me anything about the money. The house was an anniversary present. I just assumed he was making lots of money at work. I don't even know how much the house cost. Blah, blah, blah." Patti stood and stretched. "They don't believe a word, of course."

"Don't you have a lawyer?"

"I'll get one if I need to."

"What about Larry's?"

"Redbirt? Lot of good he did us. I'd never hire that asshole. This is an amazing business, Christopher."

"I know."

Patti laughed and sat on his lap. "Arthur says you're interested in getting started down here."

"Yeah. The problem is, I don't know anybody."

' "Not yet anyway," Patti said enigmatically. "Are you thinking about grass or coke?"

"Cocaine."

"Could have fooled me," Patti teased. "Last night, when I gave you a hit, I thought you were going to sneeze it all over the bathroom."

Meadows chuckled quietly and kissed her cheek. Patti looked at him appraisingly. "I'm not sure I believe you. Hell, you could be a cop for all I know." She pecked him on the nose. "'Cept you're too skinny."

She got up and started clearing the breakfast dishes. Meadows grabbed her around the waist. "Stop, I'm gonna spill something," she protested, but Meadows led her back to the bedroom, where he swiftly unbuttoned the shirt. He leaned over and began kissing the freckles on her breasts.

"Damn," Patti muttered.

"What'd I do?"

"Listen."

"Another boat," Meadows said. "So what?"

"So we better get dressed fast. That one's stopping out back. It's probably Manny."


MEADOWS SQUIRMED. They all sat in the living room: he, Patti, Manny and Manny's friend, Moe. "Call me Maurice," Manny's friend had said. "Call him Moe. Everybody does," said Manny.

Manny was Cuban. Up close in the daylight he was not quite as broad or heavily muscled as he had seemed at Lenny's the night before. His friend Moe was the reverse, a six-foot-six beanpole from Mississippi whose ivory skin was raw with sunburn. He and Manny scavenged a couple of cans of Michelob from Patti's refrigerator and then plopped down, Manny in a canary-colored bean-bag and Moe on a mushy camel sofa.

"So, Patti, you must have had a good time last night 'cause I didn't see you leave," Manny said.

"Did you go home?" she shot back. "Jesus, Manny, Susan is probably out of her mind. Call her, would you?"

"Naw, she's OK. I met one of those cheerleaders. What the hell are they called now?"

"The Dolphin Dolls," Moe said helpfully.

"Right. She's gonna get me a sideline pass to the Jets' exhibition game. What'd you say your name was?"

"Christopher Carson," Meadows said.

"What do you do?" Manny demanded.

"I'm in real estate. How about you?"

Manny was all teeth. When he grinned, the rest of his face seemed to disappear.

"Manny's a businessman; Moe's a partner," Patti explained with evident caution.

"What kind of business?" Meadows aimed his question at Manny.

"Import-export."

Moe laughed, and Manny joined him. Meadows realized they both were stoned out of their minds. The shirtless Manny fingered a gold chain around his neck. A crucifix dangled into dark chest hair, matted with sweat. He finished off the Michelob and mashed the aluminum can with two fingers.

"How's the real estate business? Sold any houses?"

"I've only been down here a couple months."

"You didn't answer me."

Meadows shrugged. "I've had one sale," he said. "Down in Homestead. In a subdivision called Valencia Gardens." The development was legitimate; its architect was an old classmate of Meadows.

"One sale in two months? That's pretty goddamn miserable, pal."

"Easy, Manny," Patti interrupted.

Meadows waved her off. "No, he's right. Business stinks. That's why I'm here."

"Chris is a good man," Patti said to Manny. "I told him about Larry and everything."

"That was real fucking smart."

"Hey, he's OK."

Manny gave an exaggerated shrug. "Well, then he must be OK."

"I'm gonna work on my tan," Moe grumbled. He got up and walked outside. Meadows watched him amble down to Manny's red Magnum, peel off his shirt and stretch out across the bow.

Manny stared at Meadows through small chocolate brown eyes. "You got a lot of money?"

"Let's drop the whole thing," Patti said curtly. "Manny, why don't you and Moe take off, OK? Chris and I are going for a swim."

Meadows put a hand on her shoulder. "No, I want to hear what he has to say."

"Manny, at least call Susan and tell her you're OK."

"Later, Pat. I want to find out how come your new boyfriend came to Florida."

"I got a little heat in Atlanta," Meadows said quickly. "A couple friends got popped. And I got scared."

"Tell me about it," Manny said. "Take that boy out there." He nodded in Moe's direction. "Talk about heat. Did two years at Eglin. The feds got him in a shrimp boat out of Mobile. It was packed to the decks with grass. They wanted to flip him, but Moe said no way. They told him he could walk away from it if he would only flip. Moe's a good man, and he's smart. This prick from DEA sits him down and tells him they're going to ask fifteen years for conspiracy, possession, firearms, the whole nine yards. Moe tells him to fuck off. So he gets two years and spends the whole time playing volleyball at Eglin. Not bad."

Manny dug into his jeans and pulled out an amber glassine container. He unscrewed the cap and dipped a tiny spoon. "You want a blast?"

Meadows shook his head.

"Know why Moe didn't turn over? Maybe Moe should tell this story."

"Manny, leave Chris alone," Patti said. "I don't think he's interested in any of this."

"Oh, I think the real estate man is very interested. Am I right?"

Meadows tightened. For a moment he thought Manny was going to lunge at him and break him in half like a cracker. The Cuban was waiting for some kind of answer, and Meadows realized sickeningly he could not even speak the language.

"Like I said, business is slow."

Manny cackled. "Times are tough. You should get hold of some condos. Condos move real good down here. Patti, how about another beer? Anyway, Christopher, you want to know why Moe didn't flip? Patti's heard this story."

"A million times," she said on her way to the kitchen.

"Joey Dent."

"Yeah." Meadows felt like standing under a hot shower until Manny and his friend rinsed away.

"Joey Dent was a friend. Pat knew him, too. Very heavy into the export-import, import-export business. But at a safe and respectable level. One day he does a dumb thing and goes along for the ride. A DC-6 lands at Opa-Locka one night, tries to land, I should say, but the nose gear snaps like a twig, and the plane skids off the runway. Twelve fire trucks show up. Joey Dent's legs are broken, and the pilot is dead. They haul Joey out of the plane and kablam! Two million bucks' worth of grass and ludes.

"It's four in the morning, Joey Dent is in Parkway General and in walk two DEA jerk-offs. 'Your wife, your kids, your house, your mistress, all down the toilet, Joey. Help us out, and you fly like an eagle. We'll send you off to Montana with a new name and a little ranch in the valley. It's so nice out there, Joey. If you don't help, however, we send you to Atlanta for seven years. By the time you get out your wife will be gone with the TV repairman and the kids won't recognize you.' Dammit, can you get this open? My hands are wet." Manny tossed the cold bottle of Miller's across the room, and Meadows snatched it before it hit the tile. He wrapped a corner of the terry-cloth robe he was wearing around the cap and twisted it off. He handed it back to Manny, and the smuggler drank half in four huge gulps.

"Imagine you're Joey Dent," he went on. "You've just had the shit scared out of you in a plane wreck; you're lying broken up in a hospital and loaded on Dilaudid. And these two DEA pricks tell you your life is over."

"He talked," Patti said wearily.

"Yup. Joey Dent talked. Two of the men he worked for got set up. And busted. They even did time, not much time, but they did go to the can. And Joey Dent never got to Montana. The feds gave him a new name, Jack Somethingorother, and moved him all the way from Miami to Tampa. Wasn't that generous? One day Joey didn't come home from his job at the post office. They found him in the Port Charlotte waterway. Before he died, someone cut off his tongue with pruning shears. Then they shot him in the head." Manny drained the Miller's. "So you see why Moe didn't mind Eglin at all."

"It works the same way everywhere," Meadows said casually. He had heard plenty of these stories from Octavio Nelson, bless his black heart.

"Hey, I wasn't trying to scare you," Manny said.

"Like hell," Patti hissed.

"I just wanted you to know why Moe's so . . . careful. He doesn't trust many people. He's a good influence on me. He's saved my ass more than once."

"Well, he's not going to save your ass from Susan if you don't call her," Patti said. The phone rang, and she sprang up to get it. "That's probably her now. What should I tell her?"

"You haven't seen me."

After Patti left the room, Manny leaned forward and motioned for Meadows to come closer. "What are you doing tonight?" he whispered.

"Nothing."

"You want to make some money?"

"Yeah. How?"

"Me and Moe got a big errand to run. We got to pick up some goodies, and we need a helper. Guy we were counting on bugged out. Patti says you're OK, you're OK."

"How much?"

"Five thousand."

"Are you kidding?" Meadows's incredulity was genuine.

"It's toilet paper to the people I work for," Manny boasted. "My boss appreciates risk. We're taking a small risk tonight. So you're interested, huh?"

"Well, sure."

"Don't bring a gun, that's one rule. And don't get loaded before you come, that's another. The third rule is the Joey Dent Rule. You know that one already." Manny held Meadows's gaze for a moment, then rose. "We'll pick you up here at midnight."

Patti walked back into the room. "You two getting along?"

"Sure," Manny said. "Was that Susie?"

"Yeah, and I told her you were on your way home."

Manny raised his hands and looked despairingly at Meadows. "You can't trust 'em, Christopher. They stick together like nuns. See you tonight." Manny swaggered out of the house, and Meadows heard the Magnum growl to life. When he looked out the window, all he saw was a frothy crease in the tea-colored water. The speed-boat was already around the bend.

Meadows felt Patti's arm around his waist. "He left out one," she said softly.

"What?"

"Rule number four. Named after my husband. The Larry Atchison Rule."

"What's that?"

"Don't get greedy."

# Chapter 20

THE HOUSE IN Coconut Grove disturbed Octavio Nelson the most.

The deliberate savagery with which Meadows's pursuers had destroyed the place was sobering. Nelson felt himself sicken as he and Pincus walked through the wreckage, touching nothing, marveling in breathless expletives at the thorough job.

"They must have got him, Captain," Pincus said. "I'll bet he's dead."

Nelson sat down in a slashed patio chair by the now-rancid pool, thinking back to the night of the lizard. "No," he said to Pincus. "Meadows wasn't here when they paid their visit. That is why they did all this."

"For sport?" Pincus prodded a mangled stereo speaker with one of his shoes.

"A message, Wilbur. The sort you don't forget. I think our friend Meadows knows what happened here. He won't be back."

"You sound awfully certain."

Nelson's eyes narrowed. Again the challenge, the edge of righteous doubt in the voice. It had been like this with Pincus for months, now, ever since the Cruz thing. Nelson was annoyed with it.

"What are we looking for?" Pincus asked.

"Drawings. Rough sketches."

"Of buildings? Let's check his studio—"

"No, not buildings," Nelson said. "Men. Meadows once told me he was going to draw sketches of Mono's bodyguards."

"Yeah? When did he tell you that?"

"One day when you weren't around," Nelson said, peeling a stack of soggy papers off the carpet.

"Before the airport murder?"

172

"I guess so, yeah. Shit, look at this. These are letters from his girl-friend. Those dirtbags probably went through the whole stack before they trashed the place."

Pincus peered over Nelson's shoulder. "The ink's all smeared now," he remarked. "Can't make out hardly anything."

The detectives had been on their ghastly tour of the house for ten minutes when Arthur Prim stalked through the front door.

"Finally putting in an appearance, I see," the black man growled.

"Hello, Prim," Nelson said. "Where's Meadows?"

"Don't know." Arthur kicked off his thongs. "I got a couple extra mops if you guys want to help clean up this shit. I been at it three days."

Pincus said, "When was the last time you talked to Mr. Meadows?"

Arthur chuckled, trading glances with Octavio Nelson. "Hey, I'm just the maid. I don't know jackshit." He bent over and began toss-ing chunks of rotting food and fragments of glass into a plastic garbage sack.

"It's OK," Nelson said. "We're not looking to bust your friend. We couldn't."

Pincus stared at his partner.

"If you see him, tell him it's OK to come up now. Tell him I've closed the investigation into Sosa's death."

"That's the airport thing, right?" Arthur asked warily.

"Yep."

"Why'd you quit on it?" Arthur said.

"Yeah, why?" Pincus echoed.

Nelson stifled him with a scorching glare and faced Arthur. "Look, all we got is a body in a car, some blood at the airport and no goddamn eyewitnesses. Nobody mourns Mono, nobody that I care about. I need Meadows's help."

"Shit!" Arthur Prim said.

"If you see him or talk to him, tell him I got his ass off the chop-ping block. Tell him he's got my word," Nelson said.

"I'm sure he'll be overwhelmed with gratitude, Captain. Could you move your foot? You're standing on a Neiman print, I believe."

Once they were alone again, in Nelson's car, Pincus practically exploded.

"What was all that nonsense about Sosa?"

"Just the truth."

"You aren't trying to trick Meadows into turning himself in?"

"No, Wilbur. I give him a little more credit than you do." Nelson relighted his cigar.

"You can't just give up on the case," Pincus protested. "We had good leads, good evidence. Meadows did it."

"Can you take it to court?"

"Not yet."

"Wilbur, I can't find the top of my fucking desk for the homicide files that are stacked up there. This one's about number one hundred and eighty-three on my list. Sosa was a slug. And if Meadows killed him, like you say, the guy deserves an oak cluster, not an indictment."

"But what—"

"And don't ever tell me I can't just give up on a case," Nelson snapped. "I think Meadows can be useful. He is a most uncommon witness, in case you hadn't noticed. He may even teach us something before it's over, so if I choose to misplace the Sosa file for a few days or a few years, that's too fucking bad."

"I didn't mean to start an argument. I'm just confused," Pincus said. "I don't think Meadows can help us one bit. But that's only my opinion."

"Opinions are like assholes," Nelson said. "Everybody's got one, and they all stink."

Back at the office, while Pincus carefully typed out a vandalism report about the Meadows residence, Nelson tried Stella one more time.

"Mr. Meadows will be out of the office for several weeks," she repeated loyally.

"This is a police emergency, ma'am. Where can I reach him? It's very urgent," Nelson said ominously.

"God, I don't know, really." Stella cartwheeled like a gull in a hurricane. "Maybe his parents . . . no, his girlfriend. Try the girlfriend, Officer."

"What is her name?"

"I don't remember."

"It's vital, miss!"

There was a pause. "It starts with a T or M. She's a pilot of some kind."

Nelson adopted the tone of a patient kindergarten teacher. "Do you have a phone number for the lady?"

"Yes, yes," she said. "Sometimes Mr. Meadows stays at her place. Here it is." She read off a number.

Nelson hung up and dialed, hung up again when a man in a Seventy-ninth Street massage parlor answered the phone. Stella had screwed up.

The detective scribbled variations of the original number, until he could think of no more. Using the cross-indexed city directory, Nelson matched numbers with names: G. Stein, Abraham Jones, Mark M. Flanigan, M. C. Betancourt . . .

Nelson studied the last name. Latin. The use of initials usually indicated a single woman, alone. The phone company was very diligent about discouraging obscene calls; genderless initials instead of a name was one sure way.

What grabbed Nelson's eye was the parenthetical business identification: (Pres., CAN Airways). The number was almost the same, 724 instead of 742. Stella's error was one of simple transposition, if this was the right woman.

The phone number belonged to a condominium on Key Biscayne. Nelson slipped away without a word to Pincus, who was still perched studiously over one of the secretary's typewriters.

The building superintendent at Terry's condo told Nelson he had not seen the busy pilot or her thin, quiet boyfriend for some time. When Nelson asked to inspect the apartment, the manager reluctantly accompanied him up the elevator and as far as Terry's front door.

"Listen, I don't want no trouble. A lady died here last year. . . ."

"In this apartment?"

"No, no. In the building. We didn't find her body for a week."

"Terrific. Sorta hangs in the drapes, doesn't it?"

"Yeah, well, I just don't want any commotion, OK?" said the super. "I mean, if there's something in there, can you just call the ambulance and take care of it without a commotion?"

"Gimme the key," Nelson said.

Inside, there was no trace of Christopher Meadows, no evidence that the architect had lived there recently or ever. Meadows had been meticulous in his flight, Nelson thought as he rummaged fruitlessly through the trash cans. The dishes were all in place in Terry's linoleum kitchen; the beds were made; the counters were absent of crumbs, stains and other loose clues. Nelson even searched through the laundry hamper only to uncover a bra, three small T-shirts and two pairs of bikini panties. There was no sign a man had been in the apartment.

The super, a pale, bald little fellow with shoulders like a turkey vulture, was hanging nervously in the hallway while Nelson searched.

"Is everything OK?" he called finally.

"Yeah. You can go back downstairs. I'll be down with the key in a few minutes."

"I think I ought to stay just—"

"Get lost!" Nelson commanded. "I'm not gonna rip off the TV, for Chrissakes."

By the time he worked his way to Terry's sweet-smelling bedroom Nelson was sure the place was dry. He opened the top drawer of the bedstand and, without touching, took a brief visual inventory: a round, unopened packet of birth control pills, a bottle of Bayer aspirin, some Vaseline, the instruction manual and warranty card for a clock radio and a dark green cloth that looked like brushed felt. The drawer smelled familiar. Gun oil.

Octavio Nelson picked up the green cloth and laid it on the bedspread. He leaned back and put his head down to get a side-angle view. The grease marks were promising, but the imprint was even better. With a forefinger Nelson traced the shape of a gun, from grip to barrel, on the soft thick cloth. He folded it and slipped it into the inside pocket of his sport coat.

Meadows's girlfriend obviously kept a pistol by the bed, but it was missing now. As Nelson rode the elevator down to the parking garage, he wondered somberly if T. Christopher Meadows was teaching himself how to shoot.

WINNIE LAINE, a travel agent at Tropic Suncoast Tours on Biscayne Boulevard, met the stranger for the first time on a Monday. He mentioned South America, and she gave him some brochures. Winnie was curious. The man was tall and blond, very polite, and she would have bet a week's pay he didn't speak a word of Spanish.

He came back on Wednesday and asked about Barranquilla, and she could hardly suppress herself. Well, Bogotá is very nice this time of year, she said; what she meant was: Barranquilla is a snake pit, and you must be out of your mind to go there. And the man took some more brochures, asked about airline fares and said he couldn't really make up his mind. As he left, Winnie wondered to herself what the young man would look like dressed in brown instead of gray.

She was surprised, pleasantly, when he returned on Friday. He apologized shyly for his indecision and then not-so-shyly asked her out for a drink after work. Winnie said no, but the man didn't seem to hear it. He smiled and was about to walk out when she changed her mind.

They went to a dockside bar at the city marina. Winnie spent the better part of two hours answering the man's quiet questions and not minding at all. When she finally asked a few of her own, the man told her he was an office supply salesman trying to unload a hundred used IBM typewriters in Colombia. The demand down there, he said brightly, was inexhaustible. He anticipated numerous trips, and he was merely shopping for the most economical way to get in and out from Miami. A good friend of his, Bobby Nelson, was a frequent traveler to South and Central America.

"Yes, he's one of our clients," Winnie exclaimed.

"No kidding?"

"Twice a month, like clockwork," said Winnie. "Miami to Bogotá to Medellín to Miami." She laughed. "I even got it memorized."

"I'll be darned," the man said. "I know he's on the road a lot."

"The seventeenth and twenty-eighth of every month," Winnie said. "He's one of our best customers."

"How long does he stay? Must be tough on his wife."

"Naw, three days at a time. That's all."

"What airline?" asked the man.

"Avianca."

"Bobby likes the service?"

"I guess so," Winnie said. "Of course, you don't have a big selection to choose from."

The man finished off his rum-and-Coke. "That's OK. It sounds like a good bet, right there. Tomorrow I'll call my boss to get the OK, and then I'll come downtown and buy the tickets. Maybe we can have lunch."

"That would be nice," Winnie said. Then the blond man drove her back to her town house and kissed her goodnight at the door. She never saw him again.

PEPE FALCÓN did all his deals in Holiday Inns, so his customers started calling him *Botones,* or bellboy. Pepe liked the name. As he prospered, his style changed accordingly. Where once he was content to get a single room for twenty-eight bucks, he now always made sure to get a suite, near the top, with a view. Any view would do. And after he collected his money, Botones would escort the customer out the door, pick up the phone and call a hooker, sometimes two. Then they would all celebrate.

On the summer night that Detective Ethan Bradley, Miami Homicide, was summoned to Room 713–714 of the Holiday Inn Bayside, Pepe Falcón celebrated for the last time. Then someone stuck the barrel of a small automatic handgun up his nose and blew a few brains and a lot of high-grade cocaine all over the walls. Detective Bradley noted in his report that the mess had "totally ruined a very nice seascape hanging on the west wall."

A few hours later a truck driver heading north on Interstate 95 with three tons of assorted vegetables noticed a car in flames on the highway apron. He braked his rig, hopped out and doused the late-model Oldsmobile until his portable fire extinguisher was empty. The trucker got on his CB and called for help when he noticed something very funny on the upholstery. A Florida highway patrolman waited for ninety minutes to make sure the car had cooled off, then used a crowbar to pop the trunk.

Inside was the body of a man named Hilarión Escandar, a young Colombian national. Detective Sergeant Ray Lesnick, Miami Homicide, was given the task of searching the corpse. He found approximately fifty-five thousand dollars in U.S. currency, two dozen raw emeralds, three different driver's licenses and an airline ticket that showed Escandar had arrived earlier that evening on a flight from Lima. The Dade County medical examiner would later determine that the twenty-four-year-old university student had been shot within thirty minutes after he had strolled out of the terminal at Miami International.

Two days later a twin-engine Beechcraft landed at 1:07 A.M. at North Perry Airport. Several men waited by their cars as the cherry-striped aircraft taxied to a stop. The pilot got out, carrying an Ingram submachine gun and nothing else.

"Sorry, fellas," he said to his welcoming committee. "Somebody fucked up. It's all dried up."

"That's impossible!" shouted one of the men.

"I couldn't buy a fucking gram!" the pilot shouted. "Your money is in the plane." He waved the gun. "Get away from that car. Don't call me again for a long time, OK?"

An airport security guard who witnessed the incident notified the Dade County Metropolitan police, but even the Beechcraft had vanished by the time a squad car arrived. Octavio Nelson heard about the landing from a friend in Narcotics at the county, and now he was beginning to believe that his punk informer was right: There was a plague on the marketplace.

He read over Ethan Bradley's report and wondered why anyone would bother killing poor Botones, a proud, self-made man—but still a small-time freelancer who couldn't move enough coke to keep a rock band on its feet for a week. And this kid Escandar, *¡Cristo!* Nelson had talked to a sister and learned Hilarión was muling to put himself through medical school. It was a lesson, all right, torching the car and leaving all the cash and jewels for the cops to find. But a lesson to whom? The kid was a nickel-and-dimer.

"It's getting nasty out there," Nelson said, tossing the files on Wilbur Pincus's desk.

"One Cuban, one Colombian—"

"Don't forget Redbirt."

"Right, and one Anglo."

"And coke is getting scarce," Nelson said, rising from his desk. "What's your mechanical mind tell you about all this?"

"That nobody big is getting hurt."

"Bravo," Nelson cheered.

"And that somebody big is sitting on a lot of cocaine—"

"A whole shitload," Nelson agreed.

"—and they will sell it," Pincus continued, "when the time and the market are just right."

Nelson grabbed a handful of cigars from a drawer. "Come on, sport, we've got work to do."

# Chapter 21

ALL THREE sat up front in the van. Manny drove. Moe sat on the passenger side, elbow out the window and a can of Budweiser on his lap. Chris Meadows sat directly behind them in a swiveling vinyl jump seat. The van was empty, except for a layer of cheap plastic taped to the floor and side panels. "Residue," Manny had explained tersely. "I don't want a single goddamn seed in this truck when we're through."

They headed west for nearly ninety minutes, Manny steering away from the interstate highway, the Palmetto Expressway and the Florida Turnpike. "You're a paranoid sumbitch—" Moe laughed.

"Every time I been stopped has been on a four-lane," Manny said. "Cops see me driving and something goes off in their heads."

"But we're clean now," Meadows ventured.

Manny glanced over at his partner.

"So all those rules were meant just for me," Meadows said dryly.

"You really think I'd come out here with no gun?" Manny sat forward, took one hand off the steering wheel and groped into the waistband of his pants. He withdrew a small, flat automatic and held it up for Meadows to see.

Moe burped, and Meadows got a faceful of hot, beery breath. "How about grabbing me another beer?" Moe crushed the empty can in one hand and heaved it out of the van. Meadows saw it bounce off a parked Cadillac.

"Ten points," Manny said.

The van turned west on the Tamiami Trail, a treacherous and ancient two-lane highway that bisected the steamy Florida Everglades. Only ten miles out of Miami, and nothing but darkness stretched ahead. Manny flicked on the brights and goosed the van up to seventy. Moe lit a joint.

Meadows fidgeted. He had agonized all day about making the trip, but as he had lain in bed with Patti, waiting for his midnight ride, he had acknowledged something to himself: He'd never been more excited. It was one sort of gratification to see a building born, story by story, until it filled a skyline with one man's vision. That was a pleasure, but it was meticulous, faultless, too damn well planned.

For what Meadows was doing now, there were no blueprints, no textbooks, no exactitude. Running the blockade was a project that demanded guile, skill and blind luck.

The architect's nerves were haywire.

"Tell me about Atlanta," Manny said.

"Muggy in the summer, wet in the winter," Meadows replied.

"He doesn't want a goddamn weather report," Moe said.

"Tell me about business. How was business?"

"Good, for a while. The cops up there are much different. They're—"

"Meaner," Moe interjected.

"Yeah."

Manny took the joint from Moe and sucked noisily. "How do you know about the Atlanta cops?" he asked Meadows. "Did you get popped up there?"

"No," Meadows said quickly. "Some friends did."

"Ha! Atlanta's nuthin. They got damn Nazi cops in Mississippi." Moe was blasting off.

"Tell Chris about the jail in Hattiesburg. With the dog."

"That was Meridian," Moe corrected.

Meadows leaned forward. Moe was beginning to mumble, and he could barely hear him over the engine. "What happened?"

"Aw, I got busted—this was three, four years back—I got busted for possession at an Allman Brothers concert."

"He was scared shitless," Manny said, handing the soggy last shred of the joint to Meadows, who passed it along to Moe.

"That's it for this one," he said, flicking the roach out the window. "Anyway, I got this ace lawyer who got me off all the charges. I bet I didn't even pull a week, but while I was in there, the cops raided a farm where this old geezer was growing grass as high as alfalfa.

"So the cops chop it down, except for a couple real small plants, which they bring into the station for a display."

"You're not serious."

"Yeah," Moe roared, "for the school kids. They gave a tour so that the kids could see what real marijuana looked like. It was terrific. They brought a whole line of 'em just past my cell and pointed me out as some kind of fuckin' criminal—"

"Which he is," Manny said.

"But that night," Moe went on, "the police chief's dog—he was a beagle—got up on the sill and ate the goddamn grass right off the planters. Chewed it right down to the stem."

Manny tapped the brakes as a behemoth tractor-trailer rig heading eastbound weaved briefly across the center line in front of them. "Shit," Manny said, punching the horn. "He's falling asleep."

Moe didn't notice. "Anyway, the chief comes in the next day and finds the pot plants all chewed to hell, and he knows what done it. So what does he do? He locks up the dog in one of the empty cells."

"What for?"

"He was afraid the thing was going to go crazy, berserk he said, from eating the grass. So he locked the dog up, pulled up a chair, got hisself some fried chicken . . . and waited."

"And?"

"And . . . nuthin!" Moe said. "The dog puked his guts out for about two hours, and that was that. The chief finally let him out after a couple of days."

Manny, still smiling at the story, turned right down an unmarked gravel road. "So what kind of action you looking for?" Moe asked.

"I don't know what you mean." Meadows chewed nervously at his lower lip. Now, without benefit of any passing headlights, he could see nothing but darkness on Moe's face.

Manny gave an impatient sigh. The van bounced over washboard ruts, and Meadows shifted his legs to brace himself.

"Man, you *know* what I'm talking about," Moe said. "What is it you're looking for?"

"I want to buy some coke," Meadows said, laboring for a matter-of-fact tone.

"Who doesn't?"

"I need a couple of pounds."

"What?" Manny hooted. "Your timing is fucking hilarious, man." He guided the van around a manhole-sized pock in the road. Hundreds of insects swirled about the headlights, casting a rush of dot-sized shadows before them.

"I don't get it," Meadows said.

"There ain't no coke to be had, at least not in those kinds of packages. The last couple of weeks has been as bad as I ever seen it. Wouldn't you say so?"

Manny nodded. "Some guys been in the business four years can't get any more than a couple ounces. It is fucking amazing."

"But why?" Meadows asked.

"I don't know for sure, but I got a theory," Manny said authoritatively. "It's the heat and the publicity. Too much goddamn violence down here. The governor and the DEA have been screaming about it at press conferences, all these crazy killings . . . I just think the wholesalers are laying low."

Moe groaned. "There's got to be a hundred warehouses full of paste down Colombia way."

Meadows's mind raced. "Then how do I get some?"

"You don't," Manny said coldly. "When things loosen up—and they will—the regulars will get first crack at the merchandise. The demand will be so great that the price will go up—"

"Naturally," Moe said laconically.

"—and there won't be much left for anyone else."

"I can pay for it. With cash," Meadows declared.

Manny tossed his head back and laughed without a trace of a smile. "Christ man, I can show you eighteen-year-old kids in Gucci Cadillacs who can pay for it in cash. That's nothing down here."

He pulled the van to the side of the dirt road and cut the engine abruptly. Meadows waited for the men to get out, but they did not move. From a few miles away drifted the diesel whine of a big semi on the Tamiami Trail. Around the van the night hummed with insects; ravenous clouds of Everglades mosquitoes bounced off the tinted windshield. Hundreds more poured through Moe's open window. He slapped frantically at his pale, thin arms, and Manny cackled.

"I don't suppose anybody brought bug spray?" Meadows asked feebly.

"Let's get out now," Manny said. He climbed down from the van and stretched his arms. Then he jogged in place for a few moments. "Much better," he announced.

"Manny, I can't take these goddamn mosquitoes," Moe cried.

"They like white meat, huh?"

"Don't we have anything to keep 'em away?"

"Just gasoline," Manny answered. "Works nicely, *chico*, if you don't mind rubbing off a couple layers of skin."

Meadows paced the road, waving his arms about his head. Better to be a moving target, he thought miserably. The buzz of hungry bugs filled his ears, and he could feel the little bastards snare in his hair. His shirt, a short-sleeved cotton tennis number, was soaked with sweat; the humidity must have been eighty-five percent.

"What now?" he asked Manny.

"Be patient." Manny squinted at his wristwatch, then up at the sky. The trace of a gray cloud line lay low over the western horizon, but overhead it was clear, the sky sprayed with brilliant stars. Meadows marveled at the unbroken flatness of the swamp, a burr of sawgrass for miles and miles. Far to the north was a small clump of trees, probably a cypress hammock. All around the men was a cacophony of frogs, insects and God only knew what else; to Meadows, the noise was getting louder and more menacing every minute.

"I think I heard something," Moe said. He hurried to the van and retrieved a small flashlight. Cautiously Meadows followed him about fifteen yards down the dirt road. Neither braved a step into the spongy sawgrass. Moe aimed the light, and the beam fixed on an opossum, lumbering awkwardly through the tangled grass. Its eyes shone a wine-bottle green in the light. It carried its prehensile tail in a curl off the ground. The fur was sparse, a mixture of snow and gray. It reminded Meadows of his grandfather's hair, the way it looked in the hospital when the old man was dying.

"You ever eat possum?" Moe asked.

Meadows shook his head.

"Niggers do all the time. When I was a kid, we used to shoot 'em with a twenty-two and sell 'em in blacktown for a dollar apiece. They use possums in stew."

"Never tried it."

"Me neither," Moe said.

The opossum seemed stuck in the bushes. It turned its head, mouth slack, and glared at the intruders. Meadows started back toward the van. "Hey, Carson!" Meadows turned to see Moe aiming a pistol at the animal.

"Are you nuts?"

"I bet I can knock its tail off."

Meadows didn't move. "Come on, Moe."

"I don't aim to kill it."

Meadows glanced down the road, searching for Manny.

"That tail looks like an eighteen-inch finger, don't it? I know some ladies who'd favor that, don't you?"

Meadows could only assume Moe was drunk or stoned, or both. Maybe even crazy. He spotted Manny's fireplug shadow near the van and whistled. Manny didn't hear him over the tree frogs.

"Hey, Manny!" Meadows called. "Look what Moe found!"

The gun went off. Meadows wheeled and backed away simultaneously. He saw the big orange spark when Moe fired again and smelled the rich wave of powder. Manny's urgent footsteps were not far behind.

"What are you doing?" he screeched breathlessly at his partner.

Moe shrugged. "I think I killed it by accident." He lowered the pistol with his right hand and raised the flashlight with his left. The opossum lay in a heap, tongue out, mouth foamy in death.

"You asshole," Manny hissed.

"Jeez, Manny, nobody can hear a thing way out here."

"If I see that gun again, one of us is leaving here alone tonight."

Moe was about to reply when he cocked his head and motioned with his gun hand. Manny heard the plane at the same moment. They sprinted toward the van. Meadows followed, still shaky, a few yards behind.

Manny vaulted into the driver's seat and flicked on the headlights. The sound of the aircraft drew nearer, but Meadows could see nothing overhead. The plane seemed to be circling.

"Two thousand feet," Moe whispered. He still gripped the pistol in one hand.

"There!" Manny said, pointing north. Meadows spotted the airplane's silhouette. All its lights were off.

"He sees us," Moe said assuringly.

"Where is he going to land?" Meadows asked.

"He's not."

Manny killed the headlights. The airplane wheeled lower and lower, dipping like a gull. Meadows guessed it to be a small Beechcraft or a twin-engine Cessna.

"Don't take your eyes off it," Manny commanded. Meadows followed the aircraft more by sound than by sight. He and Moe stood still by the van. Soon the plane was so low that the frogs and insects became silent. Meadows could see that the aircraft bore dark blue or green stripes and could barely discern the letter *N* on the tail.

"Banzai!" exclaimed Manny, pointing triumphantly as a bundle tumbled from a small door on the plane. Then came another and, very quickly, one more. Suddenly the pitch of the engine rose, and the airplane climbed rapidly, heading south.

"Moe, did you see where they landed?"

"Think so."

Manny took Meadows by the arm. "Chris, you come with me. Moe knows what to do now. I'll whistle if we need any help. And put that fucking piece away."

"Okay," Moe said. He slipped the gun back in his pants.

Manny crashed headlong through the sawgrass. Meadows followed tentatively, one eye on the ground and one eye on the bobbing white speck of Manny's flashlight. "Hurry! Move it," Manny yelled back at him.

They reached a small clearing. Meadows stood in cola-colored water over his ankles. His hands bled from stinging, invisible gashes; the sawgrass was murder. Manny handed him another flashlight.

"Point this at the ground and nowhere else. If you hear *anything* besides me, cut it off," he said. "We're looking for three bales. As soon as you find one, haul it back to the truck as fast as you can. If you hear Moe hit the horn, drop whatever you've got and run like hell."

Meadows was grateful for the darkness; Manny could not see the fear twisting his face. The sweat clinging to his chest and back suddenly felt cold.

They sloshed through the marsh for fifteen minutes. Meadows took each soggy step as if on fragile ice; he was sure that he would step on a water moccasin or kick a sleeping alligator. He stayed as close to Manny as he could, without actually following. Once he felt something brush lightly against his left leg and yelped. Whatever it was swam unseen in the water; the flashlight revealed nothing. Meadows thrashed furiously to scare it away.

"Over here," he heard Manny say.

Two bales lay within ten yards of each other. Manny hoisted one by its twine binding and handed it to Meadows. It weighed more than fifty pounds.

"How much is this worth?" he asked Manny.

"Not much," Manny grunted. "Maybe five, maybe ten grand. Just depends on where and on who."

Meadows was puzzled. "Then how can your boss afford to pay me five thousand dollars?"

"Because he's not interested in the grass." Manny stepped gingerly over a fallen cypress fence post. "We're carrying about a half million dollars' worth of cocaine. You can't see it because it's stashed in cans in the middle of these bales, where the cops would never think to look."

Meadows quickened his pace.

"If we get busted," Manny continued, "we get what? Maybe eighteen months for possession. Possession of what? Grass. The bales go right into the county incinerator, and no one gets burned for any heavy time. My boss is a smart man."

"Hold up a minute," Meadows said. "Let me catch my breath." In front of him, Manny stopped and set the bale down. The only sound was Meadows's breathing.

"I thought you said there was no cocaine around," he said finally.

"No, I said it was scarce. And I said you probably couldn't buy as much as you wanted."

"I want to buy some of this," Meadows blurted.

Manny didn't answer immediately. Meadows thought he could see him smiling. "This is not for sale."

"Why not?" Meadows demanded. His heart raced. He was so damn close.

"Because someone is waiting for it. It's been bought and paid for, you asshole. Don't tell me it works any different in Atlanta. This isn't a fucking flea market, Carson."

"I know, but—"

"You know what happens if a shipment turns up short," Manny said, lifting the bale again.

As they trudged toward the road, Meadows carefully appraised his options. It didn't take long. Running off with any of the cocaine would be fatally stupid; he would be shot as surely and casually as the opossum. Even if he got away, he had no car and no boat and, most important, no place to put the dope.

A second option was disarming his two partners and stealing both the shipment and the van. That would be brilliant, he thought grimly. What's a couple of more killers chasing you when you've already got some lunatic Cubans on your trail?

The third option was to shut up, comply with Manny's orders and hope for a there's-more-where-that-came-from handshake when it was over. That, Meadows concluded, was the wisest course.

"We'll put these in the van; then I'll go back and find the other one," Manny said.

Then he stopped in his tracks. Twenty yards away the van's horn sounded twice. Then they heard Moe crash into the swamp.

"Shit," Manny croaked. He dropped the bale, spun and raced back into the marsh, lifting his legs high to clear the water and grass. Meadows imitated in near panic. They stumbled for fifty yards before Manny stopped and dropped to one knee, wheezing like an old man. Meadows crouched beside him, and he saw the nine-millimeter automatic in Manny's right hand.

"*¡Cristo!*" Manny muttered. His voice was tense, his eyes moist and fierce. Meadows was close enough now to see the fear.

The Everglades were silent.

The architect's heart jackhammered against his ribs. He cursed himself for leaving Terry's pistol in his room.

Manny raised himself to a semicrouch and peered through the night toward the gravel road. He fanned the mosquitoes out of his eyes.

Meadows heard the sound of an automobile, the rocks crunching under rubber as it slowly approached. Manny ducked. The car stopped, and its engine cut off. A door slammed, then another.

Meadows heard several voices at once. He looked over at Manny apprehensively. The stocky young smuggler raised the handgun, tapped it against his cheek and smiled a rictus grin.

FOR HOURS THEY huddled together silently until Manny fell asleep in a fetal curl on a bed of matted sawgrass. Meadows crouched, knees in the warm muck, afraid to move. He strained to listen, but there were no sounds from the dirt road where the strange cars had stopped.

Hunters, Meadows prayed. But what could they be after out here? Rabbits, opossums, raccoons. Not much else. And hunters would be making noise; they would be shooting at *something*—rats, beer cans, maybe even Moe.

No, it has to be cops, Meadows decided, waiting for us to come out. He felt like pummeling Manny in his sleep.

Another airplane flew over, this one with its full complement of lights winking green and red as it descended toward Miami International. Meadows thought of Terry; she was due back in a week, and he couldn't wait to tell her everything.

If only he could get out of the Glades.

At dawn the sound of a car's ignition roused Meadows from a cramped and miserable nap. His pants were soaked with urine-warm marsh water. His arms itched feverishly; his flesh was a topographical disaster, welts everywhere.

Manny was awake, too. He lay still, his head on one arm, listening as the car drove off. "OK, Chris, let's move." His voice was raw. The steel-blue handgun was out again.

They crept toward the dirt road, pausing every five or six steps to listen. Suddenly Manny rose to his full height and leveled the gun toward a tall thicket.

"Don't move!" he ordered in a low voice that cut the morning stillness.

"Shit, Manny, put it away." It was Moe. He was a wreck; the insects had made a banquet out of his pale skin. His face was splotched with scarlet, a razor cut arced over one eye and his shirt was shredded at one sleeve.

Manny helped Moe to his feet, and they trudged toward the van with deliberate haste, Meadows trailing warily. There were no other cars or trucks on the dirt road, and soon the van was heading east on Tamiami Trail, back to the city. The sunrise spilled luminous pink over the Everglades, and flocks of cattle egrets rose out of the heavy grass.

"What in the hell happened?" Manny said finally.

"You guys saw the car, didn't you? I thought it was cops."

"Who were they?" Meadows asked.

"All I know is what I heard," Moe said. "As soon as I saw the head-lights, I dove into the grass and just laid there. I didn't move a fuck-ing muscle."

"We heard voices," Manny said.

"Yeah, yeah. Two guys and a chick. I think they were balling her all night."

Manny pounded his fists on the steering wheel. "And for that we spent six hours in the goddamn water? Jesus!" he mumbled furi-ously in Spanish.

Moe scratched a welt on his upper lip. "Look, man, I didn't know if they had guns or what. What was I supposed to do, ask 'em to wait a few minutes while we loaded some dope in the truck? Shit, they could've ripped us off, or killed us, or took the license tag and turned us in . . ."

Moe got a warm beer from the cooler and popped it open. "We could go back and look for the stuff," he suggested, "before it gets too light."

"No way," Manny said. "All it takes is one pilot flying a little too low, and we're had."

"Will Alonzo be pissed!" Moe was getting depressed.

Manny slipped on a pair of black wraparound sunglasses that reminded Meadows of the Tonton Macoutes in Port-au-Prince. "I'll be talking to Alonzo tonight," he said, "at Rennie's party. Chris, you like parties?"

Meadows shrugged. A few moments ago he had suppressed near jubilation at surviving the night and retreating safely. Now he was daunted by a terrible new fear. He could imagine this Alonzo, who-ever he was, fingering him as a conspirator. What if he didn't believe Manny's story? What if he suspected that the three of them had stashed the dope? *His* dope. Meadows realized he needed Manny's cunning now more than ever.

"You want to come tonight?"

"Sure," Meadows replied. "It beats another evening out there in the black lagoon."

"I think that's a damn good idea," Moe said, burping. "I think all of us ought to be there together."

They drove due east, and ahead of them the rising sun hung like a bright red egg. Manny flipped the visor down. "Don't sweat it, Moe," he said. "Alonzo understands this kind of thing. I've never fucked him over before." The words rang with a forced confidence. Meadows traced a quick glance with Moe.

"You'll like Rennie's party," Moe said.

# Chapter 22

"NASTY CUT."

Meadows's hand went to his face. He fingered the thin gash that traced a capital $C$ on his left cheek—a souvenir of his night in the swamp.

"Shaving?" asked Rennie McRae.

"Yeah."

The porky young lawyer guffawed, and his nose reddened. "Manny! Buy your friend a brand-new razor. An electric one, too." He shoved a fifty-dollar bill into Manny's right hand. "Your friend obviously has very bad hands," McRae said.

Meadows studied Manny for a cue. The Cuban took the money and shoved it in a pocket. "I'll buy him a good one," he said jovially, "and shave him myself next time."

McRae laughed appreciatively and waddled off to liven up his own party. Meadows polished off his Jack Daniel's in four hot gulps. He sat down alone on a sofa; he guessed at least a hundred people were in the apartment.

"Rennie's a very popular guy," Manny said. "He's a great lawyer, Carson. The man knows the law. Hell, he's kept me and Moe out on the streets."

"Then he must be a wizard."

Manny sagged down next to him. "Look at you, *idiota*. I take you to a fancy party, introduce you to important people, and you sit there like some kind of constipated—"

"I'm tired, OK?" Meadows scanned the crowd skittishly, afraid he would spot a familiar face.

Manny wrapped a taut arm around his shoulders. "You still bummed out from last night?"

193

"Oh, no, Manny, it was a ball. I've always wanted to spend the night in the Everglades with a billion mosquitoes sucking my blood, lying there in the water, waiting for some alligator to swim up and bite my nuts off. And what I really love is not getting paid for it."

Manny lifted his hands. "Hey, no dope, no money." He lighted a cigarette and leaned back. "We know where we dropped the stuff, and I bet we can find it again."

"Be my guest." Meadows sighed. "There's probably only about twenty-five DEA agents staking it out right now, waiting to see if we're stupid enough to come back."

"No," Manny said. "I don't think so. I'm telling Alonzo that we're going back. Maybe tonight, after the party?"

"Shit," Meadows groaned standing. "I'm getting a refill."

Meadows got up and started toward the bar. The people crammed into McRae's condominium were mostly young, tan and very loaded. The women were stunning and abundant. One look around the place told Meadows it cost at least $300,000. The carpeting was to thick it seemed to cover the tops of his shoes. On his way to the bar he passed a knot of chattering people; they hovered around a small table in the living room, chopping away at a small rock of coke presented elaborately on a silver tray. Moe was in line for his share.

"Fuckin' Manny has to show up two hours late," he was grumbling. "I coulda been into this stuff all night long if only we got here on time."

But Manny had been insistent. The party had started at ten, but he had not wanted to go until midnight. "I want to give Alonzo enough time to mellow out," he had explained. "He's much more agreeable after a couple of ludes."

It was a wonderful logic, Meadows reflected. He admired Manny in many ways, not the least of which was his finely tuned instinct for survival.

Meadows returned to the couch and waited for the summit with Alonzo. A slender woman with long dark legs and frizzy auburn hair sat next to him.

"Hi. My name is Jill."

"Hello, Chris Carson." Meadows shifted the drink to his left hand and held out his right, awkwardly.

"I fly for Southeastern."

Meadows smiled politely. Sweet Jesus, a stewardess. For a moment he wished he was back in the Everglades.

"I'm in real estate. I just moved down here. . . ."

"That's funny," Jill said. "I swear we've met before, here in Miami. Has your hair always been that long?"

"For a couple of years now." He turned away abruptly; his mind scrambled for an excuse to get up and leave.

"It was at a party out on Key Biscayne—"

"I don't think so," Meadows said curtly.

"You know the Clarks?"

"No," he lied. "Excuse me, please. I'm going to get another drink."

Meadows fled the room. His neck was damp with sweat. He racked his brain for any recollection of Jill Somebody but came up empty. He would have remembered her. She was mistaken, certainly, but it made Meadows edgy. It was just more bad luck.

Carrying a fresh Jack Daniel's he launched a search for a bathroom. He found a door, knocked twice and went in.

*"Buenas noches."*

Meadows started to back out. "Sorry."

"Don't go." The man was dark with a thick Pancho Villa mustache, porky, gregarious. He sat on the toilet with his pants up, a girl on each side.

"My name is Bobby," he offered. "This is Candy, and this is Maria. We were just having a quick hit. Want some?"

Meadows lifted his drink. "Better not," he said politely. "Thanks anyway."

"Come on, baby," said the girl name Maria. Meadows guessed her age at fifteen, tops. She wore designer jeans and a diaphanous halter top. Her nipples, Meadows mused through a fog of bourbon, looked like walnuts. She lifted a small mirror toward his face.

"Careful, careful," said Roberto Nelson.

Meadows set his glass down near the sink.

"One little toot," teased Maria.

Meadows nodded. "OK," he said, and instinctively turned to lock the door behind him. Instantly Roberto and the two girls whooped with laughter.

Meadows caught himself laughing along with them. "Well, you never know where you might find DEA," he joked.

A dumb move, he scolded himself. Thank God these clowns are too high to care.

Meadows took a rolled twenty-dollar bill from Roberto and snorted two short lines, tossing his head back. Roberto smiled a broad, perfect grin. "*Bueno,* eh?"

"*Sí,*" Meadows replied.

Then the coke kicked in, and the jolt was stunning. Suddenly Meadows could *hear* his heartbeat. He felt like swimming a thousand laps, jogging until he dropped, fucking himself unconscious. He felt, in a word, sensational.

Maria was trying to disco in the shower. Roberto joined her. Meadows feared that the two of them would become stuck in the stall or, worse, that Roberto would try to hump Maria standing up and the two of them would come crashing through the glass doors and kill everyone.

"Do you live in Miami?" Meadows asked the girl named Candy.

"Forget it," Roberto shouted from the shower. "She doesn't speak English, *amigo*. She's Colombian."

Candy smiled and nodded. Then she scooted over and stationed herself on Meadows's lap. There were three lines left on the mirror; Candy snorted all of them, one after the other. Then she started to sing, a high, off-key rendition of some long-lost *salsa* hit. Meadows's ears stung with each note. He felt hot. Although she couldn't have weighed more than ninety pounds, Candy sitting on his lap reminded Meadows that he'd best find an unoccupied bathroom as soon as possible. He squirmed from her featherweight embrace and made for the door.

"Thanks, man," he called to Roberto.

"For sure," Roberto answered. Through the dimpled glass of the shower door, Meadows could see Roberto's fat pink buttocks. The cheery Cuban's pants were at his ankles. Maria's giggles and sighs echoed off the tile as Meadows slipped out into the hallway.

The next door was locked. The one after that was ajar. Meadows gave a light rap with two knuckles.

"Come on in," boomed Rennie McRae. "Ah, Mr. Carson, sit down. Please."

McRae reclined behind a broad mahogany desk. A narrow shaft of white light from a typing lamp cast a bright sphere on the wood surface, where McRae's hands were at work. Meadows sat down across from him and waited for his eyes to adjust to the darkness.

McRae turned back to his task, barely glancing up at his nervous visitor. "I do this privately, Mr. Carson, because many of my friends are scared by the sight of needles." The lawyer used a small silver spoon to scrape flakes from a huge lump of cocaine. "I don't do this because I'm ashamed of it or because I'm afraid of the cops. This is my house."

McRae's voice was rising excitedly. Meadows watched uneasily as he flicked a small pocket lighter and steadied the spoonful of powder in the bluest tongue of the flame. McRae's hands began to shake feverishly, and Meadows thought he was about to drop the whole kit.

"I'll go through the motions of offering you some."

Meadows lifted a hand. "Thanks anyway."

McRae grinned. "This is excellent coke."

"Yes," Christopher Meadows said.

"Seventy-five percent pure. Of course, by the time it reaches our friends in Little Havana, the precious little disco swingers . . . well, the customers don't get quite the same quality. Let's just leave it at that."

"You're a dealer?"

"No, my friend. I'm the dealer's attorney. That's even better. I know faces I shouldn't know, names I should forget, dates I could never possibly recall under oath but could recite to you right now with absolute certainty. So I get a very good price on cocaine."

Meadows flinched at the sight of the syringe.

"I'm new down here," he said. "I guess Manny told you."

"He didn't have to," McRae said. Gingerly he slipped the needle into the melted coke and drew its syrup into the syringe. "I know *everybody* in Miami."

"Then you must speak Spanish."

"Sure. Who do you know? Just Manny, right?" McRae's laughter burst out like the low bark of a big Doberman. He knotted a burgundy necktie around his left arm, above the elbow. He gave Meadows a hard stare.

"Don't worry now. The needle is as clean as a whistle. I got it directly from my doctor." He chuckled again and smoothly inserted the needle into a fat vein. Meadows looked away squeamishly.

"My, my," the lawyer sighed. The needle lay on the desk. He swabbed at his arm with a cotton ball and rolled down his sleeve. "Jesus, that's good!"

Meadows started to stand, but McRae motioned him down. "I didn't invite you in here for a lesson in pharmacology." His voice was dry, and there was no laughter. "I heard about your camping trip last night. Real bad luck, huh?"

Meadows's jaw tightened. McRae lit a joint. He didn't offer it across the desk. "Manny's in some deep shit," he said evenly. "It's not your fault."

"With Alonzo?" Meadows's nerve jangled.

"Oh, yes, and worse than that." McRae's eyes moistened as the coke propelled him. He sucked deeply on the joint.

"Who else?"

"The names would mean nothing to you. They would mean nothing even in Atlanta. Alonzo, a shit, a lackey . . . the Diego brothers, even Ignacio."

Meadows's eyes flickered. "Why?"

"This is Manny's third fuck-up in as many months. Three strikes and you're out. Half a million in coke down the commode. You've got to understand what's been going down in Miami the last few weeks . . . everybody relies on such careful planning. Everything must be very precise."

"We know where it is," Meadows blurted. "I'm sure we can find it again."

"Settle down." McRae raised his hands amiably. "It's not your fault. I tell you this because you *are* new in town, and I'd hate to see you get in trouble so soon." The lawyer rolled his head back and forth. "Jesus H. Christ, this is wonderful."

"I don't know enough to get in trouble."

"Of course you don't. Didn't your friends give you any tips before they let you come down here?"

"They told me that a banker ran the show," Meadows said boldly. "A Cuban banker. That's all."

"You got smart friends. What else?"

"They said to thank God I wasn't a Colombian."

McRae roared. "That is priceless! Really."

"Rennie?"

Meadows turned lethargically in his chair. A beautiful blond woman with drowsy eyes stood at the door. "Sorry to interrupt."

"No, baby, come here," McRae said gently. He pulled her to his lap. "Mr. Carson, this is Donna. One of my secretaries."

"That's not entirely true," Donna said. She began to tickle Rennie McRae. He giggled like a four-year-old.

A pajama party, Meadows thought, just what I need.

"You been naughty, haven't you?" Donna teased. "You been cooking up the white powder in here."

"Please, please," McRae spluttered.

"Gimme some."

"It's all gone."

"Naughty boy. Stop pinching my tits."

They acted as if Meadows were invisible.

"Give me some powder," Donna said, leaning across McRae's vast lap. With authority she yanked one of the desk drawers, and it slid open.

Meadows froze. His eyes fixed on a sack of cocaine, a lump so big that it glistened in the dim light of the den. It was at least a pound.

McRae slammed the drawer. "Not now, baby, we have company. Don't worry, he says he is definitely *not* Colombian."

"That's good," Donna said, finally looking up at the architect. "You don't look Colombian."

"Damn right. He's breathing, isn't he?" McRae laughed until he wheezed. "Most of my clients are not fond of Colombians. Get off me, luv. I can't breathe."

The lawyer had surrendered all prudence to the cocaine. Meadows felt it was a good time to push even harder.

"Explain this Colombian thing."

"Greedy fucking peasants. Farmers! Moving in on the business. Surely you had trouble like that in Atlanta."

Meadows nodded. "Blacks and whites. Friendly southern competition."

"It isn't friendly down here. It's the Cubes and the Colombians," McRae said. "He tried to warn them. A little rip-off on one of their freighters a few months back. But it went bad, and they wound up killing one of the local boys. That led to an ugly thing in Coconut Grove—"

"I read about it."

"Damn shame," McRae said remorsefully. "Brought all kinds of heat."

Donna flung her brown arms around McRae's neck and gave him a long kiss. It was not long before they forgot about Christopher Meadows once more.

The architect stood quietly and edged toward the door. "Rennie, thanks for the warning," he said.

The chubby lawyer pried Donna loose momentarily. "Anytime, buddy. I hope you know what to do: Cut yourself loose, fast."

"I intend to," Meadows replied.

"No more camping trips."

He found a bathroom, then a fresh drink, and wandered out on the patio. A twenty-four-story shoe box over Brickell Avenue, Meadows thought sourly, designed by some fathead Swede. A $300,000 view. Across the water, the peach light of the sodium streetlamps glinted off the Seaquarium's geodesic dome, home of Flipper, the porpoise. To the north was the skyline, shining over the boulevard. It did not look grand and wonderful, Meadows admitted. He searched the towers for the Coral Key Bank. Soon his thoughts returned to the cocaine.

"Hey, Chris."

It was Jill.

"Are you pissed off at me or what?"

"No, of course not."

"You went for a drink and never came back."

Meadows smiled weakly. "Sorry. I got sidetracked with our host."

"Oh. Well, there's some guys looking for you."

Meadows quickly strode back inside. He found Manny and Moe in a corner and between them a gangly, coarse man pointing a smelly cigar. Meadows sat down next to Moe, and Manny introduced Alonzo.

The two Cubans jabbered at each other in Spanish. Meadows picked up only pieces of the exchange but was reassured by what he heard. "He's a good man," Manny was saying. "He was with us last night, and he didn't blow up."

Alonzo answered in English: "You men had some problems, eh?"

"We got spooked, is all," Moe said thickly.

"We got interrupted," said Manny.

"It was my fault," Moe continued. "I hit the horn 'cause I thought there was cops coming."

Alonzo said nothing.

"He did the right thing," Manny cut in. "There was another car. We couldn't see anything."

Alonzo tapped the cigar until a chunk of ash dropped into Rennie McRae's extravagant carpet.

"Chris, you were along for the first time?" Alonzo asked.

Meadows's tongue felt like sandpaper. "That's right."

"Ever done anything like that?"

"Not quite like that, no." They all laughed, but the tension did not dissipate.

"I can find all the stuff, Al," Manny volunteered after a brief silence. "Just give me a night or two."

Alonzo shook his head, and Manny responded urgently in Spanish.

"No, not now. There is to be a meeting." Alonzo switched to Spanish himself. "There will be no business for a few days. Everyone is to take some time off. The big man wants to put an end to the craziness."

Moe nudged Meadows and made an exaggerated shrug; he didn't understand a word. Meadows rolled his eyes, playing along, but strained to listen. He could tell Manny was angry.

"What good will a meeting do? Nothing will change. The Colombians are here, my friend. They want the business, they take the business. Mine, yours, the Diegos . . . we go to meetings while they go to the fucking bank."

"Quiet now," Alonzo said reproachfully. "How does a delivery boy become so wise?"

Manny was silent. Meadows felt his heart pounding.

"*El Jefe* is such a big shot," Manny argued, "he will never know if you let me sneak out there and find the stuff."

"And why wouldn't he?" Alonzo said coldly. "He knows that it's missing."

Manny rose and stalked off.

"Forgive me," Alonzo said in English. "A minor dispute. Moe?"

"Huh?"

"Sometimes your friend Manny has a very bad memory. He forgets who runs the show."

"Yeah, I understand," Moe said sullenly. "Al, I already said I'd take the blame."

"Blame is no longer important. Just see that Manny follows my advice. No deals for a while. At least until after the meeting this weekend. There will be important arrangements, I'm sure." Alonzo coughed a small cloud of blue smoke. "How well do you know Manny?" he asked Meadows.

"I just met him the other day." Meadows knew that Moe was paying close attention. "He seems OK."

Some of the party guests were crowing along to a Jimmy Buffett tape. Alonzo raised his voice to be heard. "Manny loses his temper sometimes. He gets impulsive. Don't get impulsive," he said. "Stay cool, and there will be more work coming your way."

Alonzo patted Meadows on the arm, and the architect smiled appreciatively. He made up his mind he would have nothing to do with any of them. The shadow game was over.

"What happens now?" Moe asked.

Alonzo shrugged. "They'll get it all straightened out, I guess. *Pargo con salsa verde,* and they'll split up the world over the *cafecitos. Dios,* nobody cooks snapper like Cumparsi."

"Cumparsi?" Meadows asked.

"A restaurant, man. You have to be Cuban to know about it." Alonzo moved his hand in circles over his belly. "No place like it in Little Havana."

Meadows needed an excuse to go back down the hall, and it took a few minutes to find it: Jill, standing by the bar with a Saab sales-man. Emboldened by the cocaine and the bourbon, Meadows put an arm around her waist and led her away. "My, aren't we friendly all of a sudden?" she said.

Meadows approached McRae's den and craned his neck around the half-open door. The room was empty. He could hear the lawyer's voice clear from the living room, bellowing the chorus of "Changes in Latitude, Changes in Attitude."

"Good," Meadows murmured. "A little privacy." He closed the door and twisted the lock. Jill stood with her arms at her side, look-ing up at him with a puzzled expression.

"I don't understand you," she said in a sultry whisper.

Meadows kissed her hand. "Take off your top. We haven't got much time.

They undressed hurriedly and made love on the carpet. Mead-ows moved mechanically, regretfully. His thoughts caromed from Mono to Terry to Octavio Nelson and, painfully, to Sandy Tilden. It was over in ten minutes, and he and Jill lay together briefly, damp and panting and covered with fuzz from the thick shag.

"That was nice," she said, too politely. "I've gotta get to a bath-room."

By the time Meadows could pull his trousers on Jill had already slipped out the door. Still shirtless, he hurried to Rennie McRae's desk. He found the cocaine in the same place, the top drawer on the left side. His hand already was on the plastic bag when he spot-ted the gun, hidden in the back of the drawer. Meadows recoiled as if it were a diamondback.

Meadows considered pocketing the chrome pistol but decided against it. The gun probably could be traced.

He lifted the bag of cocaine, twisted it shut and deftly tied off a half hitch in the neck. It was now a compact satchel roughly the size of a softball. Meadows was sure it was heavy enough to break glass if he threw it hard.

Meadows pawed through some drapes directly behind McRae's desk to a glass door that opened onto a small balcony. He unlocked the door and carried the coke outside into the humid night air. Peering over the railing, he gauged a target area. Seventeen stories below, he could make out an ixora hedge and, beyond that, a small tract of sodded land. There was a palm tree near a bench, which faced Biscayne Bay.

If the bag landed too far from the building, anyone walking along the waterfront might notice it. Meadows decided that it was the hedge or nothing. If he missed, a quick exit from McRae's party would be imperative so he could grab the dope before someone else did.

He scouted for pedestrians and saw no one. The only sounds were traffic from the boulevard and muffled music from the condominium. Meadows leaned over the railing and dropped the plastic bag of cocaine on a straight line with the ixora bushes. He heard them rustle when the bag landed, but he couldn't see it.

Meadows turned and took one step toward the glass door before he was paralyzed by the sight of a silhouette through the curtains. The figure was moving around the desk, making no effort at stealth. Meadows heard a man's voice, and his pulse hammered in his temples. It was McRae, looking for another fix.

The lawyer sagged into the chair at his desk and began foraging through the drawers. Through a crack in the drapes, Meadows had a clear view of the back of McRae's head, the ruddy bald spot at the crown. He could also see his own shirt, shoes and socks crumpled in the corner, and he prayed that McRae didn't.

"Goddammit!" the lawyer grunted.

Meadows held his breath. McRae fumbled through the top left drawer. He set the chrome-plated pistol on the desk with a crack. He was furious.

"Jesus fuckin' Christ!" McRae roared, lurching to his feet. Any second now he was going to see the clothes, and then he was going to search the room. . . . Meadows's nerves were strung tight as piano wire. His eyes swept the desktop and fixed on a paperweight, a large glass apple.

He slipped through the curtains and padded silently up to McRae, who was still facing the door. With his right hand, Meadows seized the back of the lawyer's moist neck and shoved him forward. The fat man's legs cracked against the desk, and he spilled face down, whimpering in confusion.

Meadows was rooted behind him, mashing McRae's face into the wood. The architect's left hand swiftly swept the pistol onto the carpet, then found the glass apple.

"What the fuck is going on?" McRae spluttered, wrenching his head to try to see his assailant.

But Meadows held on desperately. Clumsily he brought the glass apple crashing into the side of the lawyer's head. It was not a particularly forceful blow, and Meadows knew it. He was not left-handed.

McRae's hand grabbed at his arm, and frantically Meadows smashed McRae again. This time the paperweight exploded on impact. Meadows lost his grip, and McRae rolled off the desk and fell on the carpet, moaning. His eyes were closed, and his scalp was bleeding.

Miraculously Meadows's hand was not cut. He walked to the door and locked it.

McRae lay gurgling like a baby. With no small effort Meadows rolled him onto his belly. He tied a handkerchief around the lawyer's head as a blindfold.

Meadows hastily examined the injuries and decided McRae would live. His hair was gooey with blood, but all the lacerations seemed superficial. His breathing was deep, loud and almost regular.

Meadows dressed as fast as he could, his hands quaking so badly that he could hardly button his shirt. He checked McRae one more time. The battered lawyer seemed to be snoring. Meadows found the light switch and darkened the study before closing the door behind him.

He passed Jill in the living room and squeezed her waist. She was hitting on the car salesman again.

Moe was passed out under a glass coffee table. Meadows shook him by the shoulder, but it was no use. He looked around for Manny and found him on the sofa with Alonzo.

"I'm gonna take off," he said.

"I'm about ready myself," Manny said. "All the coke is gone, anyway. I'll walk down with you."

"That's OK; you go ahead and talk with Alonzo," Meadows said.

Alonzo got up. "We're finished anyway," he said. "Chris, it was nice meeting you."

"Same here."

"I'll get Moe," Manny said.

"OK, see you downstairs," Meadows said, heading for the door.

The building was designed with an elevator at the end of each hall. As loaded as they were, Manny and Moe surely would choose the one closest to McRae's condo. Meadows reasoned that if he could get there first and grab the elevator alone, it would give him a three- or four-minute lead time to find the cocaine and stash it. He would have a bigger margin if Manny wound up carrying Moe.

The elevator was on the tenth floor when Meadows pushed the button. He listened nervously for the sound of the door at McRae's apartment. When the elevator came, he strode in and mashed the Close button repeatedly.

When the door opened downstairs, Meadows dashed through the lobby into the parking lot. Stealthily he circled the building to the waterfront. He scanned the face of the co-op until he found the seventeenth-floor lights of McRae's condo. He searched the balcony for shadows and saw nothing. The den was still dark.

Meadows trotted to the ixora hedge and began to search, concentrating on an imaginary zone directly beneath McRae's balcony. He worked by the faint yellow light of the distant skyline. It was enough.

The bag of cocaine lay unbroken in a tangle of roots and leaves. Meadows retrieved it, checking it for leaks. Carrying it close to his body, belt level, he walked with deliberate nonchalance toward the parking lot.

One glance upstairs, and his pace quickened. The lights in Rennie McRae's study came on.

Meadows turned the corner of the building and sprinted for his car.

## Chapter 23

OCTAVIO NELSON WRAPPED a pillow around his head like a helmet.

"Octavio, wake up, *llamos*," his wife implored.

"Ten minutes," Nelson grunted.

"Now. Your brother's on the phone. I think you better talk to him."

Nelson staggered to the kitchen for coffee. Roberto could wait a few goddamn minutes. What was he doing calling up at nine o'clock on my day off? What was he doing calling up at all? That one Nelson knew.

Roberto didn't bother with hello. "Octavio, they put a bullet in my car."

"What a shame. Your fancy sedan?"

"Jesus, listen to me. I walked outside this morning, and there's a hole as big as a bowling ball in the door on the driver's side. I can put my fist through it. They must have used a cannon. Right in front of my house, Octavio!"

"You want me to make a report?"

"No, *hermano*." Roberto was whimpering now. "I want your help. They think I stole some stuff."

"Stuff?" Nelson seemed amused. "You mean cocaine?"

"At a party. Some lawyer had a pound or so stashed in his desk, and somebody ripped it off. They think I did it."

"Did you?"

"No! Christ, I'm not stupid, Octavio. I know these guys. I see them every day. I'm not about to fuck 'em out of their dope. I know what happens to people who do."

"Obviously they don't trust you, Roberto." The coffee burned in Nelson's stomach.

"I was in the room for about two minutes. With a chick. That was it."

"Sounds like a storybook romance," Nelson said.

"God, Octavio, I'm not jerking you around. These guys mean to kill me. You should see the car."

Nelson felt very tired. He almost hung up. "What do you want from me?"

"I've got to go out of town for a couple of days. I need a ride to the airport."

"Call a cab."

"They're probably watching the house. A taxi is no good. A taxi won't discourage them."

"Oh, but a police escort will? I see." Octavio Nelson was boiling. "Where are you?"

"At the house."

"Alone?"

"Almost," Roberto Nelson answered.

"Send her home. I'll be there in twenty minutes."

"Just like that?"

"Yeah. Don't go anywhere," Octavio Nelson ordered. Then he hung up and drained the last of the harsh, hot coffee.

A FILE WAS NO good unless it was neat.

That was one of Wilbur Pincus's convictions about organized police work, and that was why he always typed his notes. In a cardboard box in a suit closet of his apartment, there were forty or so spiral notebooks. All of Pincus's initial casework, long since reduced to typed memorandums.

Except for one. It was a blue notebook with the numbers 10-17-80 and the letters *WP* on the cover. Only half the pages were full, but the notes inside pertained to only one case.

Pincus knew the facts by heart; if it had ever gotten to court, he would have needed absolutely no coaching from the state attorney. Of course, it never did get to court, never would. . . .

There was a deal involving about ten pounds of cocaine. It was about to go down in a parking lot outside a suburban mall, fifteen minutes from Miami. Octavio Nelson got the tip from one of his "phone freaks" and decided on a lark to check it out. It was a long shot, so he didn't ask for a backup.

Pincus and Nelson waited ninety minutes, changing parking spots every now and then, circling the lot in Nelson's Dodge. A burgundy van arrived, and one man got out. He walked to another car, a blue Chevrolet Malibu, and used a key out of his pocket to open the trunk. He lifted an Adidas athletic bag, dark blue, closed the trunk and toted it back to the van.

"Let's go," Octavio Nelson said calmly, opening the door. The detectives briskly crossed the parking lot and approached the van.

*"Buenos días,"* Nelson greeted the driver.

*"Buenos días."*

Nelson flashed his badge. "I want to talk to you."

"Sure," the driver said. He was only nineteen or twenty. He wore a cranberry Dior tennis shirt and a pair of blue jeans. His sideburns were cut very high, and the modest shadow of a new mustache darkened his upper lip.

"Can I see a driver's license?" Nelson asked.

"I'm sorry, man. Don't have it with me." The kid shrugged and gave a forced laugh.

"I'm sorry, too," Nelson said. "What is your name?"

"Aristidio Cruz."

"Wilbur, start checking around the stores. Find out who owns the blue Malibu," Nelson said. "I'm going to talk to Mr. Cruz some more."

Pincus thought it would make more sense just to sit on the Malibu and wait for the owner, but he didn't say so. He pulled out his notebook and went into the shopping mall.

He wrote:

> *Interviewed D. Petri, W/M, DOB 4-3-50. Owns Danny's Pizza Shack. Says he doesn't know anything about Chevrolet in parking lot.*
>
> *Interviewed Susan Lesser, B/F, DOB 3-21-48. Stylist at Pep's Poodle Emporium, ph. 555-4457. Ms. Lesser says blue Malibu has been parked outside for at least two days. Doesn't know who it belongs to.*
>
> *Interviewed Joy Burns, W/F, DOB 8-8-52, ph. unk. Works as silkscreen operator at custom T-shirt booth. Says the blue*

*Chevrolet in quest. has been parked at mall at least two days. Ms. Burns says she is sure because her boyfriend noticed it one day when he picked her up from wk.*

Pincus walked out of the mall to tell his partner what he had learned. He saw a figure lying on the pavement near the burgundy van and broke into a run.

He later wrote:

> *Found subject, Aristidio Cruz, W/M, DOB unk., address unk., lying in parking lot bleeding profusely from head. He was unconscious and showed rapid breathing.*
>
> *Capt. Nelson stated that when he asked subject for identification, subj. suddenly opened the door to the van, which struck Capt. Nelson in chest and arms. Capt. Nelson stated that he ordered subj. Cruz to get out of the van and put his hands up, but that subj. Cruz attacked him with fists.*
>
> *Capt. Nelson further stated he struck subj. Cruz several times with his fists, which failed to subdue him. Capt. Nelson stated he then got his Kel-Lite and was forced to strike subj. Cruz numerous times before he could put the handcuffs on.*
>
> *Capt. Nelson asked me to call Metro Fire Rescue. A search of subj. van, Fl. tag JOG-737, produced: one Head tennis racket, three Wilson tennis balls, two towels, three (3) marijuana cigarettes and one Adidas athletic bag containing 8.7 pounds of white powder substance in plastic bags. (Substance later tested out as mixture of cocaine and lidocaine.)*
>
> *Subj. Cruz transported to Flagler Med. Center. Charged with resisting arrest w/violence and possession of controlled subst. w/intent to distribute.*

That's what Pincus meticulously wrote in the blue notebook. That is not precisely what found its way into the official arrest report or what the internal review board heard.

"Do me a favor," Nelson said that afternoon after the ambulance had left. "The headhunters are going to want to know if this was excessive force. Tell 'em you saw the guy come at me."

"But I didn't."

"Look, we just made the biggest coke bust this month. That Cruz guy is a scum. I got a file this big I can show you—"

"He can't be more than twenty years old," Pincus protested.

"Means nothing," Nelson said. "I got lots of work to do and I don't have the time to waste in all these goddamn 'use of force' hearings. I'm asking you to do me this one favor."

They had not been partners long enough to read each other's minds, or long enough to enjoy that peculiar we're-all-in-this-together bond. Pincus was wary, but he was also green.

"It's no big deal," Nelson said, "and someday you'll need me to do the same thing. That's just the way it works."

"OK," Pincus said after a few moments. "But there's one thing I don't understand. If this Cruz guy was so wild, where'd you get the time to run back to the car and grab the Kel-Lite?"

"Well," Nelson said, chewing on the end of his cigar, "that happened right after you went into the mall. Before he went nuts on me. I asked him if I could have a look in the van, and he said sure. That's when I got the flashlight."

"Then he came at you?"

"Right."

So Pincus hedged on the report, hedged even more when one of the internal review guys asked him what he saw and downright lied on his affidavit: "Subj. Cruz then attacked Capt. Nelson and began striking him as this officer approached scene. . . ."

Cruz himself gave a remarkably different version, but no one in the department seemed to pay much attention. Cruz was unable to give his statement for three months, until he was out of the hospital and the speech therapy had sufficiently progressed, and by that time almost everybody had forgotten about the case.

Wilbur Pincus was not one of them.

Over the months he added a few details and thoughts to what already was in that blue notebook:

> *Kel-Lite brand police flashlight. Wt. 6.5 pounds.*
> *Cruz medical charts, signed by Drs. Jacobsen and Krew, UM neurology, cites traumatic head injuries caused by rptd. blows.*
> *12-18-80. Resisting w/violence charges vs. Cruz dropped by Dade State Attorney Office per OK of Nelson.*

*2-10-81. Cruz coke trial pstpd. due to hospitalization of def.*

*4-7-81. Cruz enters negotiated plea of poss. of controlled sub-
stance in exchange for two-year max.*

*9-8-81. Cruz out w/time served.*

Long after the Cruz case was closed, Pincus continued to puzzle
over why Octavio Nelson needed his flashlight to search that van
on a day when the afternoon sun was like a torch.

One day, as he flipped again through his notes at home, Pincus
decided it was time to unpack the little Smith-Corona portable his
folks had given him when he had graduated from the academy. He
typed straight from the notebook, adding more details when they
came to his mind, correcting all mistakes with a patch of Eraso
type.

A file was no good unless it was neat.

OCTAVIO NELSON GLARED at his brother. "It's broken," he said.

"It's ninety degrees, Octavio."

"The air-conditioning has been shot for three years in this car. I
don't mind it anymore," Octavio Nelson said. "You want to get out
and call a limousine?"

Roberto Nelson shook his head. He scanned Biscayne Bay,
admiring the peacock sails of a small regatta tacking north. He did
not look directly at his brother; he knew there was going to be
another argument.

"Where is Suzanne?" Octavio Nelson demanded.

"New York," Roberto replied. "Maybe Montreal."

"Does she know you're leaving?"

"I left her a note. I'll be back by the weekend."

"Where are you going?"

"On business." Inwardly Roberto Nelson groaned. In front of
them the drawbridge rose on the MacArthur Causeway. A mam-
moth barge nuzzled by three smoky tugs waited in Miami Harbor
to cross through. Roberto Nelson would be trapped for at least fifteen minutes with his own brother, and he knew what was coming.

"Have you seen Mami lately?"

"No."

"She's looking better."

"Good." Roberto reached for the dial to the dashboard AM radio, but his brother seized him by the wrist.

"No," Octavio Nelson said disapprovingly. "If we listen to anything, we listen to that." He nodded at the General Electric police-band receiver. It was turned off. "You're in trouble, *hermano,* no?"

"*Sí, un poquito.*"

"Where are you going?"

"I'm not running way if that's what you think. Is that your theory? Cops got to have a theory, am I right?"

Octavio Nelson laughed contemptuously. Such an indignant fellow, his brother. So proud. And such a private person, so secretive.

"Mami asks about you all the time." He let it go until it settled in Roberto's eyes.

"What do you tell her?"

"I lie."

Roberto Nelson turned sharply and fixed on his brother for the first time.

"What do you tell her?" he repeated.

"That you're quite the entrepreneur, quite the import-export wizard."

Roberto turned away, flushed.

"She wondered, you know how Mami does sometimes, how her little boy could afford such a house. I told her you sell a billion dollars' worth of rattan furniture every year. I told her you're the *best* in Miami."

The bridge was down. Octavio Nelson punched the accelerator, and mercifully the car cooled with the breeze of its movement. They made the rest of the trip in silence.

As Octavio Nelson banked the old Dodge through the big curve into Miami International, he saw the five ungainly parking towers and thought of Christopher Meadows. Damn it, where was he? If he was walking around with a gun . . . Yesterday, out of desperation, Nelson had tried calling the girlfriend's place on Key Biscayne and then, on a wild chance, the architect's house in Coconut Grove. He'd gotten no answers. Meadows was underground, and Nelson was more than a little concerned about how and when he would come up for air.

His mind turned to other business: that Señora Lara who had called twice the past two days, both messages urgent, but neither leaving a return phone number. Something he'd want to know, she'd said. Well, there was plenty he wanted to know, starting with . . .

"This is fine."

"What?"

"You can drop me here," Roberto said.

Nelson eased the car to the curb under the orange and white Avianca Airlines sign. Roberto got out and struggled with the sticky back door until it squeaked open. He carefully lifted his suit bag and smoothed out the wrinkles. He closed the door and leaned over through the passenger window so abruptly that his sunglasses nearly slipped off.

"Thanks for the ride," Roberto said.

"Sure," said Octavio Nelson.

"I'll call you when I get back."

"Call a cab instead," growled the detective. "A cab with air-conditioning."

The two men parted, Roberto for the ticket counter and his brother for home.

The time was exactly 11:28 A.M.

This was meticulously recorded in a blue notebook by Detective Wilbur Pincus, sitting in his own car near the Eastern Airlines baggage stand, his mouth as dry as plywood as he watched the send-off.

# Chapter 24

"I'll try him again," Terry said. She slipped on a pair of clogs and snowshoed through the hot sand to where the public phone stood in the lee of the old brick lighthouse. A tender breeze off the sea rustled the coconut palms. The tide was high; the water, sparkling and fresh. It was an idyllic scene. Terry was not feeling idyllic.

"*Con el Capitán Nelson, por favor.*"

"*Es el que habla.*"

Terry switched to English.

"You are a hard man to locate, Captain. This is Señora Lara."

"Ah, yes. I got your messages, *señora,* but I have been very busy, in and out, and you didn't leave a number. How can I help you?"

"I have some information for you."

"Oh."

"About someone you're looking for."

"Yes." Nelson's response was flat, emotionless.

"In the *barrio,* people call him *el Jefe.*"

"Oh, a businessman, perhaps?"

"Don't play games, Captain. We both know what kind of business."

"*Bueno.* Tell me more."

"Not on the phone."

"How?"

Terry allowed a hint of impatience to creep into her voice. "If I give you this information, it must be in complete confidence."

"Of course."

"We must meet."

"All right."

"At Southland. Tonight at eight o'clock, in the main mall. Come alone."

"Very well. How will I know you?"

"You won't know me. I will know you."

*"Bueno."*

"One more thing, Captain."

"Yes?"

"*El Jefe* killed my brother. I want you to get him for me."


CHRIS MEADOWS LAY on his back, chin high, toasting in the afternoon sun. Terry slipped off the light shirt that covered the top of her white bikini and gazed at him with affection. The longer hair made a difference, and the resolved set of the face. Meadows had changed. The gentle, intellectual architect was there still, perhaps, but it was sunken into something leaner, tougher, something that tasted of recklessness and danger. With a delicious shiver Terry lay down beside him.

"He took the bait," she announced.

"Good." Meadows did not open his eyes. He might have been drowsing, but Terry knew better. Meadows was weighing angles, checking distances, building, demolishing and rebuilding a tower of deceit.

"I rehearsed so hard that I might have been a trifle theatric at the end," Terry ventured, "but I think it went well."

"Um."

"I am sure he'll come, and alone."

"Fine."

"He sounded very exotic, your Captain Nelson, very exciting; like someone I could really fall for."

"Yeah, right."

Terry sat up in exasperation. "Chris!" she rebuked. "I am not a rock or a grain of sand."

Meadows opened one baleful eye.

"Terry," he said in a way that made plain that was all he was going to say.

"You have never been ignored until you have been ignored by a lion." Terry snorted more in jealousy than petulance. "I am going for a swim."

THE PIECES WERE FALLING together nicely. It would not be the most beautiful structure he had ever designed, but it might be his most inspired, Meadows decided. Nothing of soaring beauty, but not a house of cards either. It did not have to be permanent, simply strong enough to endure one man-made storm.

There was still one vital arch missing, of course, but he would find that in time. One last arch should not be beyond the reach of T. Christopher Meadows, AIA, tempest maker.

It was only two days since he had fled the lawyer's party for Terry's apartment, stinking of sweat and excitement and gingerly carrying the satchel of stolen cocaine. Terry had been waiting, fresh and fetching in one of those long-sleeved dress shirts. And angry.

"Chris! It's three o'clock in the morning. Where have you been? Why weren't you here when I arrived?" Arms akimbo, hair tousled, legs planted like a boxer, she had surveyed him suspiciously from the doorway of the darkened bedroom, as though trying to decide whether to embrace him or slug him.

"What have you done to your hair? What happened to your face? What's in the bag?"

"Is there anything else, or can I say, 'Welcome home'? I wish you'd told me you were coming, but I'm glad you're here."

"I didn't know myself until this afternoon. Tell me what is going on, *carajo*."

"It's a long story."

The cocaine bag in hand, Meadows walked quickly to the tiny kitchen. Terry stalked after him. He poked through the refrigerator freezer compartment. Ice trays, a chicken, something in tin foil that looked like a fish, about a half dozen packages of frozen vegetables. He pulled one out from the bottom of the stack. Brussels sprouts. Perfect. He dumped the sprouts into the sink, fitted the cocaine into the box and restored it to its frozen home. Terry watched wide-eyed, momentarily stunned into silence.

"Now," said Meadows in satisfaction, "give me a big kiss and make a pot of coffee."

"I do not want any coffee, thank you, and I am through kissing you until you start making sense. What's in the box?"

"Cocaine."

That stopped her.

"Cocaine?" She echoed weakly.

"Like I said, it's a long story. Please make a pot of coffee." As Meadows went to shower away the taste of theft and stewardess, a clatter of pots and a monologue of rude Spanish bobbed in his wake.

As dispassionately as possible Meadows recounted what he jokingly called the "survival surrealism" that had climaxed with his theft of the cocaine. He left out only Patti and the stewardess. If Terry suspected, she said nothing, interrupting only once to suggest they climb into bed to be more comfortable. She listened quietly for a long time. *"Querido,"* she said finally as dawn tinged the Atlantic, "this is not like you. None of it."

"It's a bit like getting caught out in a bad storm, isn't it? You run and run, looking for a place to stay dry, but there isn't any. And after a while it suddenly occurs to you that being wet isn't so bad, that you might even come to enjoy it."

"Brrr!" Terry shivered dramatically and pulled the mauve sheet close around her. "Now what will you do?"

"Well," Meadows replied pensively, "I have nearly all the materials I need, so I think I will build a house for Señor Bermúdez and all his friends—a special kind of house."

"It would be easier if you were *latino,*" Terry said.

"Why?"

"Then you would kill them, one by one, until they were all dead and you felt very good."

Meadows laughed. "I'd rather do it the American way."

*"Bueno, mi amor."* Terry snuggled closer. Her fingers traced lightly across his chest, then danced slow circles around his navel. "You do it your way, and I will help you," she whispered. "But now you will help me, yes? Not too gently."

MEADOWS RAISED HIS arms above his head and rolled over onto his back on the crisp white towel. Adrenaline coursed through him. Things were moving now, moving well. But he would have to be careful. Meadows was juggling too many balls. No, not balls, grenades. If one of them slipped, they might all explode. Still, there was no other way. He had to take risks.

Manny and Moe and emptied-headed Patti were all risks. Chris Carson had dropped from their lives without a good-bye. What would they make of that? Would they conclude that the thin and nervous novice from Atlanta had stolen Rennie McRae's coke? Had McRae caught a glimpse of him, or would they simply puzzle it out once their systems had flushed away the fogging dope and alcohol? Once they knew, would they come looking? Meadows thought they probably would. He could not judge how well they would look, or how hard. It didn't matter. Ignore them. They were minnows, and he was fishing for shark. All Meadows needed was a little more time. If they came while he lay low in designing frenzy on Key Biscayne, too bad for them.

The cocaine itself also troubled Meadows. It was like a dead rat, lying there in Terry's refrigerator. Sooner or later it would smell. He had not wanted to involve Terry. Now there seemed no other way, and that troubled Meadows. Ignore that, too. Deep down, Meadows knew, she was tougher and stronger than he could ever be.

And so was Octavio Nelson. There was no way he could be ignored. Meadows would have to take him head-on. That would be a trial and a danger. Nelson was the foundation on which Meadows's structure of revenge had to rest. But could Meadows trust him? Probably not. Certainly not beyond the Cuban cop's own self-interest.

Meadows watched the coconut fronds rustle in a light breeze off the sea. The night before, he had paced the beaches of Key Biscayne with Terry and Arthur. Terry thought Nelson could be trusted in his promise to forget about the Mono killing. Arthur believed otherwise.

"Nelson is shrewd and mean, and he will use anything he's got on anybody he knows to get what he wants," Arthur had pronounced.

"But he is *latino*," Terry had objected. "If he gives his word, Arthur, then somehow he will keep it."

"Only if it's convenient."

Meadows had cocked half an ear to the debate around him on the deserted beach. He thought Arthur was right, but he had taken no side. Mono would be academic to the plan Meadows was devising. Nelson would see that. Even if he had lied to Arthur, events would persuade Nelson that the Mono killing was not worth pursuing.

With the right enticement, Meadows could snare Nelson and use him as calculatingly as Nelson had used Meadows at the funeral parlor. Locked away in Terry's apartment, Meadows had what Nelson wanted most: the lifelike sketches of a peasant, a man with a cauliflower ear and a double-faced bastard with a dazzling smile and a rose at his lapel. Or perhaps triple-faced. That flamboyant José L. Bermúdez and the faceless *Jefe* were the same man, Meadows knew without question. Was Bermúdez also "Ignacio" to some of his doper minions? Meadows thought back to McRae's avuncular lecture. McRae had said the name Ignacio with the same reverence some reserved for God or the president. *El Jefe*-Bermúdez-Ignacio. The name was as irrelevant as Mono. Whatever he was called, Meadows would destroy him.

The sketches were vital for that. He would scatter them like chum and watch Nelson rise in pursuit like a hungry swordfish. Meadows could afford to give away the identities that Nelson craved because he had more than that. Meadows knew that Bermúdez and the Colombian chieftains would meet in Miami to formalize their alliance. He had learned that from McRae. And from what Meadows had heard from Alonzo, he suspected the cocaine summit would be soon.

Meadows couldn't know for sure how soon until he found the missing arch. He would dedicate tomorrow to it. A two-hour search by telephone that morning had been fruitless. Meadows was sure Alonzo had said "Cumparsi's." He had said it was a restaurant, but Meadows had been unable to find it in the phone book or through Information.

"Cumparsi." Meadows rolled the name over his tongue. He must have heard it wrong. But it was close, surely. Still, there had been no listing under *Cu, Ca,* or *Co.* He had even checked the *G*'s and the *Q*'s.

Tomorrow he would look in earnest. A bell captain at one of the big hotels might know. Or one of Clara Jackson's colleagues at the *Journal*. If necessary, Meadows would drive block by block through Little Havana until he found it. After that it would only be a question of hammering the roof in place.

Meadows pushed himself to his feet on the sunny beach and walked toward where Terry swam, a pouting white speck in the warm blue sea.

# Chapter 25

MEADOWS HAD CHOSEN the shopping center for its anonymity. It lay like a huge, gap-toothed cash register at the juncture of two featureless highways south of the city, a palace of plastic and plasterboard. Two squat department stores anchored the monster to its asphalt peneplain. A broad mall, glass-roofed, a quarter of a mile long and lined by lesser shops, throbbed like a phallus between them. The mall had become middle-class suburbia's replacement for the neighborhood: Bored housewives rendezvoused breathlessly with sallow lovers on its benches; heart-attack victims sought rejuvenation on measured strolls along its floral carpet. Long-legged teenagers whose fathers had stolen hubcaps dueled silently with pimply store detectives for stereo tapes. Meadows hated the place, but he would use it, just as he would use Nelson, Terry and himself to destroy José Bermúdez. Chris Meadows had known the grip of compulsion before, but before, it had always been professional, a virus assuaged by an all-night stand at the designing board. The fever that enveloped him now was deeper-seated, more consuming. It left him cold with anger and cunning, and he wondered if he would ever purge it.

"I'm afraid I have a bit of stage fright," Terry admitted. They had been walking arm in arm through the crowded mall, a scouting foray. Now Meadows stopped and looked at Terry. She wore a denim skirt, a crisp white blouse and fisherman's sandals. She was ravishing.

"What is there to be nervous about? He looks just like the sketch I drew for you—a good-looking *Latino*. In this crowd he'll stand out like a gorilla. Besides"—Meadows grinned—"looking the way you do, he'll probably head right for you and figure if you're not the mysterious Señora Lara, then the hell with her."

"Don't be stupid. Suppose he doesn't want to talk to you?"

"He'll want to, don't worry."

"Maybe," Terry replied uncertainly, "but I feel just like I did before the curtain went up on the big play when I was in school."

"And when it did, I bet you were fine. What role did you play?"

"Pizarro."

"Pizarro the *conquistador*?"

"It was an all-girls school, *boludo*."

Perhaps as a slave to his conscience for all the trash he sold up front, the owner of the Book Baron in the Southland Mall had built a quiet room at the back of his shop reserved for Floridiana. Meadows had browsed there before, always alone. And he was alone again when he heard Terry approaching.

". . . and so, of course, everybody knows God must be Brazilian. Who else repairs at night all the mistakes we make by day?"

Octavio Nelson laughed. But when he stepped into the tiny room, his grin was only a formality.

"*Hola, amigo*," Nelson said to Meadows, hand outstretched, "how's the floor covering holding out?"

It was a bad moment for Meadows. Floor covering? What was he talking about? Meadows had summoned Nelson to talk about summary justice, not rugs. Then it came to him. A young *Latina*, lovely and importuning. A dead aunt and a rosary. Nelson was trying to throw him off-balance, the bastard.

"So that's your idea of surveillance, a lady in black," Meadows said. "She wasn't even around when I needed her."

"Neither was I, and I'm sorry," Nelson said. "One of my men got shot, and I had to go. There was no time to get you."

"Sure. Who got shot, Pincus?"

"No, unfortunately," Nelson muttered. "García. He works undercover. He was playing Wyatt Earp for some waitress at a doughnut shop, and he shot himself." Nelson looked at Meadows. "I didn't think you'd believe me."

Meadows stared back at him for a long moment, then sighed. "Shit," he said finally. "I think I do. It sounds too stupid to be a lie."

He glared at Nelson. "You know I could have been killed in that place. How would that have looked in your file, getting a witness murdered?"

Nelson gave him a look. "I said I was sorry."

"Sorry! You go chasing off to nursemaid some idiot while I'm waiting for a knife in my ribs?"

Nelson shook his head. "These things happen." He pretended to scan the titles on the shelves. "So how does it feel to swim with the sharks, Meadows?"

Meadows calmed down. "So far so good. I swim fast."

"You damn well better. Now what it is you have to tell me?"

"First," Meadows said, "tell me the status of the Mono case."

Nelson laughed, his cigar tilting. "*Coño.* Mono's ancient history. Nobody cares who killed that asshole. Didn't your friend Prim pass along the message?"

"What about Pincus? Pincus cares."

"Forget Pincus."

"You guys have been busy, I bet. Lots of killings, rip-offs. The cocaine is dried up," Meadows said casually. "Hardly a snort left in town."

Nelson said, "So you've done your homework."

Terry pawed distractingly at a book about orchids. She must have been biting her tongue to avoid asking about the floor covering remark and the unexplained "she." Meadows vowed to brain her if she interrupted now.

"Are Mono's two pals still hunting for me?"

"No way. I mean, if they bumped into you on the street and recognized you, they'd kill you on general principles. But they aren't looking for you." Nelson snorted. "They're busy as hell, raking in the overtime. And do you know something else? They're better than Mono ever was. Gun, knife, garrote, you name it. Slick as *sandía.*"

"Do you know who they are?"

"Not yet."

"And the big man. What was it you called him? *El Jefe?*"

Nelson shook his head.

"Jesus, it's not your year, is it?" Meadows scoffed.

"Chris," Terry blurted, "that's not fair."

It was Nelson who responded. "*No se preocupe, señorita.* He's right; there have been better times." Nelson turned to Meadows. "You finished gloating yet?"

"Tell me about Ignacio," the architect said.

Nelson whistled. "Now I *am* impressed. That's the street name for *el Jefe.* Where it comes from, I don't know."

"Does anybody know who he is?"

"Nobody I've busted. Believe me, I've tried everything to get the name. I've had some very serious discussions about it with some of these little pukes."

"I almost believe it," Meadows said grimly.

He almost gave it away then. He wanted to shout the name. He wanted to throw it like a saucer of spoiled milk into the face of the bitter cop who had so frightened and humiliated him.

Meadows fought back the urge. "I do have some things to tell you. That's why I had Terry call. I think the less you have to do with me officially, the better."

Nelson's eyebrows rose quizzically.

"I know who the new torpedoes are, Nelson," Meadows continued. "And I think I know who your mysterious Ignacio is."

Nelson jammed his hands in his pockets and said nothing. He would save the sarcasm for after the architect's little presentation.

"They were there at the funeral parlor, just like you said," Meadows went on. "I saw them all."

Suddenly Nelson was taut. "Why didn't you tell me? *Por Dios!*"

Meadows smiled. "You don't wait for me, I don't wait for you."

Nelson's dark face grew even darker, and fists balling, he stepped forward as Meadows faded back. Terry gasped. Simultaneously a voice spoke up: "Is this where I can find *River of Grass* by Marjorie Stoneman Douglas?"

She was the color of damp tobacco, elf-sized, with frizzy gray hair and a believer's mouth. Closer to seventy than anything else. Meadows didn't look, but he would have bet she was wearing sneakers.

"No," Nelson snapped.

"Do you work here, young man?" She turned to Meadows.

"No."

"Oh, dear! Well, I must have that book for Tuesday's ladies discussion group, and this is where Esther said she bought hers."

"Not here," said Nelson.

"Try outside," said Meadows.

"Well, this is the Floridiana section, isn't it?"

Terry was magnificent.

"You are in the right section, madam, but I am afraid the book is out of stock. We should have it next week. I'll be glad to save you a copy."

"Oh, that's too late," she said with a perplexed glance at Meadows and Nelson. She left as silently as she had come, and some of the sudden tension whooshed out behind her.

"What is this all about, *amigo*?"

"Part of it is about that long, boozy talk we had one night on my porch. It seems a long time ago."

"I remember."

"You said that you would kill *el Jefe* if you ever caught him, and I told you that would be wrong—but now I understand how you could feel that way. The law's too good for people like him, or too weak . . . but it's still all we've got, isn't it? I mean, without it, we'd be no different from them, would we?"

Nelson waited silently. Terry's eyes went from one man to the other.

"Well," Meadows said, "I'm going to give you this Ignacio, so you can put a real name to his face. But I'm going to do it my way. *¿Comprende?*"

"*You* are going to give *me* Ignacio?" A growl.

"That's right. With evidence. There will be a Colombian, too, maybe several."

"Gee, thanks. You want to borrow my badge?"

"I don't foresee any violence, but I will need some firepower at the right moment. I'm assuming you can lay it on quickly."

Nelson's cigar pitched onto the green linoleum floor.

"You're out of your goddamned mind," he said. "I don't believe this. Shit, you didn't know cocaine from coconuts the first time I saw you in the hospital. And the last time, outside the funeral home, you were scared enough to wet your fancy pants. And now you're telling me you're going to *deliver* a scumbag I have been chasing for nearly two years. You're acting like you got shot in the head, not the leg."

Again Terry intervened. "What he says is true, Captain. *De veras.*"

Nelson shifted his gaze to the girl. Could she be involved some-how? Where was Meadows's pipeline? He clawed at the left breast pocket of his guayabera for a fresh cigar.

"Look," he said more gently. "I know what you've been through, and I appreciate your wanting to help. But these people . . . they'll chew you up like cornflakes, Meadows. If you know who they are, tell me and I'll get them. You get out of town."

Meadows sighed impatiently. "No way," he said.

"Look, we'll do it nice and legal. I'll read them their rights in Spanish and English both, OK? Good old textbook justice."

"Did I say that's what I wanted?"

Nelson grumbled in exasperation. He ran his hand through rough black hair. He sucked glumly on the cigar.

"Nothing happens for a week, that's the deal," Meadows said sternly. "Your word of honor."

"Impossible. The pressure we're getting from the mayor's office is incredible. Murders are very bad for tourism, Meadows. You give me the names and I've got to move."

"No names. Sketches. You can't go out and arrest a soul with just a drawing for evidence, can you?"

Nelson bit down hard on the end of the cigar. He wished there was a place to spit in the bookstore.

"A week," Meadows continued, "and you'll have all that you need. The sketches will be delivered soon. I didn't bring them here because I didn't know how things would go."

"You're crazy. Both of you."

"Wait. You'll see. And when it's over, we'll all go out and cele-brate. We'll go to Cumparsi's."

"You keep surprising me, Meadows. Not many Anglos know about that place. It's a deal. Help me put this Ignacio away, and we'll go to La Cumparsita. My treat."

"Fair enough," Meadows smiled. Ssssnap. He felt the way Terry might after an all-night flight with the runway in view. The instru-ments were all in green. The gear was down and locked. All that remained was to bring it in.

"Can you tell me any more about what you're planning?" Nelson implored. "It would help me get set up."

"In a few days."

"Where do I find you in the meantime?"

"You don't. Stay away from me altogether. That is, if your career means anything to you at all. When the prosecutors ask afterward, you'll want to be able to say you didn't know anything about it until it happened. When I'm ready, Señora Lara will call."

"I sure hope you know what you're doing," Nelson said in a troubled voice.

"Oh, I do."

"Well, be careful with the pistol," Nelson said. He watched the words take the wind out of Christopher Meadows.

"What pistol?" Meadows asked hoarsely.

"The thirty-eight," Nelson replied. "Be real careful. I can tell you don't like guns."

Meadows swallowed hard. Terry was staring at him. "Here's some bedtime reading," he said abruptly, handing the cop a gaily wrapped package.

NELSON FELT DAZED. His head throbbed. He had gone to the shopping center without expectation. Señora Lara, he had decided, would be a crank or an angry wife who had read someplace that cops made good lays. Well, she had been spectacular. And the elliptical architect had been simply bewildering: castles in the air. Had Meadows flipped out? It would be tempting to believe that, but he hadn't seemed crazy—just single-minded and as idealistic as ever.

With a sigh Nelson wrestled open the glove compartment of the police Plymouth and dragged out the aspirin. Then he turned on the dome light and opened the package Meadows had given him.

The book was called *Shark Fishing in Florida Waters*. Nelson was about to toss it into the back seat when he felt the folded paper inside the cover.

There were three sheets: a peasant, a boxer with a bad ear and a man whose well-known grace and power seemed to leap off the page. When he fanned out the three sketches on the steering wheel before him, Octavio Nelson realized his hands were shaking.

LATER, AS THEY LAY in bed, Terry nibbled at Meadows's right ear. "I think you are brilliant, *querido*. But now that he has the sketches, do you really believe Nelson will wait for the week he promised you?"

"No, of course not. He might get Cauliflower Ear and the Peasant, and if he does, so much the better. But he won't get Bermúdez in a week—the man's wound his cocoon of legitimacy too tightly around him."

Terry was silent for a time.

"Chris, that pistol Nelson talked about," she said at last. "It's mine, isn't it?"

"Yes."

"How did he know about it?"

"I've been thinking about that. I think Nelson must have come here one day while you were flying and I was in Fort Lauderdale."

"If he knows about this apartment, then he probably also knows we are here right now."

"Yeah, but he won't bother us now. He has too much else on his plate. He'll wait to see how things develop."

Terry shivered.

"He scares me, Chris."

"He doesn't miss a thing. But for now at least, he's no threat."

"And your insistence on letting justice have its way with Bermúdez? Do you think Nelson believed it?"

"I hope so." Meadows left the second half of his response unspoken: I almost believed it myself.

Terry's fingers marched like soldiers with a mission along the inside of Meadows's thigh.

"Sometimes, *querido*," she whispered, "you scare me, too."

# Chapter 26

JOSÉ L. BERMÚDEZ pressed the button for the twentieth floor. His hand explored a breast pocket of his pale suit. The speech was still there. One of the secretaries would have to retype it before noon. He hit the 20 button again, and the elevator doors whispered together, then stopped.

A huge black hand had inserted itself.

Bermúdez hit the Door Open button. "I'm sorry," he said hastily. "I didn't see you."

"That's all right," a voice answered. A massive barn door of a black man strolled into the elevator. He wore a neat dark suit with a silvery tie on a French shirt. A lush, symmetrical Afro cut sprouted from his head. A finger the size of a small blackjack tapped the 19 button.

Bermúdez stared up at his early-morning companion.

"Excuse me," he said. "I can't help but asking, but do you play pro football?"

Arthur Prim smiled bashfully.

"I thought so! For the Dolphins, right?" Bermúdez was jubilant.

"The Steelers," Arthur said.

His eyes fell on the brown leather briefcase the banker carried. He studied it for a few seconds, then looked up at the indicator light as the elevator hummed toward the top of the building.

"The Steelers have a fine team," Bermúdez offered.

Arthur nodded confidently.

"I'm a Dolphins fan myself. I have season tickets on the forty," Bermúdez said. "I haven't missed a game in two years."

"Yeah?"

The elevator doors opened on the nineteenth floor.

Bermúdez suddenly set down the briefcase and extended his right hand. "I'm José Bermúdez," he said. "Nice to meet you."

Arthur Prim shook his hand. "I'm Terry Bradshaw," he said, stepping off.

FROM NIGHT TO NIGHT the dream changed little. Always the colors were brilliant, beginning with the crystal blue ocean.

Meadows was swimming offshore with a full, lazy breast stroke, his head out of the water. The beach was deserted except for two figures, a small girl with shoulder-length blond hair and a lovely tanned woman in a dark bathing suit. They were running hand in hand, and the sound of the girl's giggling and her mother's husky laughter drifted like music out to the architect. He paddled to shallower water until his feet met the grainy bottom. Standing upright, he shouted and waved happily with both arms.

The girl and the woman stopped running and waved back. The little one yelled something. Meadows put a hand to his right ear, to show that he was out of earshot. They strolled toward the water, and the little girl shouted again, this time cupping her tiny hands to her mouth.

Meadows was still too far to hear. He began to move out of the water, skating his legs against a mild undertow. "Just a minute," he shouted, but the words died in a mounting rush of engine noise.

Meadows scanned the clouds but found no airplane. Looking down the beach, he located the source of the roar, a red Ford Mustang. It churned along the water's edge, its fat tires spitting beach sand with the exhaust.

"Look out!" Meadows called to the woman and her daughter. But they would not take their eyes off him. They smiled and waved stupidly. Meadows pointed with both arms.

"Watch out for the car! Get in the water, hurry!"

Out of nowhere the little girl produced an ice cream cone and held it out, motioning for Meadows to come get his present. He thrashed toward the beach, and the splashing of his legs drowned in the earsplitting approach of the car, a blur now, one hundred yards and closing fast. Behind the windshield Meadows could see the forms, but not the faces, of two dark men.

The offshore current suddenly seemed to hug his midsection, driving him back a step. Using his arms, Meadows lifted each leg and pushed forward toward the beach. He knew he would never get there in time.

*Couldn't they see the car?*

The woman and the little blond girl watched him curiously, smiling. They thought he was clowning around, trying to make them laugh.

Meadows was only a few yards from shore when his legs buckled and his feet went out from under him, cleaned out by some invisible cross-block. He went down in slow motion, a horrid freeze-frame image of the girl, her mother and the speeding car locked in his eyes.

A terrible cry sprung from Meadows's lungs as he fell, but it died in his throat as his head went under.

*Run,* it said.

When he came up, the woman and her blond daughter lay in a broken, bloody heap on the beach. The red Mustang was stopped fifty yards away. The two men were unfurling a canary-colored beach towel to lie down on.

Meadows dug his fingers into the wet-cement sand and dragged himself out of the water, crying. He stood up, weaving, and made his way to where the bodies lay.

The little girl's eyes, as green as his own, seemed to stare past him into the boiling sun. Blood ran in thick trails from both nostrils.

Meadows fell to his knees, sick and dizzy. He keeled sideways, and his head hit the beach with no sound. He scrabbled pathetically at the packed sand, and he lifted two handfuls, letting the grains sprinkle down on his face and hair. He noticed that it was not sand at all, but something flaky and white.

"Cocaine," Meadows said aloud, closing his eyes. Dunes of cocaine.

The last thing he heard was the noise of a car being started.

He awoke, as always, damp in an acrid sweat and clutching for Terry. But her half of the bed was empty. Still trembling, Meadows shambled toward the kitchen, where he heard her voice on the phone. He folded himself into a hard-back chair at the table and tried to shake the dark fog of the dream.

"Yes, *señorita,* is this La Cumparsita? *Bueno.* I am calling for Señor Bermúdez . . . yes, yes, I am one of his secretaries." Terry giggled. "Oh, yes, he has several."

A real pro, Meadows thought proudly. She's perfect.

"Señor Bermúdez would like to verify his reservation for tonight . . . oh? Don't tell me he got it wrong again. Oh, my. Yes . . . certain. You're sure. *Sí.* Thank you very much."

Terry hung up. "How about some orange juice?" she asked.

Meadows nodded and started to talk.

"It's tomorrow night," she said solemnly. "Eight o'clock. And you were right. The reservations were in his name." Terry opened the refrigerator and began gathering the breakfast items. Meadows could not see her face but he heard her voice.

"It was just like you said," she murmured.

Meadows stood up and stretched so hard his elbow joints cracked audibly. He was wide awake.

THE YOUNG BLACK woman behind the counter beamed when she saw him. "It's been awhile, Christopher."

"Yes, Sally." Meadows smiled back. "You look terrific."

She shrugged. "I guess the jogging helps. Haven't seen you on the course lately. You been in town?"

"In and out," Meadows said casually. He started to mention the leg injury but thought better of it.

"What do you need?"

"There's a Cuban restaurant on Twenty-seventh Avenue near Seventh Street. It's called La Cumparsita. They are expanding the operation, and they'd like me to redesign the whole thing. Trouble is, they can't find the working papers."

"The owners?" Sally said. "Lord."

"Well, it's changed hands once or twice," Meadows said, groping. "I guess the blueprints got lost in the shuffle."

"Well, that's what your friendly county building department is for," she said. "Give me that address again."

Sally was back in five minutes with a sheath of yellowed papers that curled themselves at the edges when she tried to set them on the counter. Meadows peeled through them until he found the contract documents.

"I can make a copy for you," Sally offered. "Won't even charge you the twelve-dollar fee."

"It's up to twelve?" Meadows said with mock surprise. "I think I can handle that, Sally, but does it still take two weeks to get blue-prints duplicated?"

"At least. I can move you to the top of the waiting list."

"You're wonderful," Meadows said warmly. "But I'm afraid I need these today."

Sally looked puzzled. "Your clients are in a hurry, huh?"

"No, *I'm* in a hurry, Sal. This is going to be a real drag, and I'd like to polish it off as soon as possible. Get on to more exciting things."

"I can't remember the last time you did a restaurant," she remarked.

"Oh, I just don't brag about them like the other guys." He carried the drawings to a long table at the end of the room and spread the blueprints out. To keep the corners from springing up, Meadows laid his briefcase across the top edge and a chipped glass ash-tray across the bottom. He set an onionskin sketch pad on his lap and, with a finely sharpened No. 2 lead pencil, began to duplicate the working plans for La Cumparsita's restaurant. He'd never had much of a gift for guessing dimensions, so he used a slide rule to ensure that his freehand plans were true to scale.

The blueprints were dated February 17, 1957. Meadows winced. There was no telling what random changes had transformed the interior since then.

It was just a hole in the wall, Meadows mused. Sixty by thirty, table space. A small bar running twenty feet along the east wall. The kitchen was like a cell, ten by thirty with an exit.

The drawings indicated rest rooms at the south end, with a fire exit in between. There was a small room, three by three, next to the women's rest room. Meadows guessed it to be a pantry or janitor's closet.

He duplicated every detail, including the dimension of the lot, the parking area and the front easement, which faced busy Twenty-seventh Avenue. When he was done, he carried the papers back to Sally.

"It was good seeing you again," he said.

"You, too," she replied. "I like your hair like that."

Meadows felt himself redden.

"You want me to send the copies to your office?"

"What?"

Sally laughed. "I mean, you aren't going to work from *that,* are you?" She motioned to the sketch in his hand.

"Oh . . . no," Meadows fumbled. "This . . . this is just to fiddle around with until the blueprints come. I've been doing a lot of work at home lately."

Sally nodded.

"Yeah, send the copies to the office," Meadows said, heading toward the door, "as usual, Sally."

JOSÉ BERMÚDEZ TOOK one sip of thc Chablis and winced; his wife's hand tugged at his elbow.

"Please," she said in faultless English. "Act like it tastes fine."

"This is goat piss," Bermúdez muttered. He set the glass down and smiled across the table at Mayor Rubén Carrollo. To the mayor's right was a county commissioner; to his left, an executive from the University of Miami. Next to the executive was the publisher of the *Miami Journal,* J. B. Deene, accompanied by an editor whose name Bermúdez had already forgotten. It was quite a table of dignitaries.

"Your speech all prepared?" Carrollo asked.

Bermúdez nodded and tapped his chest. "Always I am a bit nervous when I have to talk to a big crowd."

"Better get used to it," Carrollo said, winking.

Donna Bermúdez beamed.

"Ladies and gentlemen . . ." The voice came from a stumpy red-faced man at a podium, not far across the hotel ballroom. Behind him, fastened to a ghastly green curtain, was a banner that said United Charities of Dade—Hop on the Bandwagon!

"I am proud to introduce our keynote speaker for today's kickoff luncheon."

Bermúdez speared a baby tomato in his salad and ate it off the fork. He looked around the ballroom and counted a half dozen people yawning. Already, he mused.

Carrollo leaned across the table and whispered, "I thought you handled yourself very well in Washington last week."

"Thank you," Bermúdez said. "I only told the truth."

"Of course."

"I cannot stop people from depositing money in my bank," he said. "What would happen if I asked every customer where he got his cash?"

Carrollo shook his head and reached for the wine. "I thought the questioning was very unfair. After everything you've done for this community."

Bermúdez seemed to be heating up. "I told them that what they wanted was impossible. I am a businessman, a banker, not a damned narcotics agent!"

". . . and, of course, we can thank him for the Downtown Community Center," boomed the man at the podium, "the Bayside Seniors' Park, and—in large part—for the children's leukemia wing at Flagler Memorial."

"Jesus," said Donna Bermúdez. "You've got a piece of lettuce on your suit." Her husband scowled and flicked it away.

"Ladies and gentlemen, this year's chairperson for the United Charities of Dade, Mr. José Bermúdez!"

Bermúdez rose, waved once to each side of the ballroom, then threaded his way through the tables toward the lectern. He waited for the applause to die, then slipped the speech from his inside suit pocket.

"We have had a most difficult year in Miami," he began. "Civil disturbances, a worrisome decline in beach tourism and unprecedented violence in the streets. Some of my dearest friends are considering leaving South Florida, but I have told them, and I will tell you: It is at times like this that we need each other the most. That, my friends, is what United Charities is all about. Friendship and need . . ."

"A very good speech," Mayor Carrollo said to Donna Bermúdez. "Did he write this himself?"

"Yes," she replied. "He stayed up last night working on it. This means a great deal to José."

"We are fortunate to have him," the mayor said warmly.

". . . and by giving generously, by working hand in hand, we can remedy many of the social ills that have plagued our community, and we can bind the painful wounds of racism, of alienation, of lawlessness . . ."

In the back of the ballroom two men stood together by a set of double doors through which uniformed waiters crashed every few seconds.

"So that's your man?" said the first one.

"Yes," said the second, swallowing hard.

"He don't look like a killer, but who does?"

"I want you to remember his face," the second man said.

"No sweat."

At the table the mayor touched the hand of Donna Bermúdez. "Did José tell you I plan to run for the State House?"

Mrs. Bermúdez stopped listening to her husband's speech and focused on Carrollo. "Yes, he did. We will do everything we can. You can count on us." She delivered the words momentously. The mayor took a deep breath and touched his heart graciously.

"He's almost done," said the first man in the back of the room. "Let's take off." He wished they had not come.

The second man did not move; each of Bermúdez's platitudes seemed worth a thought. The irony was splendid.

"And nobody knows better than those of us who came here to escape tyranny, to embrace freedom, to make our own way," Bermúdez concluded, "what opportunity is all about, what compassion is all about . . ."

"Let's go," the first man said impatiently. "Come on, Chris, before he recognizes me."

"Arthur," said the second man morosely, "he wouldn't know *me* any more than he knew Sandy. I could walk up to him now—"

"Don't even think of it."

"I could walk up to him right now and blow his head off, and even when I pulled the trigger, he wouldn't know what on earth was happening," Meadows said. "He wouldn't have a clue. That's the beauty of this whole thing."

Outside, Arthur Prim shuffled toward the car, distracted. Meadows pointed to a brown Seville parked in front of the hotel.

"Look at that. That's his car, Arthur, and look where it's parked. Blocking a whole cab lane!"

"Take it easy, man."

The heat rose in discernible waves off the sidewalks of Miami Beach. They crossed the street with a gaggle of old women, some toting open umbrellas to escape the sun. When they got to the rented Thunderbird, Meadows rolled down the electric windows to vent off the hot air. The two men stood by the car, waiting until it was bearable inside.

"I finally appreciate your problem," Arthur said to Meadows. "That guy in there—no cop would ever believe it."

"Do you?"

"Yeah."

"Even after what you just saw in the ballroom?"

"*Because* of what I just saw," Arthur said, clapping his huge hands together. "That's the good thing about growing up in Liberty City. I knew junkies that could make you believe they were preachers. To this day I think some of them were."

"This man is a murderer."

Arthur stopped laughing and ducked into the passenger side. "I know, man," he said.

Meadows drove them west toward the city. There was an FM station that played classical music, but his one-handed effort to find it on the car radio was futile.

Arthur idly opened the glove compartment and saw Terry's gun. "Why you keeping this here?"

"I thought it would look worse if it was under the seat," he stammered, "if I got stopped by a cop or something."

Arthur slouched back against the headrest and raised his eyes upward. "Lord help us."

"Jesus, what good would it do me in the trunk?"

"Are you still practicing?"

"Yes." After three afternoons of firing the pistol Meadows's arm ached below the elbow. He was developing a callus on the fleshy part of the palm of his hand. Progress, however, was evident: His aim was now more than adequate—if perforated beer cans were any testament. The .38 caliber Smith & Wesson was not yet a friend, but it was no longer a stranger.

"None of the goons were at the speech today."

"No," Meadows said. "I guess I shouldn't have expected them. Bermúdez isn't that stupid."

"That's OK," Arthur said. "From your descriptions, I think I'll know the motherfuckers as soon as I lay eyes on them."

Meadows glanced over at Arthur and smiled for the first time in a while. "They're hard to miss," he said, "but then so are you."

After crossing the Venetian Causeway to the mainland, Meadows headed south on the interstate toward Coconut Grove. "I meant to thank you for looking after the house."

Arthur shrugged. "I cleaned up what I could, drained the pool . . . shit, it was a mess. Never seen anything like that."

Meadows's jaw tightened. Arthur gazed out the windows as they whipped by Miami's abbreviated skyline. A few stubborn out-of-season buzzards circled the spire of the old downtown courthouse, lighting occasionally on a ledge over the jail.

"Chris, there are other ways to do it." Arthur gave his friend a hard look. This would be the last time to mention it.

"I want to do it this way," Meadows said.

"People die every day, man. Car accidents, suicides. People get drunk and drown."

Meadows shook his head. "No."

Arthur slapped Meadows on the knee. "OK. Your way."

Meadows guided the car down an exit ramp and decided to take the scenic route, shady Bayshore Drive. He thought fleetingly of driving by the house, just for a look, but discarded the idea. There was no time.

Soon the joggers and trendy cyclists outnumbered the automobiles. Purposely he slowed his speed and lowered the window. The breeze off the bay was a marvelous tonic; a bright fleet of bare-masted Sunfish rocked at anchor off Dinner Key.

"Why don't you let me off here?" Arthur said.

"I can give you a lift up to Grand Avenue."

"Naw, I'd just as soon walk. Do a little socializing."

Arthur squeezed out of the car at the next intersection. He lumbered around to the driver's side, heedless of traffic, and leaned over at Meadows's window. For a moment Meadows thought the big man was going to say one thing, but he said another.

"Well, it's going to be interesting."

"Yes."

A sports car behind the Thunderbird honked. Arthur bent over and slapped his ass in defiance. "Every fucking body is in a hurry," he said. "Me too. I gotta go shopping. Chris, be seeing you."

"Tomorrow night," Meadows said, touching the accelerator.

DONNA BERMÚDEZ HAD lots of shopping to do after the luncheon. The pool demanded new patio furniture, something that would not crack in the summer sun.

"Fine," José Bermúdez said. "You drop me off at the bank and go over to Mayfair for a few hours."

"Can't you take the afternoon off?" She flipped down the sun visor on the passenger side of the Seville and primped in the small mirror.

"No, I'm sorry. I've got calls to make." He turned the temperature control as low as it would go. The collar of his shirt was wet enough to wring by hand.

"It was a grand speech," Donna said proudly. "The mayor thinks you're really something."

"Our mayor is an *idiota*."

"José!"

Bermúdez reached across the car and let his hand wander up his wife's dress.

"How much can I spend today?"

"Not too much," he said, "but buy something nice."

She smiled and said nothing when his hand reached her panties.

"Don't forget the cocktail party tomorrow night. At Rubén's."

"I won't be able to make it," Bermúdez said, withdrawing. A county bus was stalled on the causeway in front of them; he could only guess how much the good people in the back row had seen.

"Why not? I was looking forward to it."

Bermúdez took a deep breath and feigned disappointment. "A customer is arriving from South America, and I must meet with him. He has a huge account with the bank, millions."

"How about afterward?"

"Donna, I'm afraid it will be another late evening. I'm sorry."

"So you'll miss dinner again," she said disapprovingly.

"Yes. The old fool insists on a restaurant in Little Havana. The food is wretched—they make the fish taste like tacos—but there is a waitress of his liking."

"Jesus," Donna Bermúdez hissed. "For that you miss a big party."

"Darling, have a little sympathy," José Bermúdez said through his teeth. "For me, the entire evening will be a terrible bore."

# Chapter 27

AVIANCA FLIGHT 6 from Bogotá and Medellín, scheduled to touch down at Miami International at four-thirty in the afternoon, was delayed an hour by bad weather. This was a matter of small consequence to Roberto Nelson; no one was meeting him at the airport. An hour one way or another was unimportant.

The airliner was dodging a small thunder cell over western Jamaica when Roberto finally persuaded the striking dark stewardess to scribble her name and phone number on a cocktail napkin.

"You are based out of Bogotá, no?"

"That's right."

"I travel there often," Roberto said.

"Oh? You are a businessman then?"

Roberto's teeth gleamed. "That's correct." He congratulated himself for splurging; it always paid to fly first class. The flight attendants in the coach section always seemed brusque, too busy to socialize.

"Will you be in Miami tonight?" he asked, wondering silently if Suzanne was home yet.

"No. It's a turnaround, I'm afraid. We go back to Colombia in two hours," she said with practiced disappointment. "Are you sure I can't get you something to eat or drink? You're the only passenger on the aircraft who didn't want supper."

Roberto patted his midsection. "Thanks anyway," he said, "but I feel a little queasy. I better wait till I get my feet back on solid ground." The flight attendant nodded sympathetically and glided down the aisle.

Queasy! Who wouldn't be? Roberto thought to himself. This was a survival mission, nothing less. That *hijo de puta* McRae and his fucking cocaine. Call *me* a thief!

Roberto seethed whenever he replayed the confrontation.

"I didn't rip you off, Rennie. I am not foolish."

"Two dumb lies," McRae had replied, his face swollen and beet-blotched. "There's no point in arguing. You've got a week to redeem yourself."

"But I didn't take it!"

McRae had waved him off with one hand. "You replace the stuff, and I forget about the inconvenience and the bump on my head. Now get out of my office before I kill you."

"You go fuck yourself," Roberto had said.

Then they'd blasted his Mercedes, and that was all the encouragement he'd needed. Foolish is what he would have been if he had ignored that kind of warning.

"I brought you something." It was Illeana, the stewardess. She held out a small plastic tray with a glass of water and a package of Alka-Seltzer tablets.

"You're very sweet, but I think I'll be OK when we land," Roberto said.

"We've got Dramamine, too."

"No, thanks," Roberto said, touching her hand.

He was dying for a double scotch, but that would have been stupid. His stomach actually was beginning to churn.


U.S. CUSTOMS Inspector W. K. Junior Hillings walked up to the athletic-looking blond man and tapped him lightly on the shoulder. The man folded the sports section of the *Miami Journal* and tucked it under one arm.

"Yes?"

"It just landed."

"Good. Let's go."

Hillings led Wilbur Pincus to an office overlooking the congested customs inspection lobby in the bottom level of Miami International. The first arrivals off Avianca 6 were queuing up behind some flight attendants from BOAC out of London.

From where Pincus sat, he had a clear view of each line. He noticed everyone whose luggage was marked with the orange and white flight tags of Avianca.

Roberto Nelson slung his suit bag across his back. He no longer cared about wrinkled clothes; his business was finished. The line before him moved slowly. His watch read 5:45. His stomach roiled.

Sourly Roberto thought how unpleasant the next few days were going to be. Afterward, he would eat a whole pig.

"Excuse me, sir." A man in a government uniform with a small silver badge touched Roberto's arm. "Could you come with me, please?"

"Sure," Roberto Nelson said amiably, "but I really don't want to lose my place in line."

"Oh, don't worry," Junior Hillings said.

Roberto followed him to a small stale room where two other inspectors waited impassively. Hillings closed the door. "We're going to search your luggage," he said.

"Can I ask why?"

"Just routine," said one of the other officers, a huge red-haired man who was built like a refrigerator. He took the suit bag from Roberto Nelson and laid it on a table. Roberto shrugged and sat down in a chair.

"Please," Hillings said, "you're going to have to stand up for a body search."

Roberto scowled. He rose and, facing the wall, spread his legs, leaned forward and braced his hands high over his head. "I believe this is the proper position," he said snidely over his shoulder.

"Oh, that's fine," Hillings said politely, "but let's try it with your clothes off. Please."

"No!" Roberto wheeled, reddening. The third inspector, a lean black man with biceps like bread loaves, took a step forward and squared his weight like a boxer.

"Mr. Nelson, if you don't cooperate, there will be a lot of trouble and paperwork for everybody." Hillings sighed.

"I'm an American citizen!"

"Naturalized American citizen," Hillings corrected, waving Roberto's passport. "It doesn't matter. By law we could do a body search on Nancy Reagan if we wanted."

"Take off your clothes," said the red-haired man.

"I want a lawyer."

Hillings shrugged. "You're wasting your time. We can keep you tied up for days."

Roberto quavered; that would be a disaster.

"OK," he said after several moments. His stubby, thick fingers fumbled at the buttons of his white silk shirt. "But make it quick if you can. It's Saturday night, and I got to meet some people. You understand, don't you?"

Seconds later Roberto's shirt, socks, Brittania jeans, snakeskin belt and Dingo boots were on the table. A gold digital watch, a heavy bracelet with the initials *RN* and three rings—one set with an emerald—were placed in a bag and sealed. The black customs inspector was examining Roberto's neck chain with its fourteen-carat pendant, a solid gold razor blade. He held it up and dangled it for Hillings to see.

Roberto was naked, spread-eagled again. His jaw set and he fought to keep his eyes from watering. He could feel the warm breath of the red-haired customs man on his back. It made his body hair prickle and stand up.

The inspector checked behind Roberto's ears, then inside them. He felt Roberto's armpits, wiping his hands afterward on a paper towel.

"Take one step back, please," he directed. "Now bend over."

Roberto whimpered, and the bitter thought of his brother seized his mind. For this he would never forgive Octavio.

The red-haired customs man spread Roberto's buttocks and examined his rectum. Bent over like a football player at scrimmage, Roberto felt dizzy. The customs man seemed to be taking his time.

"I don't feel very good," Roberto said.

"We're almost done," Hillings told him.

Roberto cringed and felt himself shrink when the inspector touched his scrotum to lift his testicles.

"Jesus," he cried. "Be careful."

"That's all," Hillings said. "You can get dressed now and take a seat."

Roberto's suit bag was open on the table. He dressed hastily, stepping into his jeans so clumsily that he almost ripped the seat out. He felt hot; his mustache was damp and salty.

The black inspector was studying a wide florid necktie. He laid it flat on the table and ran his hands across, smoothing the fabric.

"I think we ought to open this up," he said. He handed the tie to Hillings, who examined it and shook his head.

"No, it's OK. Anything else?"

"No."

"Did you check the boots?"

"The heels are OK," the black inspector reported.

"Mr. Nelson, are you declaring anything upon reentry into the United States?"

"You've got the form I filled out on the plane, so you know the answer," Roberto said.

"Did you buy this tie in Colombia?"

"Hell, no, I got it at J. C. Penney's in Miami Beach. Sorry if you're not crazy about the style."

"Excuse me," Hillings said, walking out of the room.

Pincus was pacing in an office down the hall. It was so stuffy that he had taken the unusual liberty of loosening his tie and unbuttoning his shirt.

Hillings walked in and said, "Nelson's clean."

Pincus sagged against a desk, knocking over somebody's framed picture of the wife and kids. "Did you check . . ."

"We checked everywhere, Wil. His mouth, his ears, his asshole."

"His hair. Did you check his hair?"

"Christ," Hillings said. "How much could you carry on your scalp? Come on, man, I know the difference between dandruff and cocaine. This is my job, remember? I do this five goddamn days a week. The man is clean. We gotta let him go or all of us are going to court."

"Shit," Pincus said. "It doesn't make sense."

Through the window he spotted Roberto Nelson, huffing across the lobby with his suit bag.

"I better go," Pincus said, rising. "Junior, thanks for the favor. I swear I thought he was muling."

"It's OK, Wil," Hillings said. "Who is this guy, anyway—some dirtbag or a big shot?"

"A little of both."

Pincus saw Roberto clear the double doors of the Customs exit, and he followed, striding quickly. Automatically the doors closed. Seconds later Pincus walked through them into the steaming underground transportation plaza. Roberto Nelson was not in sight.

The curb was packed with people, yammering at porters in a variety of languages. Taxis careered heedlessly through the throngs; buses groaned and farted as they lurched through the insane traffic. The atmosphere was thick with carbon monoxide and sweat.

The taxi lines were long; Pincus guessed that Roberto was hunting for the shortest one. The detective quick-stepped through the crowds, watching for a porcine profile with a brown suit bag over the shoulder.

After five minutes he decided it was hopeless and gave up. Roberto Nelson most likely was going home anyway. Pincus knew where to find him.

But what if somebody were meeting him? That, Pincus brooded, would be most significant. Especially if the somebody was his brother, Octavio. If that was the case, Roberto probably was already long gone.

Pincus headed toward his car, parked in the short-term lot across from the customs waiting area. He had deftly negotiated two treacherous lines of outbound airport traffic when he heard the screams of a young woman.

Pincus broke into a sprint. The cries bounced off the concrete. Probably a goddamn purse job, the detective thought. He fumbled in his jacket for his City of Miami badge and ID. He hoped it would be sufficient to prevent the airport security people from shooting at him while he ran.

A crescendo of automobile horns told Pincus the trouble was no more than fifty yards away. A logjam of baggage-toting travelers clogged one of the taxi stands, forming a disorderly circle. Pincus decided to leave his pistol in the shoulder holster; you never knew when some itchy-fingered nut would try to use it on you.

Panting, he threaded his way through the crowd. "Police officer, excuse me . . . police officer, please let me through . . . police officer . . ."

"Get an ambulance!" A woman shouted. "Somebody's been hit by a cab."

Pincus broke through. He flashed his badge at an airport security man, who eagerly deferred, pointing at a figure prone on the pavement near a black and orange taxi.

Pincus wordlessly knelt next to Roberto Nelson and felt the chubby neck for a pulse. He found one, but it was weak. Pincus rolled him over on his back.

Roberto saw the end of the world through half-open eyes; the lids fluttered erratically, almost comically. His mouth frothed, and his neatly clipped mustache was flecked with drool. His cheeks were hot.

"Mister, I did not do." It was the cabdriver, a lanky Haitian with tears in his eyes. "I promise, I did not do. The man, he fell down in front of my taxi car."

Pincus raised a hand and nodded. "Can we get a doctor here? Somebody!" No one in the crowd volunteered, and the airport security guard ran off for help.

Pincus leaned over and spoke crisply into Roberto Nelson's right ear. "Roberto, can you hear me? I'm a policeman. Can you hear me?"

Roberto's jaw moved up and down. Only a gurgle came out. His body became stiff, and he began to writhe sideways on the pavement, his flesh grating over the dirt and small rocks. Pincus stretched himself across and lowered the full measure of his weight, but Roberto continued to thrash beneath him.

"It's epilepsy," somebody in the crowd said.

Pincus pinioned Roberto's arms to his side and held on with all his strength. Then the man became still. The raspy breathing stopped, and Roberto's eyes rolled back in his head like stained eggs.

A woman in the crowd whispered, "My God."

Wilbur Pincus had seen enough to know it was futile, but he pounded and pounded on Roberto Nelson's chest until the ambulance came and the paramedics told him what a good try it had been.

# Chapter 28

HIS NAME was Victor, and he was a man of opulent appetites and impeccable taste. Some said he was Basque. Others thought he was Greek. How he had come to Miami, no one could say, but it clearly was not his first port of call. Among his languages, Victor counted English, Greek, French, Cantonese and a Spanish of indeterminate origin. Argentine, perhaps.

Victor was a hideous figure, over three hundred pounds and bald as a balloon. He loved truffles, scallops and young boys, usually in that order, but that was largely a matter between Victor and the dark Cuban youths who came and went in his kitchen.

That Victor was not better known in Miami was a matter of unspoken conspiracy among the Cuban professionals who frequented La Cumparsita. Victor was, they recognized intuitively, one restaurant critic away from chic Anglo hordes who slummed in the *barrio* in their fractured Spanish the way another generation of fashionable whites once cruised Harlem.

Either you knew about La Cumparsita or you didn't. His customers preferred it that way, and so did Victor. There was a menu, but it was only in Spanish, and only first-timers ever consulted it. All others trusted in Victor. He practiced personal service, and some said that merely the sight of him waddling over in a maroon velvet tuxedo to tout that night's specialties was worth the startling prices he charged for them.

It was a small restaurant, but Victor had resisted the temptation to expand. The self-impressed diners made him money enough, and his kitchen rewarded him with everything else he needed.

Victor was in fact a Shanghai-born White Russian who traveled on a Panamanian passport of doubtful provenance. But it had served him well in all corners of the earth, and everywhere he had gone he had massively sampled the cuisine and carefully studied the ambience in which it was served.

La Cumparsita, whose stake he had acquired in a brief liaison with an Austrian woman of more money than sense, was a blending of all Victor had learned.

He had chosen a quiet side street for his dream, in the *barrio* to be sure, but one tree-lined step removed from the bustle of Southwest Eighth Street. He had screened the parking lot from the restaurant with a thick hedge of southern pine breached by the single flagstone path. La Cumparsita itself Victor had divided into two distinct beings, each with its own atmosphere.

Running along most of the left side of the building and reached by a door toward the rear was a discreet bar. It was dark enough for lovers and friendly enough to soothe hungry customers waiting for tables inside.

The main dining room, twelve carefully arranged tables, was Victor's masterpiece. It combined the atmosphere of a rich man's club with the air of bounty and quality. From France had come the idea of wicker baskets with colorful assortments of fruits and vegetables. They faced diners as they came through the carved oak door marked only by a small sign in engraved bronze.

To the left stood a large freezer with eye-level glass panels, a copy of one Victor had once seen in Buenos Aires. Thick sides of beef, racks of lamb and hanging ducks awaited a master's touch. The freezer's complement to the right of the entrance was a lobster pool and a salt-water tank where Victor's Catch of the Day whiled away their last few minutes. Order snapper, or pompano, or yellow tail, and a smiling chef in a tall hat—or Victor himself if you were an important customer—would gracefully scoop it from the tank with a net. Victor thought of the fish tank as his Hong Kong standby. Keeping the fish alive was tricky and tedious, and the tank cost him the earth, but it was worth its weight in gold.

The restaurant décor was elegant and subtle: pewterware, goblets, English crystal and damask tablecloths. Candles at each table in silver holders. The chairs were cushioned wicker, as plush as the service, as ample as the portions.

Victor had a genius for plants, and he moved them around to shed privacy or fantasy as whim and circumstance demanded. That night he had built a screen of potted palms in the far corner of the room, obscuring the last table there from all but the most determined gaze. That would be Señor Bermúdez's table.

Victor treasured his patronage; it was like an imprimature among the Cuban elite. Sometimes Bermúdez came with his family and was expansive, table-hopping, ordering champagne for his friend there, brandy for that happy couple there.

Other times, like tonight, he demanded privacy. A large table, but set for two, he had said; his guest would be a distinguished foreign visitor whose good will meant millions for Miami. Bermúdez had politely listened to Victor's suggestions and then ordered what he always ordered: Maine lobster cocktail, hearts of palm salad, blanquette de veau, a Lafite Bordeaux 1970, mineral water. For dessert he would eat Danish bleu with English biscuits and a ripe pear. Then he would drink Courvoisier and espresso until midnight.

Victor cast his eye down the list of reservations. Bermúdez would be the undisputed VIP that night. The rest were regulars with two exceptions, a rough-sounding man named Gómez, who had asked for a table for four, and a Señora Lara, who had sounded delightful and said she had been recommended by a Mexican diplomat who came regularly once a month with his mistress. She'd booked a table for two and asked for a window. On a routine Thursday night such as this, it would be no problem. Victor smiled benignly at a sad-eyed grouper in the sparkling tank and lumbered into the kitchen to check on his newest dishwasher. He was newly arrived from Cuba and a trifle skittish, poor dear.

JOSÉ BERMÚDEZ wondered moodily whether there was any such thing as a perfect rose. He had ordered a dozen, to be sure of getting one he liked, and still he was not satisfied. On close examination they all were flawed in some tiny way. He would change florists. Choosing the least offensive among them, Bermúdez meticulously affixed it to his lapel. The splash of yellow winked cheerfully from the gray sharkskin. Bermúdez smiled at the hall mirror, which obligingly confirmed his eminence. He was ready then, ready for the elegant dinner that would climax all the work, all the planning, all the years of posturing in a country that was not his own.

Market forces. How the *gringos* loved to talk about their precious market forces. At business school, at the bank, that was all they ever talked about. *Idiotas*. They would drown, mewling like doomed kittens, clutching helplessly at the straw of private enterprise and the market system. How stupid they were. Even after what the Arabs had done to them, even after the smelly Semites in their absurd burnooses had milked them dry, the *gringos* did not understand. Competition was as obsolete as democracy. The twenty-first century would be the age of the cartel, the unforgettable era of the new monopolists, when men who were strong and farsighted and, yes, ruthless would control the globe. And José Bermúdez would be one of them. Beginning tonight, at dinner with the jaded Colombian patriarch.

The old man was essential for now. He was powerful, smart and dangerous. He would make an instructive partner until, a year or two from now, Bermúdez was strong enough to devour him. Then, like a line of tumbling dominoes, the pace would quicken. His five-year plan was to monopolize a steady flow of cocaine into the United States from a seat in the United States Senate he would purchase with cocaine money. In the five years after that . . . well, anything was possible—wasn't it?—in the land of free enterprise. The mirror returned Bermúdez's broadest smile.

The Colombian could have no cause for complaint tonight. Bermúdez's promised destruction of the cocaine competition in Miami had been as smooth as the skin of the old man's flower girls and as violent as their sexual urges. Enough had died to chase the others away. And the old man had kept his bargain. If there was any cocaine left in Miami, it was old stock. All that remained now was to set the new price and solidify the new lines of supply.

Like the old man, Bermúdez himself would be far removed from the commercial side of the business. He had recruited a small group of young Cubans, all of them college-trained, all of them hungry, to handle that; a modern management team that would obey utterly a shadowy voice called Ignacio. All that remained for

Bermúdez himself would be the occasional policy decision and short trips to diplomatic banks in Panama and the Bahamas.

Bermúdez paused for a moment in the circular graveled drive to run his fingers lovingly over the gold *JLB* demurely inset on the driver's door of the chocolate Seville. He loved the car and the sense of power it gave him.

He savored the drive downtown to pick up the old man. On the way it occurred to him that the monogram might be a bit much, a trifle *nouveau riche*. He decided to have the initials painted out. After tonight it would not be long before self-advertisement would be superfluous for José Luis Bermúdez.

THE MAN WITH the cauliflower ear drank deeply from the bottle of dark rum.

"I will not wear it," he announced. "I have not worn one since my mother's funeral."

"It's a fancy place, *hermano;* you have to," the Peasant insisted.

"I don't care how fancy it is."

"We have to look good for the Colombians. We have to baby-sit them while Ignacio talks with their boss. He wants us there."

*"Al diablo con los colombianos."*

"They are our friends now, and Ignacio said we had to look good. He said it twice," the Peasant cajoled, smoothing his own shiny brown suit. *"Vamos."*

*"Mierda.* Show me how to tie the fucking thing."

"CHRIS, THAT'S TOO much make-up. I already look like a strumpet."

"That's right. A little more around the eyes. And take off the panty hose."

"What's wrong with my panty hose?"

"You can see where the stocking ends at the top through the slit in the skirt. It destroys the effect."

"Whoremonger!"

———

"WHERE THE FUCK is Pincus?"

"He ain't here, Captain; called in sick," the intercom squeaked.

Sick my ass, Octavio Nelson thought foully. The devious little twerp was up to something, and it was auditioning for the DEA.

"How many men does that leave us?"

"Nine, if you're comin'."

"I'm coming."

Oh, I wouldn't miss the T. Christopher Meadows Surprise Party for anything in the world, Nelson thought savagely. Especially since I think he's right.

It had been three days since the meeting with Meadows, and Nelson had worked almost nonstop. He had shown two of the architect's sketches to cops and snitches and a few brave witnesses. Nelson sensed that another day or two of legwork would enable him to attach names to the faces. After that it was only a question of finding the dirtbags and rousting them.

The sketch of José Bermúdez was Nelson's personal treasure. He had shown it to no one. At first he had disbelieved that Bermúdez could be the street boss "Ignacio," the doper's ingenious *el Jefe*. Nelson had known Bermúdez casually for nearly all of the time they had both been in the United States. He had even admired him— one exile who had adapted spectacularly.

Meadows was mistaken, Nelson had concluded in the dark emptiness of the police car that night at Southland. He had fingered the wrong man. Yet in three days Nelson had discovered enough about Bermúdez to change his mind.

He had learned from a domino player that Bermúdez kept a small private office at the back of a cigar factory near his bank. It was supposed to be a front for the banker's anti-Castro activities, but it would serve nicely, Nelson mused, as a nerve center for other, less patriotic enterprises.

Then Nelson had learned casually through other friends in the *barrio* that Bermúdez had business interests in Colombia. And he had realized, almost as an afterthought, that Bermúdez's bank office was only a staircase away from the offices of a dead cocaine lawyer named Redbirt.

But it was Nelson's wife, Angela, who had scoured the week-old

newspapers stacked in the laundry room to resurrect a lengthy article in the *Miami Journal* about the Senate Banking Committee and
an investigation of the flow of illicit drug cash into South Florida's
banks. Half the bankers in Miami had been on hand in the nation's
capital to defend their assets and cover their asses.

José Bermúdez had been there, too, explaining as best he could
how ninety-five million dollars in cash had enriched his bank in a
single twelve-month period.

Meadows's sketch tied it all together. The more Nelson thought
about it, the better it fitted. What better disguise than prominence?
If Meadows made good his promise tonight, even if he simply put
Bermúdez in the same place with the two goons, Nelson would
know for sure.

Nelson wished to God he knew what the crazy architect was planning. With his quixotic taste for law and order, whatever it was
could not be violent. Or would Meadows surprise him once more?
Nelson wondered fleetingly whether he could successfully cover
for Meadows if the architect calmly walked up to José Bermúdez
and shot him through the head.

Nelson reached across his office desk and punched the intercom. "It's almost eight. Round up the posse and let's move."

"We're ready, Captain, but Reilly had a question."

"What is it?"

"Those people inside that you told us to watch out for? Who they
with?"

Good question, Reilly, Nelson muttered inaudibly. "Let's just say
they're with a friendly force."


DR. HARRY APPEL was fourteen blocks and eight glorious minutes
out of the morgue when the beeper on his belt went off. For just
once on a Saturday night, he had hoped to slip away early, but now
his plans dissolved. He congratulated himself for not having made
any serious arrangements for the evening. In his line of work it was
hard enough getting dates.

Appel negotiated a daring U-turn at the toll plaza on the Airport
Expressway, and he was back in the office ten minutes later. Dr.

Frank Cline greeted him in the lounge as Appel unfolded a starched, clean lab coat.

"Harry, I'm sorry to call you back, but this one's got me stumped."

"Just one? Thank God. I thought we'd had another quadruple. I may get out of here at a decent hour yet."

Appel picked through his locker for a bag of prized pipe tobacco. Cline was only two years out of his residency, but Appel valued his work. Good pathologists were hard to come by.

"They found this guy at the airport," Cline told him as the men rode downstairs to the morgue. "At first they thought he was hit by a cab, but he wasn't."

"No traumatic injuries?"

"Nope." Cline held the door for his boss, followed him through and pointed to the autopsy table. Sitting nearby in a straight-backed chair was Detective Wilbur Pincus. Appel gave a friendly wave.

"Christ, Wil, what brings you out? This a VIP?"

Pincus said nothing. His face was ashen.

In a low voice Cline said, "Pincus was there when the guy collapsed. He's not real eager to talk about it. Seems he was tailing the deceased off an airplane."

Appel gave the body a once-over. He picked up Cline's chart and read from the notes. "Roberto Justo Nelson," he said aloud. "This shows an address on Hibiscus Island."

"Right," Pincus murmured.

"Frank, the toxicology isn't done yet?"

"I sent it down an hour ago. The lab is very busy."

"Call them back, and tell them to push it. I don't want to keep Pincus any longer than necessary." Appel noticed that the young detective was keeping a liberal distance between himself and the corpse. Cline left the morgue to use the phone.

Appel turned to Pincus. "This guy an informant?"

"No," Pincus said. "It's Octavio Nelson's brother."

"Shit," Appel said heavily, mouthing an unlighted pipe. "Why were you tailing him?"

"He was dealing coke."

"Is Nelson involved?"

"I think so," Pincus said gravely. "There were some peculiar circumstances . . ."

Appel lifted Roberto's bluish arms and peered at the veins. "Where is Nelson?"

"On a stakeout."

"Have you called him?"

"No," Pincus said, growing pale. "Not yet."

Appel sighed and struggled into a pair of latex surgical gloves. Cline came back and reported that the lab technicians were moving ahead on the blood testing with renewed haste.

Appel began probing Roberto's organs. Pincus turned his chair away; the wooden legs squealed like chalk on the bare tile, breaking the silence.

"Wil, was this a convulsion?"

"Yes. A seizure. There was some salivation, thrashing around. Then his heart stopped, and I tried CPR until the ambulance got there. It was too late by then."

"Was hc arriving on an international flight?" asked Appel, holding up a yard-long length of intestines.

"Right. Colombia."

Appel said, "Frank, look at this." The two men huddled over the purplish soup inside Roberto Nelson's splayed abdomen. Pincus stared at the chilly walls and rehearsed the speech to his partner. He had plenty of ammunition—the phonied towing report, the ride to the Avianca terminal. Octavio would have much to explain. Unfortunately there was nothing to connect him directly with Roberto's unsavory commerce, nothing but the blood between them. To Pincus, that was plenty. To the headhunters at internal review, it might be zero. And it might be Pincus who would be forced to explain his extracurricular spying. So be it, he thought determinedly, if that was how Octavio Nelson wanted it to go. There was always one last weapon: Aristidio Cruz. It was never too late for a naïve young detective to atone for his past sins. Pincus's honesty, however belated, might even be regarded as an act of courage.

"OK, I think we've got 'em all," Harry Appel announced finally.

"I can't believe it," Frank Cline said.

"They were easy to miss, unless you were looking."

Appel carried a stainless steel surgical tray from the autopsy table to Pincus's somber seat across the morgue. "Here," the pathologist said, "are your culprits."

Pincus swallowed hard and forced himself to study the contents of the tray: a number of gaily colored sacs, moist with blood and rank with body fluids, swollen and elastic.

"Rubbers," Harry Appel said triumphantly. "Seventeen rubbers." He used a sharp surgical tool to poke one until it split open. He spun the tool in his hand and used the cupped end to scoop a pinch of damp ivory paste and hold it up to glisten under the morgue's piercing lights. "Don't suppose you wanna take any bets on what this is?" Appel said.

"Coke!" Pincus exclaimed.

"Yeah, the lab techs, bless their lethargic little hearts, will tell us for sure. My guess is that the contents of one or more of these little beauties was discharged right into Nelson's bloodstream."

"That's fatal?"

"In large amounts, certainly. Different things can happen. Usually the brain goes haywire and stops telling the lungs to breathe. Massive respiratory failure. If that doesn't get you, some sort of heart arrhythmia probably will," Appel explained. "You see, the human body simply wasn't made to absorb this much of a powerful stimulant. It's like plugging a hundred-ten-volt toaster into a two-twenty-volt socket. You burn it up."

"I figured it was a stroke or something," Cline said sheepishly.

"Just a smuggler's special," Appel said. "Another couple hours, and he would have passed these fine. He would have been home free. This kind of constipation is deadly, Wil."

"I figured he was carrying something," Pincus said. "I had Customs do a body search at the airport."

"Well, Customs doesn't give enemas," Appel said. "You better call your partner now."

"No," said Pincus, his face as gray as the new corpse, "not me, Doctor."

# Chapter 29

VICTOR GLOWERED and tugged peevishly at his Vandyke. The boy was a tease. Either he delivered that night or he went back on the street. Victor could not abide teases.

The old grandfather clock read 8:25, and the small dining room was nearly full. The clink of crystal and the murmur of voices soothed Victor. At least dinner was proceeding as smoothly as ordained. Quiet, elegant.

Several main courses remained to be ordered. There were a few groupers left in the tank, and Victor knew he would have to push them hard, else they would probably die overnight. Wretched beasts.

"Hey!" To Victor the call was like a curse at an opera. He flinched, and several other diners' heads raised. The Gómez table again. Victor didn't know who they were, but he vowed they would never be back. Four nasty little men who should be shining shoes. Two pairs of them, really, and not friends either. In their ill-fitted suits and pointy toes they had circled like dogs at first, as though uncertain whether to fuck or to fight.

"Hey! Fat man!"

Victor hurried over.

"Yes, sir?"

"We want to eat *now*." The man in the skewed necktie spoke in atrocious gutter Spanish.

"May I suggest grouper? Grilled with a light sauce of butter and garlic, it's quite delicious."

"Not fish," said a dark man with a black mustache. He was from the second pair.

"The veal is very good tonight," Victor ventured.

"No. Chicken. *Arroz con pollo.* With plenty of black beans."

Victor brooded. Did they think they were in a cantina?

"You can make *arroz con pollo,* can't you?"

"It's not usual, but of course we can make it."

"Good. Hurry, we are hungry."

Victor turned to go.

"And more beer," the Mustache Man added.

"Not me." The man in the shiny brown suit spoke for the first time. "For me another scotch and Coca-Cola."

"Yes, sir," said Victor, mentally deciding how much he could pad their bill without causing a scene.

"And send one to the lady," the man said, gesturing toward the window where a lovely *Latina* in a skintight dress slit almost to her waist sat alone.

"The lady," Victor said icily, "is waiting for her husband."

"Send her the drink, fat man."

"That is my dessert," announced the Peasant when Victor had shambled away.

"I saw her first," complained the Mustache Man.

"She smiled at me," said Cauliflower Ear.

"What about the husband?" The fourth man was thin and wore a large emerald ring.

"Fuck the husband."

"No, fuck her."

They all laughed loudly while Victor quivered impotently.

When the red-coated waiter brought the drink, the woman shone a dazzling smile of thanks at the four men. Her tongue drew a slow and lascivious circle around full red lips.

"We are all friends now," the Peasant said tightly. "We will share her."

THE OLD MAN skillfully dipped a morsel of lobster into the cup of hot butter.

"Excellent, Ignacio, truly excellent. I congratulate you."

"Yes, it is a good place. I'm sorry you did not bring your wife."

"Next time perhaps. This is a working trip, too important for her."

"But not for your two associates." José Bermúdez gestured through the screen of palms toward the sound of merriment beyond.

"Ah, Pepín and Alberto. I seldom travel without them. Rough men, but their hearts are good."

"Yes." Make peace, but prepare for war. Canny old bastard.

"Your men seem to be showing them a good time."

"Yes."

"It is well. They should know and respect one another. I believe that specialists should always respect their peers, don't you?"

"Of course."

"And you and I, Ignacio? When do we exchange information?"

"Tomorrow. If you will come to the bank at nine. I have everything ready."

"Splendid. I have brought things for you to see, too."

"We will not be disturbed for the whole day, I promise you."

The old man smiled thinly. "And what business is it that brings me to the bank tomorrow, Ignacio?"

"Of course, I'm sorry. It is a textile agreement. You want to build a new factory in Cartagena, and we are interested in financing it. The papers are all ready, and we will sign them. In another ten days the deal will collapse in a dispute over mortgage interest."

The old man speared another chunk of lobster.

"Excellent, Ignacio. Excellent."


OCTAVIO NELSON HAD not been this tense since the long-ago afternoon he had clung to a rock with a bloody arm and prayed that the Batista patrol would weary of the hot sun. His palms itched. His stomach clenched.

José L. Bermúdez's big Seville rested peacefully in the parking lot. Nelson had seen that much in his first quiet prowl through the darkness. But what was happening inside La Cumparsita? Was Meadows there? Nelson had not seen him go in. Who else was there, and what were they doing? If Meadows had only given him a little more notice, he could have wired somebody and sent him inside.

Nelson skirted the pale circle of light from the restaurant windows and walked along the left side to the door leading to the bar.

"Reilly, have you got a watch with a second hand?"

"Yes, Captain."

"Are you sure you know what to do?"

"Captain, relax, I'm not stupid. Exactly one minute after we hear you guys go in the front and the back, me and Bloom seal this door. Our people slide out the door in the meantime, right?"

"How many people?"

"Three people, Captain. Two guys and a gal. Relax, willya? You're makin' me nervous."

"OK, Reilly, OK. Sorry."

Nelson returned to the front of the restaurant to await Meadows's signal.

*Jesus,* he thought silently, I would give my soul for a cigar.

"NOW THAT'S SOME nigger," the Peasant smirked. All four men turned beerily toward the door.

The black man who stood there seemed seven feet tall, an effect encouraged by a gigantic wide-brimmed hat topped by a gaily trailing ostrich plume. The hat matched the leisure suit and the shoes. They all were shocking pink. A heavy gold medallion peered comfortably from the rippling black chest. The black man froze the restaurant.

"Good evening all," he proclaimed to no one in particular and strode to the table by the window. He bussed the solitary *Latina* firmly on the cheek, ran proprietary fingers lightly across her lap and squeezed into the chair opposite her.

Victor came quickly. The evening was becoming bizarre.

"My good man. A planter's punch to match my suit, if you please, and a cup of black coffee to match my true love's eyes."

Victor felt giddy. At the Gómez table the tension was suddenly electric. The two distinguished men in the far corner took no heed. They were talking business.

"Arthur," asked Terry from between her teeth, "where did you get those clothes?"

"Chris told me to be ostentatious."

Terry suppressed a giggle.

"What time is it?"

Arthur ignited a quartz watch, and the numbers glowed fiercely against his wrist.

"It's exactly five minutes to takeoff. Sit back and enjoy the ride."

"I'm nervous as a cat, Arthur."

"Honey, when Chris Meadows builds something, it stays built. Everything will be fine."

"Those men are animals, swine."

Arthur looked over at the four men. They looked back through angry obsidian eyes. Arthur smiled and waved a big left hand, a gesture of greeting or contempt.

"When I was playing my way through college, it took more meat than that just to slow me down. Here, drink from my glass—that'll make them even madder."

VICTOR WAS UP to his arms in salad when a voice at his back surprised him. He whirled, and two handfuls of Bibb lettuce and fresh-cut cucumber flew like confetti.

"I'm so sorry. I didn't mean to startle you," said the intruder, a tall man with sandy hair and cool green eyes. He wore a gray workman's shirt with Dade County stitched over the pocket.

"What are you doing in my kitchen?" Victor blustered. "Who are you, anyway?"

"The name is Kelly, and I'm with the county building department. We had a call about a possible structural problem on your side of the building. Apparently one of the beams buckled. I knocked a couple times, but no one answered. The kitchen door was open."

"I've got a roomful of customers out there," Victor said irascibly. "Come back tomorrow afternoon."

"You the owner?" the inspector asked.

"Of course."

"This afternoon one of your people told the other inspector to come back tonight. Here I am. I won't disturb your customers; it'll be quick."

Victor dried his hands on a towel. Structural problems, he fumed. Nobody had mentioned a word to him.

"Look, Inspector," he said reasonably, "why don't you have something to eat here with us in the kitchen and a nice cold glass of wine and then we can work out a more suitable time?"

"You offering me a bribe?"

Victor foamed. "No, of course not. But I do have an obligation to my customers. Inspection tonight is quite out of the question."

"OK, wise ass, we'll play it your way. I find this building to be structurally unsound. Shut it down. Now."

"But, but . . ." Victor surrendered with what little grace he had left. "Please go ahead and do your inspection. I am sure you will find everything in perfect order."

With a grim bureaucratic shake of his head Chris Meadows strode through the swinging doors of the kitchen at the rear of the dining room. He turned hard left and walked the seven paces to where the blueprints had told him the small men's room would be. Luckily it was empty.

Meadows locked himself into the only stall. He spun the combination locks on each side of the expensive brown leather briefcase and took from it a small laundry bag. It took only a second to strip off the inspector's shirt. It went into the bag.

From the briefcase he extracted a bright yellow T-shirt. The rococo lettering on the front read Viva Me. He put it on and added a pair of wraparound sunglasses with mirrored lenses. The chrome-plated pistol he tucked carefully into the waistband of his twill trousers.

Meadows made sure that the rest of the briefcase was as it should be and then wiped it carefully, inside and out, with toilet paper. The laundry bag he dropped into the tank behind the toilet. Meadows tousled his hair and checked his watch. Right on time.

Meadows had his hand on the stall door when he heard someone come into the bathroom. He cursed silently and decided to wait.

After thirty seconds Meadows chafed with impatience. After a minute he writhed. After a minute and a half he could wait no more. The unseen man's capacity was astonishing. To wait longer would throw off the carefully arranged timing Meadows had worked out with Terry and Arthur.

Meadows opened the door to the stall and came face-to-face with Cauliflower Ear.

The gunman had just turned from the urinal; his hands were still groping at his fly. His zipper was down. Meadows could smell the beer on his breath from three feet away. Was there a dawning glimmer of recognition in the man's bloodshot eyes? Meadows couldn't be sure, but the risk was too great.

Meadows dropped the briefcase, snatched the pistol from his pants and jammed it, barrel first, into the gunman's groin. Cauliflower Ear took an involuntary step back and doubled in pain.

"On the floor, *macho*," Meadows hissed. "On the floor now, or you will never use it again."

The gunman slumped to his knees, dazed. Savagely Meadows twisted the bloated ear. The man yelped in pain and flopped onto his belly.

Meadows reversed the pistol and hit the gunman once so hard across the temple that the jolt raced up Meadows's arm and ignited a cord in his neck. Cauliflower Ear was silent.

Unconscious or dead. It didn't matter. Meadows collected his ragged breathing and looked at his watch again.

"Not yet, Arthur, please. Just a few more seconds; that's all."

Meadows returned the gun to his pants, checked his appearance in the mirror and picked up the briefcase. After twisting the lock in the bathroom door so it would bolt behind him, Meadows strode purposefully into the dining room.

Arthur hadn't failed him.

Every eye seemed riveted on the black giant who stood at the table by the window. Feet planted, plume waving, arms extended as though in benediction, Arthur was in fine fettle.

"Innkeeper!" he demanded in a rich baritone that filled the room and ricocheted off the walls. "More wine for the virgins and an aphrodisiac for my lover."

At the rear of the restaurant Meadows turned left again and strode unobserved nine paces to the corner table. He skirted the protective screen of palms and sat down, briefcase at his feet.

"Ignacio, man, sorry I'm late. If there's no food left, I'll just help myself to a drink," Meadows said.

José Bermúdez had a forkful of veal halfway to his mouth. It stopped there for a long heartbeat.

"I'm sorry, you must be mistaken," Bermúdez said finally.

Meadows reached across to a silver salver on the table and tore off a chunk of French bread.

"Mistaken? Really?" he said, spewing crumbs. "Who's the spic?"

"This man, who is he?" the old Colombian demanded in Spanish.

"I don't know."

Meadows laughed caustically. "You don't know? Really, José. I mean, Ignacio . . . forgive me, a slip of the tongue." Meadows drained Bermúdez's wine with a loud glug. Color ebbed from the banker's face.

"Leave instantly or I will call the police," Bermúdez demanded. His voice was shrill.

"The police. Now that's funny. What is this, fellas, the amateur hour?" Meadows propped the sunglasses on the top of his head. "I've got your merchandise; I want my money. Simple, no?"

"I am leaving right now," the Colombian said, wiping his mouth with an embroidered napkin.

Bermúdez was trapped between two fires. "Wait, my friend, please wait. This is a mistake," he begged the Colombian.

"My mistake was coming here," the old man said, and started to lever himself up from the table. "You are as foolish as the greedy cowboys who work for you."

Bermúdez glared at Meadows. "You will die for this." He clapped his hands twice.

"*¡Violeta!*" the old man shouted.

Both were well-rehearsed signals, but neither worked, for they drowned in a hellacious commotion from the front of the dining room.

The striking salt-and-pepper couple at the table by the window had exploded.

"Honky hussy!" the black man snarled.

"*¡Ayuda! ¡Socorro!*" the *Latina* screamed.

"Two-timing bitch!"

"*¡Policía!*"

He was choking her. Everyone could see that. A waiter saw it and dropped a skillet of crêpes flambé. A fat woman diner saw it and screamed. A middle-aged Cuban businessman saw it and started over to help. The three killers saw it, and they erupted as one, toppling their table in their haste to help. They never heard their masters' summonses.

In the darkness outside, Octavio Nelson intently watched the front of the restaurant from the shelter of a large cabbage palm. One of his detectives materialized suddenly.

"Captain, there's an urgent radio call for you."

Nelson's gaze never left the restaurant.

"Not now, I'm busy."

"It's something about your brother, Captain. And Detective Pincus. They said it was very important."

Nelson stifled a groan. Wilbur Pincus and Bobby Nelson were the last two people on earth he wanted to hear from just then.

"Mike," Nelson muttered angrily, "you will go back to the car. You will tell the dispatcher you cannot find me. And then you will turn off the fucking radio. Is that clear?"

"Yes, Captain."

In La Cumparsita, Terry wriggled in apparent helplessness as the giant's weight bore down on her. Then Arthur abandoned the theatric chorus of grunts that had accompanied his assault.

"They will be here in a second," he whispered. "Do it now, Terry; there's no more time."

He released his grasp, and Terry fell back against the front window. Carefully she pressed her open palm against the glass, clenched her fist and again showed the palm.

Octavio Nelson saw it, and his English deserted him.

"*Vamos*," he screamed. "*Vamos*."

With a gentle shove Arthur directed Terry toward the front door.

He caught the first of her would-be saviors with a stiff arm under the chin. The second went down under a pink-toed kick. Arthur was grinning like a maniac as he himself started backing toward the door. Child's play. Not a linebacker among them.

Victor was apoplectic. Help. He had to get help. They were ruining him. Dazed, his eyes swollen with tears, Victor directed his great bulk toward the telephone by the door. He collided instead with the fish tank and carried it down to the soft beige carpet under him. For Meadows, the pratfall was a bonus.

He affected not to hear the madness that consumed La Cumparsita. He spoke with a tough edge.

"Look, Ignacio. I don't know what's going on here, but you wanted a delivery, and here it is. Now I expect you to transfer my fee into the appropriate account on Monday morning, first thing, as usual. Then we'll talk about a next time, if there is one. I'm beginning not to like this restaurant."

Meadows slung the briefcase on the table and rose to leave.

It was the best-quality leather case money could buy, identical to the one Bermúdez carried so smartly to work each morning—even the tasteful *JLB* monogrammed under the handle was the same. Arthur had found it at an imported leather shop in the Southland Mall.

The banker and the old Colombian stared dumbly at the briefcase. Meadows pushed it closer, knocking over a carafe of wine, closer still, until it stopped solidly against the chest of José Bermúdez, who grabbed it furiously with both hands just as Octavio Nelson walked up to the table.

*"Buenas noches, señores,"* Nelson said softly.

# Chapter 30

TERRY DROVE. Arthur sat next to her, chortling. In the back seat, Meadows exchanged the loud T-shirt for a blue cotton pullover.

"Don't forget to stop at the phone booth," Meadows said.

"Don't you think you've caused enough damage already?" Terry asked with a grin. She would prize the image of the fat man going ass over teakettle with his fish tank for as long as she lived.

"It's a good cake, but it needs a little icing."

Meadows had the quarter ready, and he dialed the number from heart.

"*Journal* city desk."

"Clara Jackson, please."

"Hold on for a transfer." There were three clicks, and then the voice of Clara Jackson.

"Clara? This is a friend down at Metro. Nelson in Narcotics just raided a restaurant called La Cumparsita on Southwest Seventh. They're still down there if you've got a photographer handy."

Then Meadows hung up. Maybe it was a dirty trick. Maybe Nelson would play it straight. But Meadows was one uptown architect who never designed anything that was not insured.

"Damn," Arthur exclaimed, "I haven't had this much fun since we upset Notre Dame."

"You fell on a fumble," Meadows said. It was done; he felt spent.

"Indeed, with six seconds left," Arthur said. "In the end zone. Two green shirts hanging onto me like pilotfish."

Terry asked, "How long before they open the briefcase, Chris?"

"Not long, I'm sure. They'll take it downtown. Bermúdez will deny it's his, of course, but we left Nelson a lot of rope to play with."

They had packed the attaché case with care and cunning. In the lining, in a place where expert searchers were sure to look, were secreted two sheets of plain white paper typed by an anonymous IBM.

One carried names like Manny, Moe, Alonzo, McRae—all the names Meadows could remember, except Patti Atchison. The second sheet held a half dozen names with a plain black line drawn through each. The names had one thing in common. They belonged to victims of recent cocaine violence.

In the zippered compartment was a smoldering handwritten letter in Spanish to *Queridissimo Josecito* from a sexy lady named Carmen who could only be his mistress. When he finished reading it the first time, Meadows had been randy as hell.

"That's some fantasy," he had muttered.

"Fantasy?" Terry's smile had been wicked. "Not fantasy, *querido*, history."

Meadows had contributed a book to the briefcase, a handsome volume called *Banking for the Eighties*. A square section of each page, 410 in all, had been carved out with a straight razor. In this space, Meadows had reverently laid the bag of stolen coke.

One additional item completed the inventory: a receipt for a dozen yellow roses. Arthur had insisted.


NELSON TOOK THE briefcase downtown, but he did not pry it open for nearly two hours. First, he had to arrange the release of the three Colombians; if their documents were in order and immigration had no interest in them, neither did he. The two Cuban gunmen Nelson would keep for a while.

A shaken José Bermúdez drove home from La Cumparsita in his monogrammed Seville. The catastrophe at the restaurant surpassed understanding. He had gone in triumph. He had left stunned, in ashes.

There would be no repairing the damage with the skittish and suspicious Colombians now. They would believe he had set them up. And they had been set up—and he along with them. But by whom?

Not by the police. He had Octavio Nelson's warmest apologies for the confusion and his most earnest promise to look for the young Anglo in the yellow T-shirt.

Still, Bermúdez thought, it would have been better had Nelson not draped a hairy arm around his shoulders there in the parking lot while the handcuffed Colombians were being herded into a paddy wagon. Most unfortunate.

Perhaps he should have gone to police headquarters with the old Colombian, stood by him, made him see that José Bermúdez had had no hand in the tragedy that destroyed their dinner and their relationship. No, his image in Miami would never have survived that; it would be hard enough to fend off the reporters as it was.

As he wheeled the Cadillac into his driveway, José Bermúdez made a mental note to order a better alarm system and to hire some respectable bodyguards.

OCTAVIO NELSON HAD never been good with locks, and it was nearly eleven before he jimmied the attaché case open with a screwdriver he found in the police locker. He sat on one of the gray varnished benches and examined the contents one by one, smiling wryly.

"Nice try, *amigo*," Nelson whispered, "but my way is better."

He heard footsteps on the terrazzo and slammed the briefcase shut. Wilbur Pincus turned the corner and stopped. His eyes were pink, and his voice was raw.

"There you are," he said to Octavio Nelson. "I've got some bad news, Captain."

MEADOWS WAS STILL asleep the next morning when Terry, cross-legged at the foot of the bed, found the story submerged on page four of the *Journal*'s local news section:

### RAID ON MIAMI RESTAURANT NETS COKE, COLOMBIANS
#### by Clara Jackson

A WILD SUPPERTIME RAID by Metro narcotics detectives Saturday night led to the seizure of nearly a pound of high-grade cocaine at a popular Little Havana restaurant.

Acting on a tip, nine detectives stormed the La Cumparsita restaurant on SW Seventh Street shortly after 8:00 P.M., according to police spokesman Jim McWilliams.

About 400 grams of cocaine were discovered in a brown briefcase, McWilliams said. Three Colombians and two Cuban-Americans were arrested at the scene. The Colombians were turned over to the U.S. Immigration and Naturalization Service, which refused to release their names.

The Cuban suspects have been charged with possession of a controlled substance, resisting arrest with violence, possession of unregistered firearms and assault. McWilliams said both men gave their names as "Juan Fernández."

Also detained briefly at the restaurant was prominent Cuban-exile banker José Bermúdez. He was released at the scene after brief questioning by police.

Reached at his home late Saturday night Bermúdez told the *Journal* he was dining with a friend when police stormed the restaurant. "I didn't know what was going on," he said. "I guess I was just in the wrong place at the wrong time.

"The police did an excellent job," Bermúdez added. "They made their arrests swiftly, and no one got hurt. They are to be commended."

Victor Volstok, the owner of La Cumparsita, was unavailable for comment.

Terry's fury propelled Meadows out of bed.

"They let him go," she cried. "Nelson, the bastard, he let him go! *¡Hijo de puta!*"

Meadows took the newspaper and read the story silently. His face showed no surprise. When the telephone rang, he stretched across the bed and snatched it off the hook. It was Arthur.

"They fucked us, man."

"I'm reading about it right now," Meadows said.

"Your cop friend is a prick," Arthur snarled, his voice thick with sleep.

"Take it easy," Meadows said.

"He bought his way out," Terry fumed. "He opened his wallet and Nelson dove in."

Meadows put a finger to his lips. Terry reddened, exasperated.

"What now?" Arthur said wearily.

"I don't know," Meadows said with a trace of a smile. "You up for some chess later?"

# Chapter 31

FOUR DAYS LATER an open grave appeared on a small rise overlooking an artificial lake. It was a prime lot in the new Catholic cemetery on the fringes of the Everglades, a gravesite befitting such an important man as José Bermúdez.

Many mourners came. Businessmen and civic leaders. Office workers and laborers. A congressman and the mayor. A bishop said the mass and read prayers over the grave. There were many Cubans and nearly as many Anglos, for the dynamic man who lay in the oak casket had bridged the gap between the communities in Miami.

The mourners placed their wreaths and said their prayers and shed their tears, and they drove away. Now only three old men remained, hatless in the noonday sun.

"So young, so young. *Que descanse en paz,*" Pedro murmured in private oration. He wrung gnarled hands that were stained a leather brown from sixty years of making cigars. It was like losing a son.

"The ways of God are strange." Raúl sniffled.

As usual, it was Jesús who took charge.

"It is for us to mourn, but it is also for us to understand," he said softly.

"What do you mean?" asked Raúl.

"It was no accident. A careful man like that. Was it an accident that our shop burned to the ground just three days earlier? Was that an accident, too? If that is what you believe, my friends, then you are fools!"

There was a long moment of silence. A duck landed noisily on the artificial lake. A backhoe began digging nearby.

Raúl stared mutely at the fresh-turned earth. Pedro's shoulders slumped in sudden, terrible realization.

"Castro!" Raúl spit.

*"Comunistas de mierda,"* Pedro whispered.

Jesús nodded grimly.

He shuffled to the edge of the grave and reached into his pocket. Then all three stiffened to attention as the paper Cuban flag fluttered from Jesús's shaking hands onto the casket.

*"Murió por Cuba,"* Jesús intoned bravely. He had died for Cuba. The old men wept.

"DON'T JERK IT, you'll pull it out of his mouth," Meadows advised mildly.

"*Carajo*," Octavio Nelson grunted, "I know how to fish. I'm just a little rusty, that's all. I'll get him."

Meadows watched the struggle from the captain's chair of the Seacraft. It was a brilliant day that tasted of the subtle Florida autumn, and they had been drifting north along the edge of the Gulf Stream where a chain of seaweed promised dolphin. Meadows felt very good.

"*Mierda.* I lost him."

Nelson plopped the rod in its holder near the stem and pulled a fresh can of beer from the ice chest.

"Why aren't you fishing?"

Meadows shrugged.

"Why should I work when somebody will do it for me?"

Nelson swallowed deeply.

"You know, you're a funny guy, *amigo.* I got to thinking about you a lot while you were away." Nelson drank again. "And what I think is that you conned me. I think that all the bullshit about law and order and justice was smoke."

"Oh?" Meadows said neutrally.

"All you ever really wanted to do was drive a wedge between Bermúdez and the Colombians, am I right? You didn't care if I arrested him. And the briefcase. That was a prop. Just like me."

Meadows stared at the sea. He picked up one of the fishing rods and aimed for the weed line.

Nelson lighted a cigar.

"Watch the match," Meadows said. "We got gas in the boat."

Nelson chuckled. "You should have seen that old fart down at headquarters."

"The Colombian?"

"Yeah, we hassled him pretty good. Strip-searched him, the whole routine. All the while he kept looking around for his pal Bermúdez. Couldn't figure out why Bermúdez wasn't there, too. He was mad enough to bite, the Colombian was."

"There's a fish rising over there. Why don't you try floating a live shrimp this time?"

Nelson ignored him. He wagged his cigar toward a distant lighthouse, a white derrick on the horizon. "Fowey Rocks?"

Meadows squinted. "I think so."

"That's where they found the body."

Meadows said, "In a shirt and tie."

"Yeah. Some boating accident, huh?"

"The papers said he left Crandon Marina with two guys in a speedboat."

Nelson shrugged. "That's what the dockmaster says."

"Any other leads?"

Nelson pursed his lips and blew smoke into the fickle sea breeze. "I don't investigate boating accidents," he said.

Meadows twisted the drag down on his reel until it was tightened to his satisfaction. "I was out of town when it happened," he said. "Arthur saved the clipping."

"And I was at my brother's funeral."

The breeze died. It was the last they spoke of José Bermúdez.

Meadows reeled in his line. His bait, a small blue runner, was dead, torn in half. A thread of violet gut hung from the wounds.

"Fucking barracudas," Nelson surmised.

"Or sharks," Meadows said, twisting the mangled fish from the hook. "You know, it's true about sharks. They'll eat just about anything. And if you cut one, the others in the school will eat it alive. I've seen it happen myself."

"Me too," Nelson said. "Every day."

Meadows scooped another runner from the baitwell and hooked him higher this time, behind the first dorsal point in the back. He stood up and cast the big spinning outfit as far as he could behind the boat. The fish landed with a muted slap. A gull circled overhead, piping hungrily.

"How was your hearing at the police department?"

"No problem," Nelson said.

It had lasted only one hour. Pincus had read in a firm voice from his blue notebook. The guy was amazing, a regular stenographer. He wrote down *everything*, Nelson marveled. Then to resurrect Aristidio Cruz, *Cristo!* Pincus had the balls of a bull elephant, that was for sure.

The hearing officer from internal review was an old academy pal of Nelson's. He had listened to Pincus for twenty minutes, then told him to sit down, thank you very much.

"Octavio, let's hear from you."

"Captain, Roberto was my brother, but I didn't know what the hell he was up to. I had his car towed as a favor, that's all. I'll reimburse the department for that. I did give him a ride to the airport, also as a favor. That I won't bother to defend. This Cruz thing I can't even remember."

"OK," the hearing officer had said. And a few minutes later: "Thanks for your time, gentlemen. I'm going to rule that there is insufficient cause for action in this case. The complaint is not sustained."

Nelson was halfway out the door when Wilbur Pincus caught up with him. "I'm sorry," he had said plaintively. "About your brother. About everything. I . . . I sent some flowers."

"That was very thoughtful," Nelson had replied, "but you should have come to the funeral. Your friend Mr. Cruz was there."

"Why?" Pincus had said, his voice fading suddenly. "How did he know Roberto?"

"Strictly business, *amigo.*"

Nelson's rod dipped, and he set the hook and hauled in a small mangrove snapper. "A few more of these, and we have dinner," he announced.

"So is Pincus quitting?" Meadows asked intently.

"Are you kidding? He's doing great, a regular star. They gave him a new partner, and already he's got a big case. Your Cuban friends we busted at 'Cumparsi's.' The one with the fucked-up ear and his buddy, the fashion plate."

"The sketches?"

"Right. Their names are Contreras and Losada. Pincus has got 'em cold. I thought I told you about it."

"No," Meadows said. "What are the charges?"

"Murder."

"Whose?"

"Your old pal Mono."

"But you told me that case was closed."

"Was. Sure was," Nelson said with a pirate's grin, "until that knife turned up in the trunk of Losada's Continental. I searched all over the airport for that damned thing, but Pincus got a warrant and went through the car—and there it was. The lab says it's definitely the right weapon."

Meadows gently raised the tip of the fishing rod, and it twitched a reply; the frantic little baitfish was still alive at the end of his line.

"Nice work," he said, reaching into Octavio Nelson's pocket for a Cuban cigar.

### A DEATH IN CHINA

An American investigating his mentor's murder finds himself ensnared in a web of lies and treachery in China, where even tomorrow's weather is a state secret. From a nightmarish interrogation to assassination by cobra, *A Death in China* takes readers on a trip with no rest stops through a world of claustrophobic mistrust and terrifying danger.

"A tautly written, fast-paced thriller that captures the real China."

—*The New York Times*

Crime Fiction/0-375-70067-6

### POWDER BURN

Architect Chris Meadows has the bad luck to see an old girlfriend get hit by a car full of drugland hitmen. He has the worse luck to see the faces of her murderers. Because in a town as violent as Miami, a witness doesn't stand a chance—especially when the cops who ought to be protecting him are more interested in dangling him as live bait.

"An explosive read . . . authentic, compelling and frightening."

—*Atlanta Journal-Constitution*

Crime Fiction/0-375-70068-4

### TRAP LINE

Key West is a smuggler's paradise. All that's needed are the captains to run the contraband, and Breeze Albury is one of the best fishing captains on the Rock. He's in no mood to become the Machine's delivery boy, however. So the Machine sets out to persuade him. It starts by taking away Albury's livelihood and his freedom. But when the Machine threatens Albury's son, the washed-out wharf rat turns into a raging, sea-going vigilante.

"A piece of nautical adventure writing worthy of C.S. Forester."

—*Ellery Queen Mystery Magazine*

Crime Fiction/0-375-70069-2